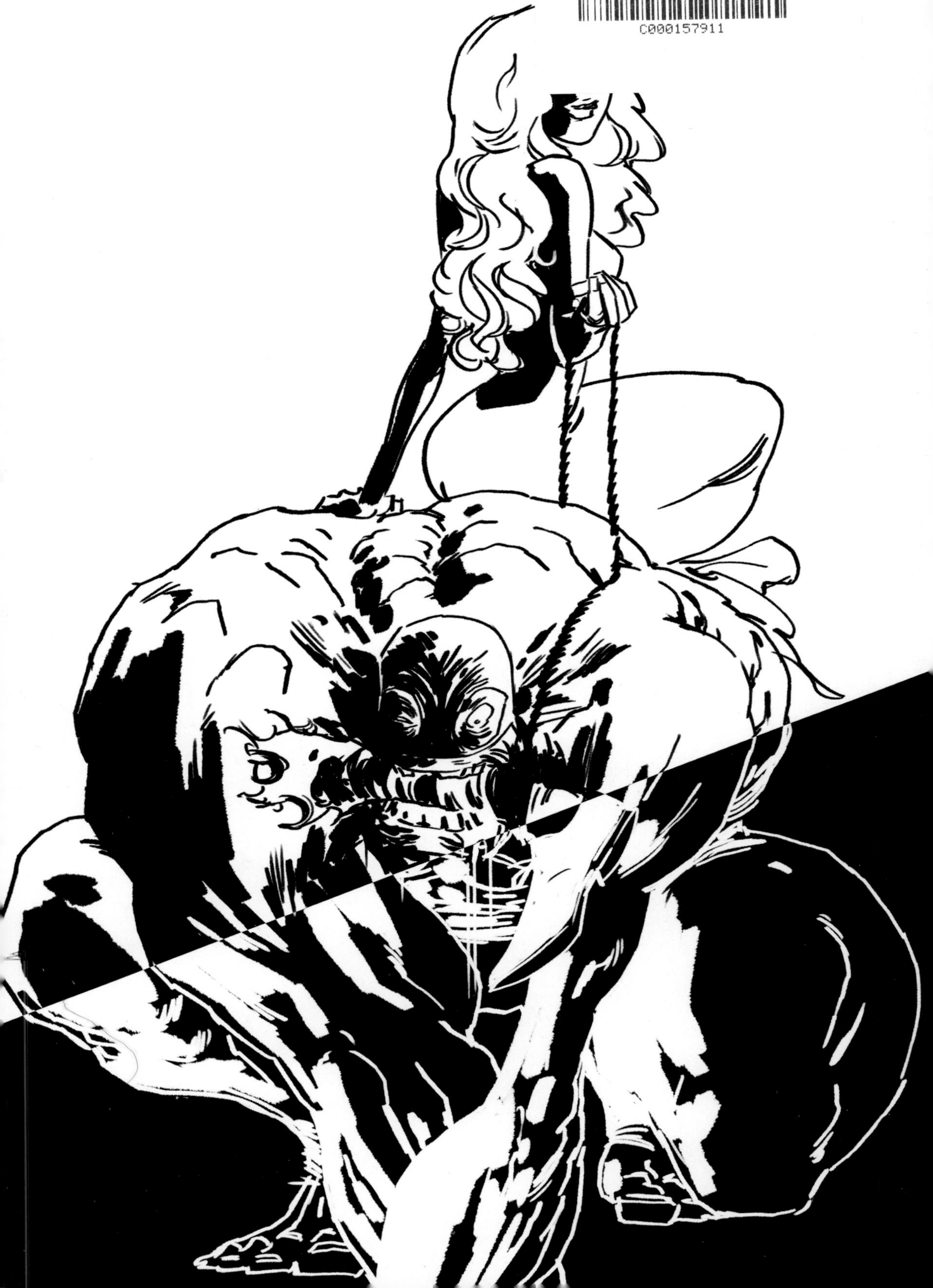

IMAGE COMICS, INC.

Robert Kirkman – Chief Operating Officer
Erik Larsen – Chief Financial Officer
Todd McFarlane – President
Marc Silvestri – Chief Executive Officer
Jim Valentino – Vice President
Eric Stephenson – Publisher
Corey Hart – Director of Sales
Jeff Boison – Director of Publishing Planning & Book Trade Sales
Chris Ross – Director of Digital Sales
Jeff Stang – Director of Specialty Sales
Kat Salazar – Director of PR & Marketing
Drew Gill – Art Director
Heather Doornink – Production Director
Branwyn Bigglestone – Controller

IMAGECOMICS.COM

COLLECTION DESIGN BY
JEFF POWELL

ISBN 978-1-5343-0338-6

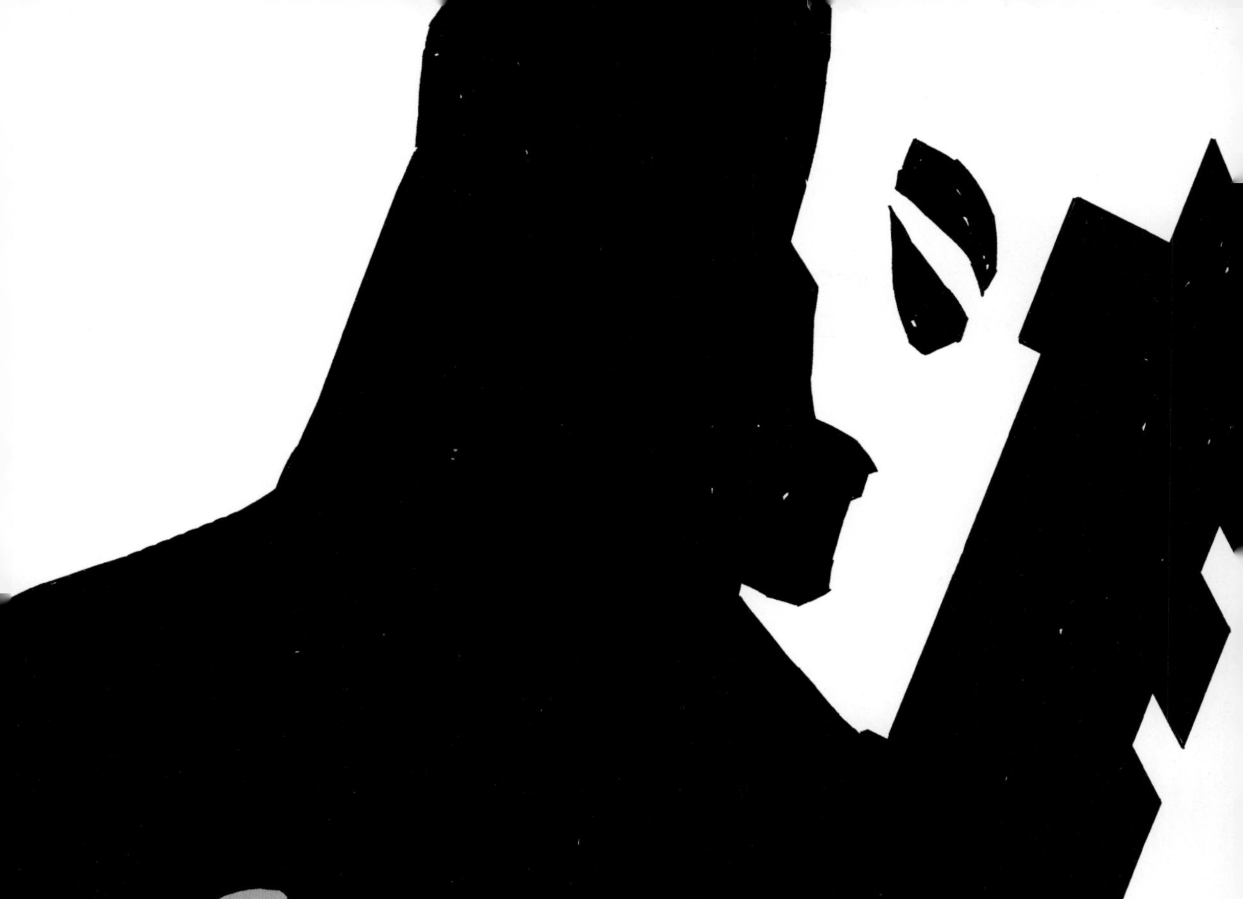

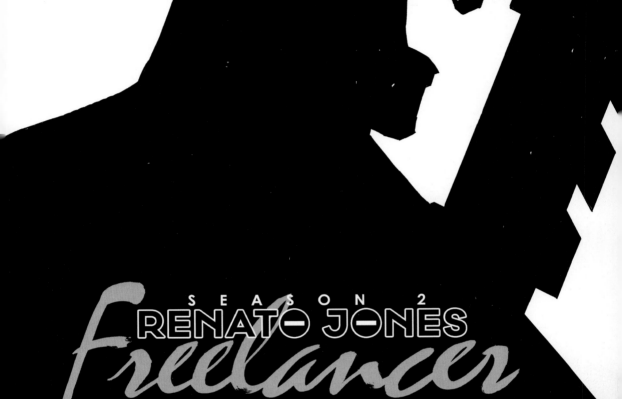

SEASON 2

RENATO JONES

Freelancer

CREATED, WRITTEN, DRAWN AND OWNED BY

KAARE KYLE ANDREWS

LETTERED BY

JEFF POWELL

EDITED BY

SEBASTIAN GIRNER

FLATS

ALICE ITO

INSPIRATION

NICOLE ANDREWS

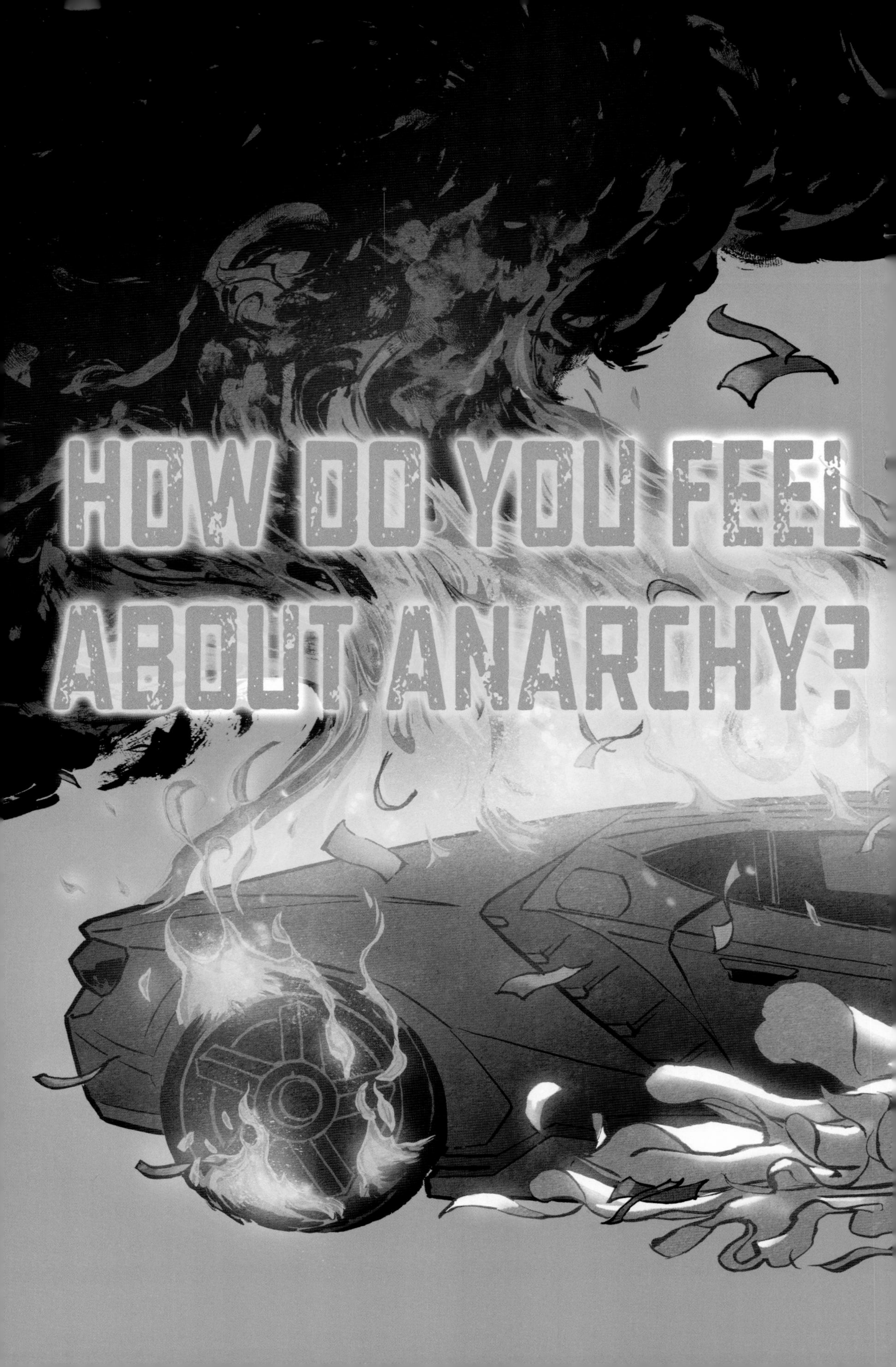
HOW DO YOU FEEL ABOUT ANARCHY?

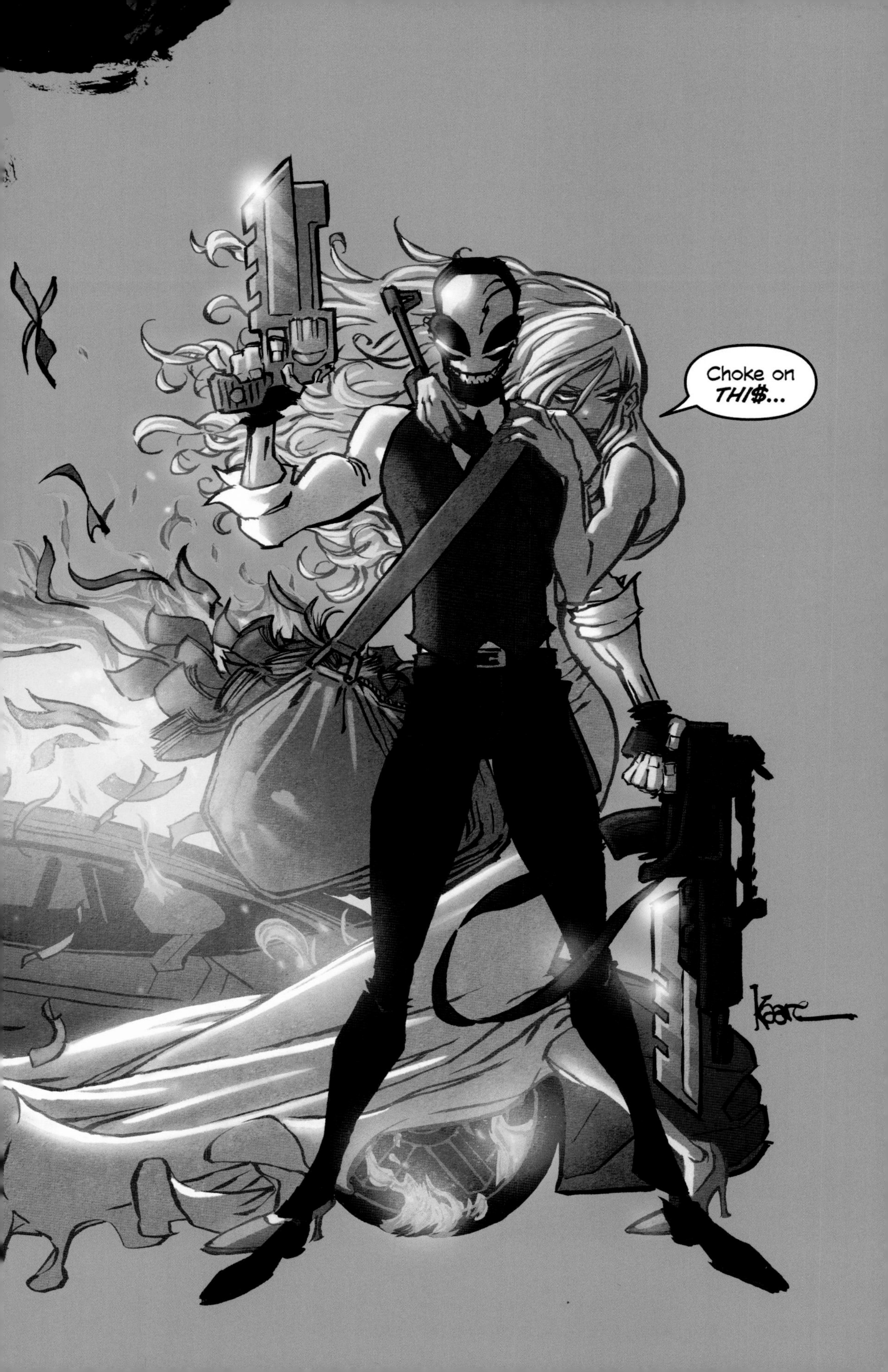
Choke on
THI$...

$$\frac{1}{}$$

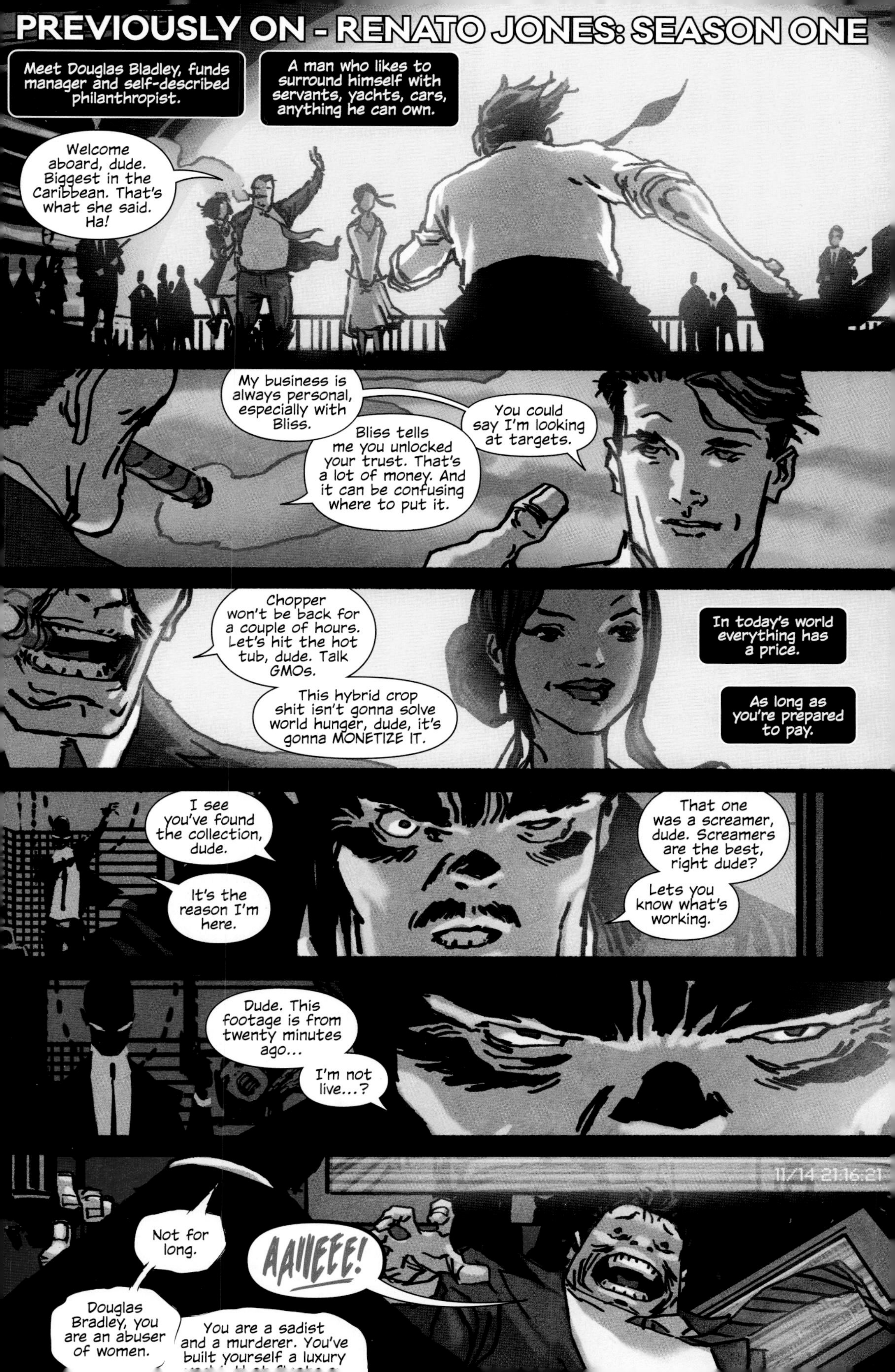
PREVIOUSLY ON - RENATO JONES: SEASON ONE
Meet Douglas Bladley, funds manager and self-described philanthropist.
A man who likes to surround himself with servants, yachts, cars, anything he can own.
Welcome aboard, dude. Biggest in the Caribbean. That's what she said. Ha!
My business is always personal, especially with Bliss.
You could say I'm looking at targets.
Bliss tells me you unlocked your trust. That's a lot of money. And it can be confusing where to put it.
Chopper won't be back for a couple of hours. Let's hit the hot tub, dude. Talk GMOs.
This hybrid crop shit isn't gonna solve world hunger, dude, it's gonna MONETIZE IT.
In today's world everything has a price.
As long as you're prepared to pay.
I see you've found the collection, dude.
It's the reason I'm here.
That one was a screamer, dude. Screamers are the best, right dude?
Lets you know what's working.
Dude. This footage is from twenty minutes ago...
I'm not live...?
11/14 21:16:21
Not for long.
AAIIEEE!
Douglas Bradley, you are an abuser of women.
You are a sadist and a murderer. You've built yourself a luxury

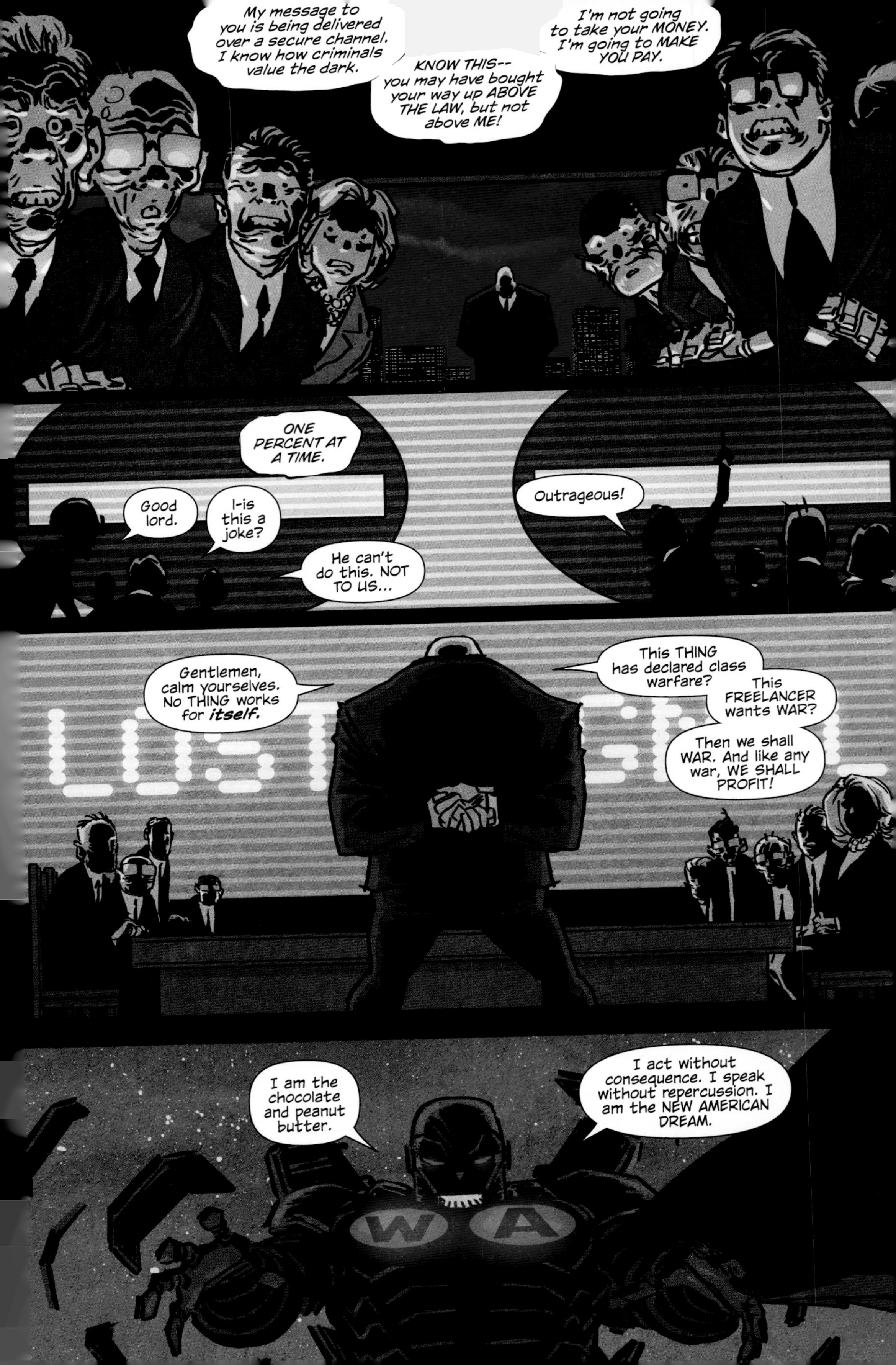
My message to you is being delivered over a secure channel. I know how criminals value the dark.
KNOW THIS-- you may have bought your way up ABOVE THE LAW, but not above ME!
I'm not going to take your MONEY. I'm going to MAKE YOU PAY.
ONE PERCENT AT A TIME.
Good lord.
I-is this a joke?
He can't do this. NOT TO US...
Outrageous!
Gentlemen, calm yourselves. No THING works for *itself.*
This THING has declared class warfare?
This FREELANCER wants WAR?
Then we shall WAR. And like any war, WE SHALL PROFIT!
I am the chocolate and peanut butter.
I act without consequence. I speak without repercussion. I am the NEW AMERICAN DREAM.
W A

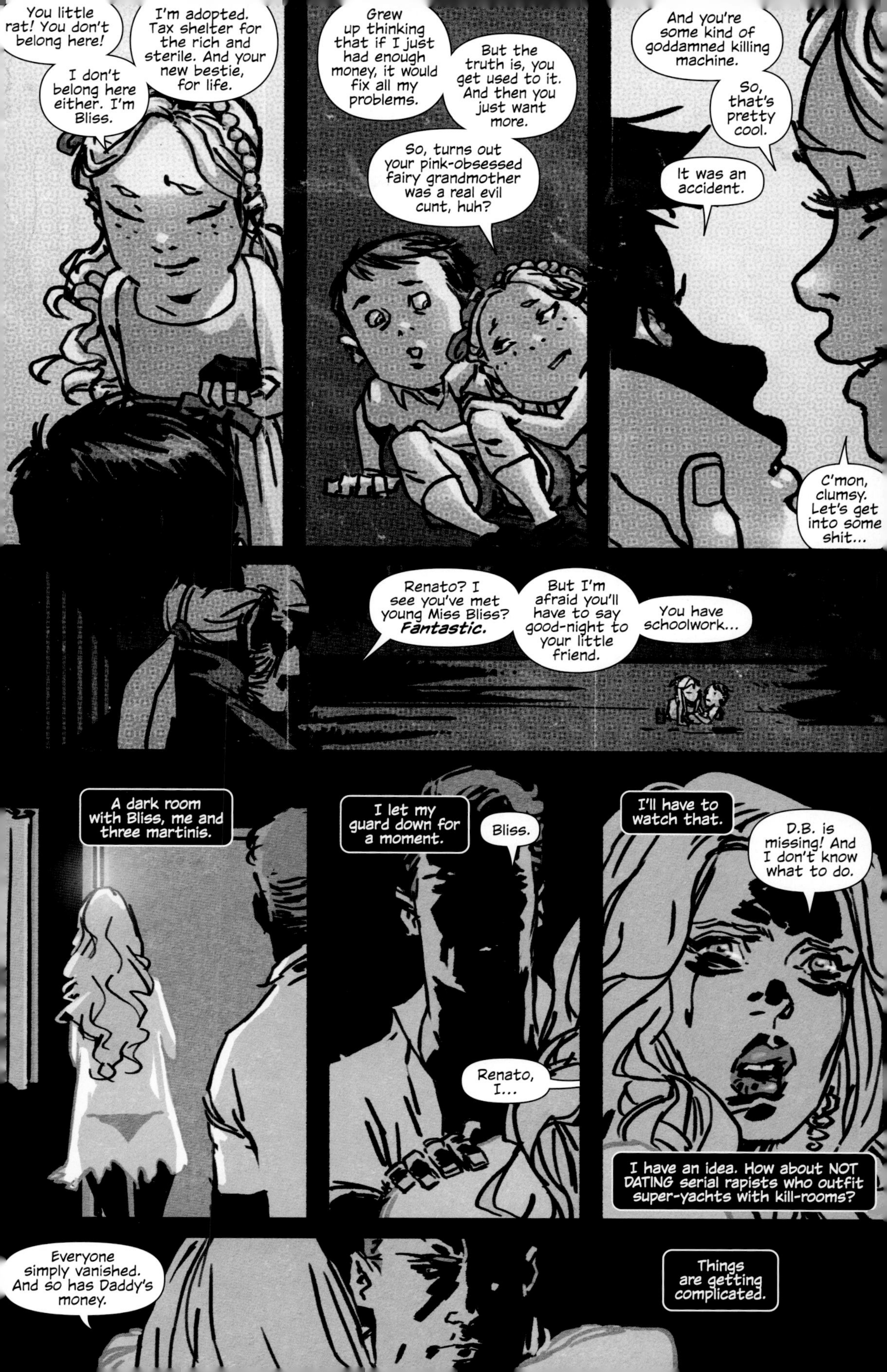
You little rat! You don't belong here!
I'm adopted. Tax shelter for the rich and sterile. And your new bestie, for life.
I don't belong here either. I'm Bliss.
Grew up thinking that if I just had enough money, it would fix all my problems.
But the truth is, you get used to it. And then you just want more.
So, turns out your pink-obsessed fairy grandmother was a real evil cunt, huh?
And you're some kind of goddamned killing machine.
So, that's pretty cool.
It was an accident.
C'mon, clumsy. Let's get into some shit...
Renato? I see you've met young Miss Bliss? Fantastic.
But I'm afraid you'll have to say good-night to your little friend.
You have schoolwork...
A dark room with Bliss, me and three martinis.
I let my guard down for a moment.
Bliss.
Renato, I...
I'll have to watch that.
D.B. is missing! And I don't know what to do.
I have an idea. How about NOT DATING serial rapists who outfit super-yachts with kill-rooms?
Everyone simply vanished. And so has Daddy's money.
Things are getting complicated.

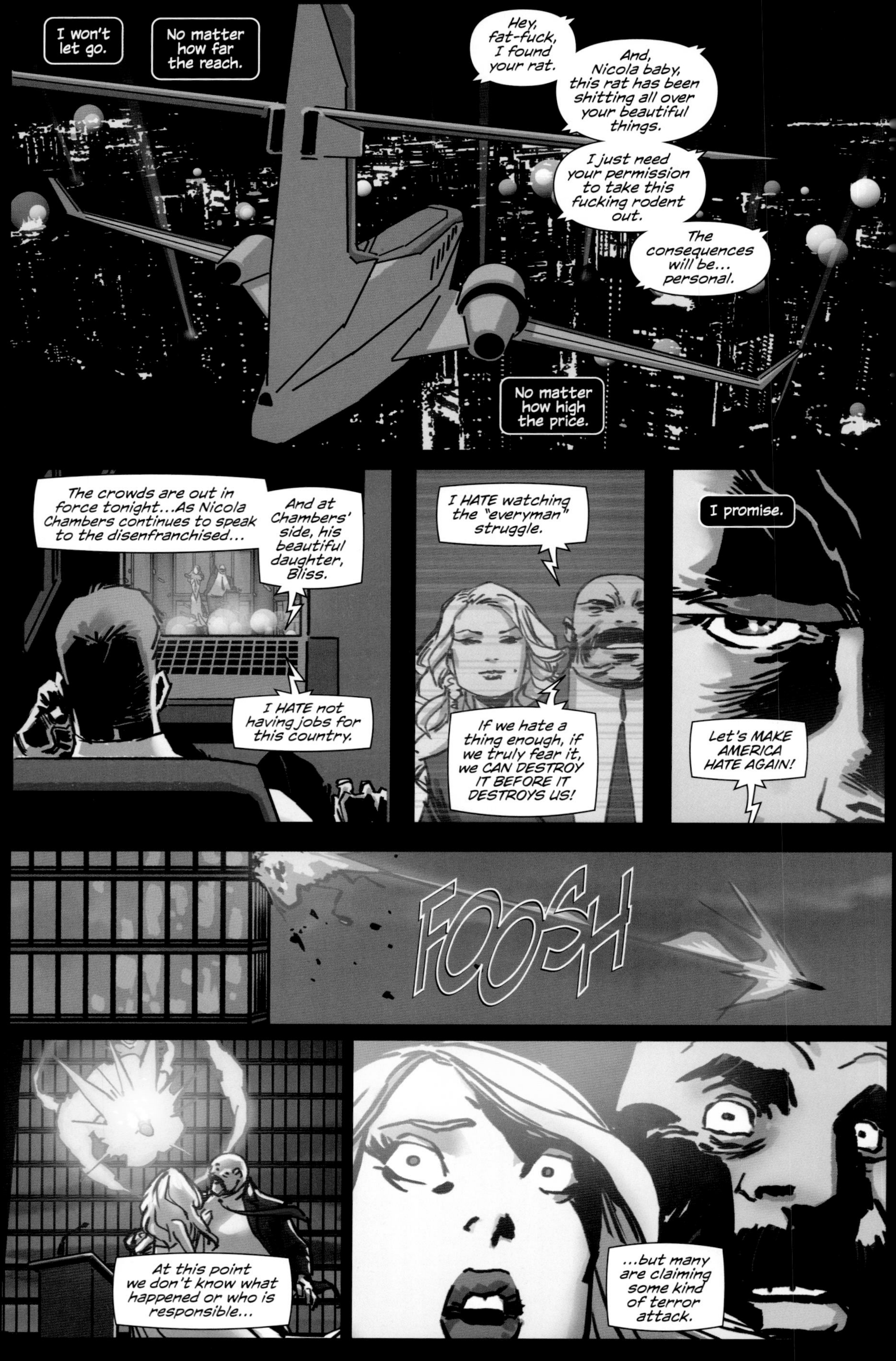
I won't let go.
No matter how far the reach.
Hey, fat-fuck, I found your rat.
And, Nicola baby, this rat has been shitting all over your beautiful things.
I just need your permission to take this fucking rodent out.
The consequences will be... personal.
No matter how high the price.
The crowds are out in force tonight...As Nicola Chambers continues to speak to the disenfranchised...
And at Chambers' side, his beautiful daughter, Bliss.
I HATE not having jobs for this country.
I HATE watching the "everyman" struggle.
If we hate a thing enough, if we truly fear it, we CAN DESTROY IT BEFORE IT DESTROYS US!
I promise.
Let's MAKE AMERICA HATE AGAIN!
FOOSH
At this point we don't know what happened or who is responsible...
...but many are claiming some kind of terror attack.

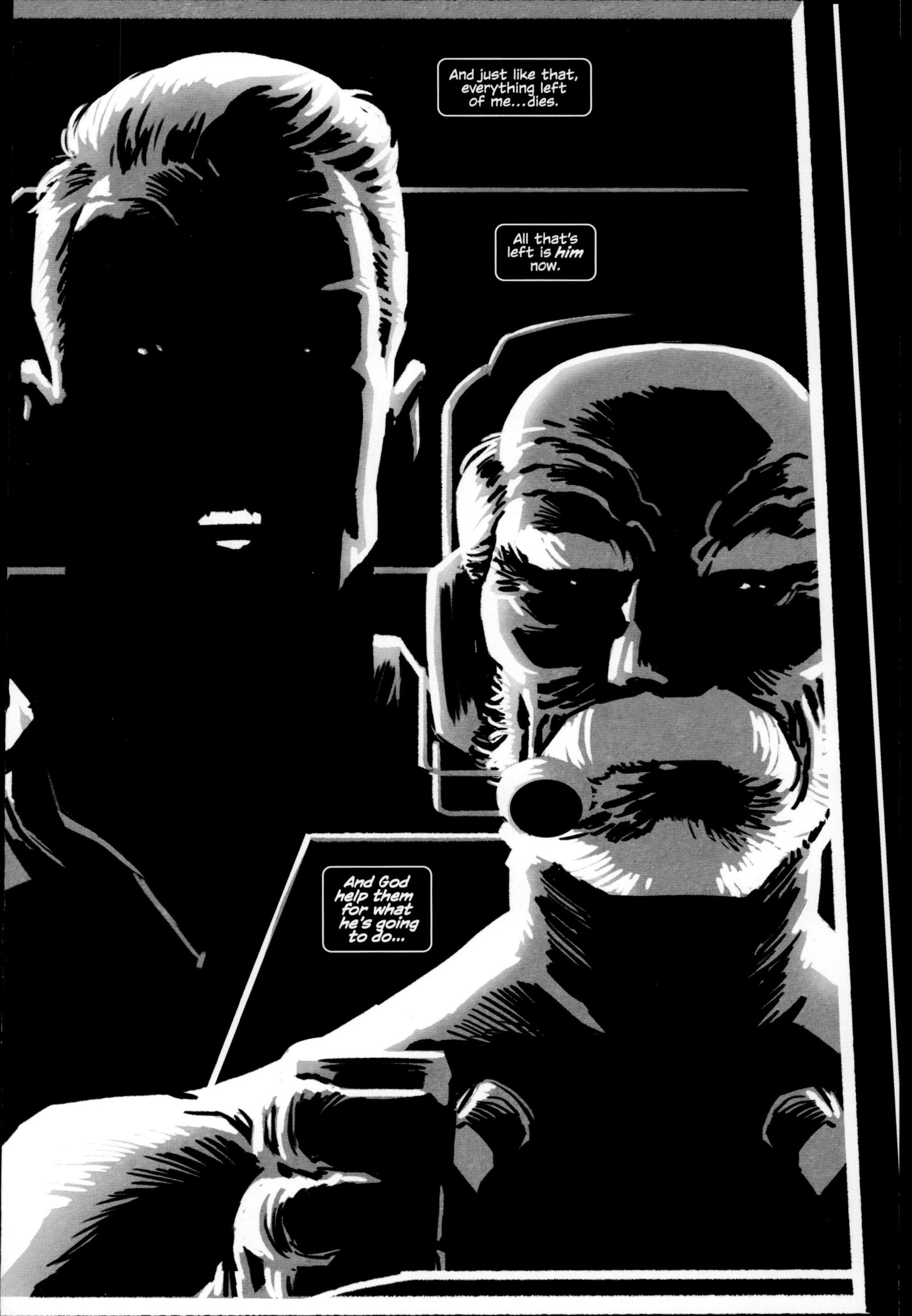
And just like that, everything left of me...dies.
All that's left is *him* now.
And God help them for what he's going to do...

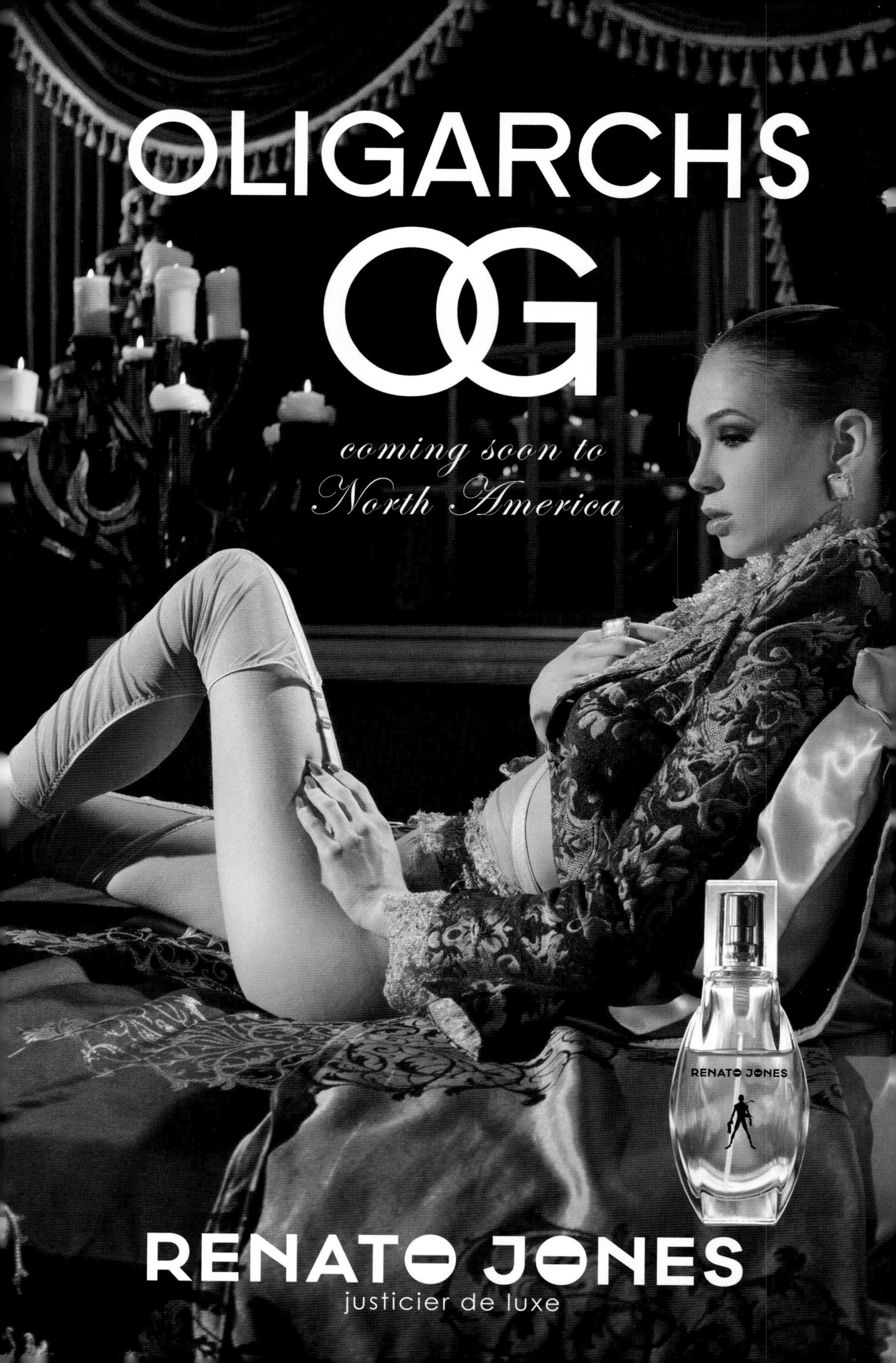
OLIGARCHS
OG
coming soon to
North America
RENATO JONES
RENATO JONES
justicier de luxe

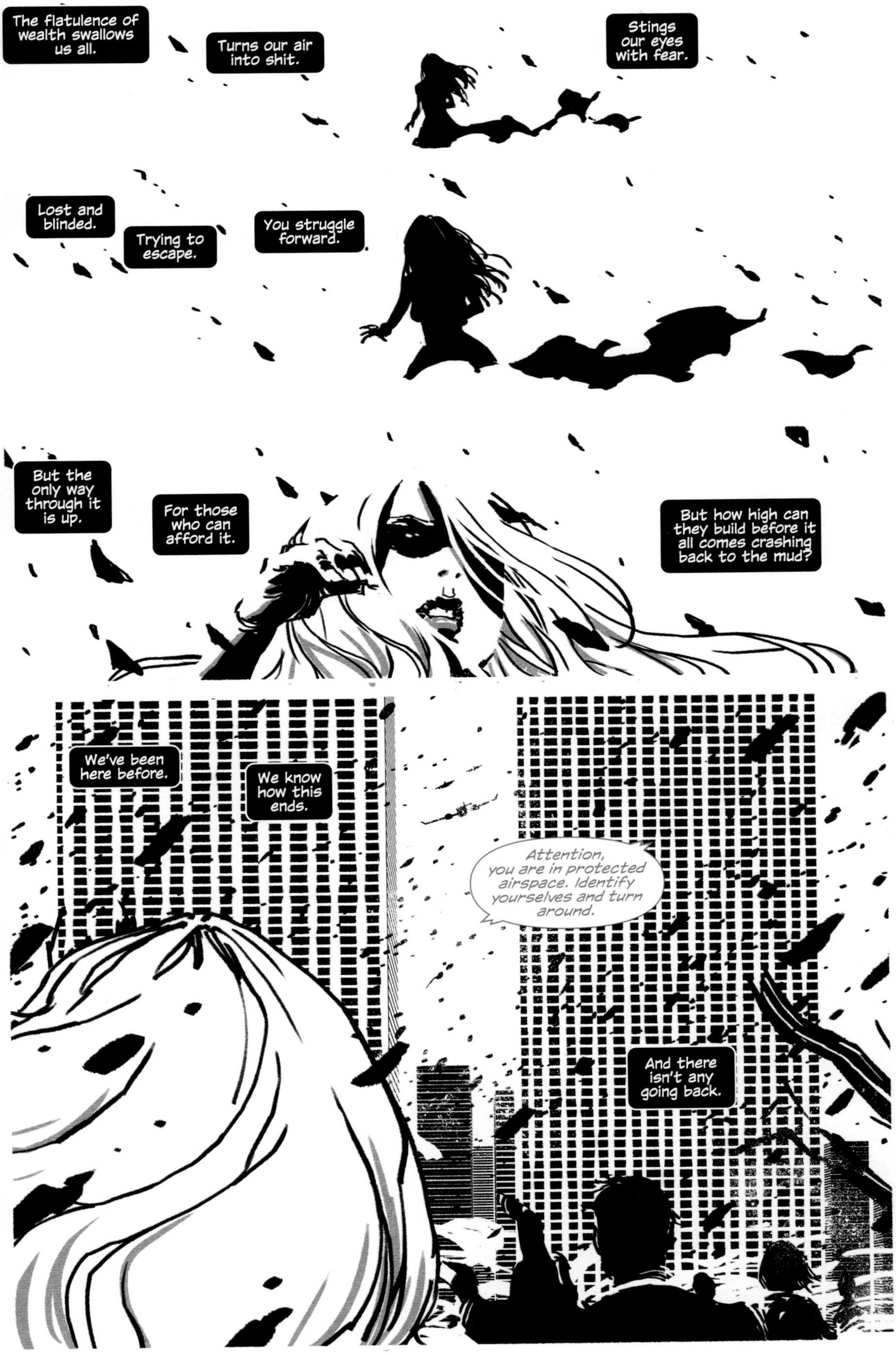
The flatulence of wealth swallows us all.
Turns our air into shit.
Stings our eyes with fear.
Lost and blinded.
Trying to escape.
You struggle forward.
But the only way through it is up.
For those who can afford it.
But how high can they build before it all comes crashing back to the mud?
We've been here before.
We know how this ends.
Attention, you are in protected airspace. Identify yourselves and turn around.
And there isn't any going back.

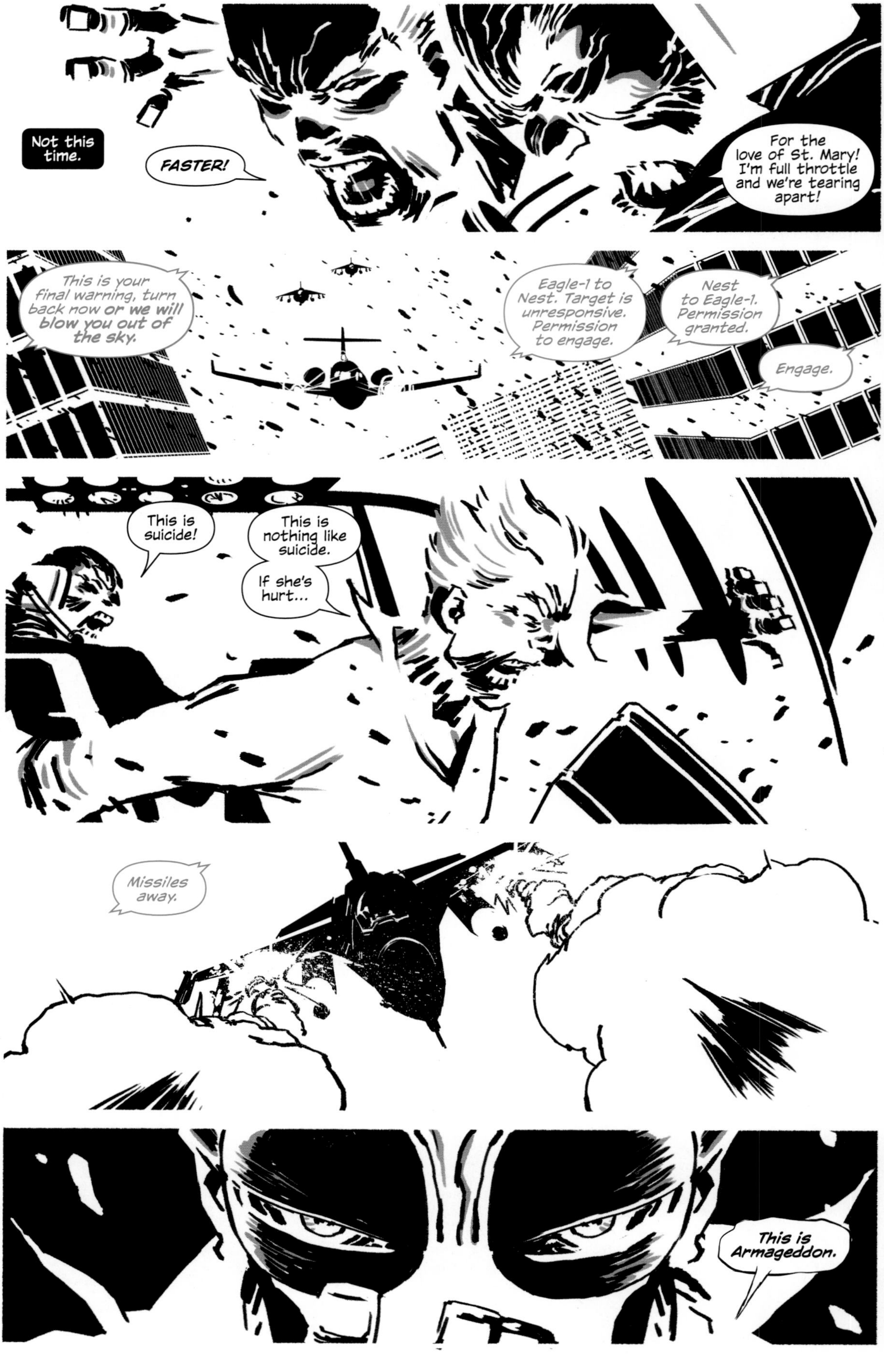
Not this time.
FASTER!
For the love of St. Mary! I'm full throttle and we're tearing apart!
This is your final warning, turn back now or we will blow you out of the sky.
Eagle-1 to Nest. Target is unresponsive. Permission to engage.
Nest to Eagle-1. Permission granted.
Engage.
This is suicide!
This is nothing like suicide.
If she's hurt...
Missiles away.
This is Armageddon.

i promised you

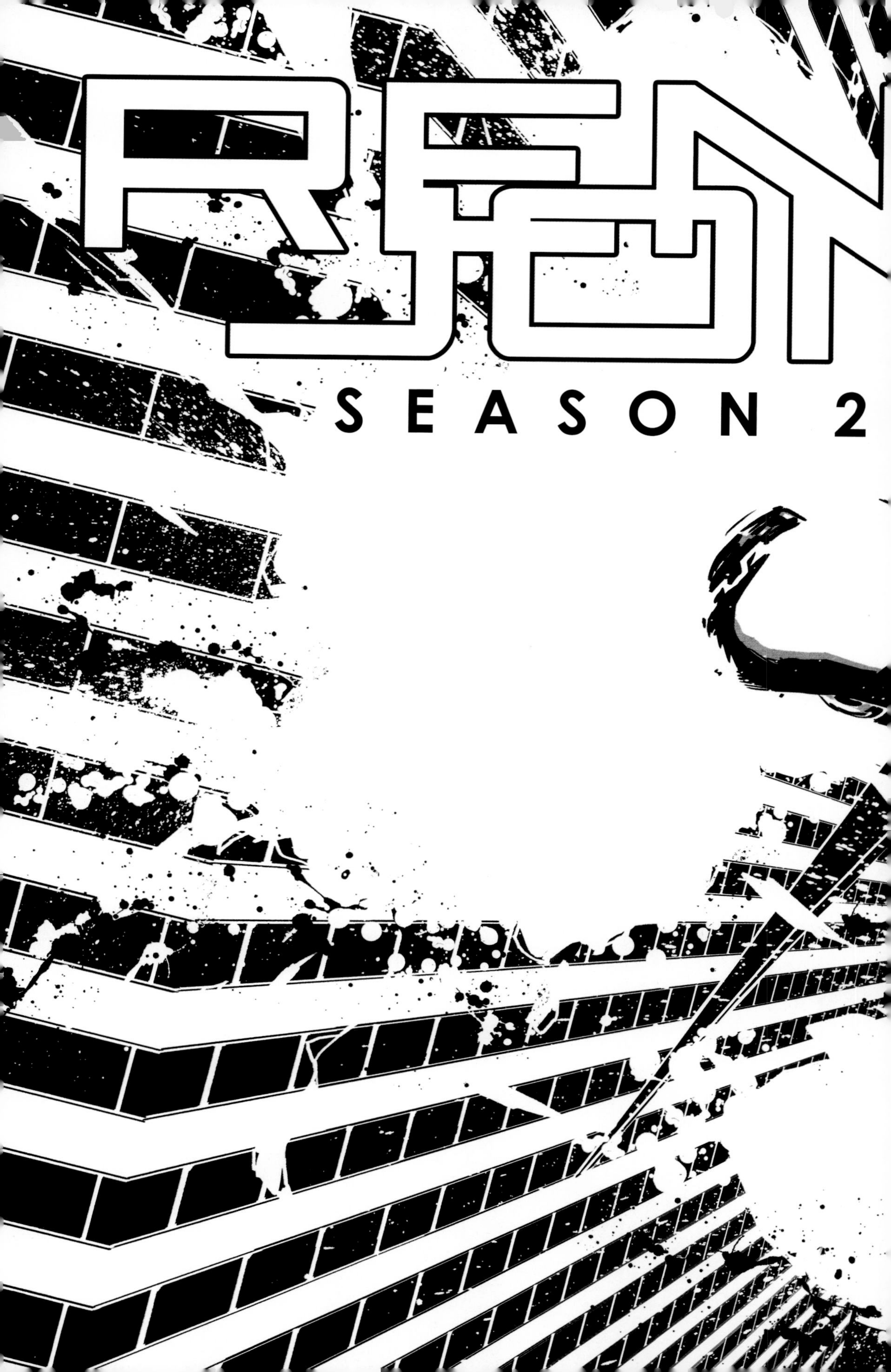
SEASON 2

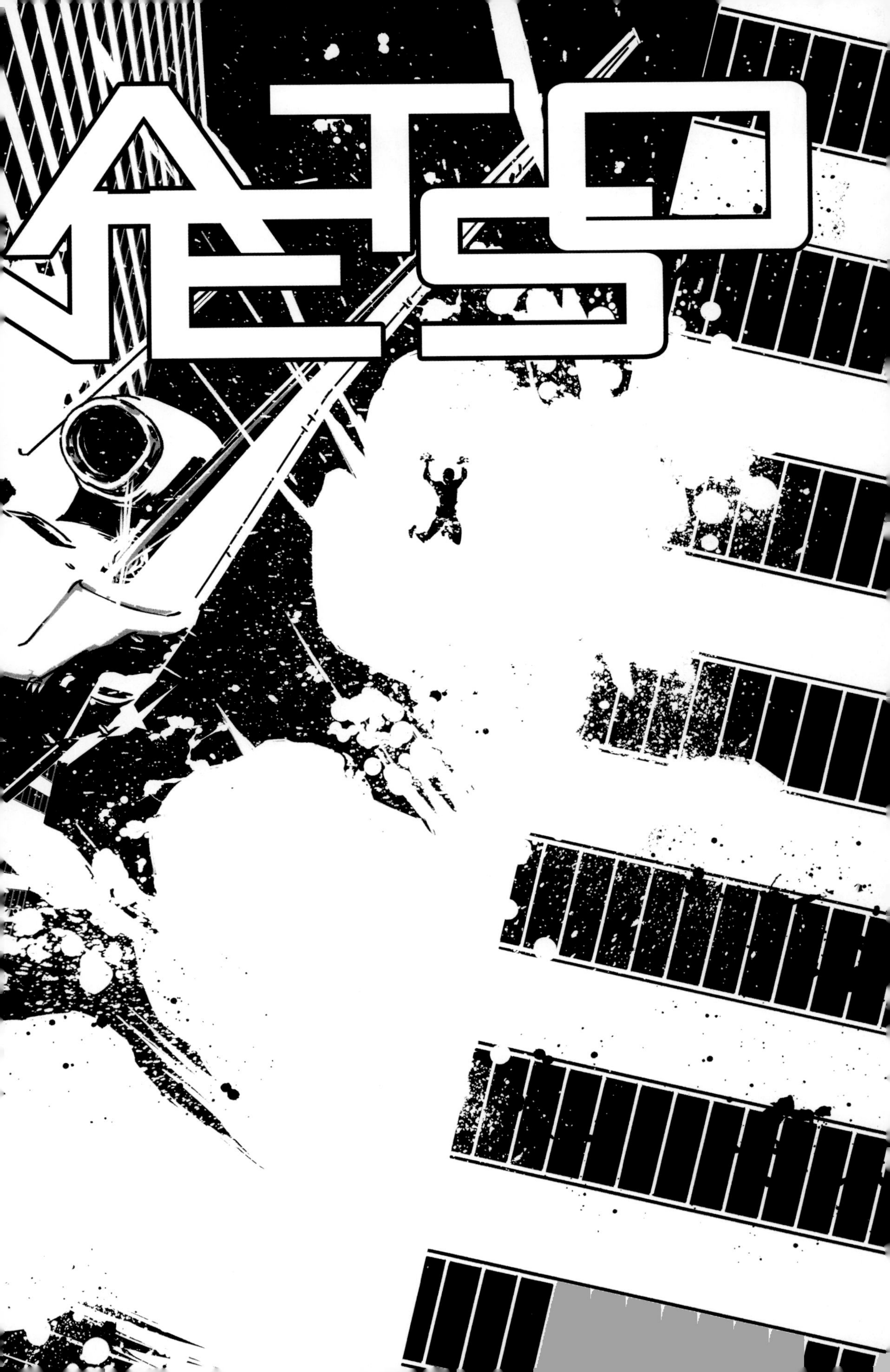

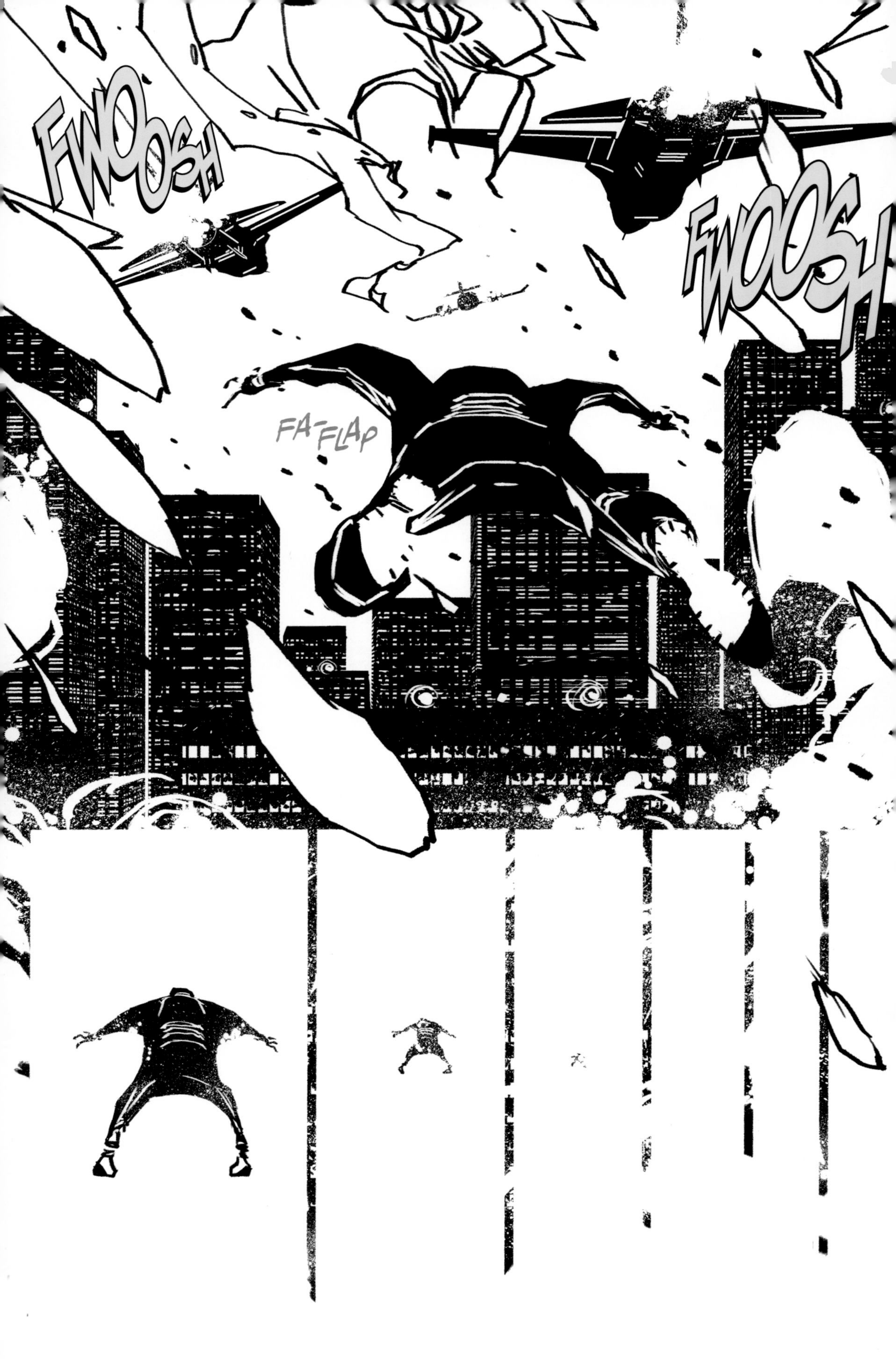
FWOOSH
FWOOSH
FA-FLAP

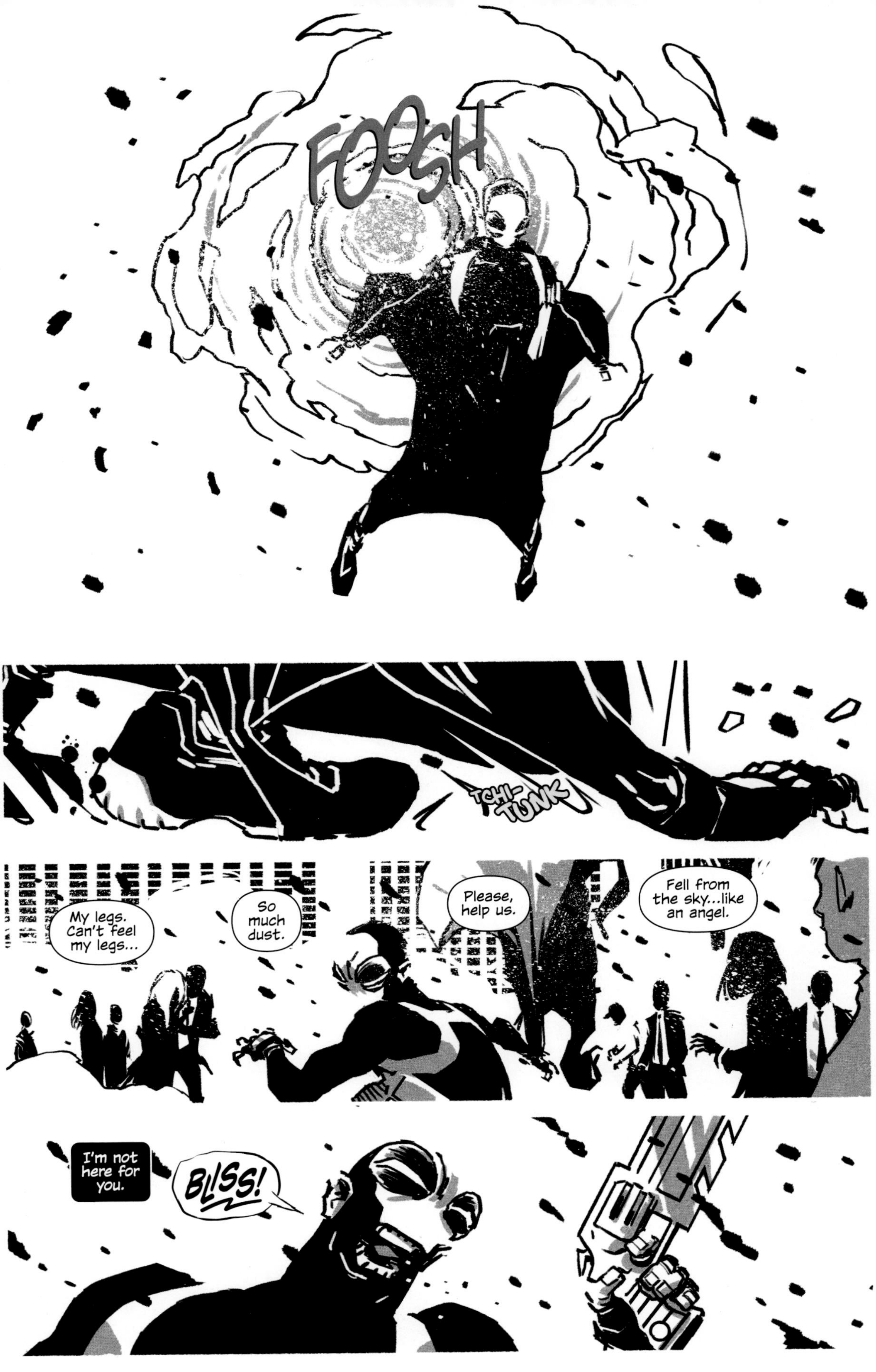
FOOSH
TCHI-TUNK
My legs. Can't feel my legs...
So much dust.
Please, help us.
Fell from the sky...like an angel.
I'm not here for you.
BLISS!

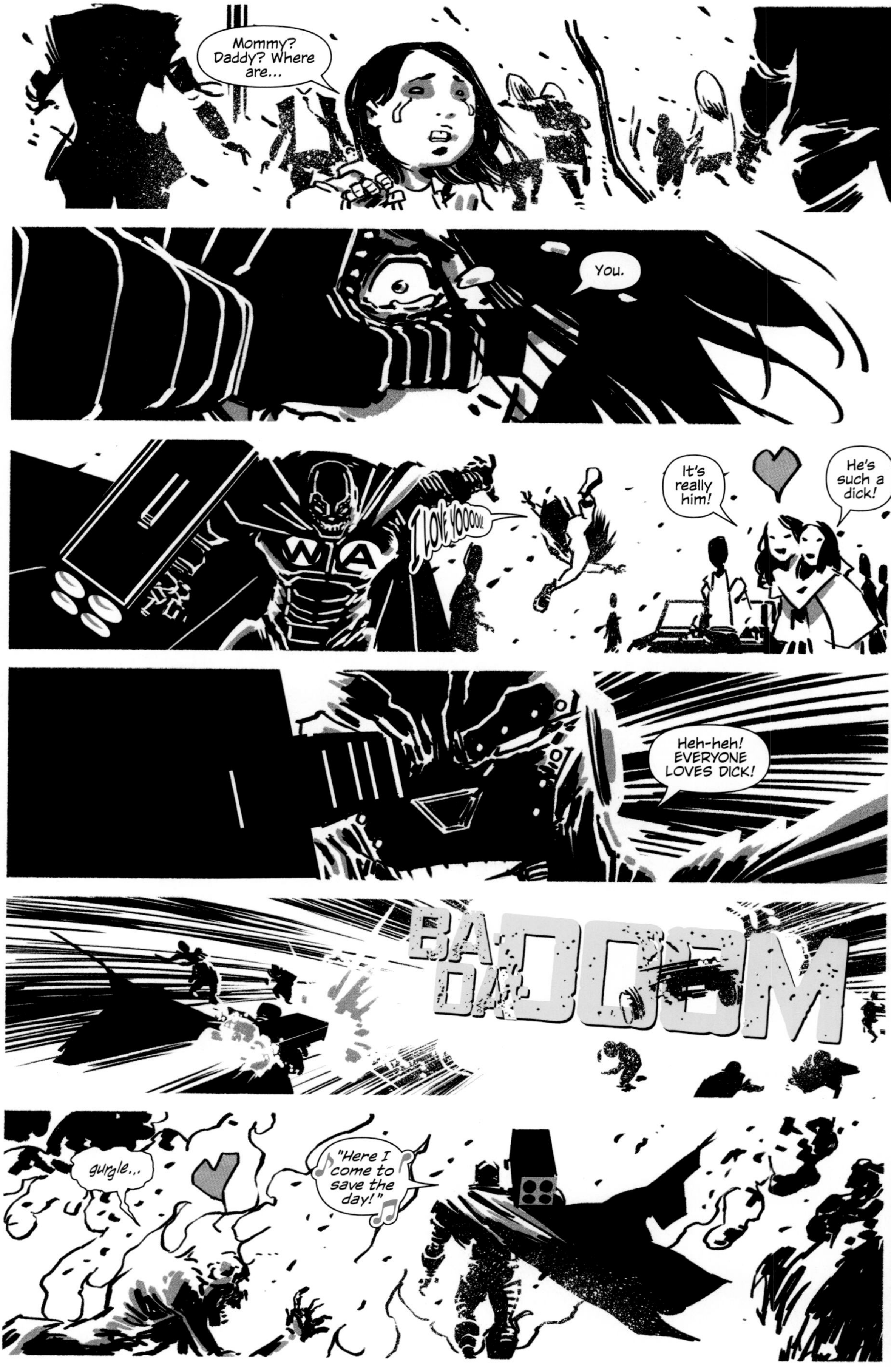
Mommy? Daddy? Where are...
You.
I LOVE YOOOOU.
It's really him!
He's such a dick!
Heh-heh! EVERYONE LOVES DICK!
BA-DA-DOOM
gurgle...
"Here I come to save the day!"

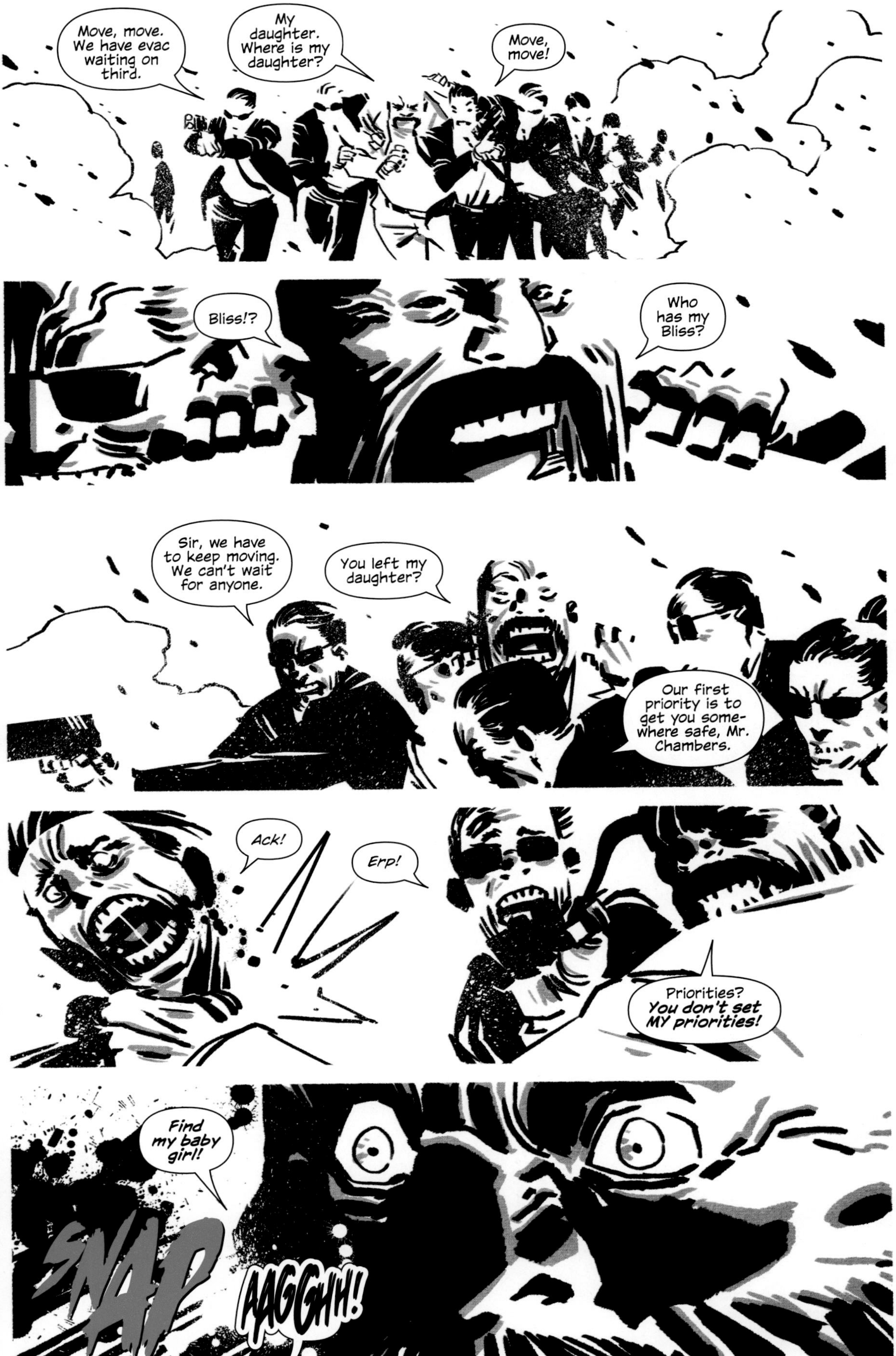

Move, move. We have evac waiting on third.
My daughter. Where is my daughter?
Move, move!
Bliss!?
Who has my Bliss?
Sir, we have to keep moving. We can't wait for anyone.
You left my daughter?
Our first priority is to get you some-where safe, Mr. Chambers.
Ack!
Erp!
Priorities? You don't set MY priorities!
Find my baby girl!
SNAP
AAGGHH!

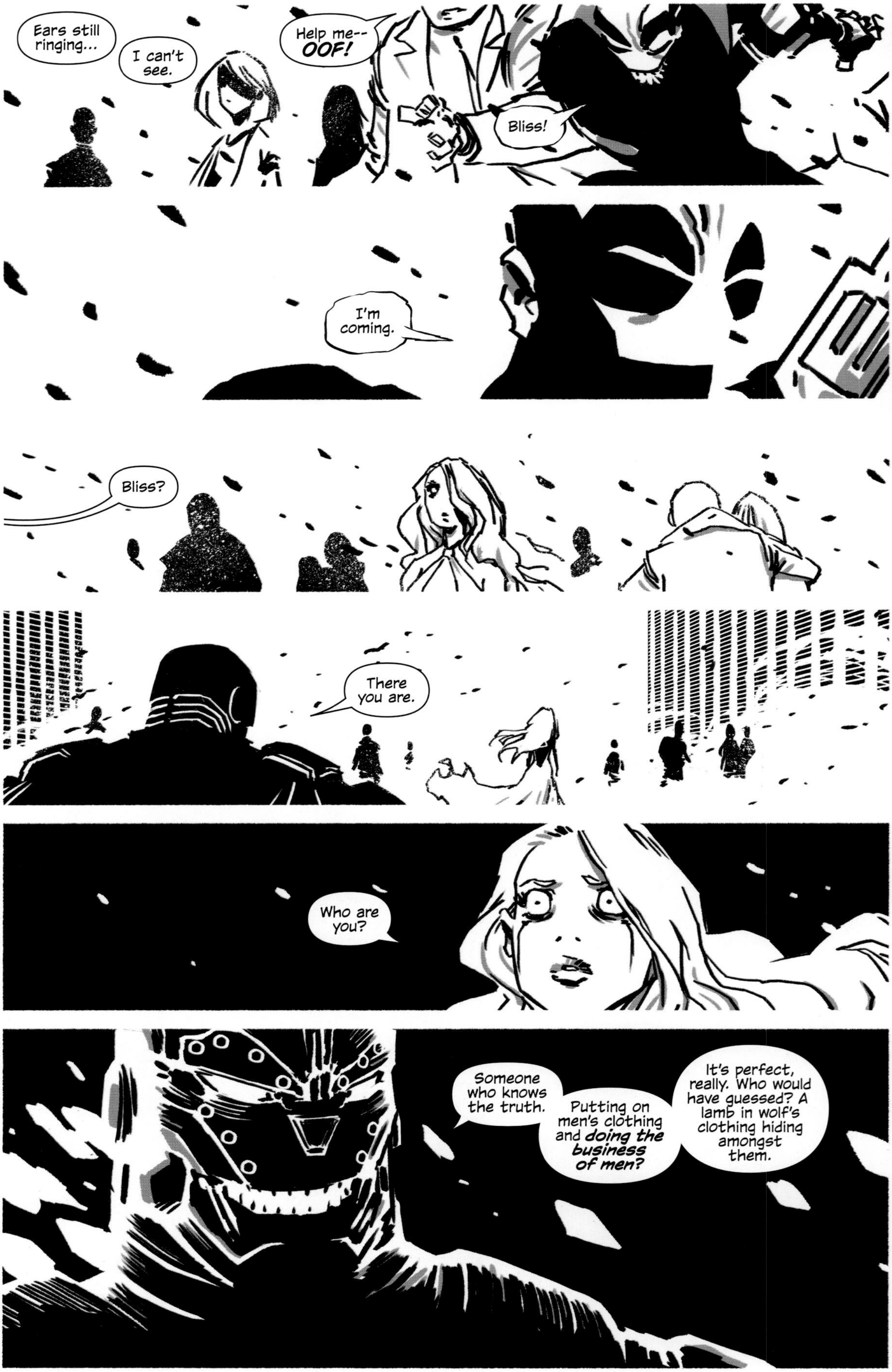
Ears still ringing...
I can't see.
Help me-- OOF!
Bliss!
I'm coming.
Bliss?
There you are.
Who are you?
Someone who knows the truth.
Putting on men's clothing and *doing the business of men?*
It's perfect, really. Who would have guessed? A lamb in wolf's clothing hiding amongst them.

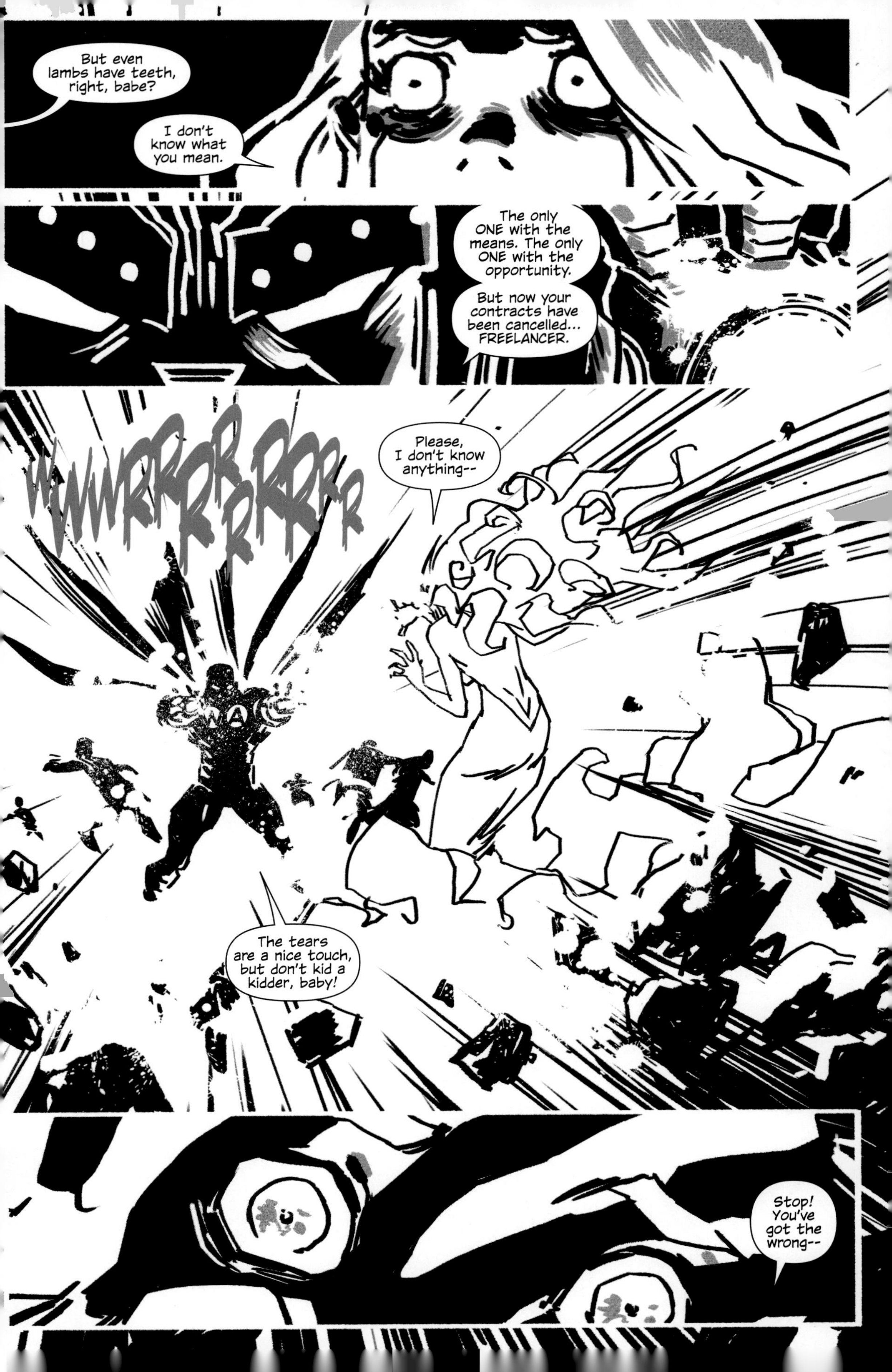

But even lambs have teeth, right, babe?
I don't know what you mean.
The only ONE with the means. The only ONE with the opportunity.
But now your contracts have been cancelled... FREELANCER.
WWWRRRRRRRRRRR
Please, I don't know anything--
The tears are a nice touch, but don't kid a kidder, baby!
Stop! You've got the wrong--

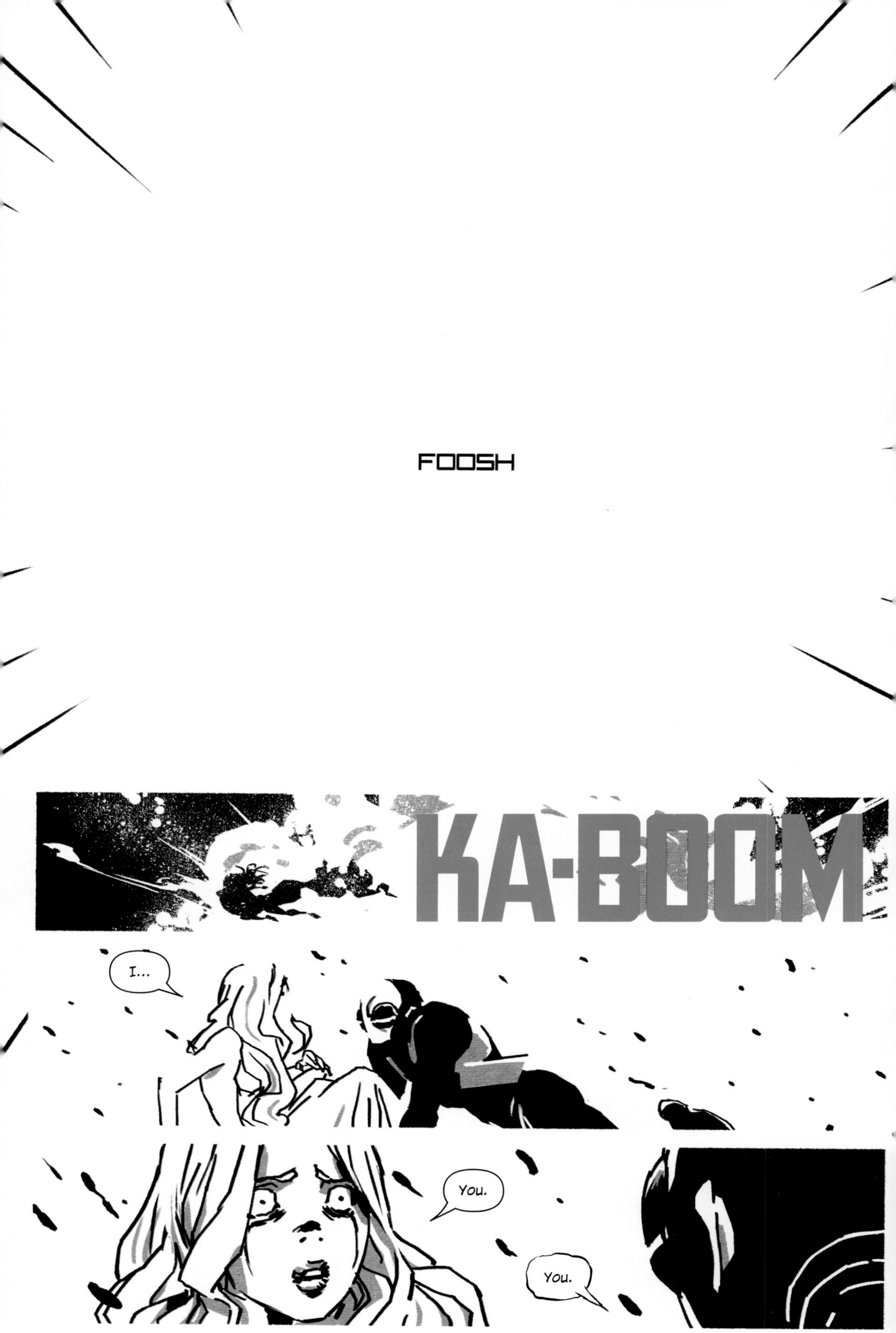

FOOSH
KA-BOOM
I...
You.
You.

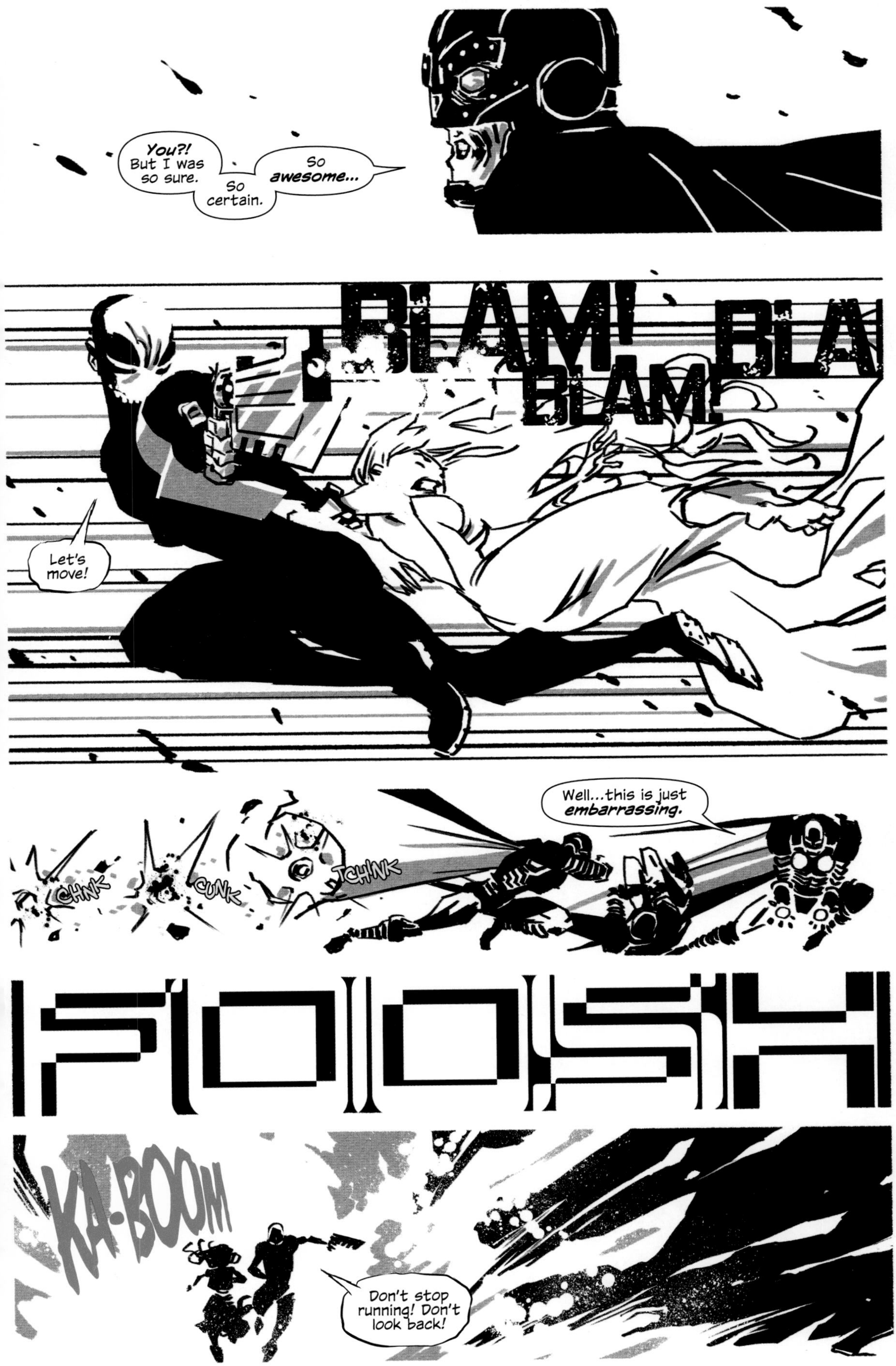

You?! But I was so sure.
So certain.
So awesome...
BLAM! BLAM! BLAM!
Let's move!
CHNK
CUNK
TCHNK
Well...this is just embarrassing.
FOOSH
KA-BOOM
Don't stop running! Don't look back!

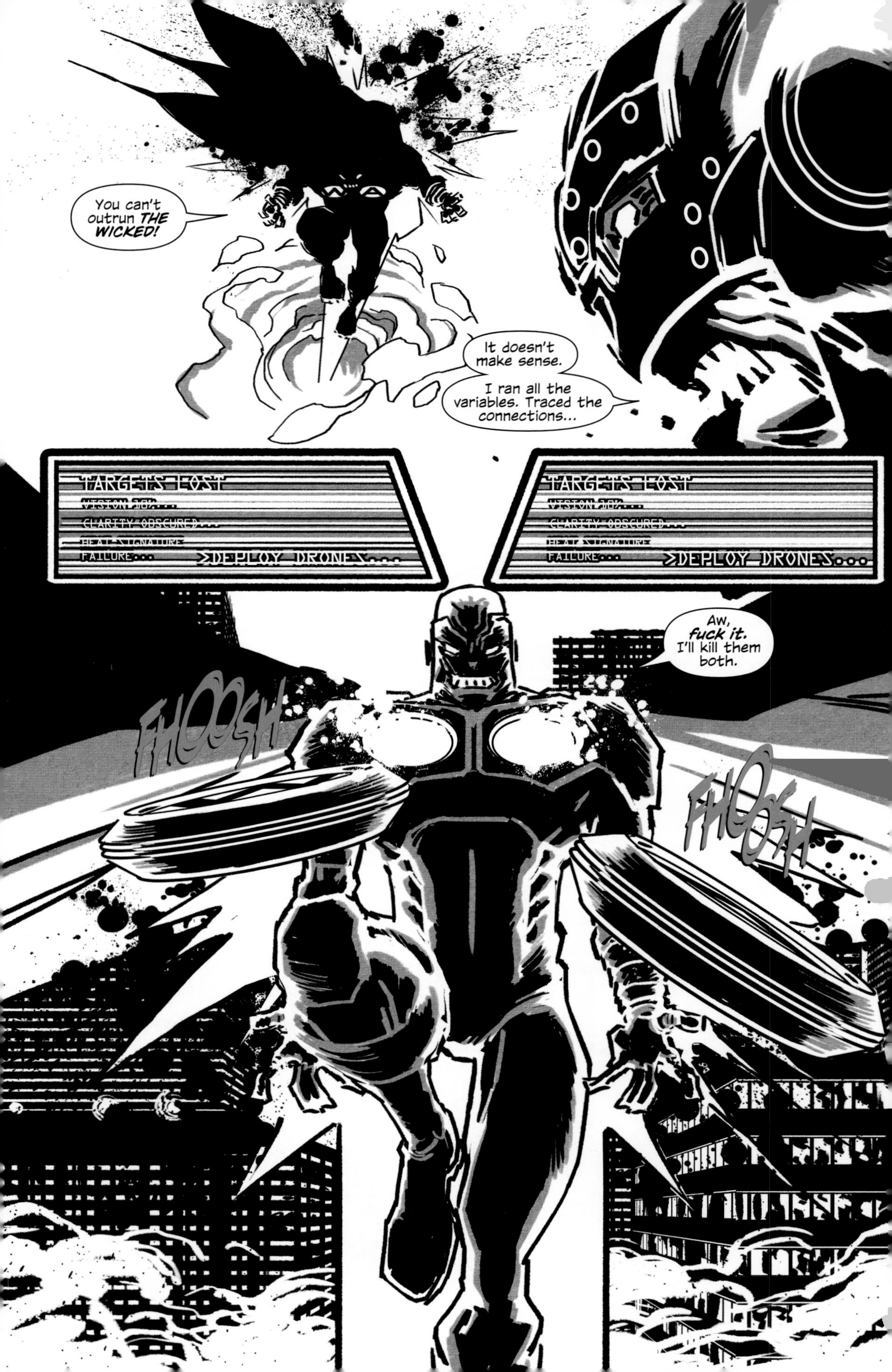
You can't outrun THE WICKED!
It doesn't make sense.
I ran all the variables. Traced the connections...
TARGETS LOST
VISION 10%...
CLARITY OBSCURED...
HEAT SIGNATURE FAILURE...
>DEPLOY DRONES...
TARGETS LOST
VISION 10%...
CLARITY OBSCURED...
HEAT SIGNATURE FAILURE...
>DEPLOY DRONES...
Aw, fuck it. I'll kill them both.
FHOOSH
FHOOSH

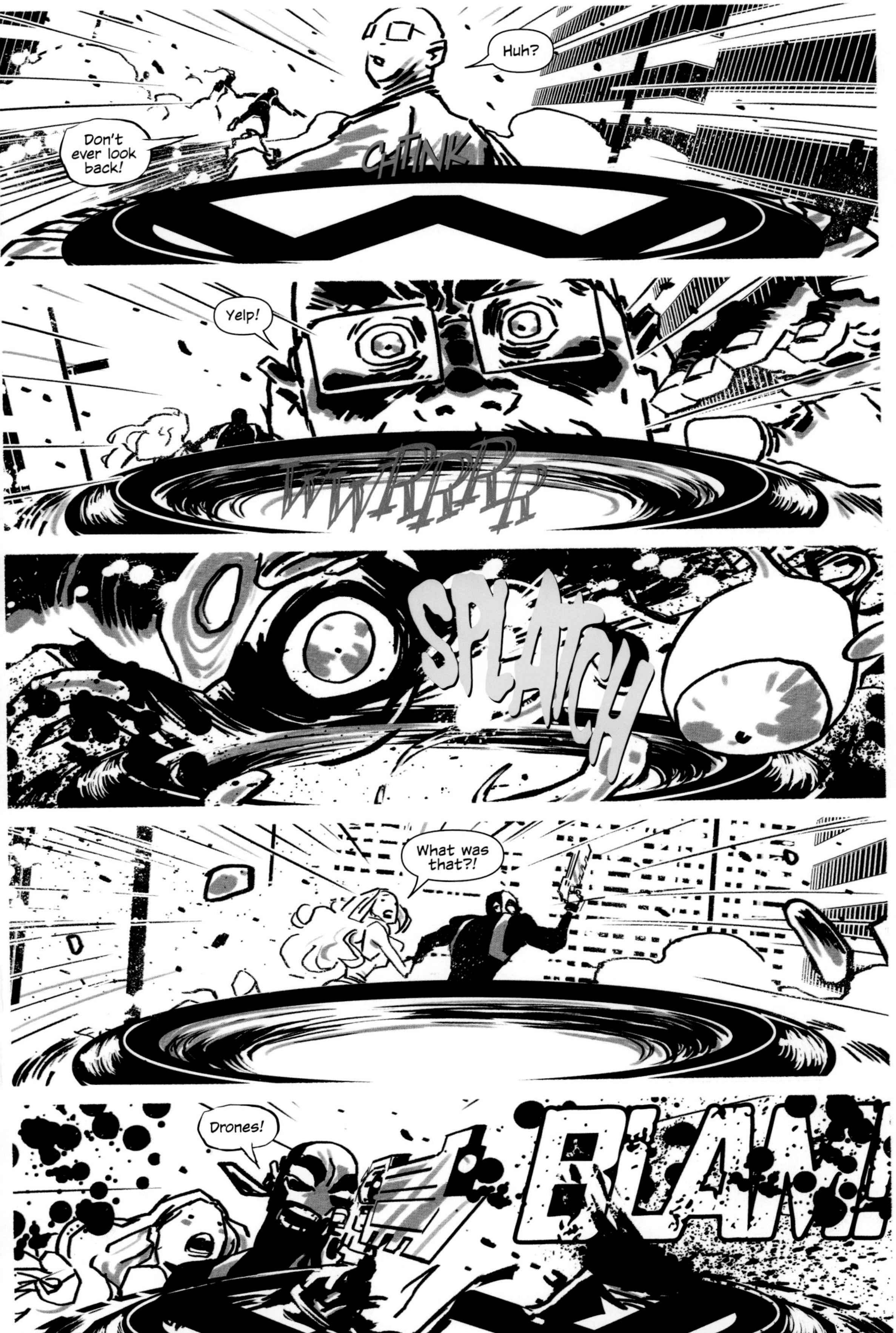

Huh?
Don't ever look back!
CHINK
Yelp!
WWRRRR
SPLATCH
What was that?!
Drones!
BLAM!

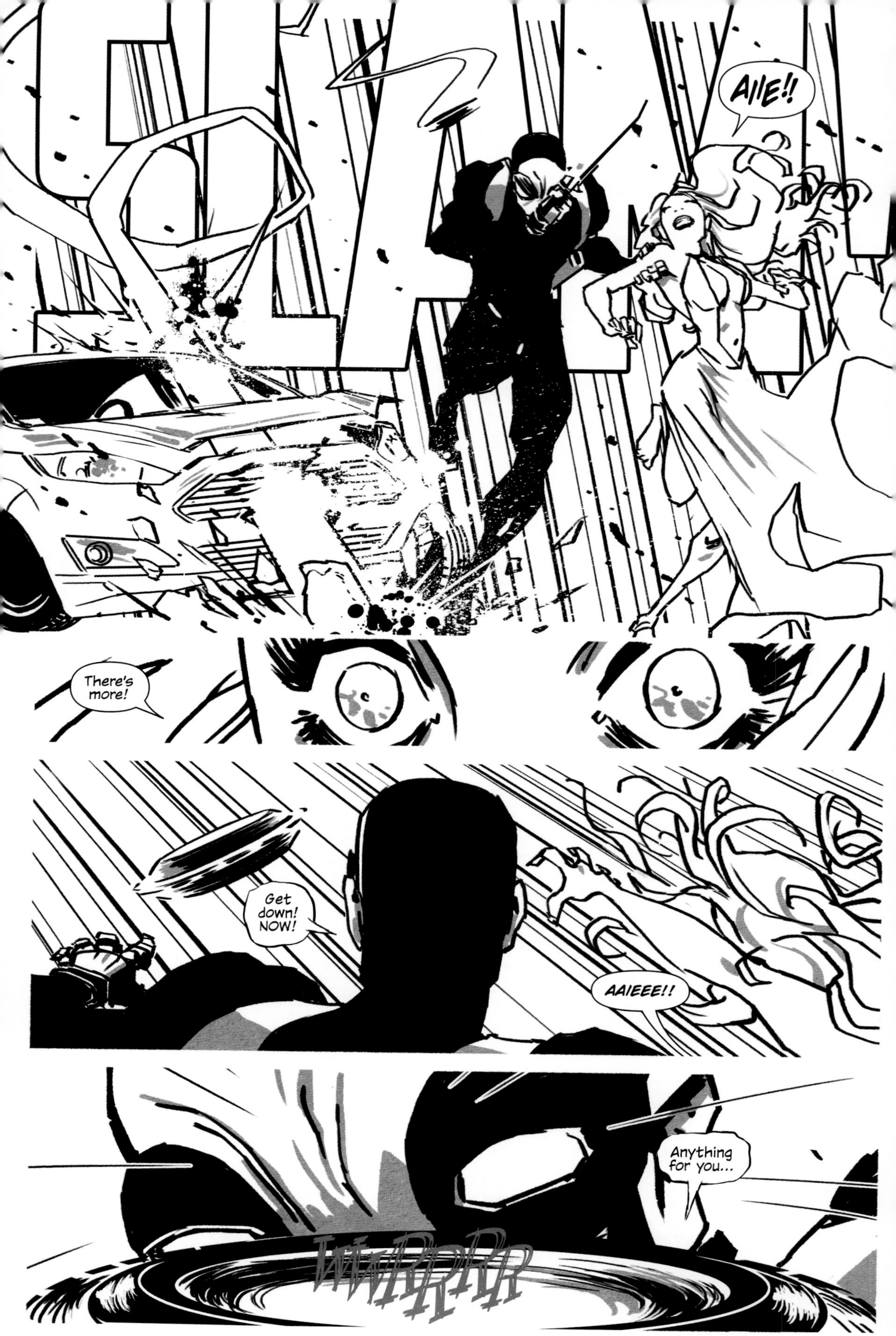
AIIE!!
There's more!
Get down! NOW!
AAIEEE!!
Anything for you...
WWRRRRR

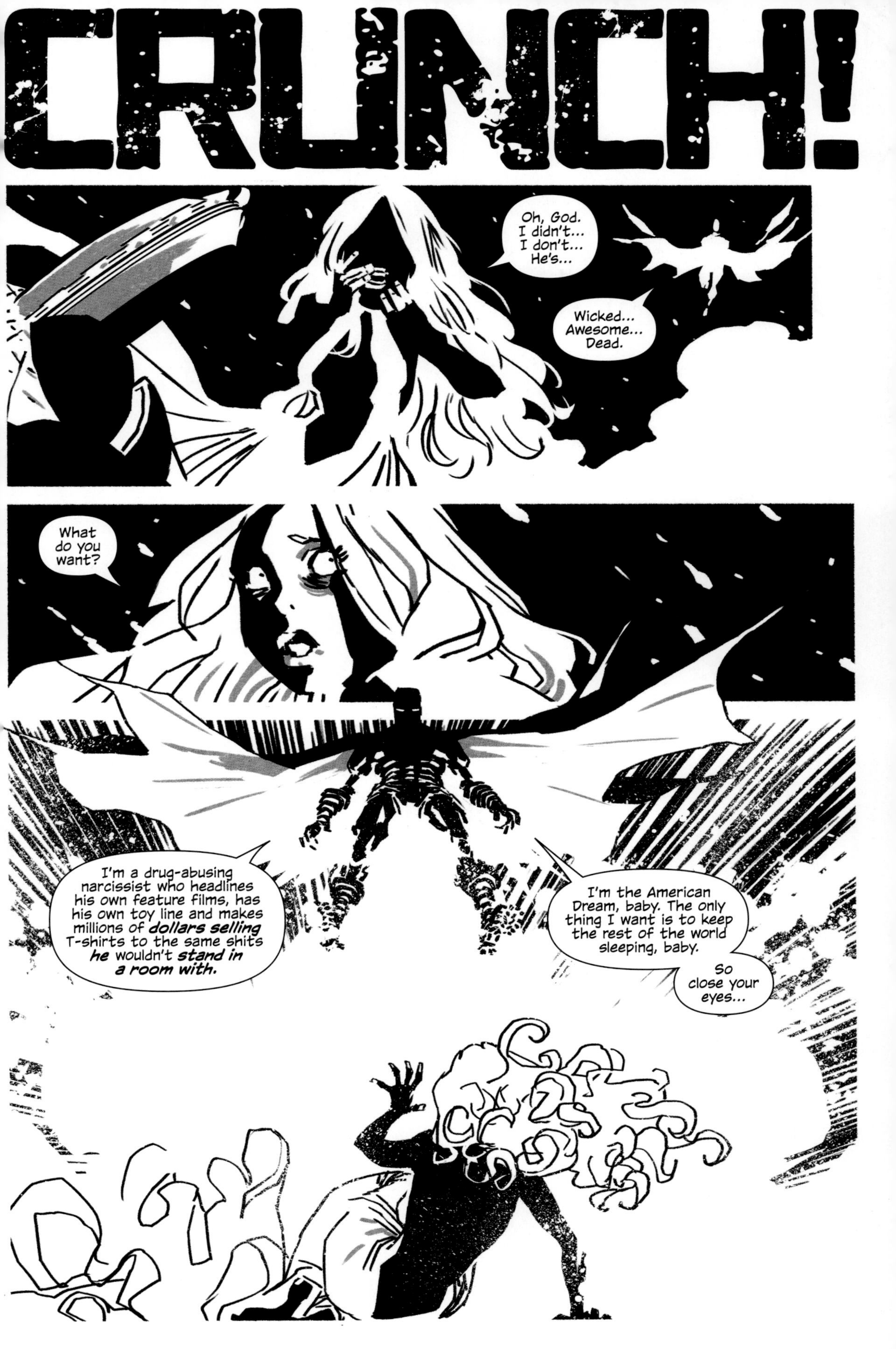
CRUNCH!
Oh, God. I didn't... I don't... He's...
Wicked... Awesome... Dead.
What do you want?
I'm a drug-abusing narcissist who headlines his own feature films, has his own toy line and makes millions of **dollars selling** T-shirts to the same shits ***he*** wouldn't ***stand in a room with.***
I'm the American Dream, baby. The only thing I want is to keep the rest of the world sleeping, baby.
So close your eyes...

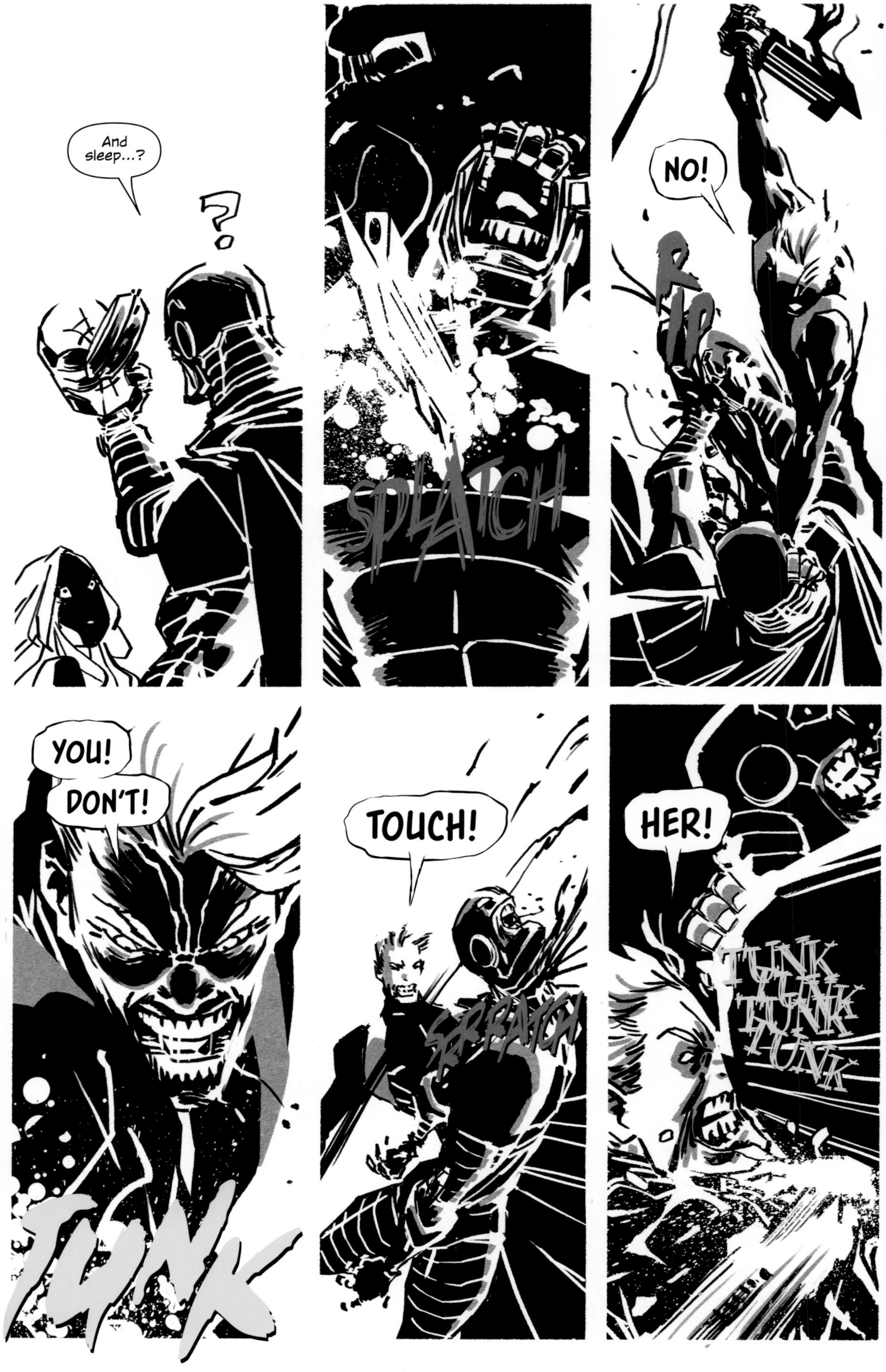
And sleep...?
?
SPLATCH
NO!
RIP
YOU!
DON'T!
TUNK
TOUCH!
SKRATCH
HER!
TUNK TUNK TUNK TUNK

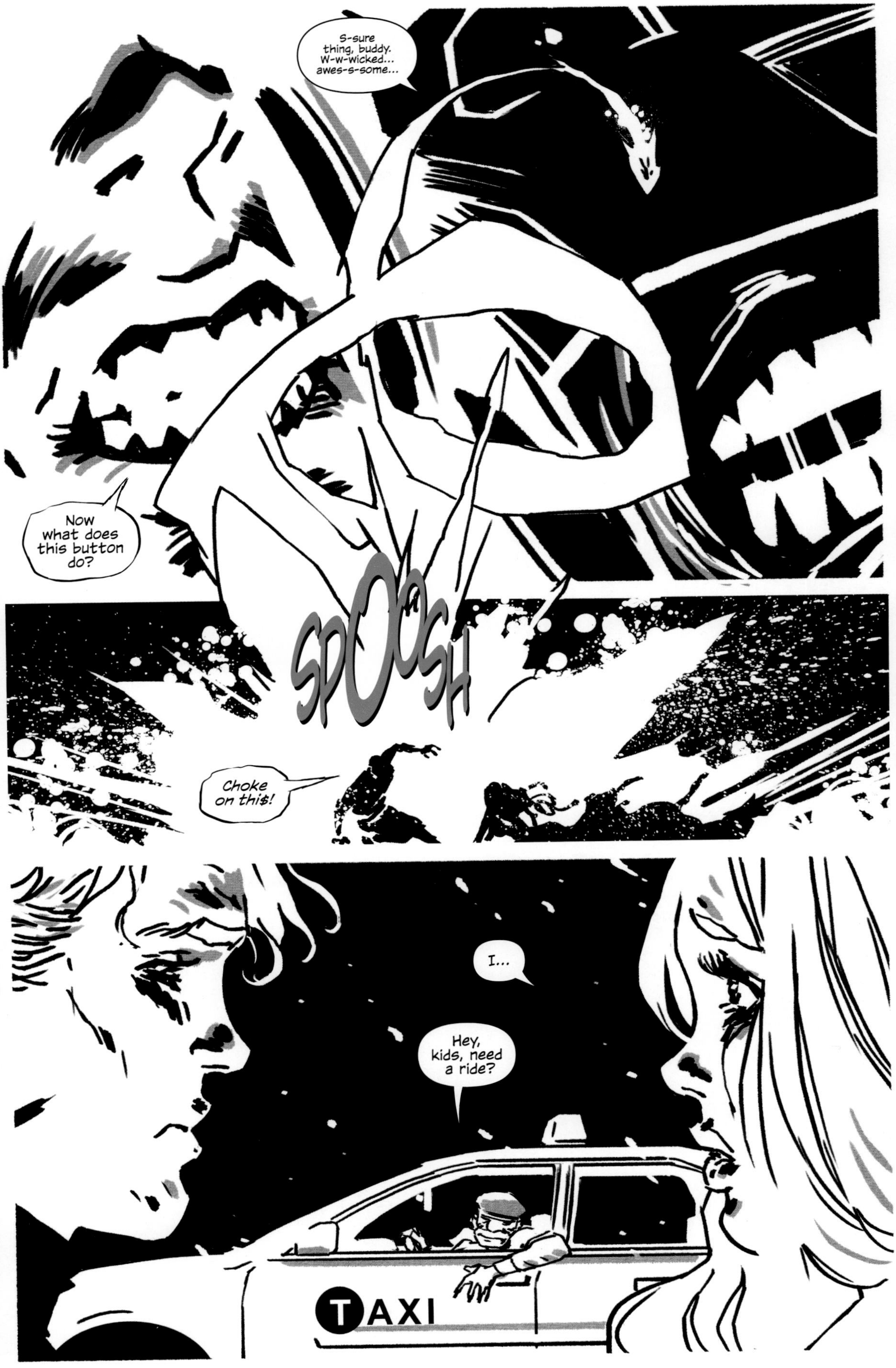
S-sure thing, buddy. W-w-wicked... awes-s-some...
Now what does this button do?
SPOOSH
Choke on thi$!
I...
Hey, kids, need a ride?
TAXI

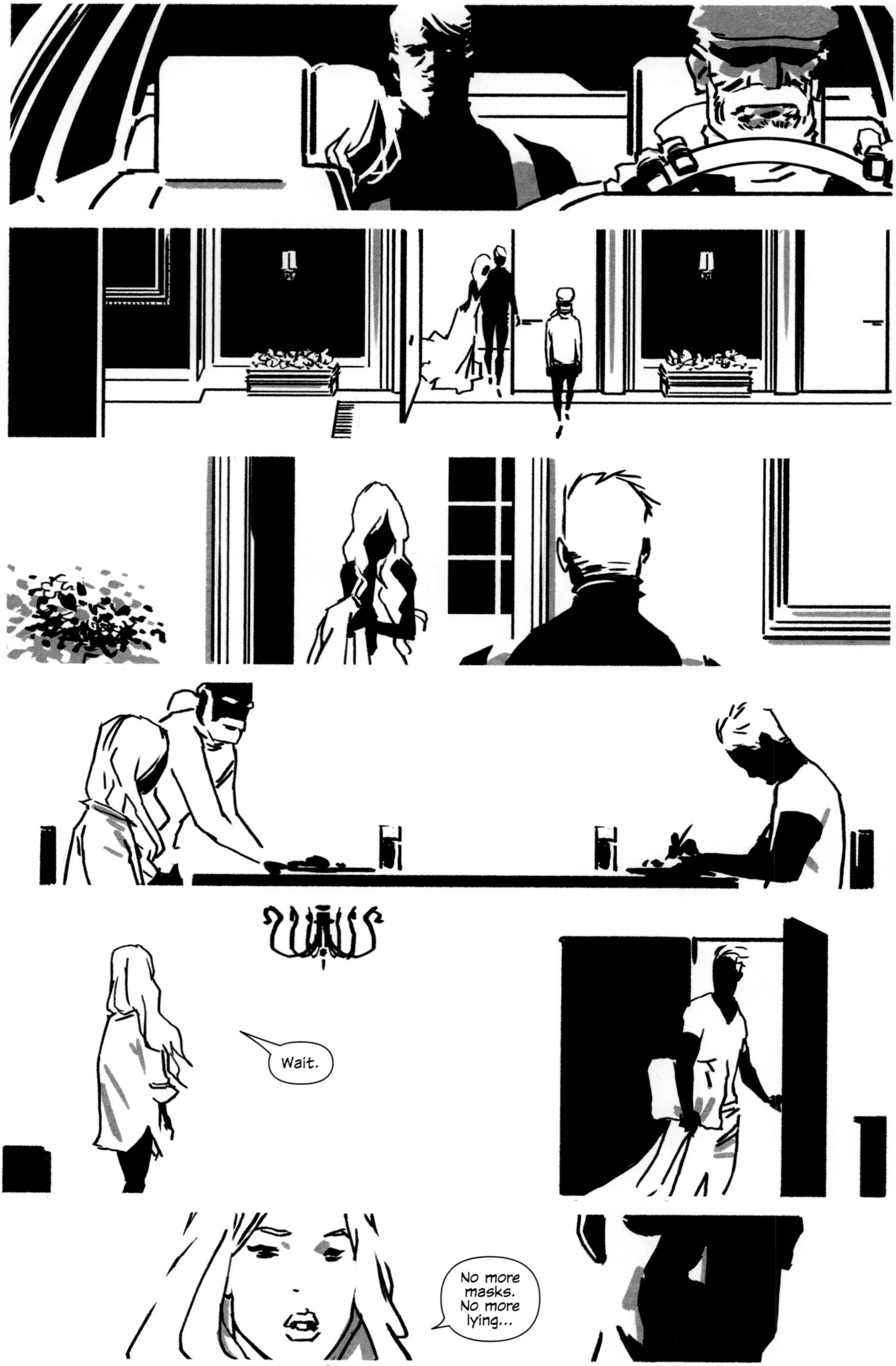
Wait.
No more masks. No more lying...

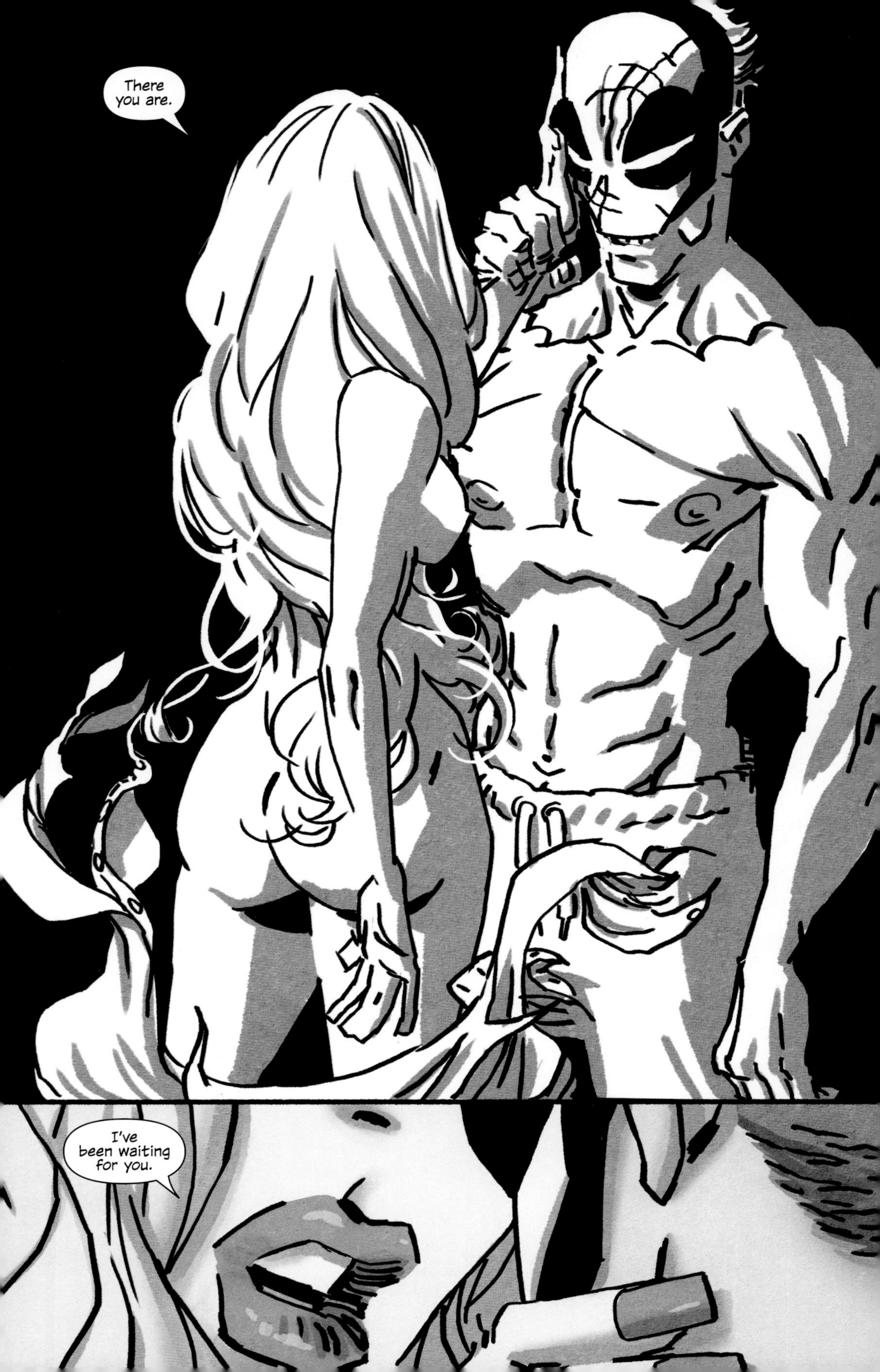
There you are.
I've been waiting for you.

And just like that I understand why I never ran away. Why I took this name. Lived this life.

You look at me now and cut right through.

I'm drowning in truth and there's nothing left to hold onto... but you.

It's always been you.

Bliss.

I followed you all the way here.

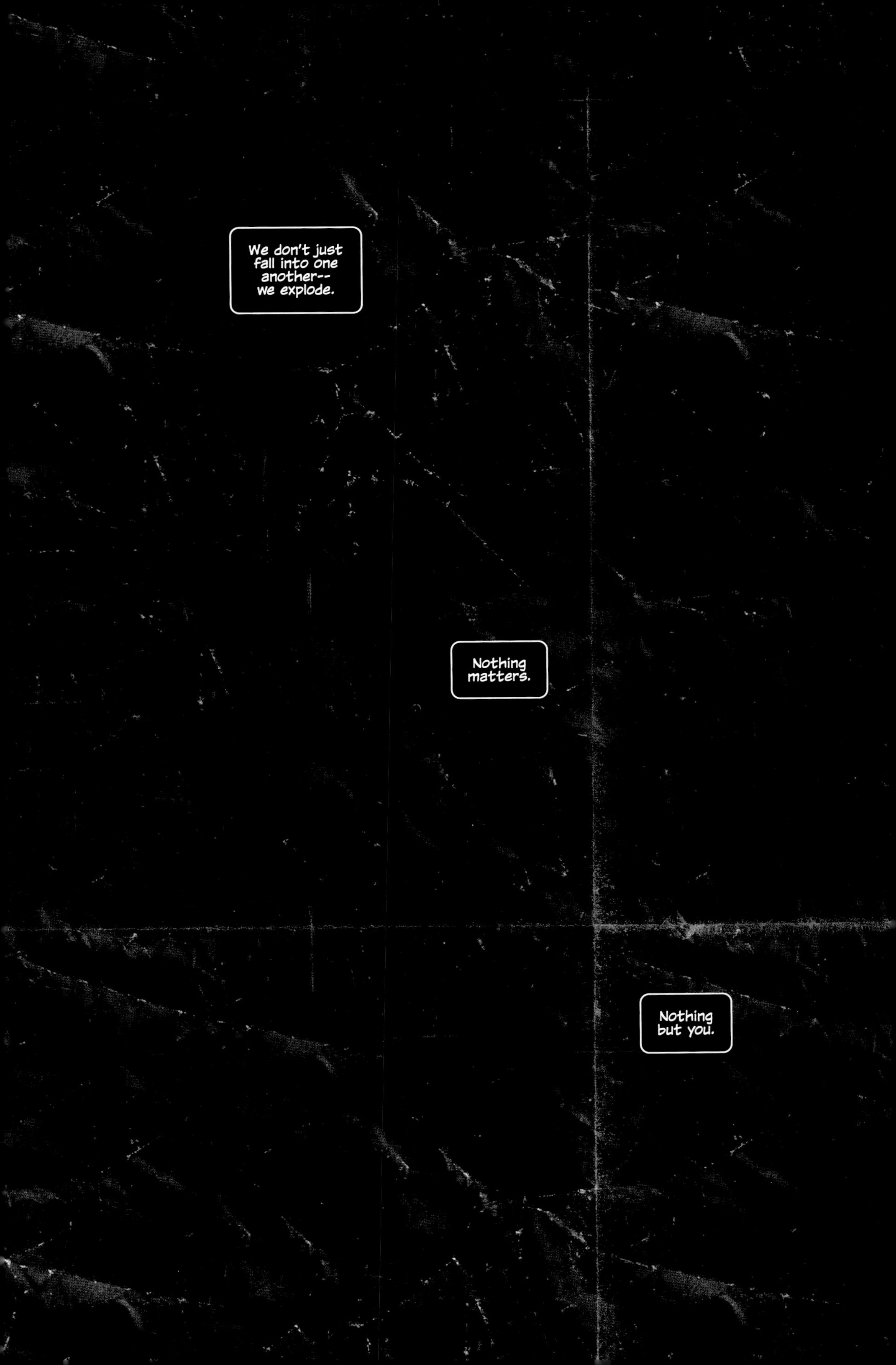
We don't just fall into one another-- we explode.
Nothing matters.
Nothing but you.

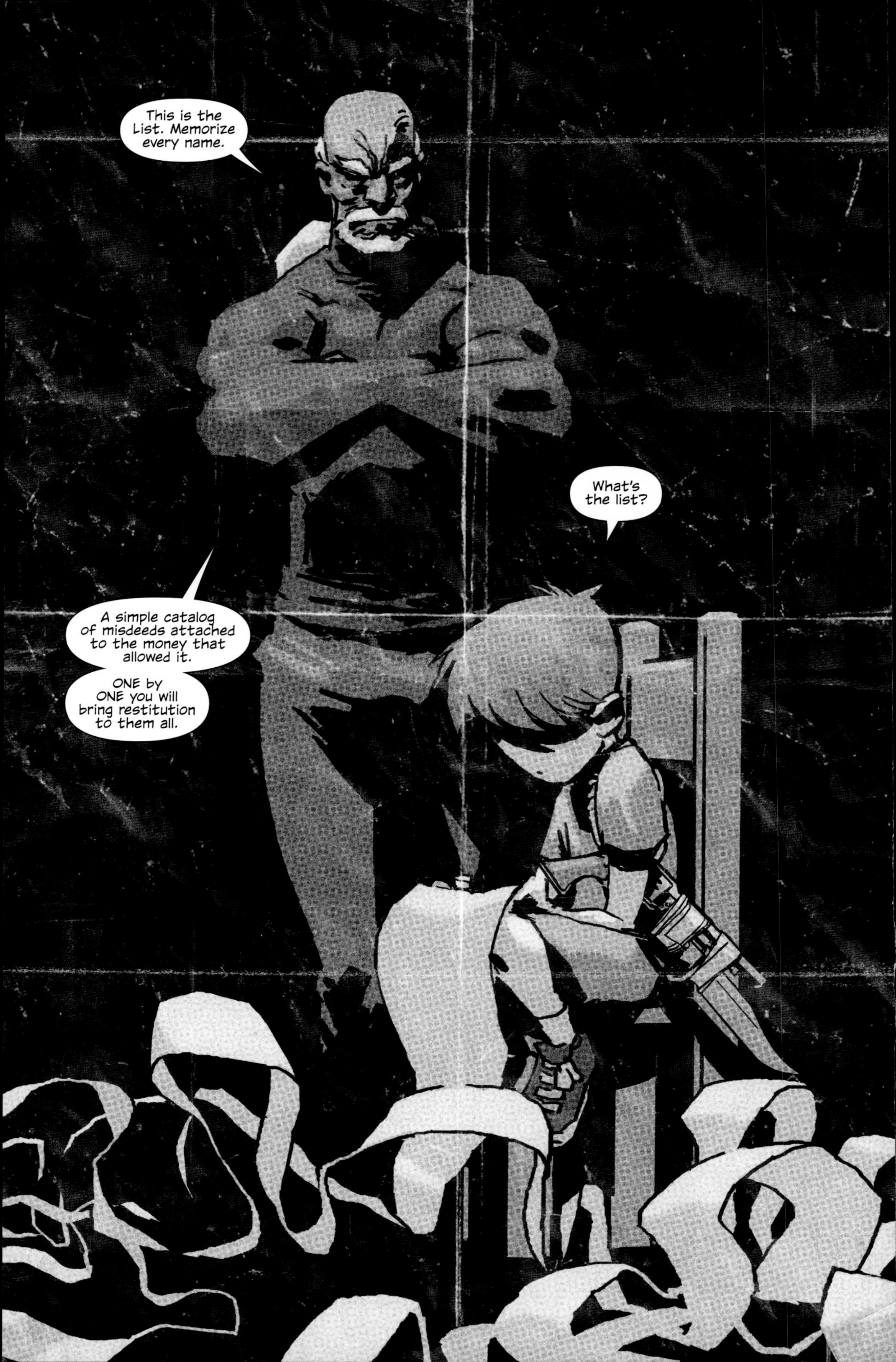
This is the List. Memorize every name.
What's the list?
A simple catalog of misdeeds attached to the money that allowed it.
ONE by ONE you will bring restitution to them all.

Jonathan Walker
Nicola Chambers

But this must be... a mistake?

She's just a kid. Like me... she hasn't done anything--

Nicola Chambers
Bliss Chambers

Yet? Children inherit more than money.

Ask the Roman Emperor. Ask the Byzantine Empire. Ask North Korea or Syria.

Monarchies are built upon those who become that which they once despised.

I warned you about her.

Nicola Chambers
Bliss Chambers

One day she will sit on top of the throne.

Bliss Chambers

And on that day she will meet you in a very

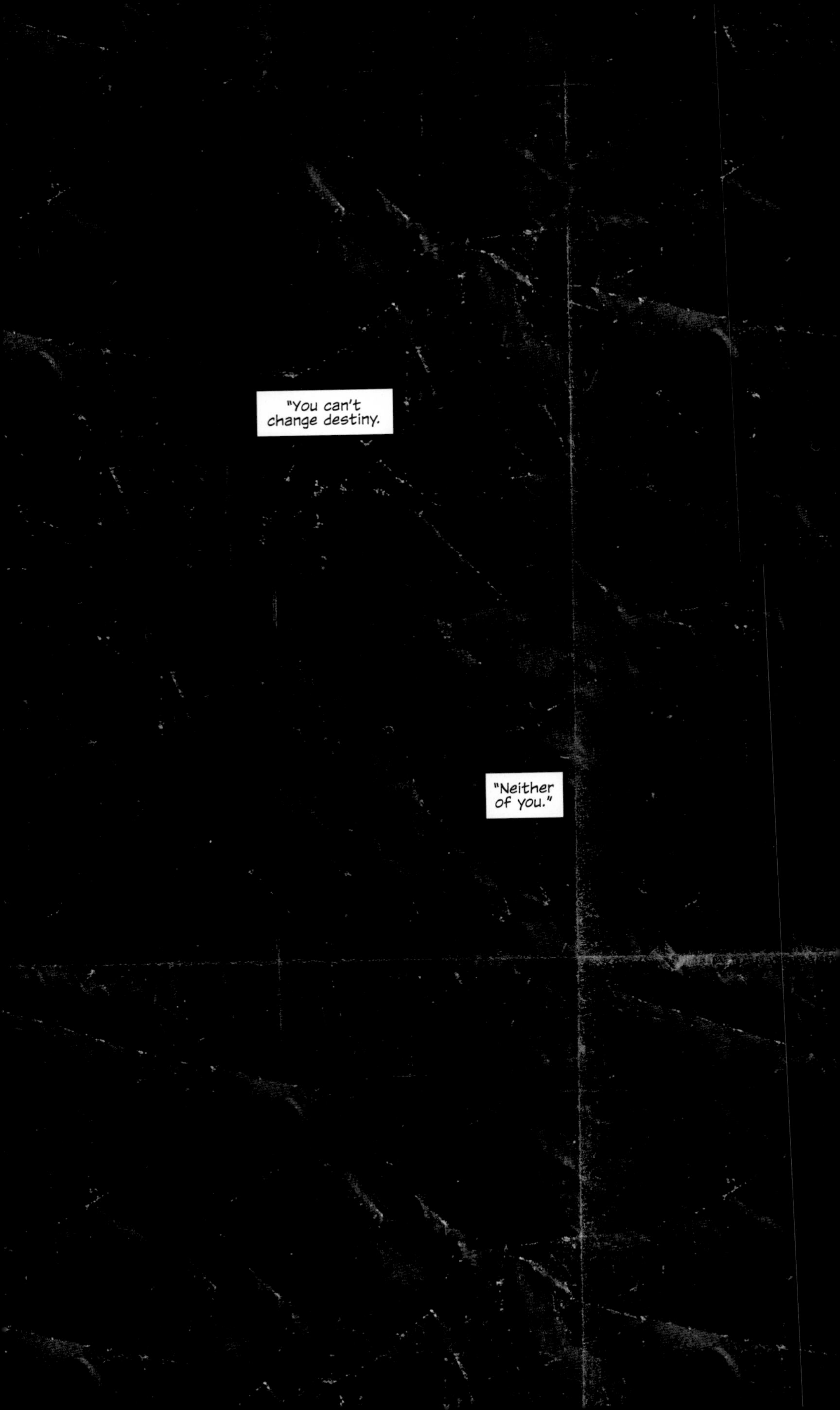
"You can't change destiny.
"Neither of you."

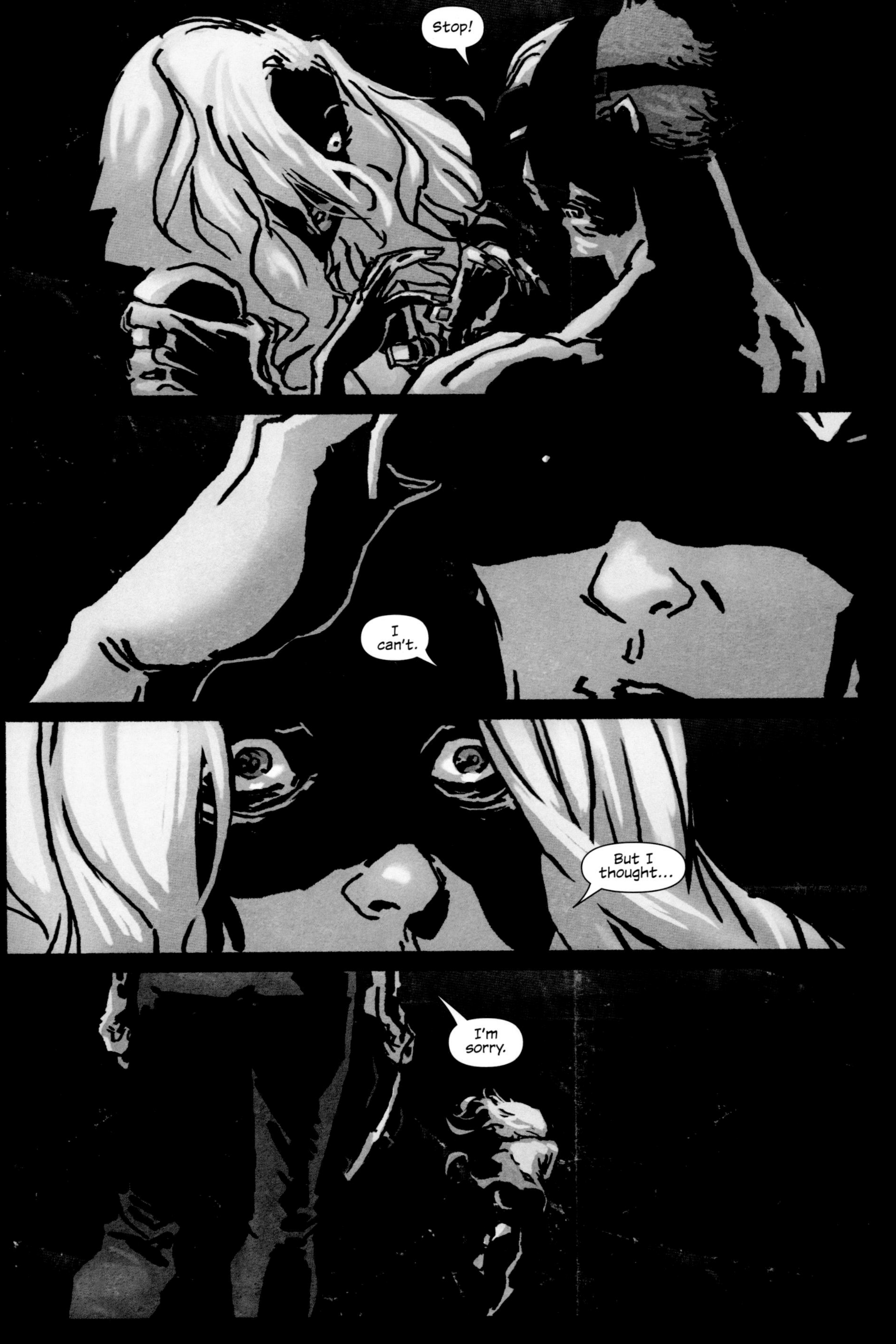
Stop!
I can't.
But I thought...
I'm sorry.

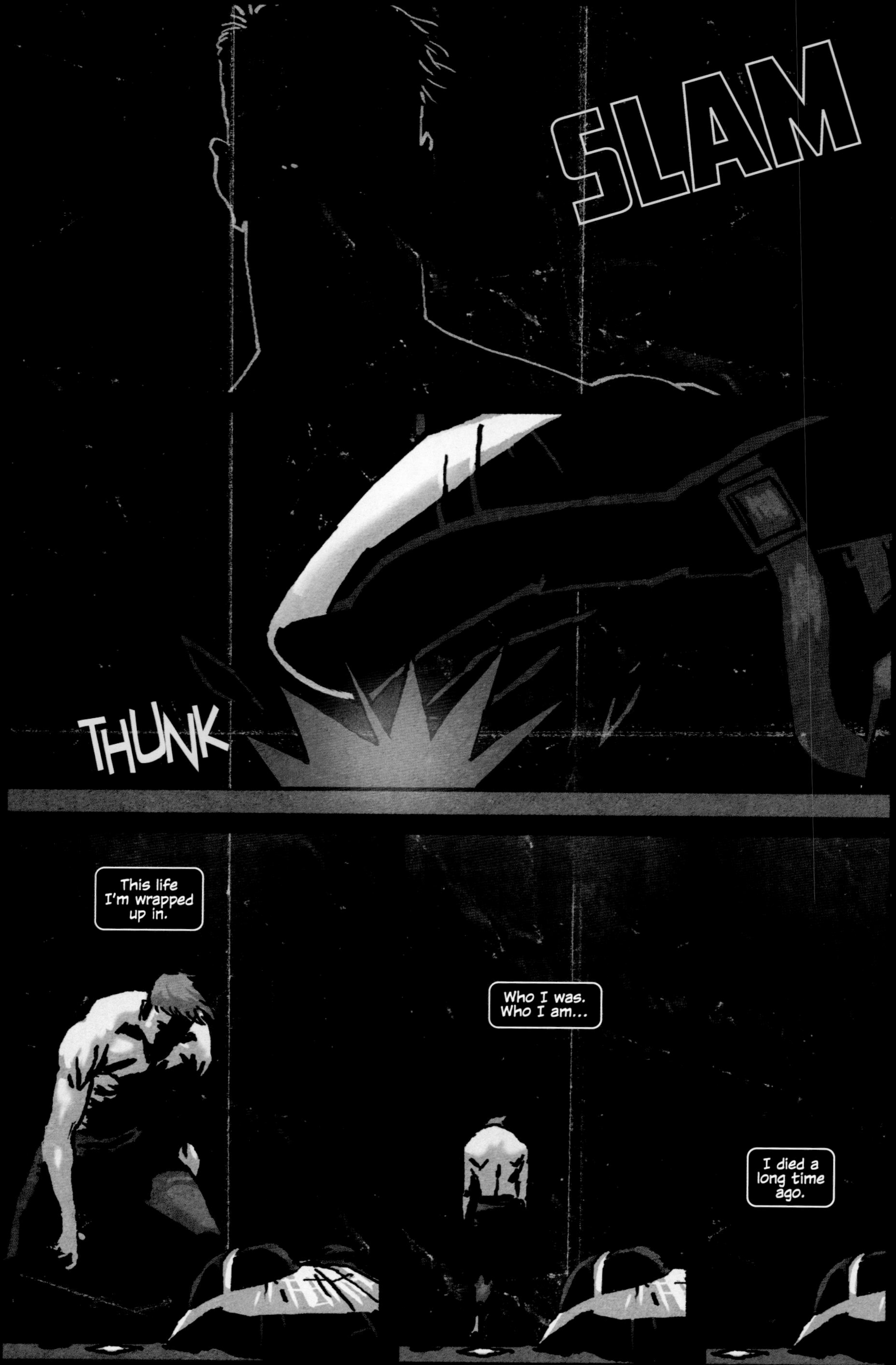
SLAM
THUNK
This life I'm wrapped up in.
Who I was. Who I am...
I died a long time ago.

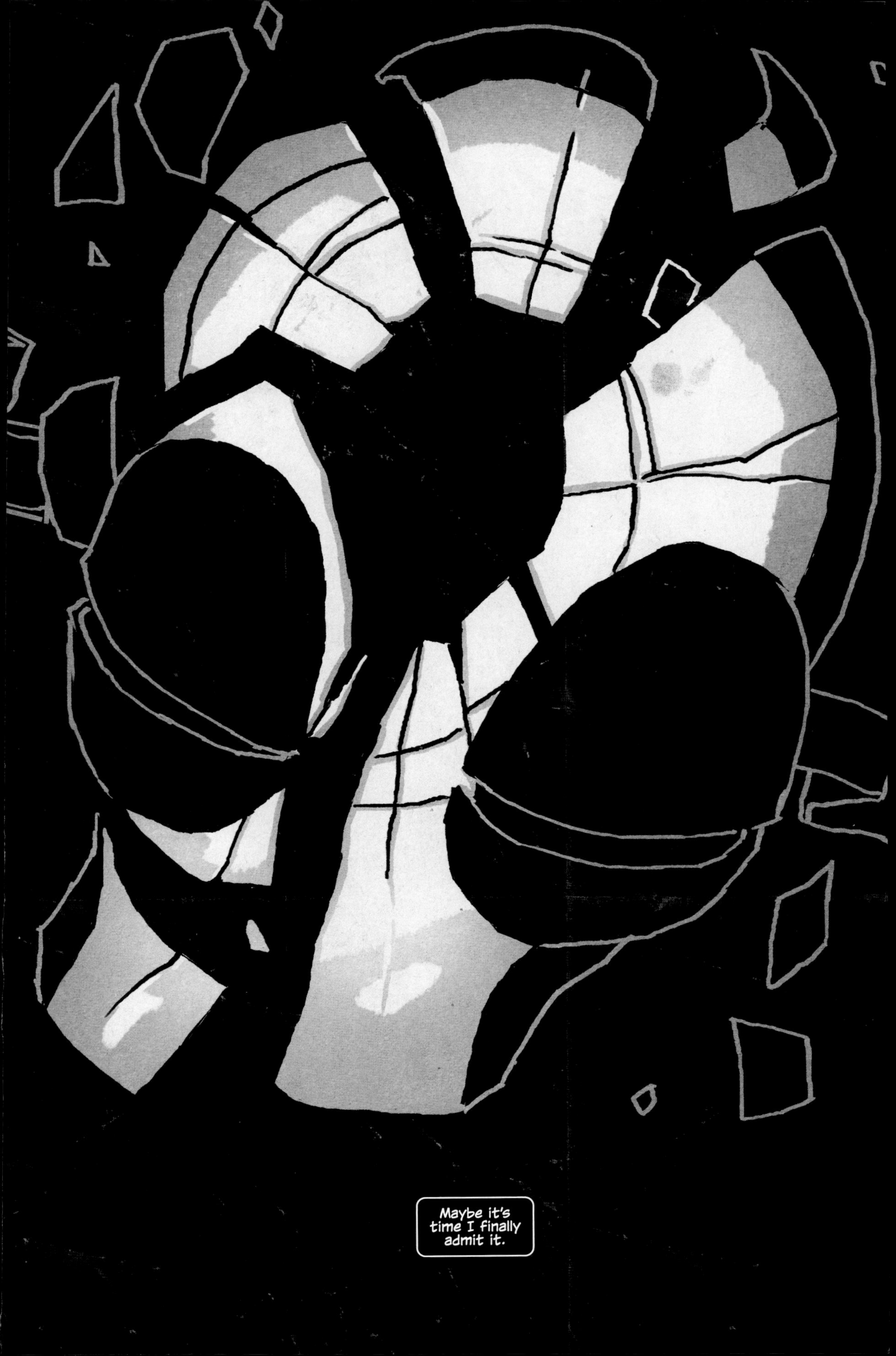
Maybe it's time I finally admit it.

there you are

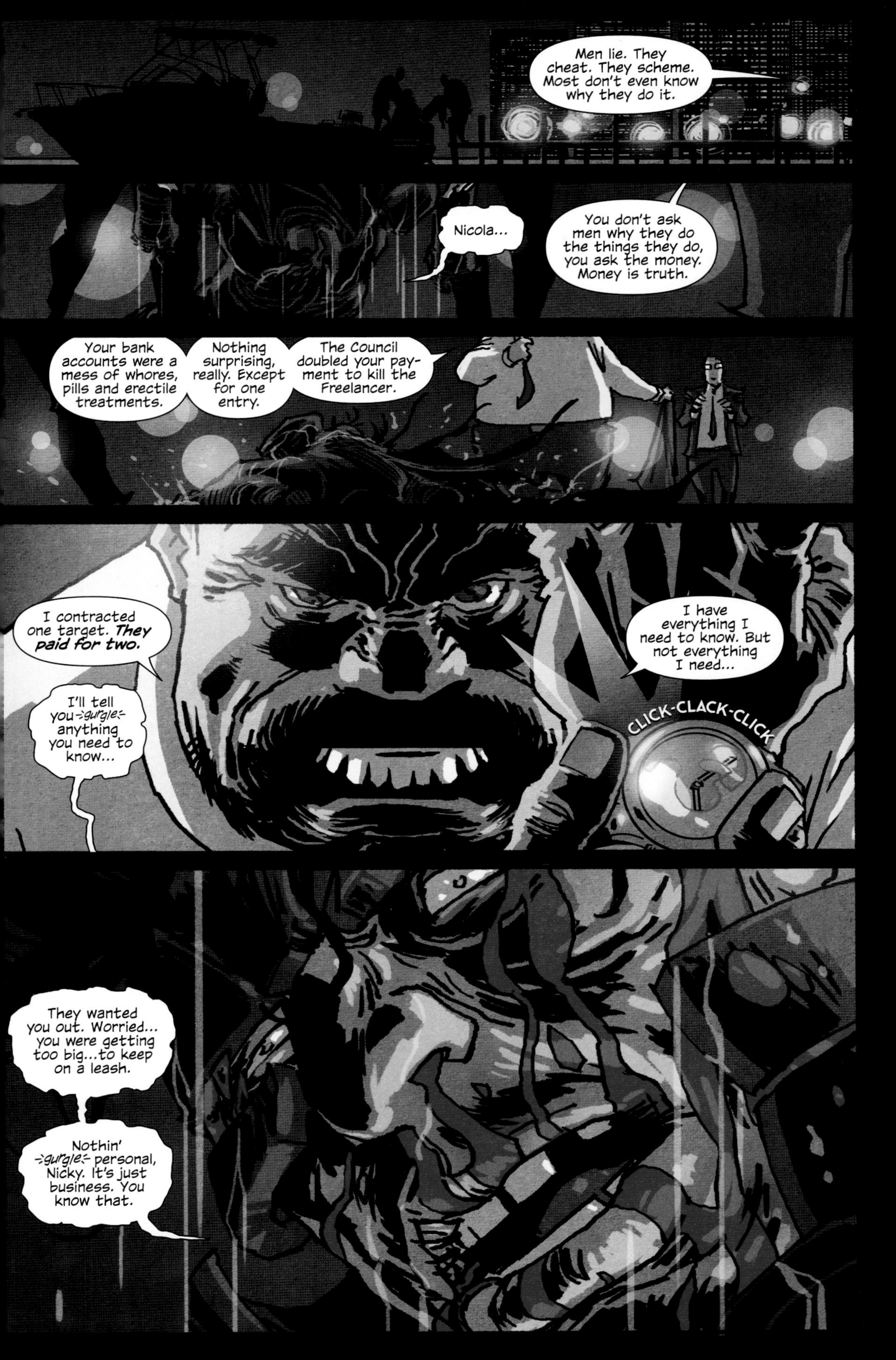

Men lie. They cheat. They scheme. Most don't even know why they do it.
Nicola...
You don't ask men why they do the things they do, you ask the money. Money is truth.
Your bank accounts were a mess of whores, pills and erectile treatments.
Nothing surprising, really. Except for one entry.
The Council doubled your payment to kill the Freelancer.
I contracted one target. *They paid for two.*
I'll tell you -gurgle- anything you need to know...
I have everything I need to know. But not everything I need...
CLICK-CLACK-CLICK
They wanted you out. Worried... you were getting too big...to keep on a leash.
Nothin' -gurgle- personal, Nicky. It's just business. You know that.

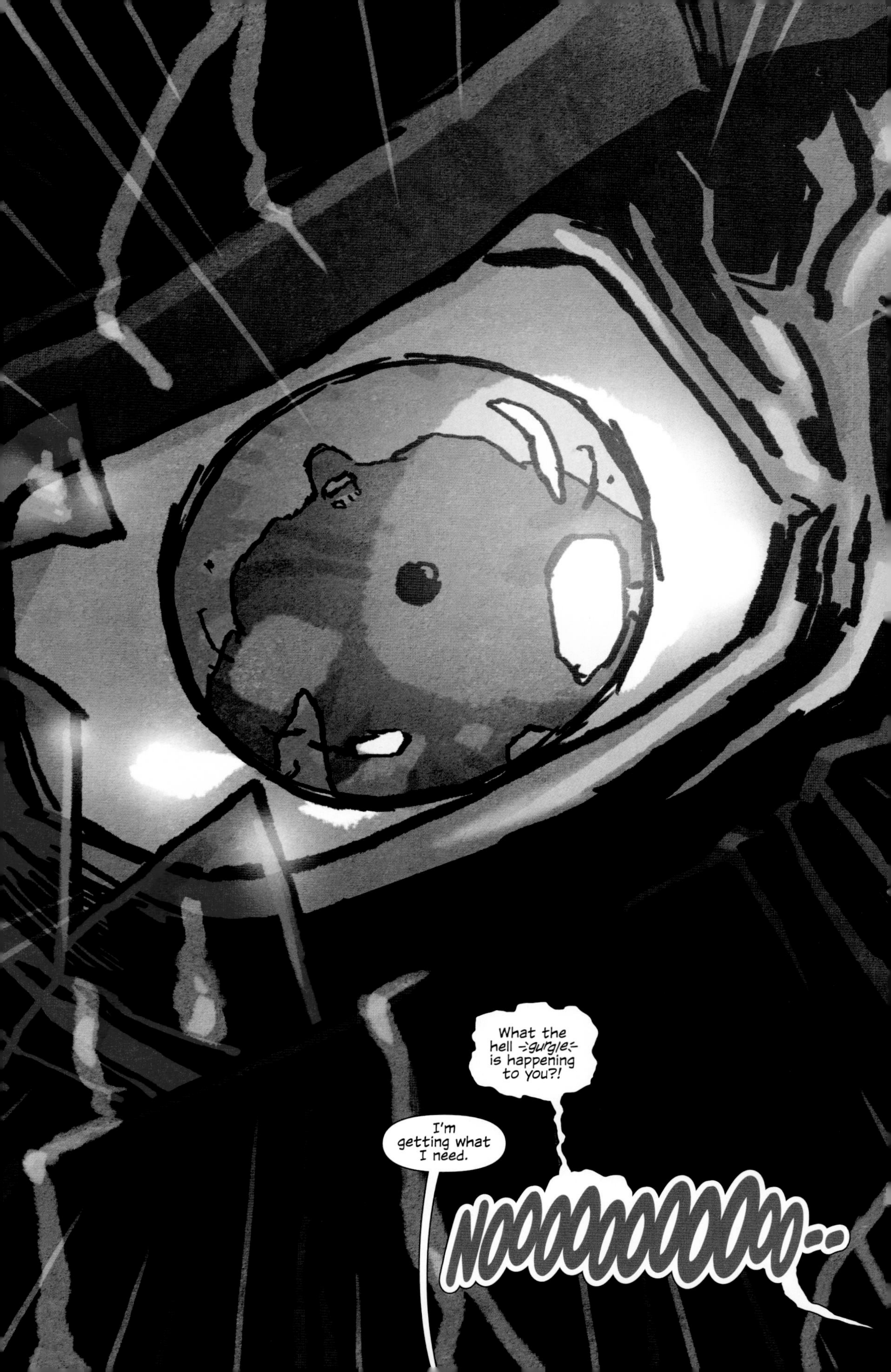

What the hell -gurgle- is happening to you?!
I'm getting what I need.
NOOOOOOOOOOO--

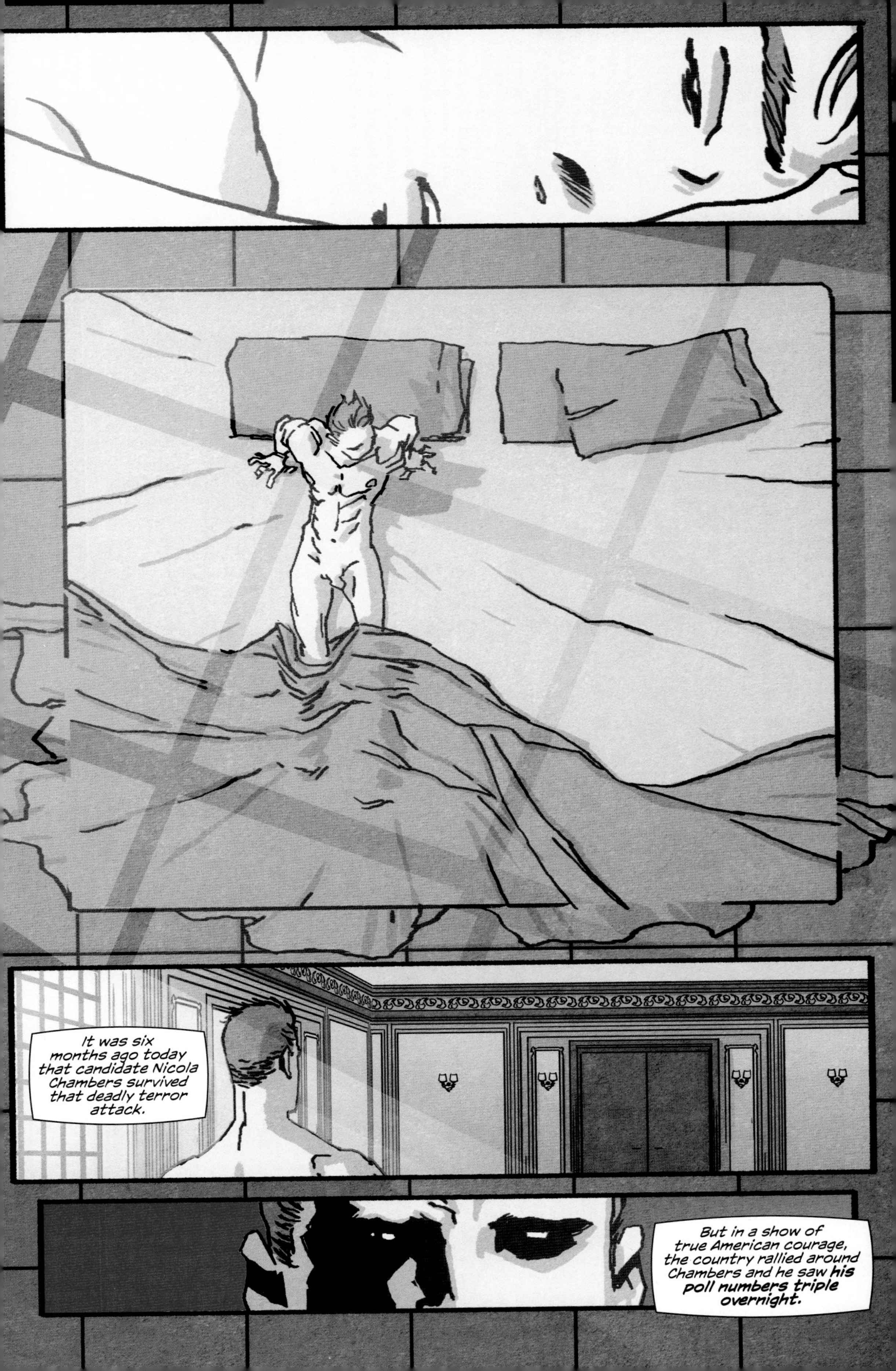
It was six months ago today that candidate Nicola Chambers survived that deadly terror attack.
But in a show of true American courage, the country rallied around Chambers and he saw **his poll numbers triple overnight.**

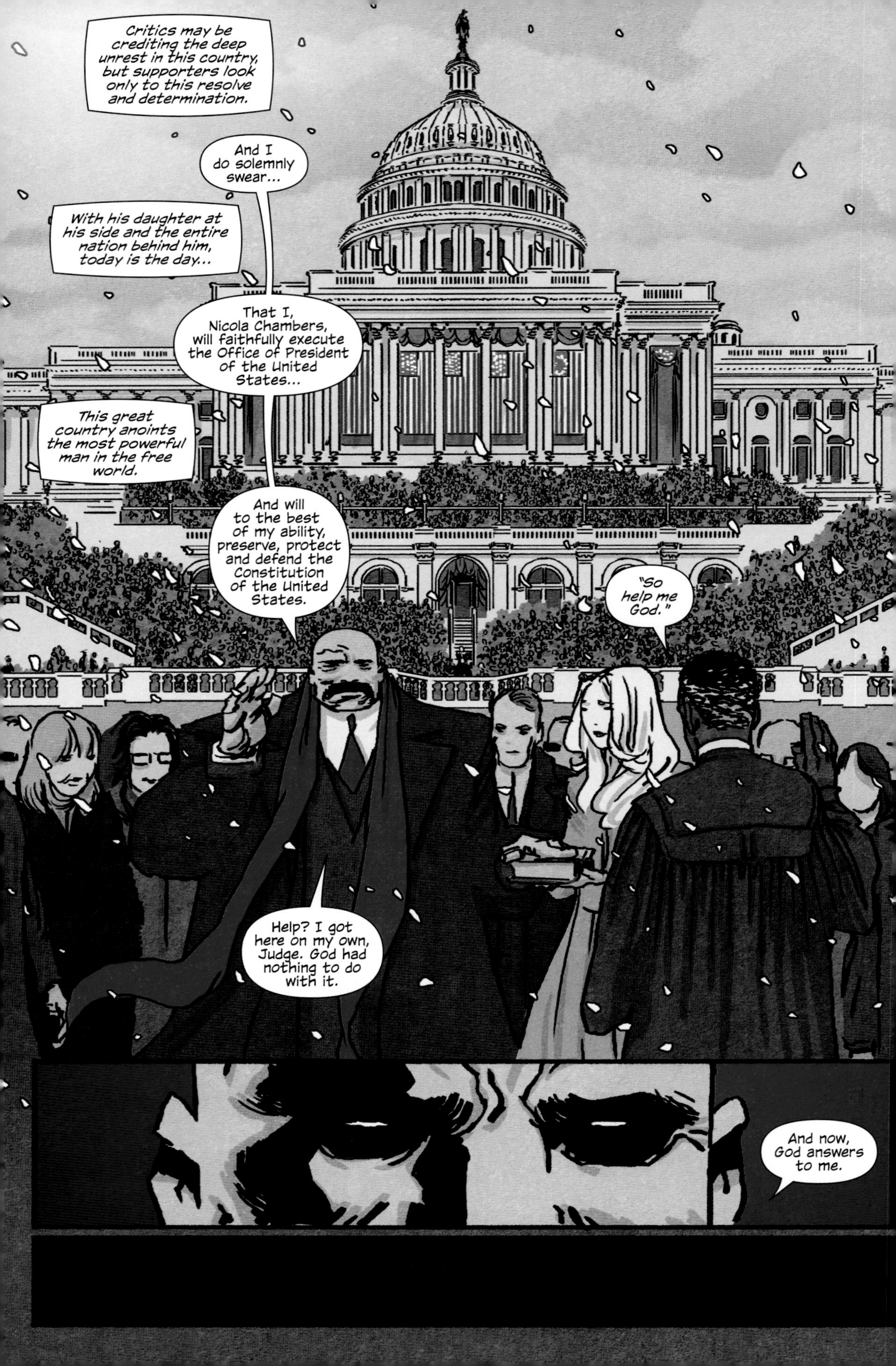
Critics may be crediting the deep unrest in this country, but supporters look only to this resolve and determination.
And I do solemnly swear...
With his daughter at his side and the entire nation behind him, today is the day...
That I, Nicola Chambers, will faithfully execute the Office of President of the United States...
This great country anoints the most powerful man in the free world.
And will to the best of my ability, preserve, protect and defend the Constitution of the United States.
"So help me God."
Help? I got here on my own, Judge. God had nothing to do with it.
And now, God answers to me.

"I'm the American Dream, baby. The only thing I want is to keep the rest of the world sleeping."

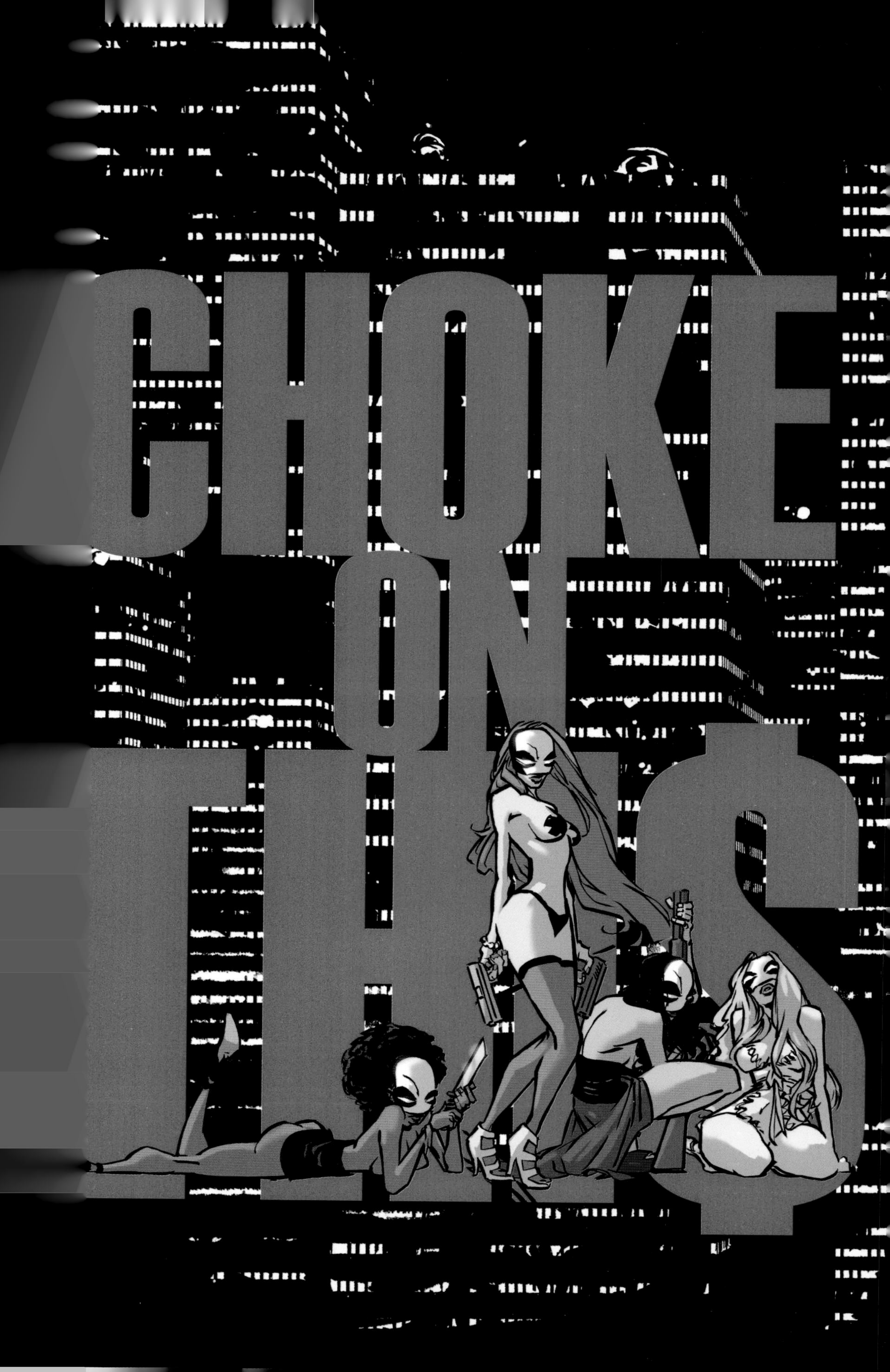
CHOKE
ON
THI$

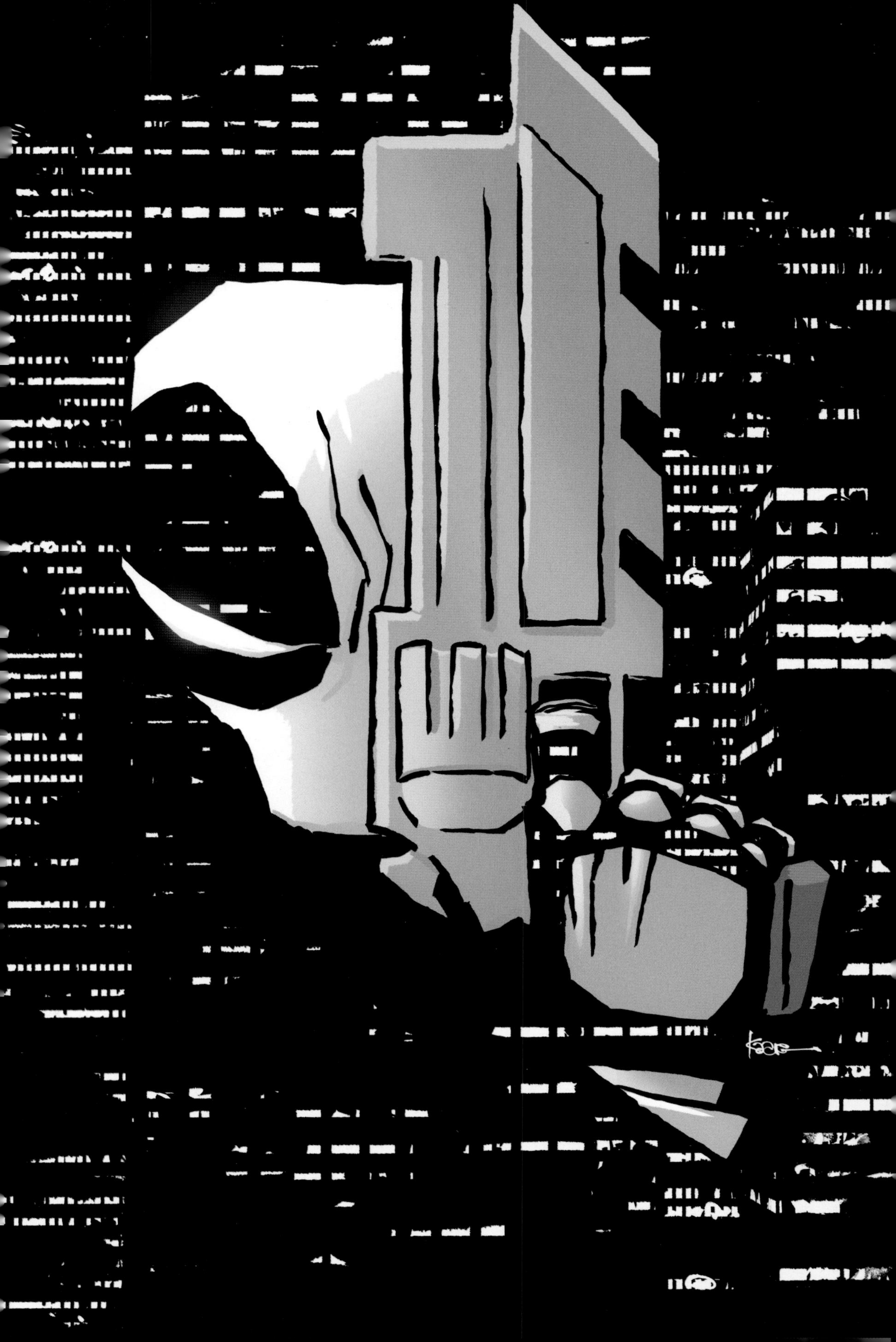

2

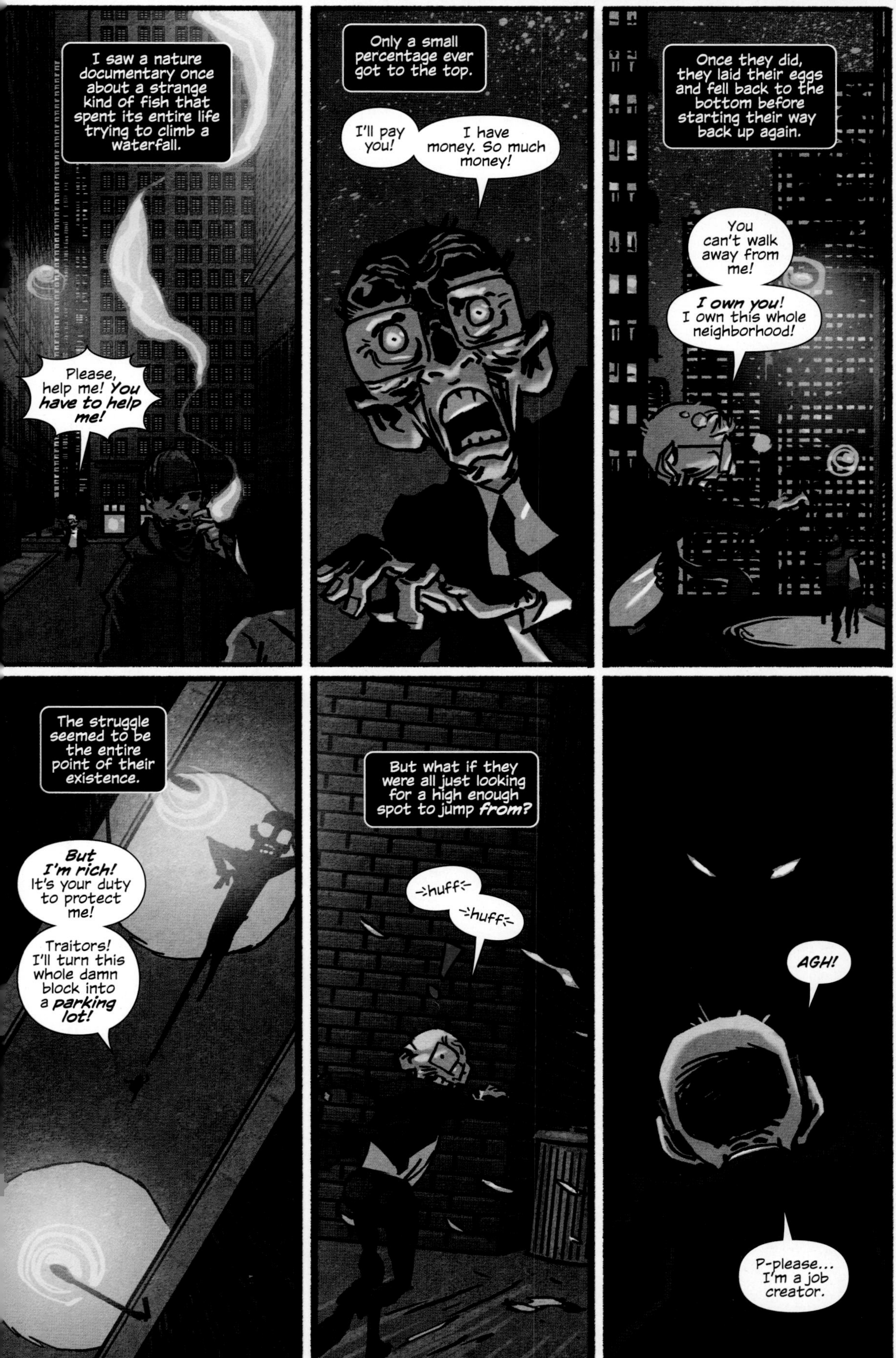
I saw a nature documentary once about a strange kind of fish that spent its entire life trying to climb a waterfall.
Please, help me! You have to help me!
Only a small percentage ever got to the top.
I'll pay you!
I have money. So much money!
Once they did, they laid their eggs and fell back to the bottom before starting their way back up again.
You can't walk away from me!
I own you! I own this whole neighborhood!
The struggle seemed to be the entire point of their existence.
But I'm rich! It's your duty to protect me!
Traitors! I'll turn this whole damn block into a parking lot!
But what if they were all just looking for a high enough spot to jump from?
huff
huff
AGH!
P-please... I'm a job creator.

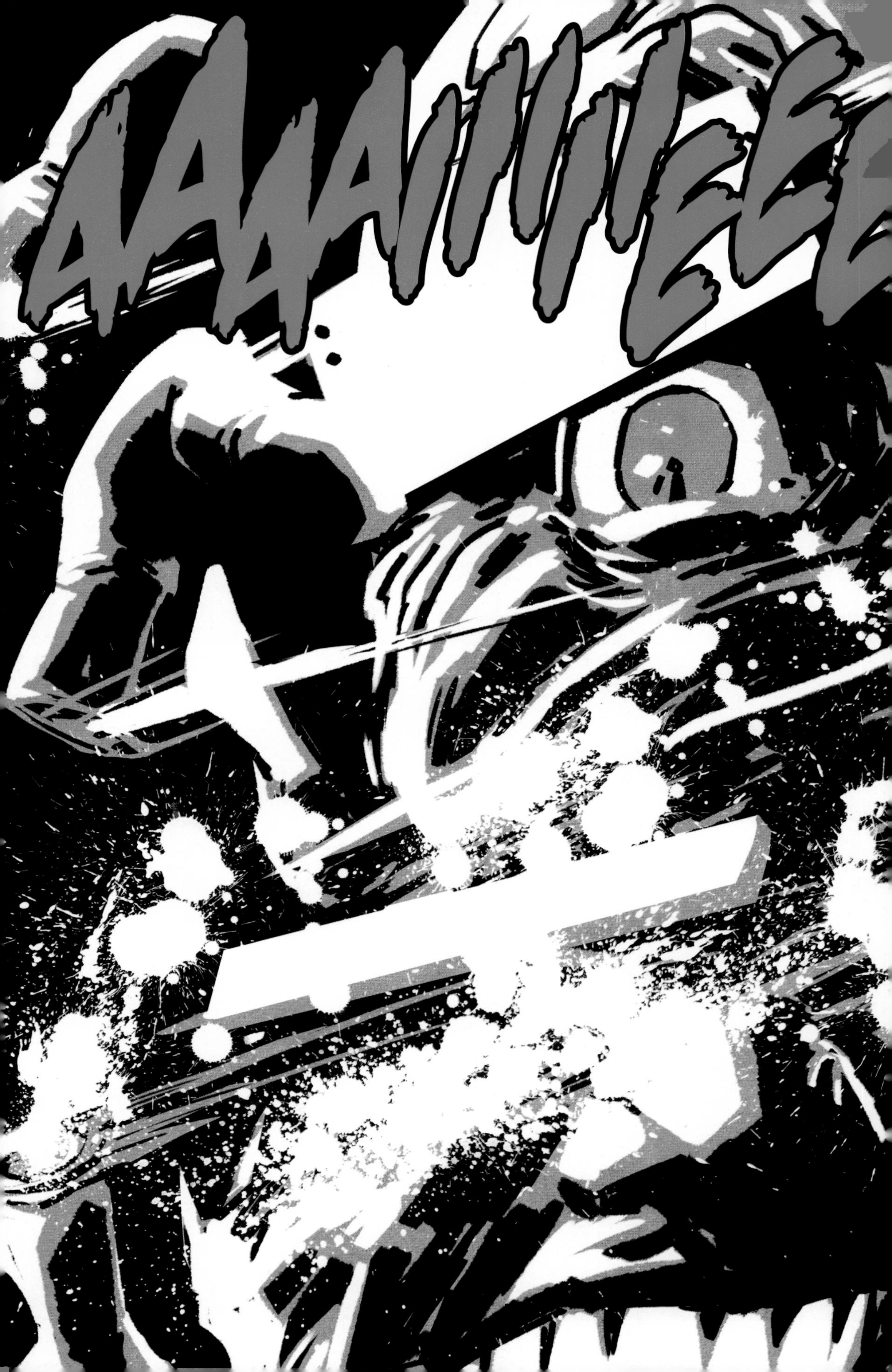
AAAIIIIEEE

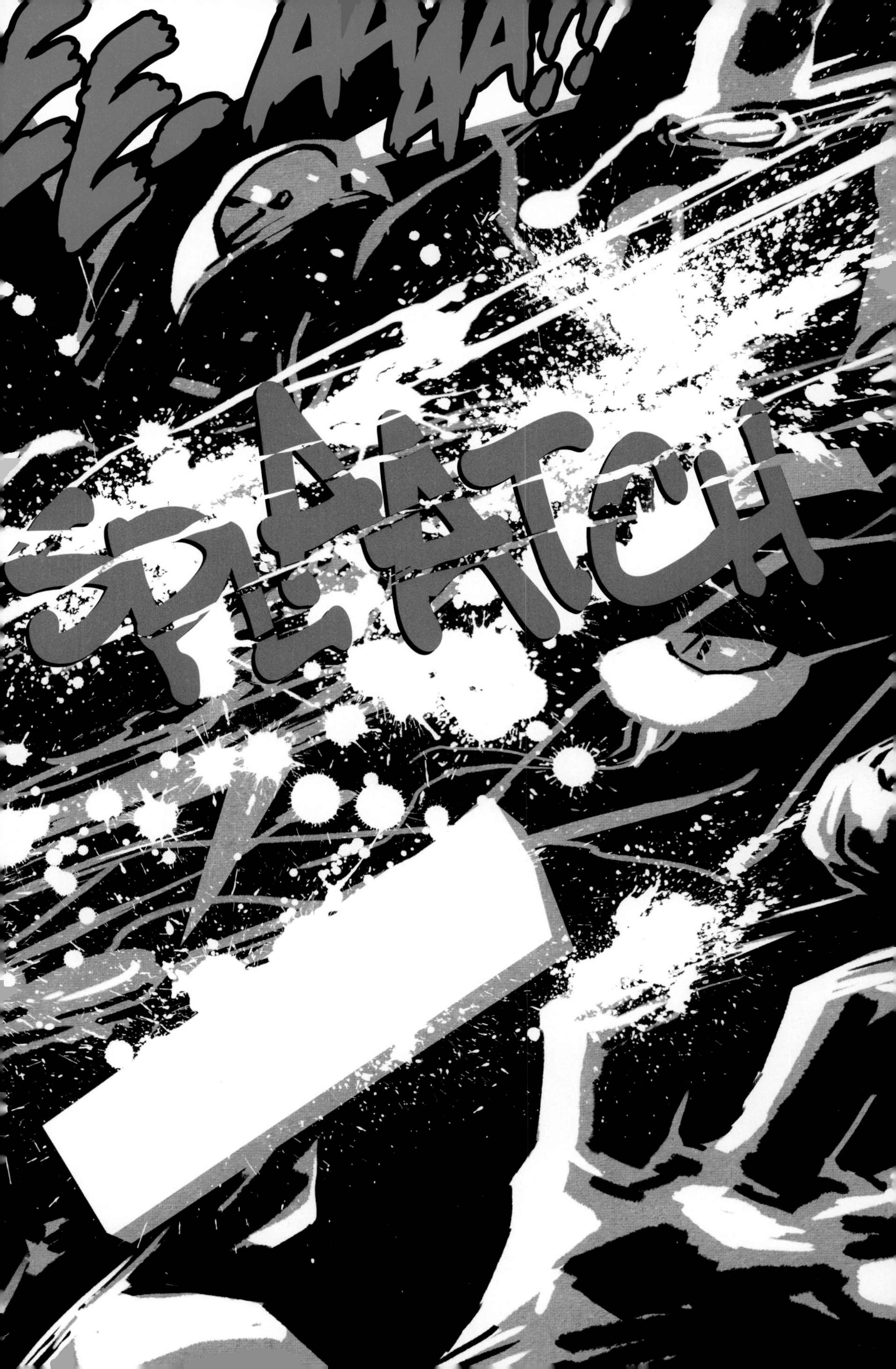
EE AAAA!!
SPLATCH

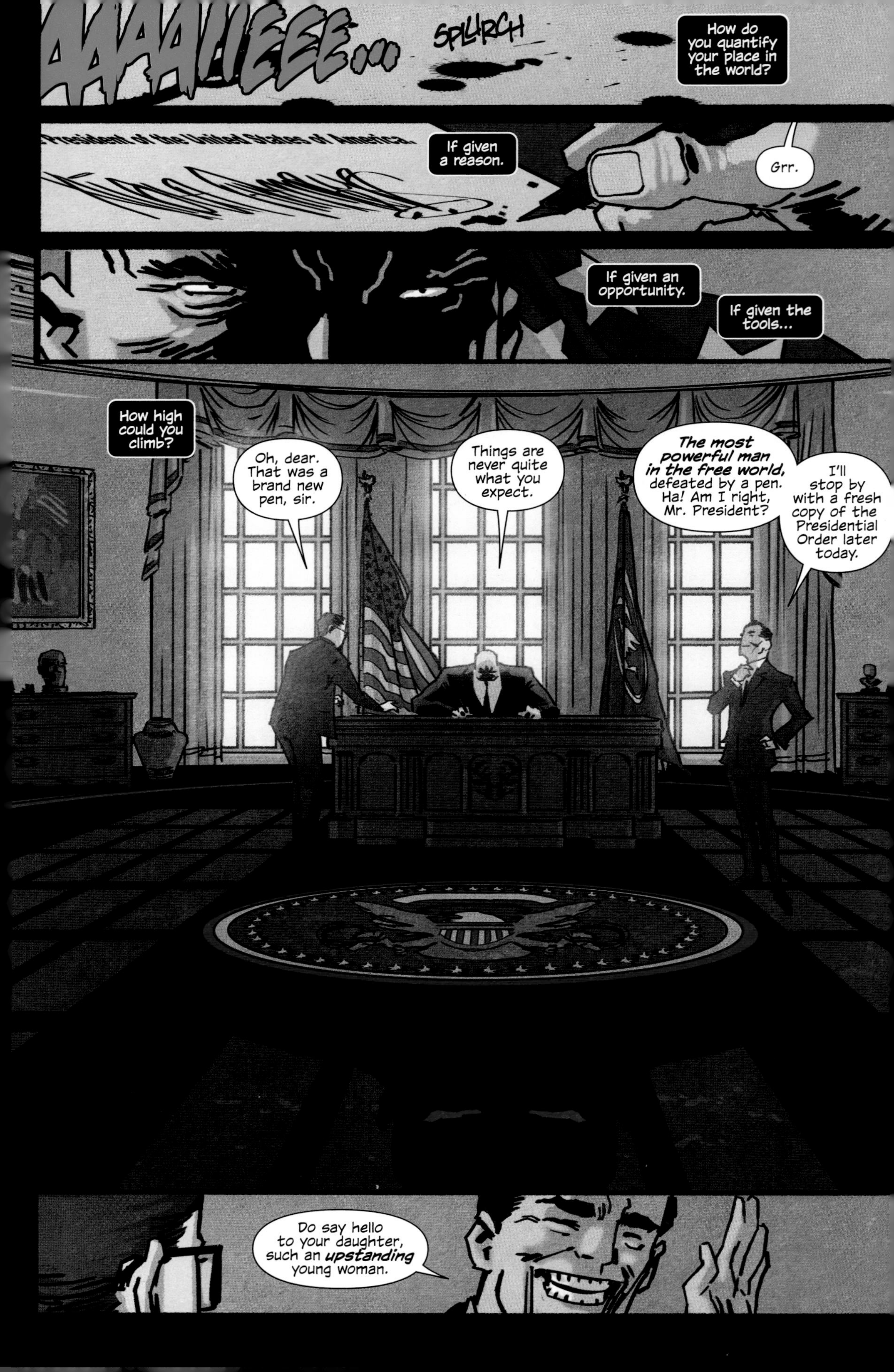
AAAAAIIEEE...
SPLURCH
How do you quantify your place in the world?
President of the United States of America.
If given a reason.
Grr.
If given an opportunity.
If given the tools...
How high could you climb?
Oh, dear. That was a brand new pen, sir.
Things are never quite what you expect.
The most powerful man in the free world, defeated by a pen. Ha! Am I right, Mr. President?
I'll stop by with a fresh copy of the Presidential Order later today.
Do say hello to your daughter, such an *upstanding* young woman.

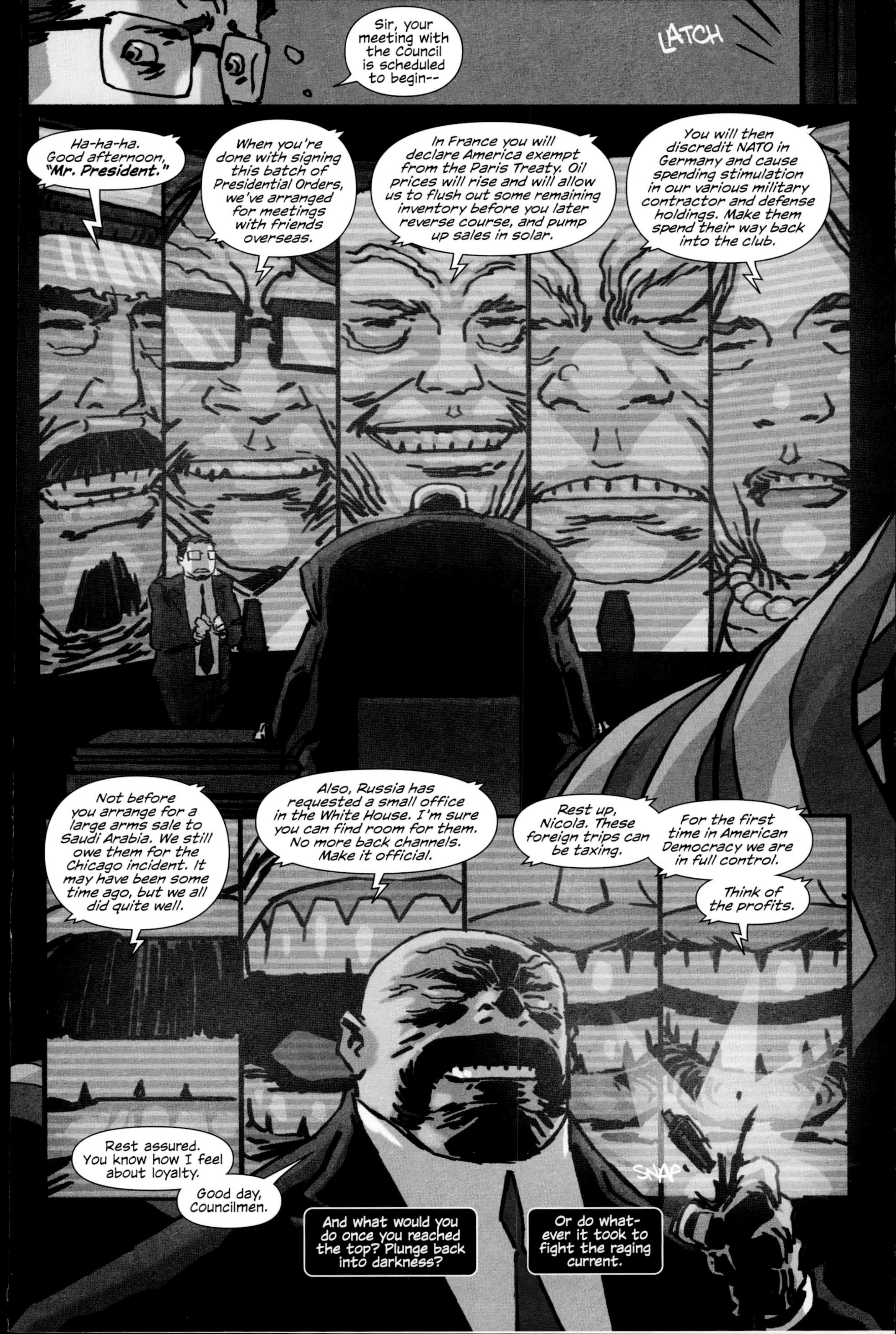
Sir, your meeting with the Council is scheduled to begin--
LATCH
Ha-ha-ha. Good afternoon, "Mr. President."
When you're done with signing this batch of Presidential Orders, we've arranged for meetings with friends overseas.
In France you will declare America exempt from the Paris Treaty. Oil prices will rise and will allow us to flush out some remaining inventory before you later reverse course, and pump up sales in solar.
You will then discredit NATO in Germany and cause spending stimulation in our various military contractor and defense holdings. Make them spend their way back into the club.
Not before you arrange for a large arms sale to Saudi Arabia. We still owe them for the Chicago incident. It may have been some time ago, but we all did quite well.
Also, Russia has requested a small office in the White House. I'm sure you can find room for them. No more back channels. Make it official.
Rest up, Nicola. These foreign trips can be taxing.
For the first time in American Democracy we are in full control.
Think of the profits.
Rest assured. You know how I feel about loyalty.
Good day, Councilmen.
SNAP
And what would you do once you reached the top? Plunge back into darkness?
Or do what-ever it took to fight the raging current.

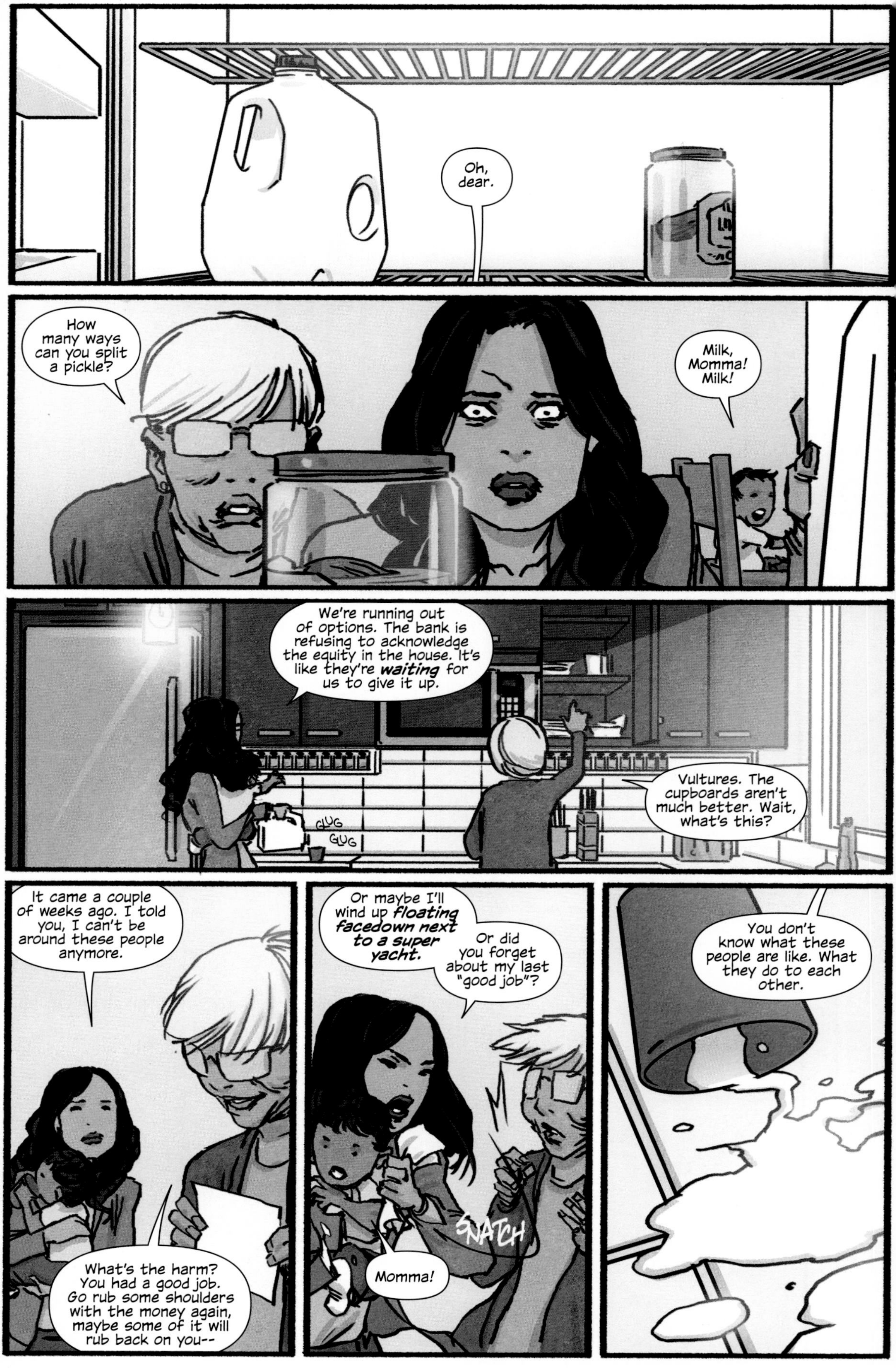
Oh, dear.
How many ways can you split a pickle?
Milk, Momma! Milk!
We're running out of options. The bank is refusing to acknowledge the equity in the house. It's like they're *waiting* for us to give it up.
GLUG GLUG
Vultures. The cupboards aren't much better. Wait, what's this?
It came a couple of weeks ago. I told you, I can't be around these people anymore.
What's the harm? You had a good job. Go rub some shoulders with the money again, maybe some of it will rub back on you--
Or maybe I'll wind up ***floating facedown next to a super yacht.***
Or did you forget about my last "good job"?
SNATCH
Momma!
You don't know what these people are like. What they do to each other.

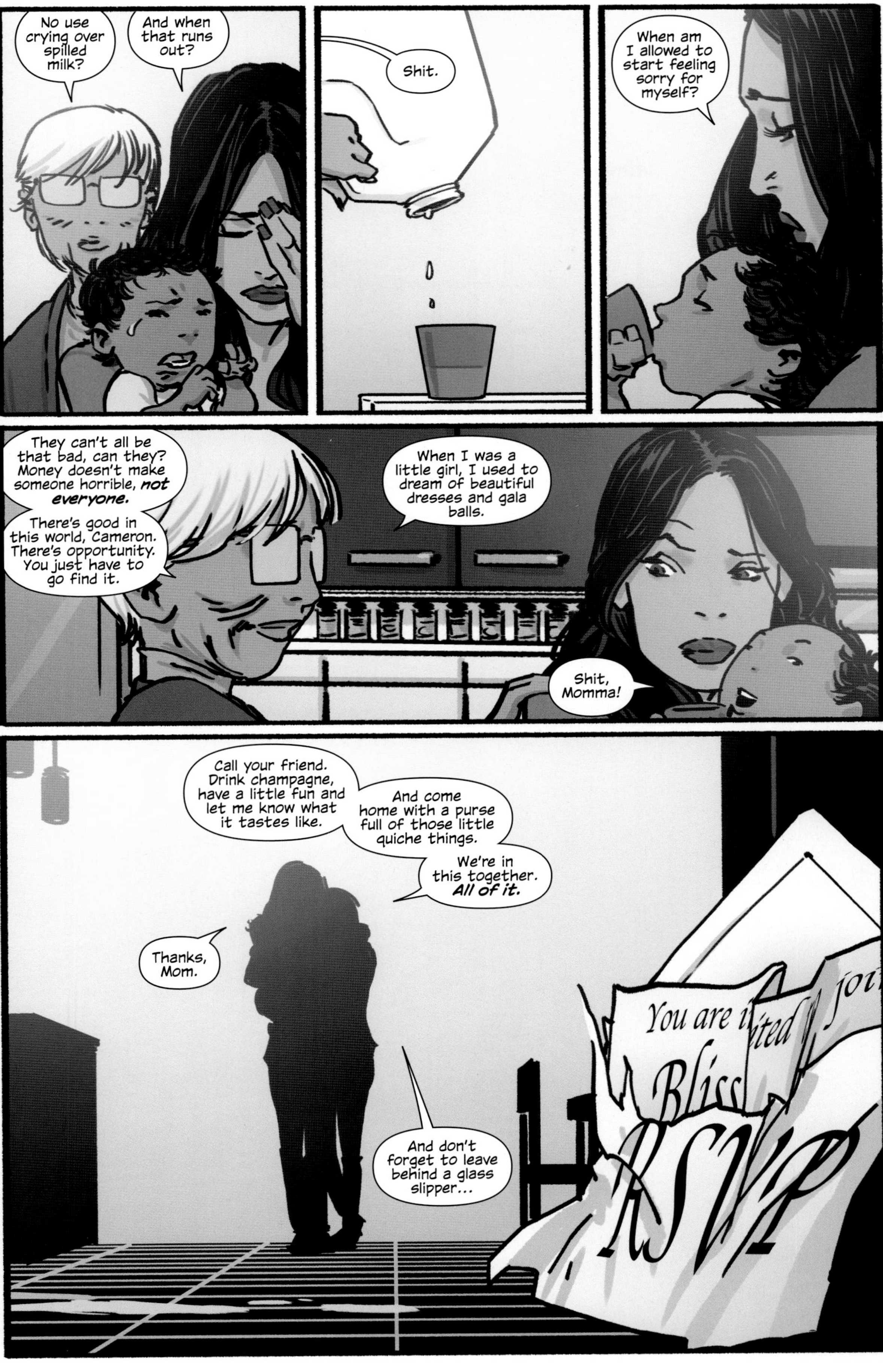
No use crying over spilled milk?
And when that runs out?
Shit.
When am I allowed to start feeling sorry for myself?
They can't all be that bad, can they? Money doesn't make someone horrible, ***not everyone.***
There's good in this world, Cameron. There's opportunity. You just have to go find it.
When I was a little girl, I used to dream of beautiful dresses and gala balls.
Shit, Momma!
Call your friend. Drink champagne, have a little fun and let me know what it tastes like.
And come home with a purse full of those little quiche things.
We're in this together. ***All of it.***
Thanks, Mom.
And don't forget to leave behind a glass slipper...
Bliss
RSVP

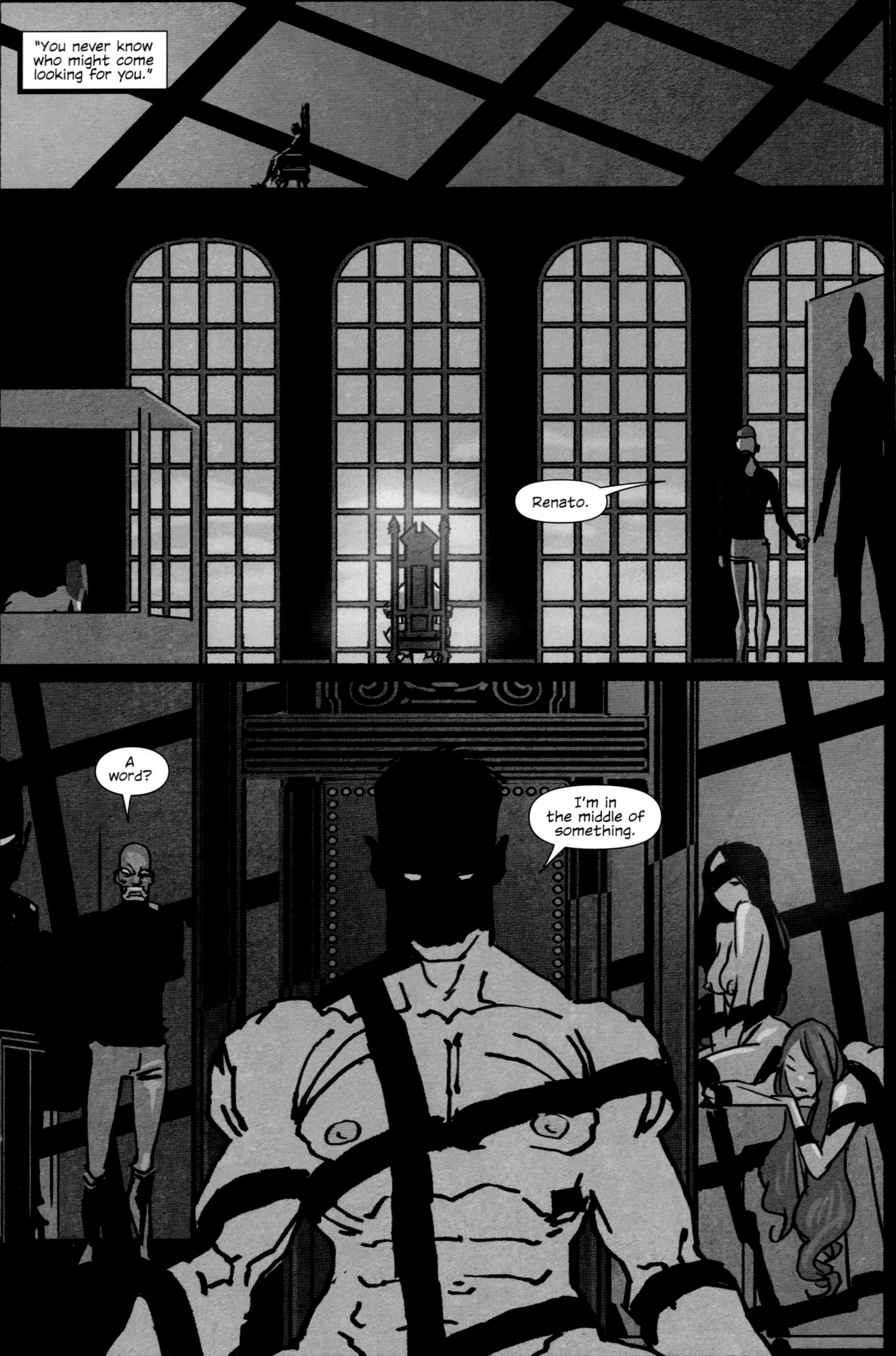
"You never know who might come looking for you."
Renato.
A word?
I'm in the middle of something.

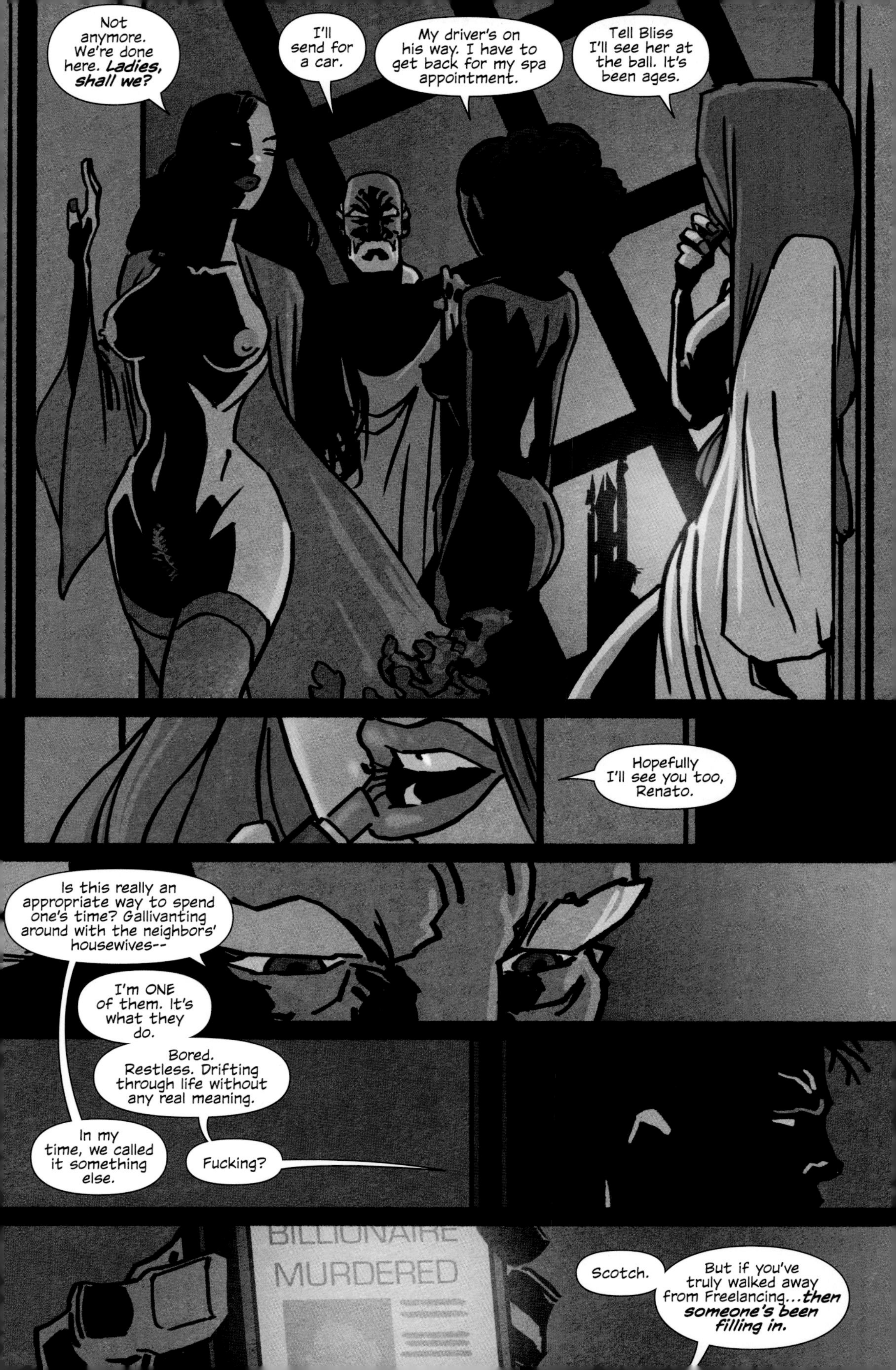
Not anymore. We're done here. *Ladies, shall we?*
I'll send for a car.
My driver's on his way. I have to get back for my spa appointment.
Tell Bliss I'll see her at the ball. It's been ages.
Hopefully I'll see you too, Renato.
Is this really an appropriate way to spend one's time? Gallivanting around with the neighbors' housewives--
I'm ONE of them. It's what they do.
Bored. Restless. Drifting through life without any real meaning.
In my time, we called it something else.
Fucking?
BILLIONAIRE MURDERED
Scotch.
But if you've truly walked away from Freelancing... *then someone's been filling in.*

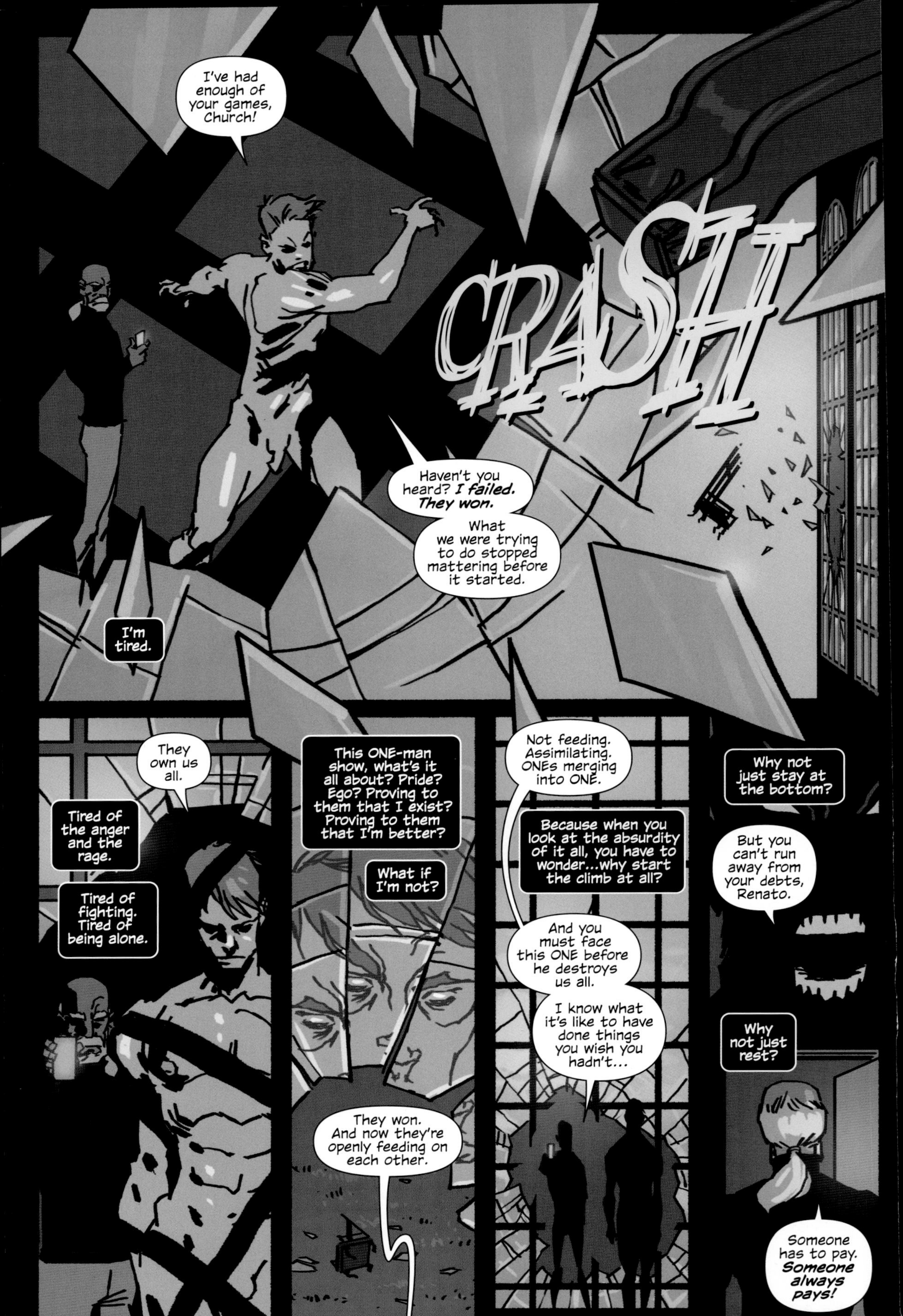
I've had enough of your games, Church!
CRASH
Haven't you heard? I failed. They won.
What we were trying to do stopped mattering before it started.
I'm tired.
They own us all.
Tired of the anger and the rage.
Tired of fighting. Tired of being alone.
This ONE-man show, what's it all about? Pride? Ego? Proving to them that I exist? Proving to them that I'm better?
What if I'm not?
They won. And now they're openly feeding on each other.
Not feeding. Assimilating. ONEs merging into ONE.
Because when you look at the absurdity of it all, you have to wonder...why start the climb at all?
And you must face this ONE before he destroys us all.
I know what it's like to have done things you wish you hadn't...
Why not just stay at the bottom?
But you can't run away from your debts, Renato.
Why not just rest?
Someone has to pay. Someone always pays!

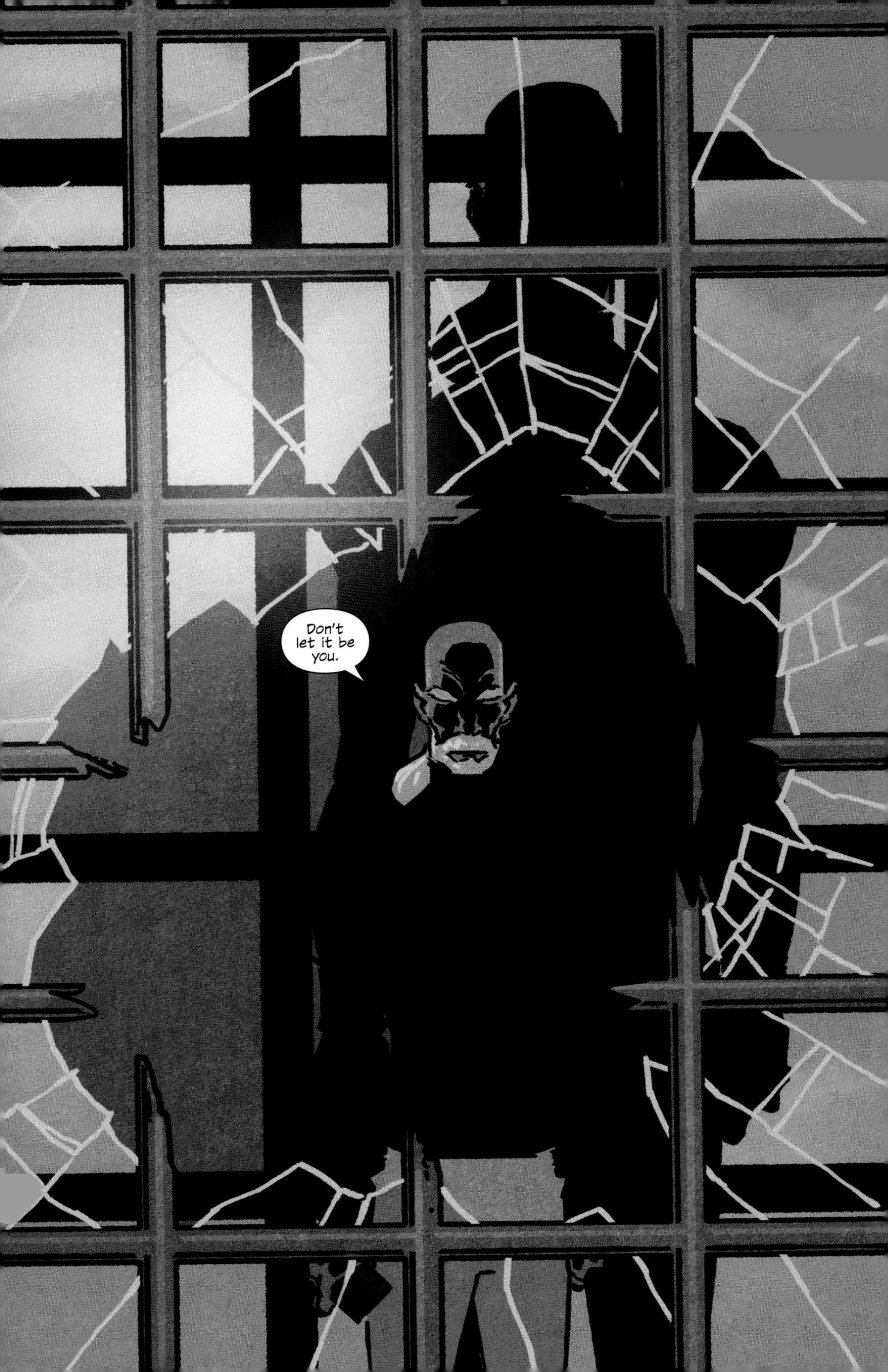
Don't let it be you.

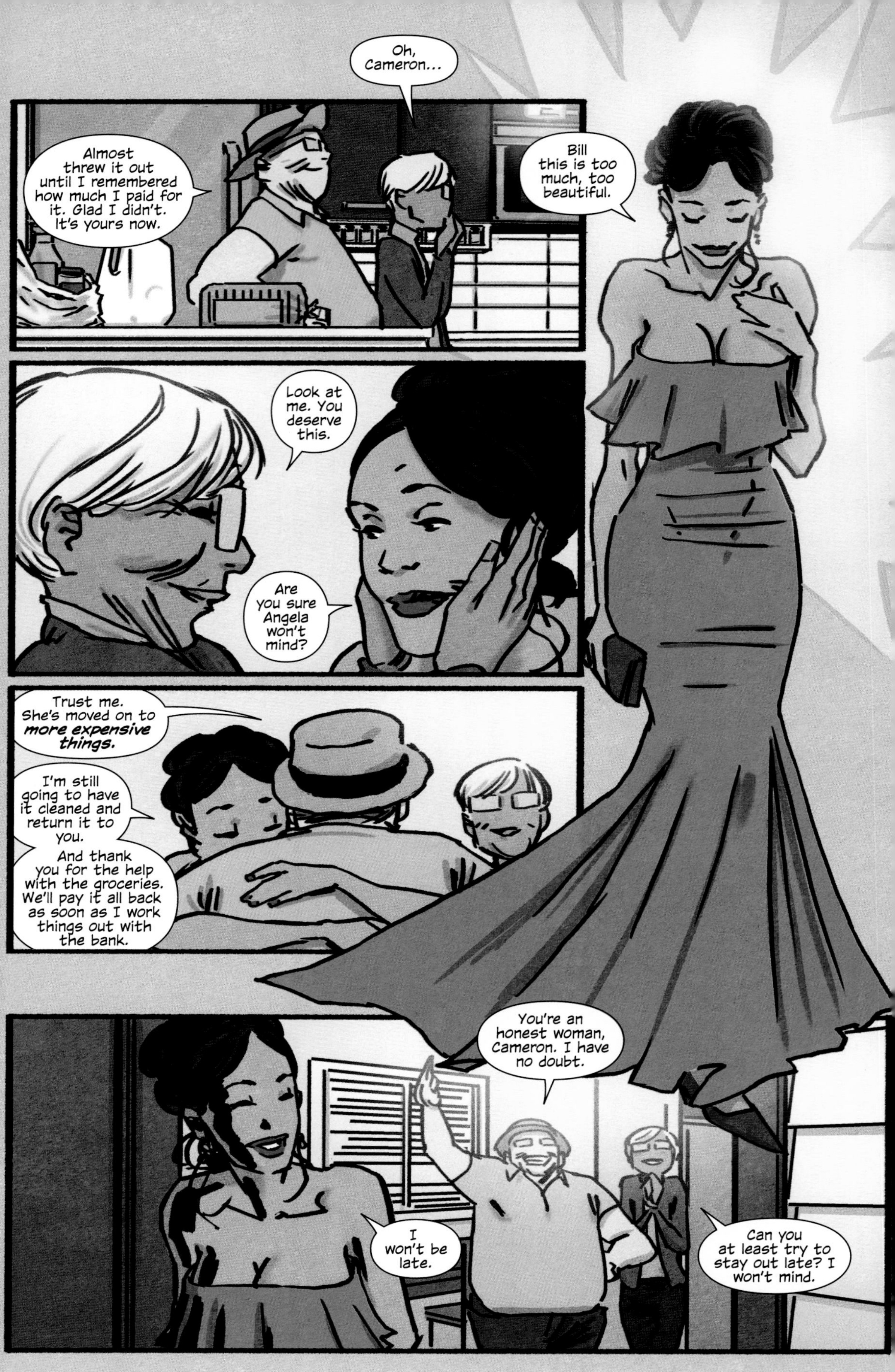
Oh, Cameron...
Almost threw it out until I remembered how much I paid for it. Glad I didn't. It's yours now.
Bill this is too much, too beautiful.
Look at me. You deserve this.
Are you sure Angela won't mind?
Trust me. She's moved on to ***more expensive things.***
I'm still going to have it cleaned and return it to you.
And thank you for the help with the groceries. We'll pay it all back as soon as I work things out with the bank.
You're an honest woman, Cameron. I have no doubt.
I won't be late.
Can you at least try to stay out late? I won't mind.

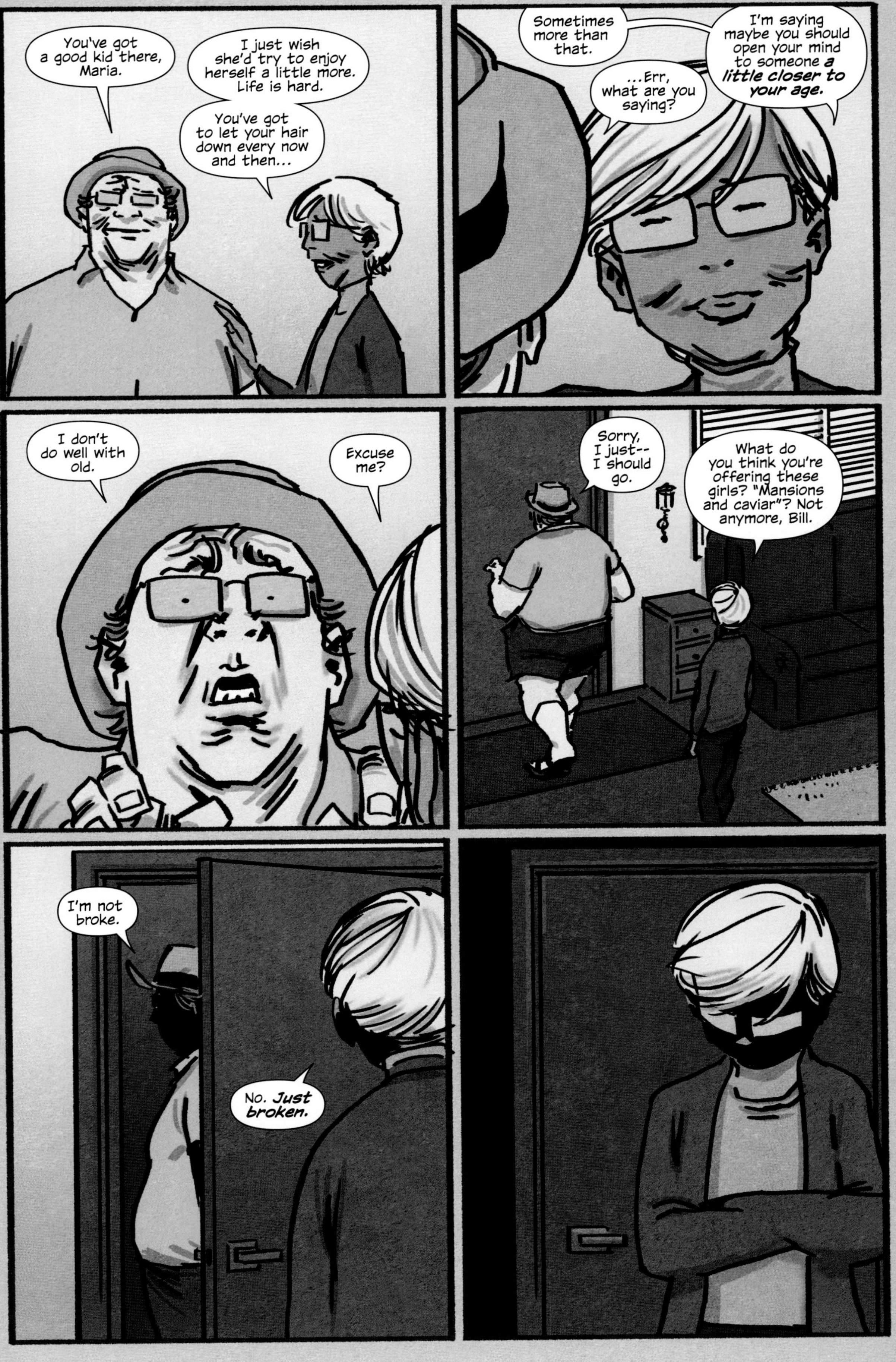
You've got a good kid there, Maria.
I just wish she'd try to enjoy herself a little more. Life is hard.
You've got to let your hair down every now and then...
Sometimes more than that.
I'm saying maybe you should open your mind to someone ***a little closer to your age.***
...Err, what are you saying?
I don't do well with old.
Excuse me?
Sorry, I just-- I should go.
What do you think you're offering these girls? "Mansions and caviar"? Not anymore, Bill.
I'm not broke.
No. ***Just broken.***

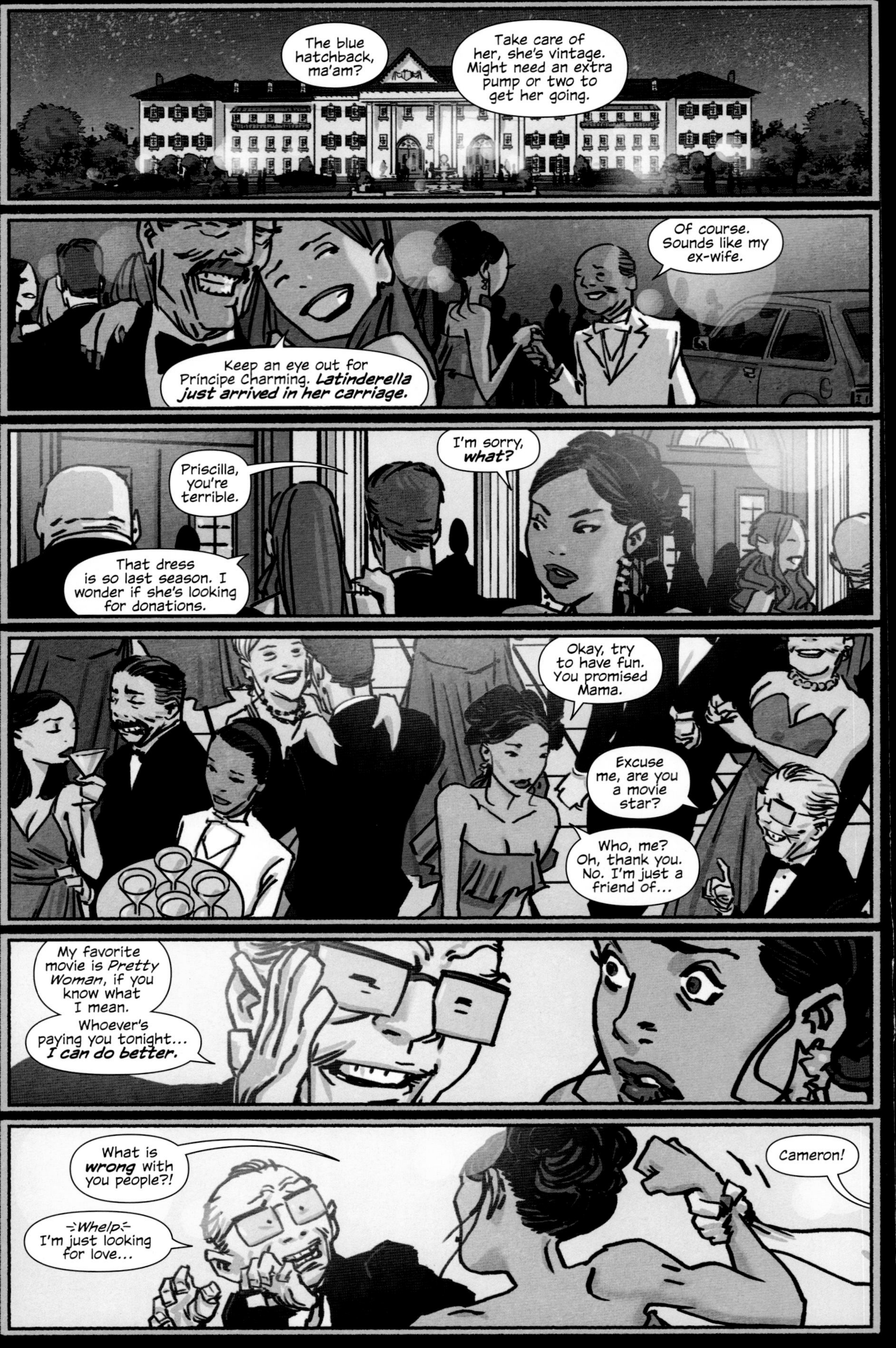
The blue hatchback, ma'am?
Take care of her, she's vintage. Might need an extra pump or two to get her going.
Of course. Sounds like my ex-wife.
Keep an eye out for Principe Charming. **Latinderella just arrived in her carriage.**
Priscilla, you're terrible.
That dress is so last season. I wonder if she's looking for donations.
I'm sorry, **what?**
Okay, try to have fun. You promised Mama.
Excuse me, are you a movie star?
Who, me? Oh, thank you. No. I'm just a friend of...
My favorite movie is *Pretty Woman*, if you know what I mean.
Whoever's paying you tonight... **I can do better.**
What is **wrong** with you people?!
Cameron!
Whelp
I'm just looking for love...

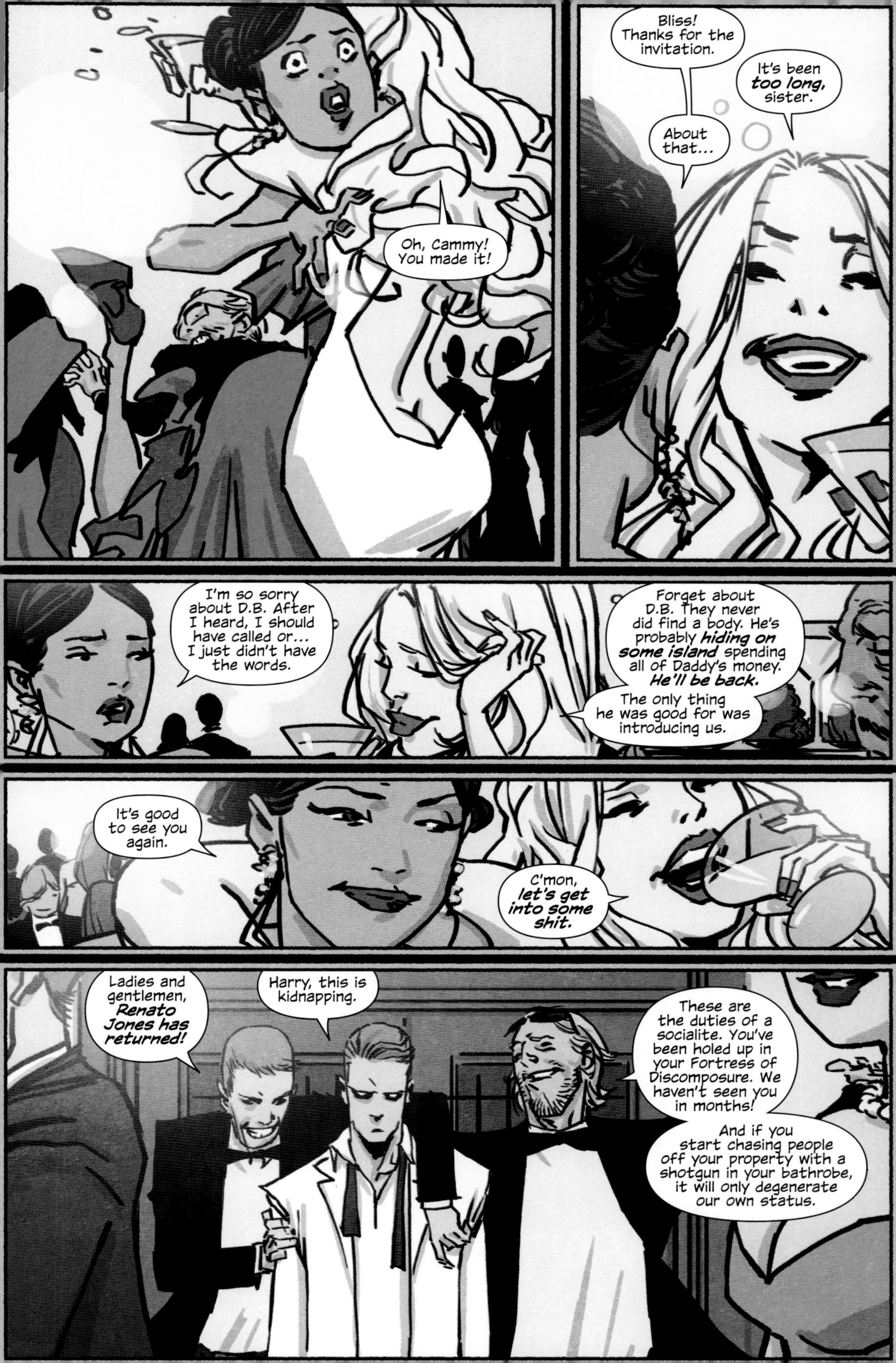

Oh, Cammy! You made it!
Bliss! Thanks for the invitation.
About that...
It's been **too long,** sister.
I'm so sorry about D.B. After I heard, I should have called or... I just didn't have the words.
Forget about D.B. They never did find a body. He's probably **hiding on some island** spending all of Daddy's money. **He'll be back.**
The only thing he was good for was introducing us.
It's good to see you again.
C'mon, **let's get into some shit.**
Ladies and gentlemen, **Renato Jones has returned!**
Harry, this is kidnapping.
These are the duties of a socialite. You've been holed up in your Fortress of Discomposure. We haven't seen you in months!
And if you start chasing people off your property with a shotgun in your bathrobe, it will only degenerate our own status.

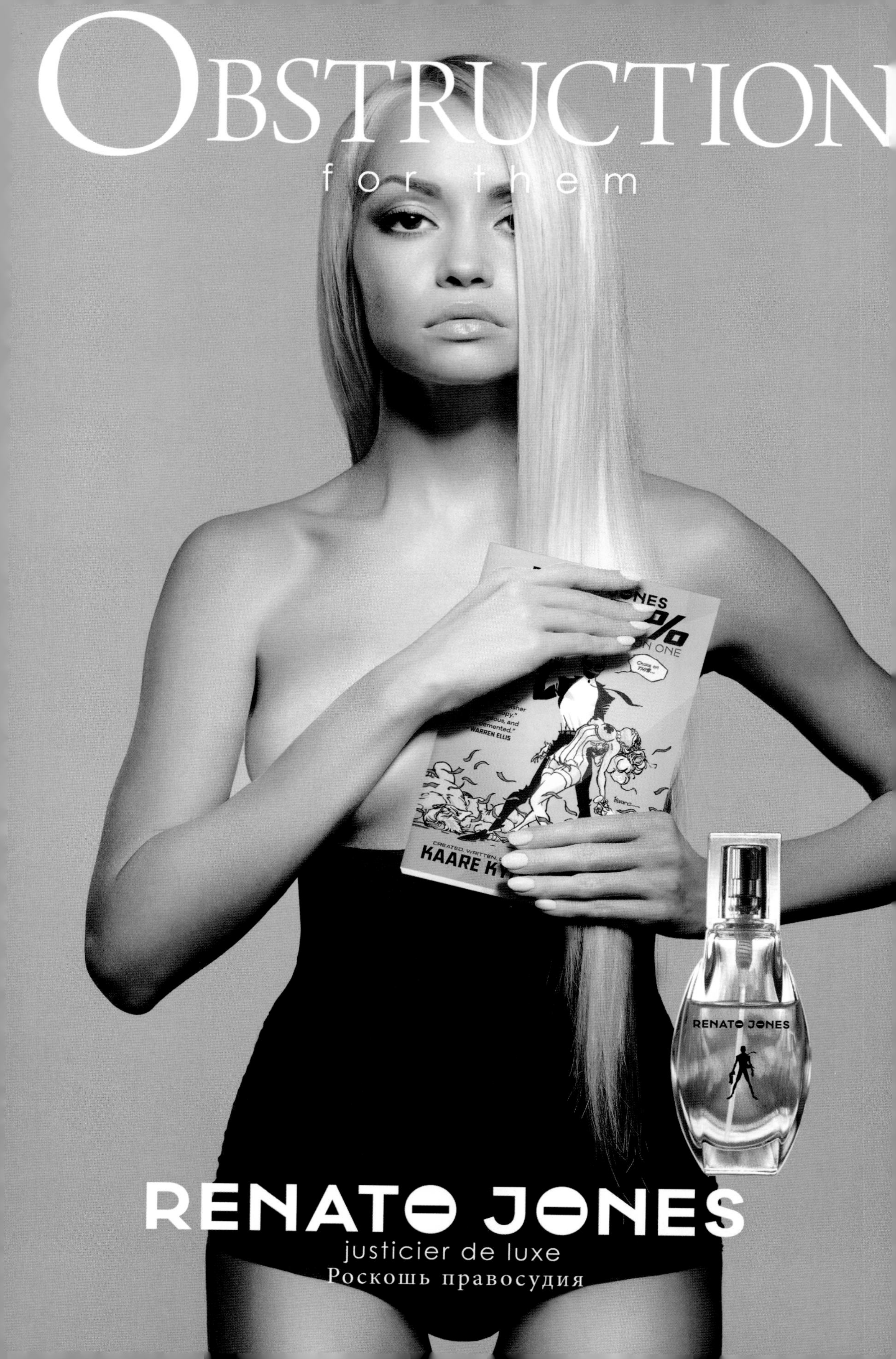

OBSTRUCTION
for them
WARREN ELLIS
RENATO JONES
RENATO JONES
justicier de luxe
Роскошь правосудия

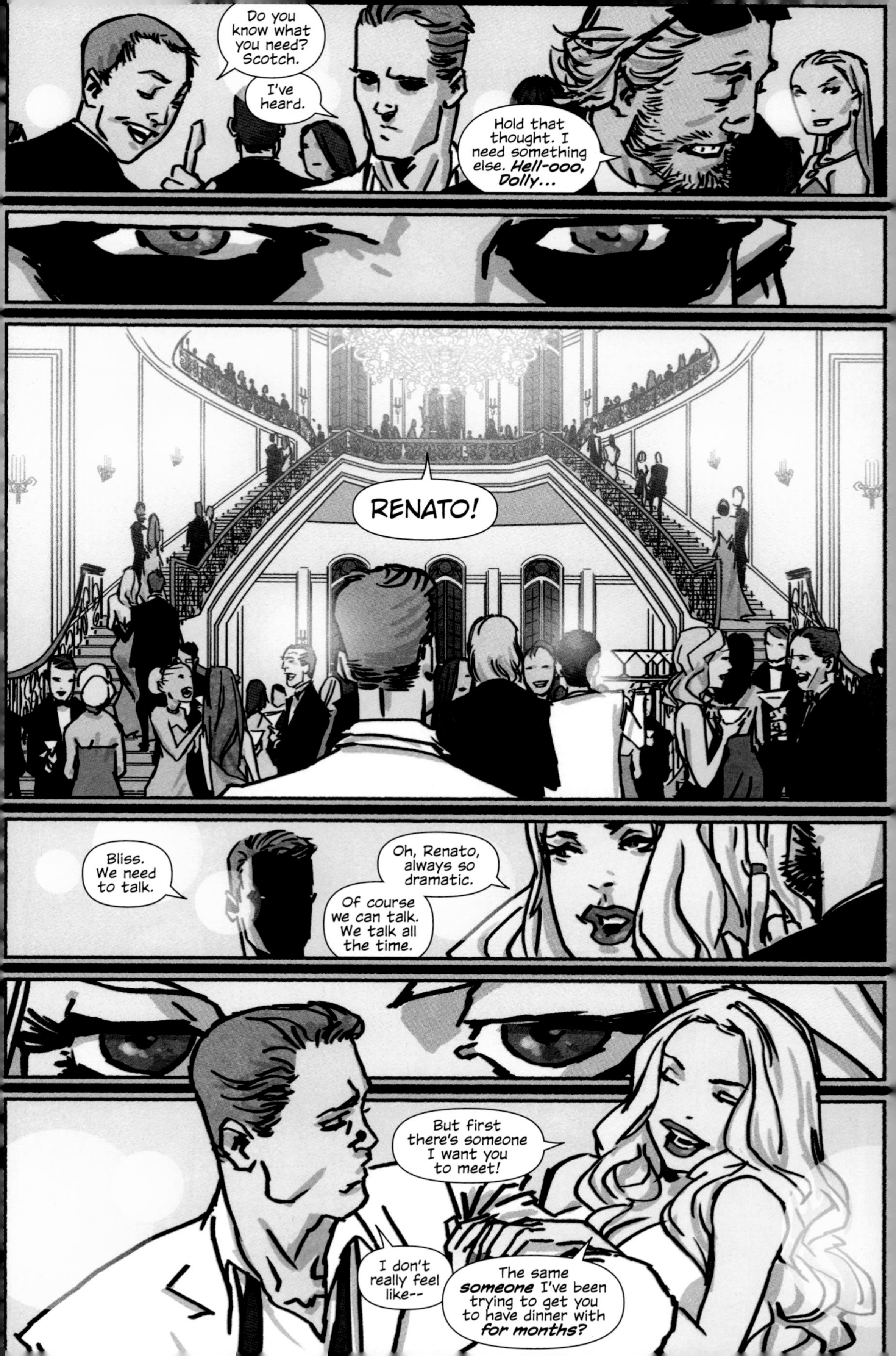
Do you know what you need? Scotch.
I've heard.
Hold that thought. I need something else. **Hell-ooo, Dolly...**
RENATO!
Bliss. We need to talk.
Oh, Renato, always so dramatic.
Of course we can talk. We talk all the time.
But first there's someone I want you to meet!
I don't really feel like--
The same **someone** I've been trying to get you to have dinner with **for months?**

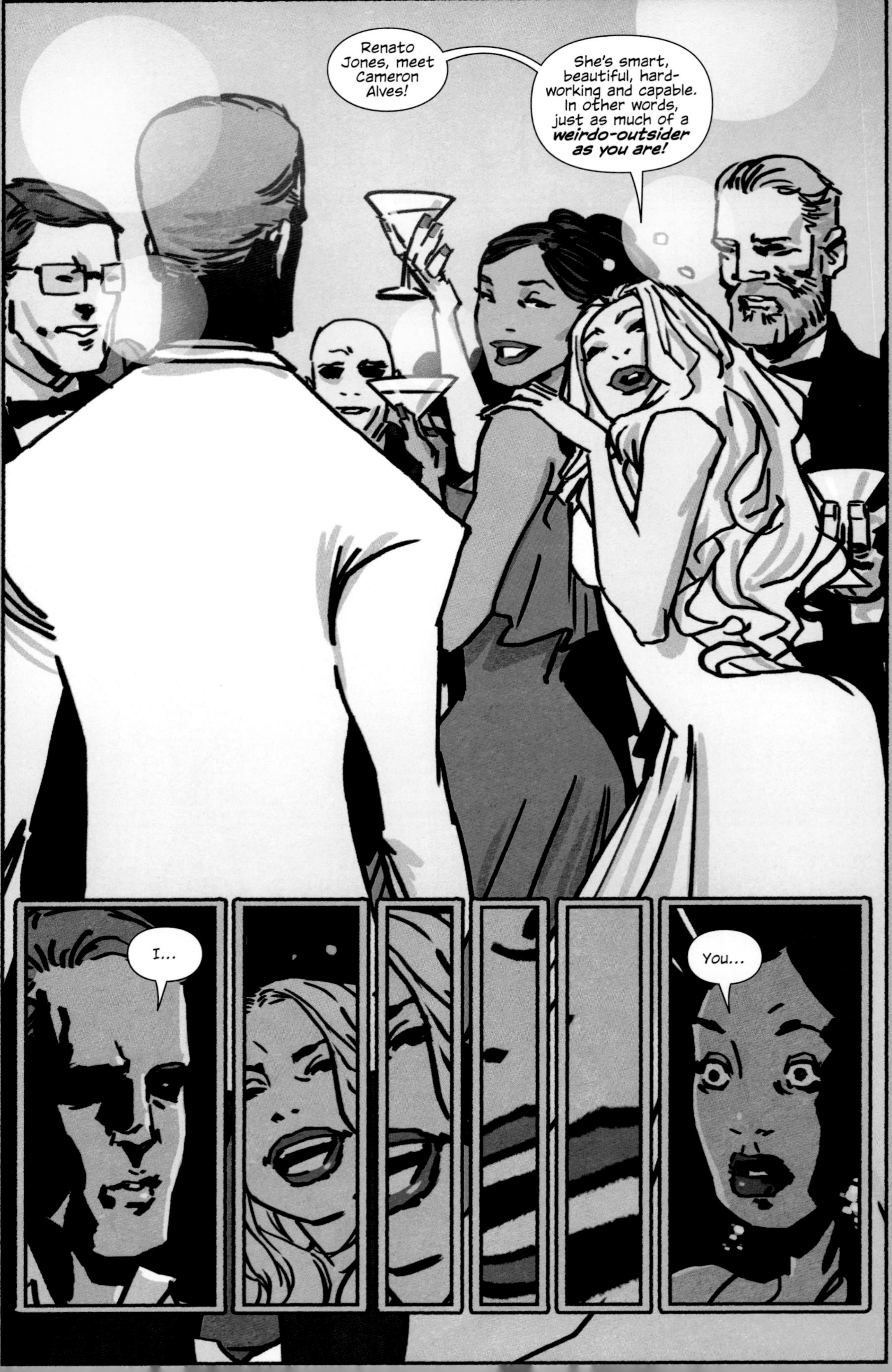
Renato Jones, meet Cameron Alves!
She's smart, beautiful, hard-working and capable. In other words, just as much of a **weirdo-outsider as you are!**
I...
You...

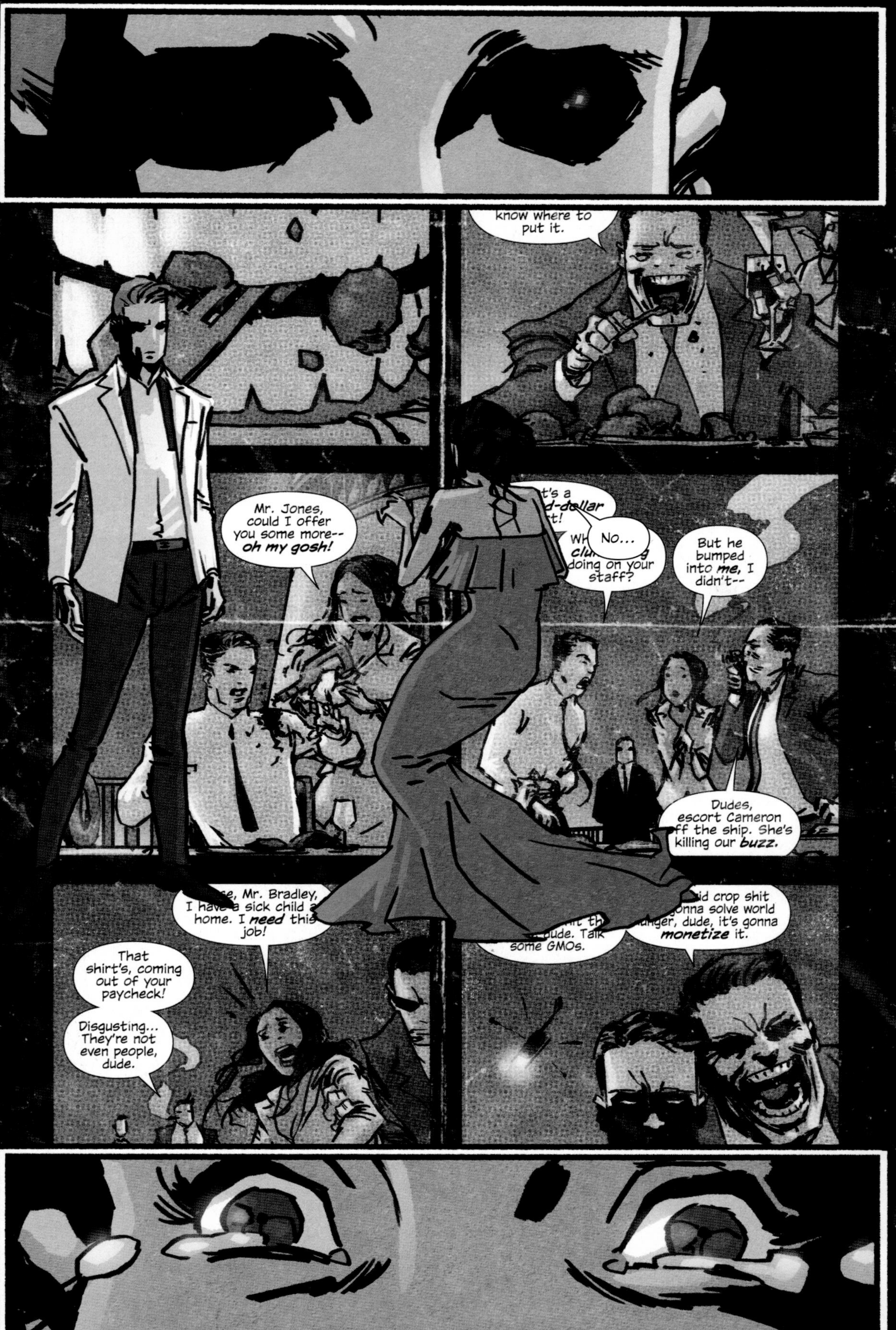

know where to put it.
Mr. Jones, could I offer you some more-- oh my gosh!
...t's a ...d-dollar ...t!
Wh... clu... doing on your staff?
No...
But he bumped into me, I didn't--
Dudes, escort Cameron ...ff the ship. She's killing our buzz.
...se, Mr. Bradley, I have a sick child a... home. I need this job!
That shirt's, coming out of your paycheck!
Disgusting... They're not even people, dude.
...t th... dude. Talk some GMOs.
...d crop shit ...onna solve world ...unger, dude, it's gonna monetize it.

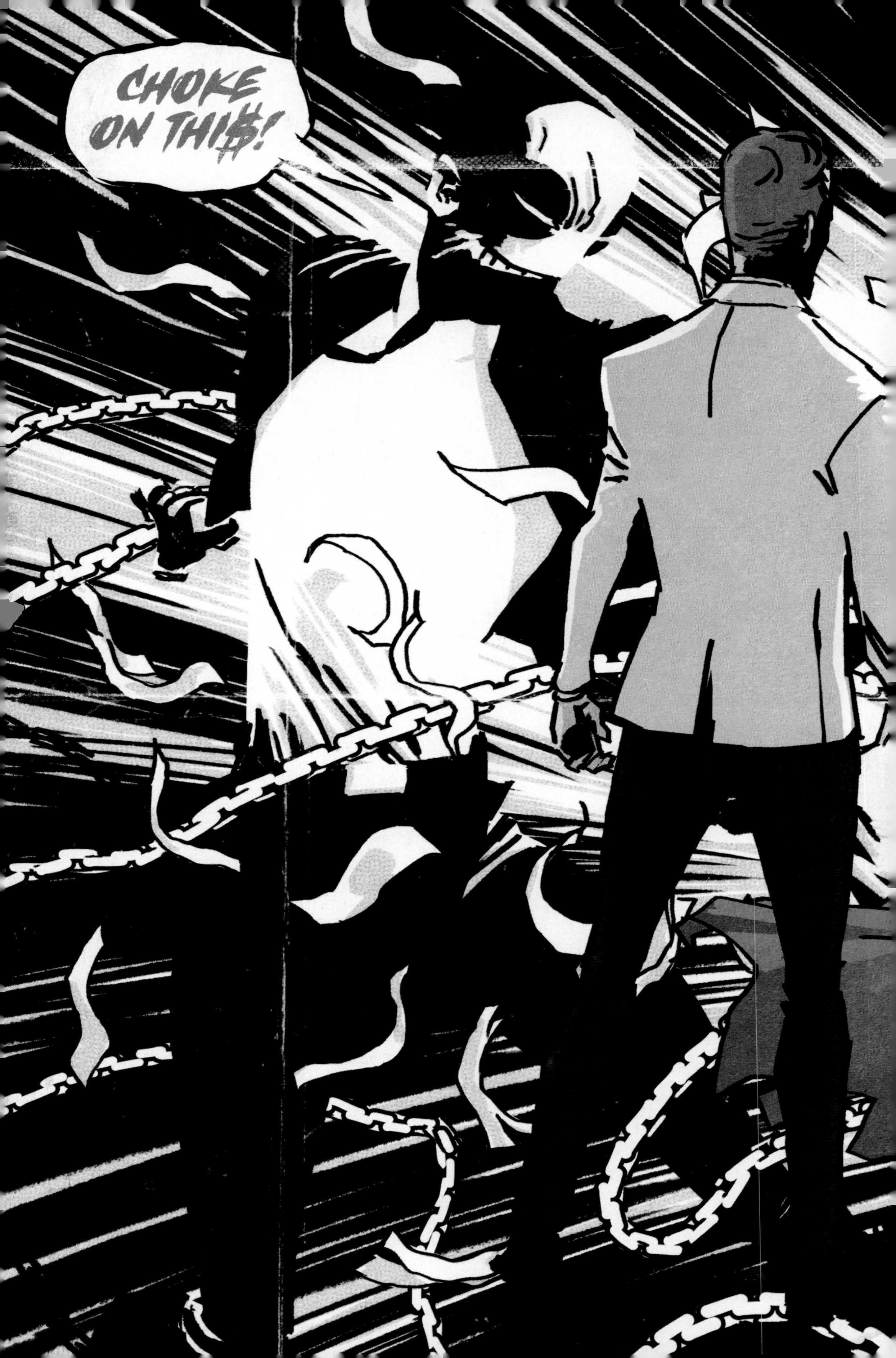
CHOKE ON THI$!

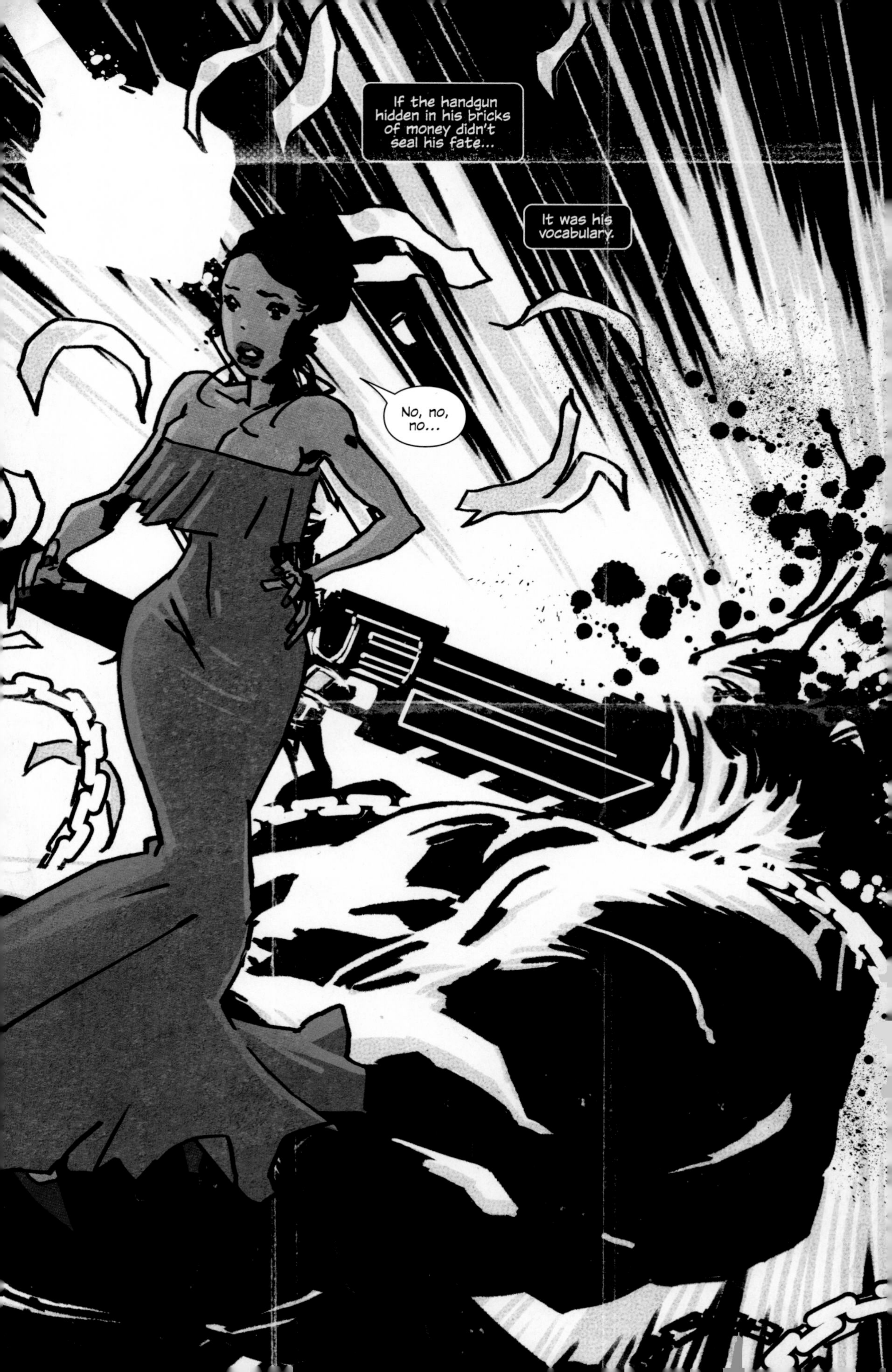
If the handgun hidden in his bricks of money didn't seal his fate...
It was his vocabulary.
No, no, no...

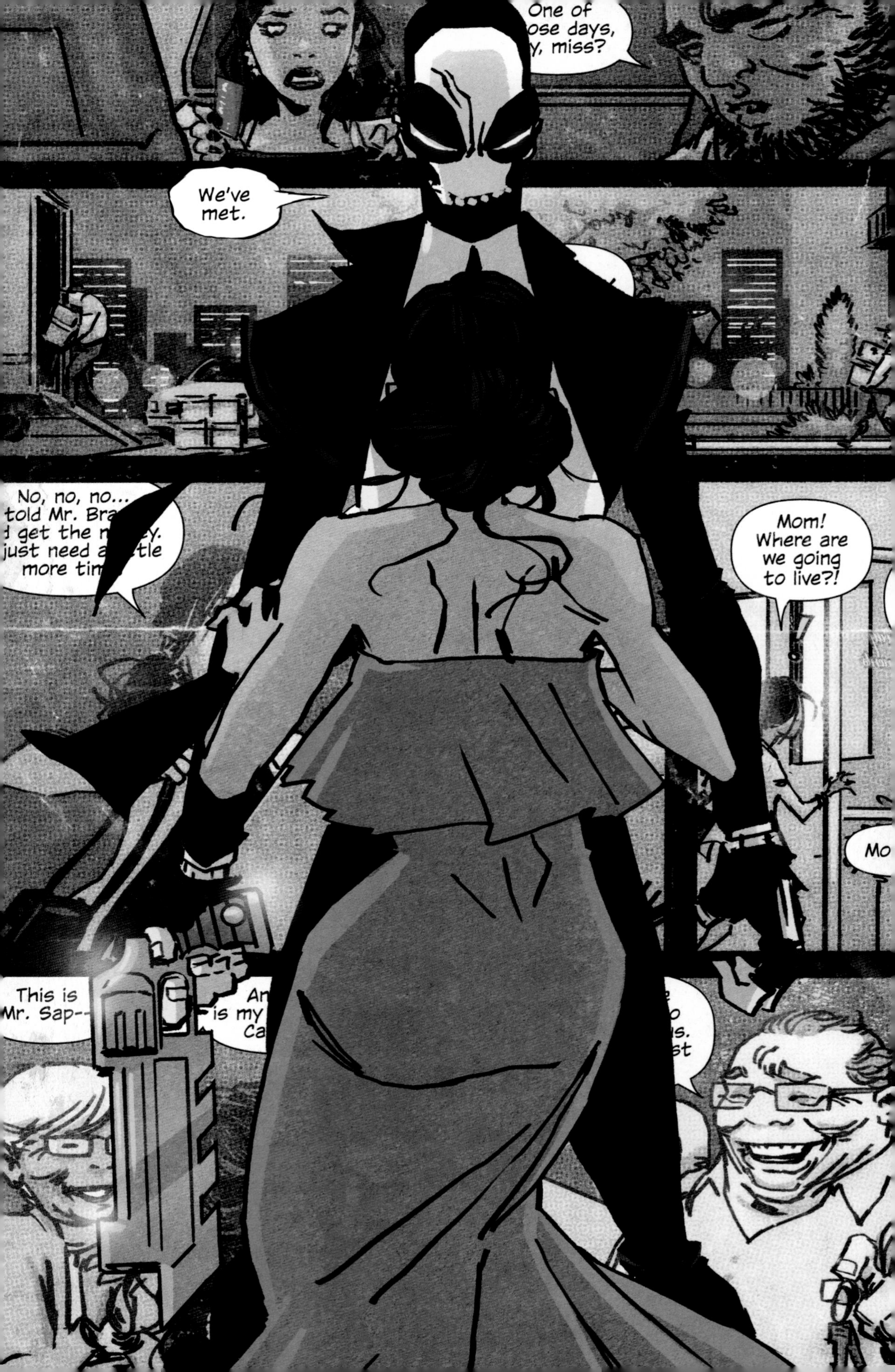
One of ose days, y, miss?
We've met.
No, no, no... told Mr. Bra get the m ey. just need a tle more tim
Mom! Where are we going to live?!
Mo
This is Mr. Sap--
An is my Ca

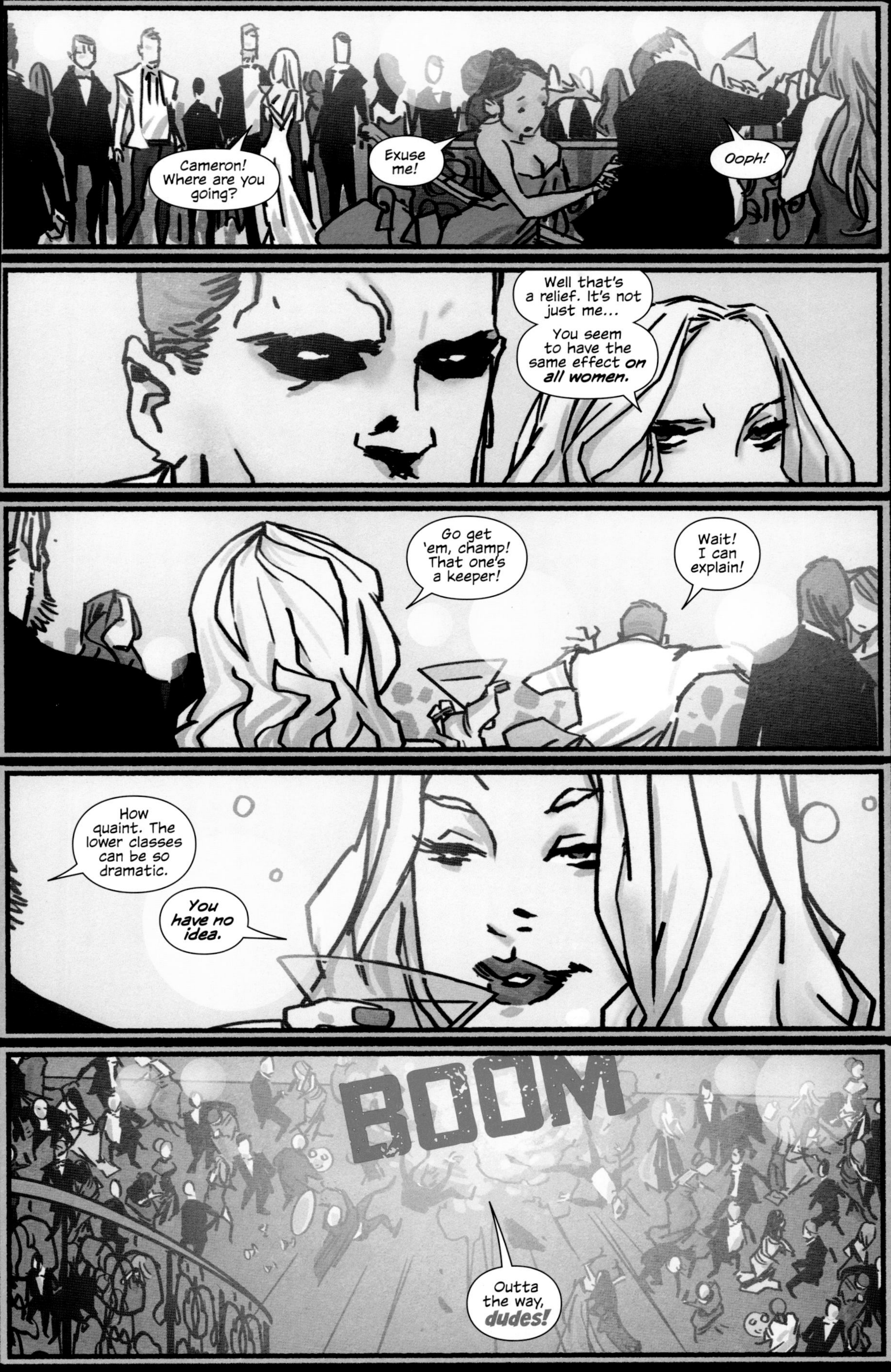
Cameron! Where are you going?
Exuse me!
Ooph!
Well that's a relief. It's not just me...
You seem to have the same effect *on all women.*
Go get 'em, champ! That one's a keeper!
Wait! I can explain!
How quaint. The lower classes can be so dramatic.
You have no idea.
BOOM
Outta the way, *dudes!*

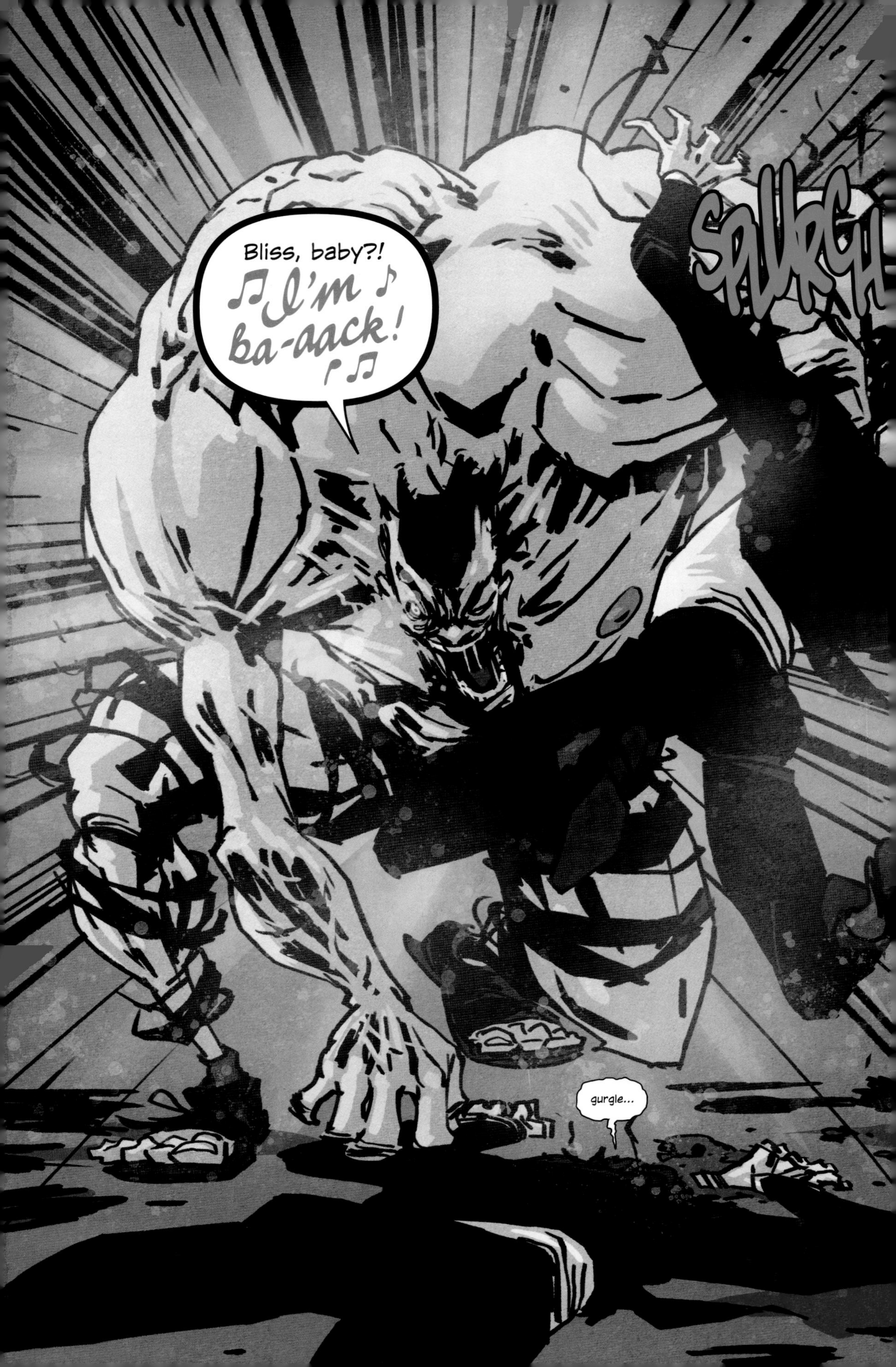

SPLURGH
Bliss, baby?! ♫ I'm ♪ ba-aack! ♪♫
gurgle...

"This
ONE-man
show,
what's it
all about?
Pride?"

"We are the reason the other half has anything at all. A mistake we are looking to rectify."

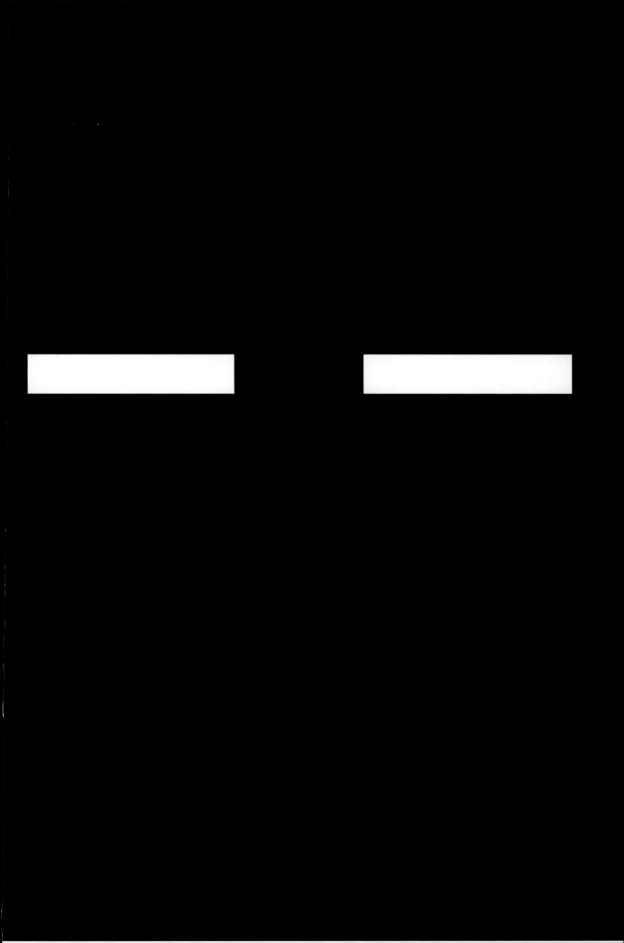

3

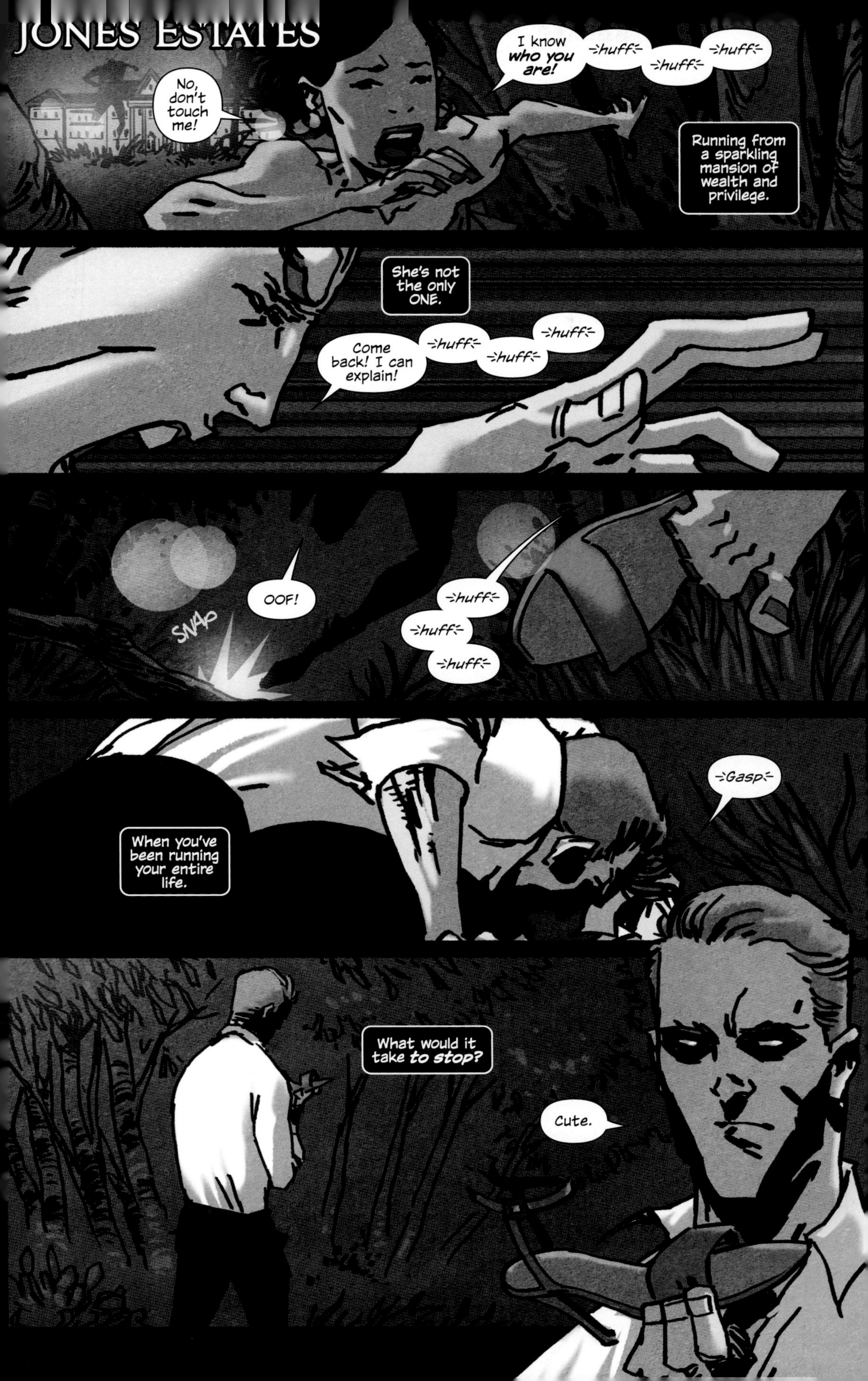
JONES ESTATES
No, don't touch me!
I know who you are!
-huff-
-huff-
-huff-
Running from a sparkling mansion of wealth and privilege.
She's not the only ONE.
Come back! I can explain!
-huff-
-huff-
-huff-
OOF!
SNAP
-huff-
-huff-
-huff-
-Gasp-
When you've been running your entire life.
What would it take to stop?
Cute.

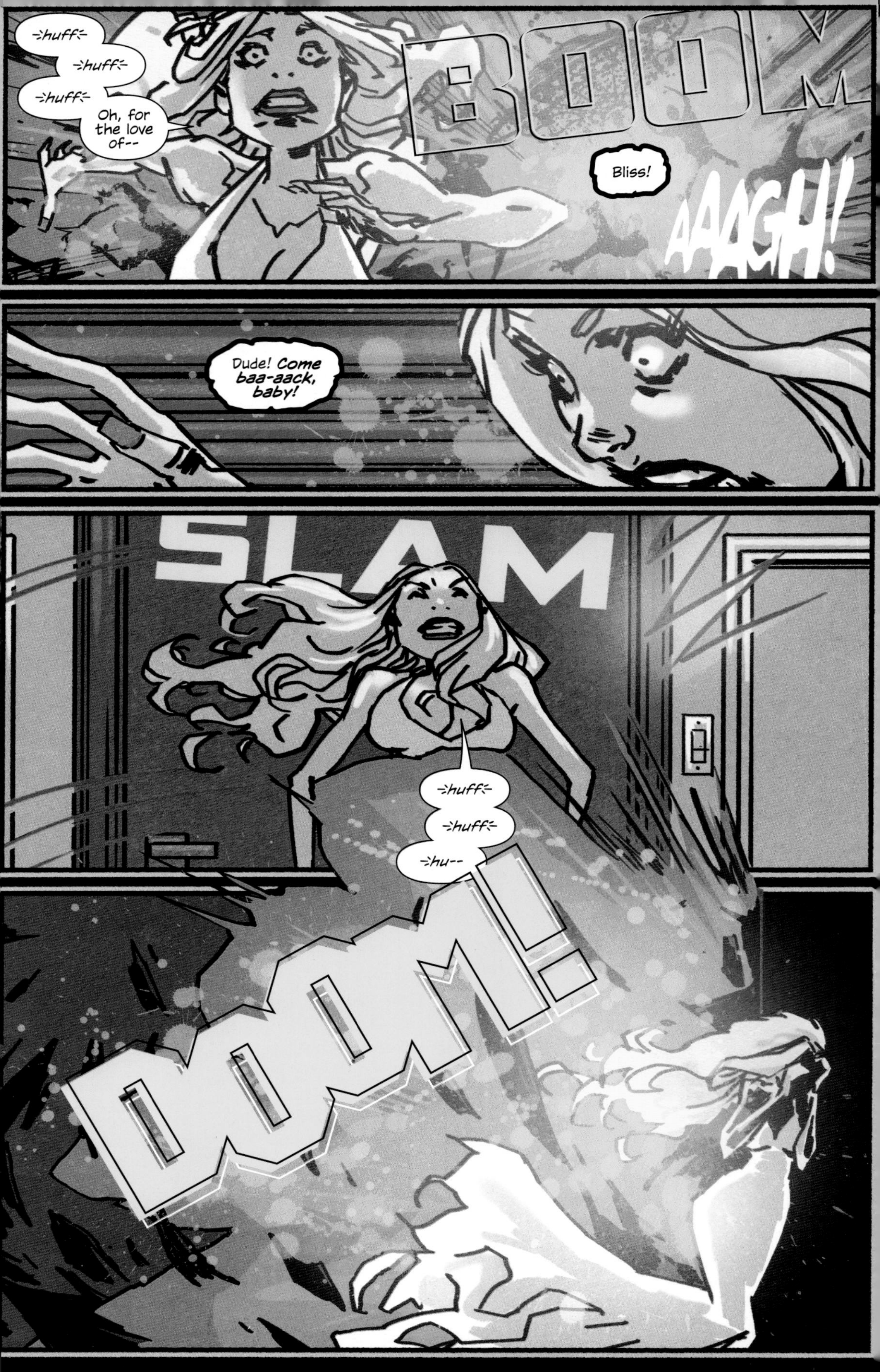

-huff-
-huff-
-huff-
Oh, for the love of--
BOOM
Bliss!
AAAGH!
Dude! Come baa-aack, baby!
SLAM
-huff-
-huff-
-hu--
DOOM!

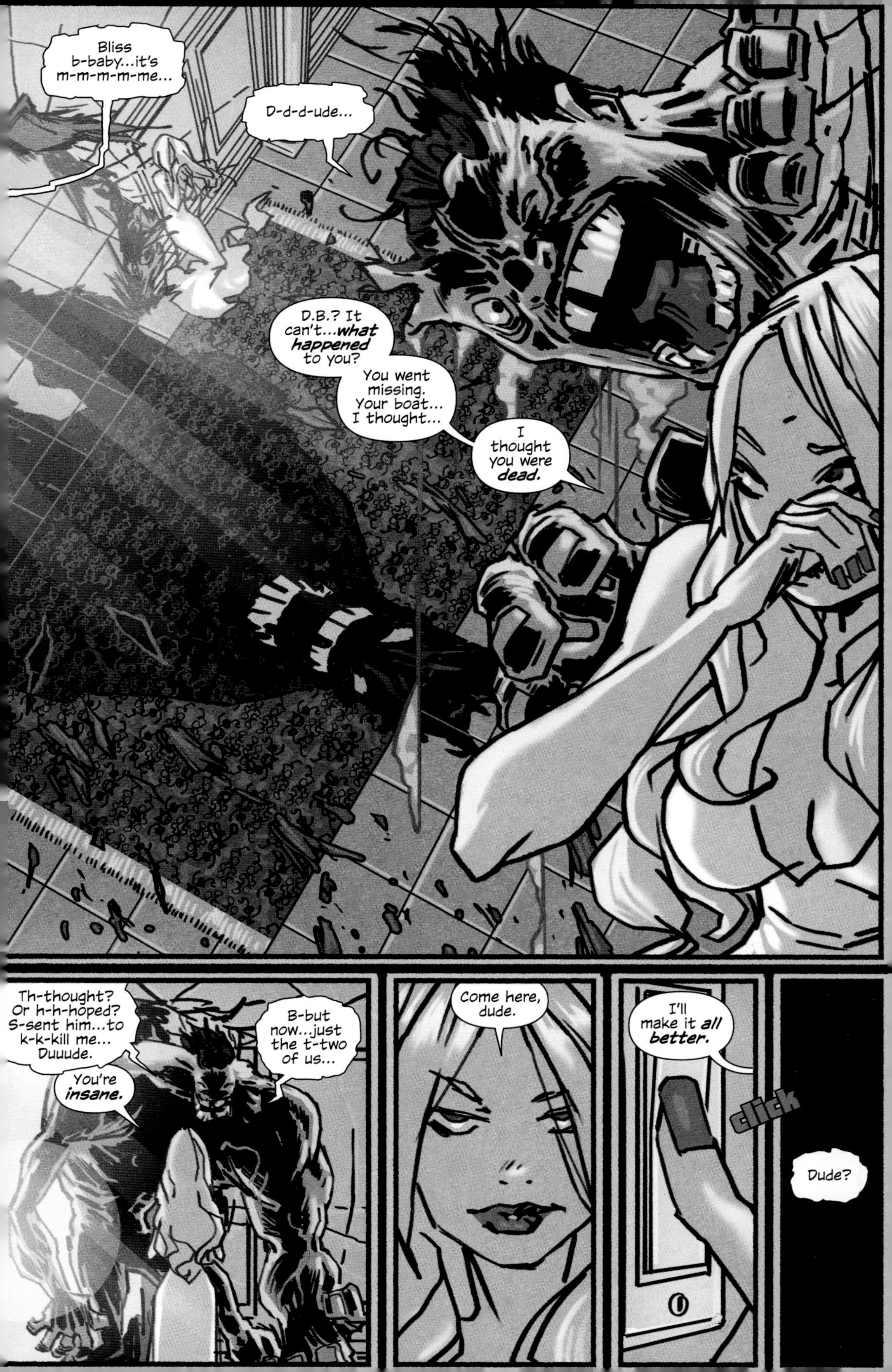

Bliss b-baby...it's m-m-m-m-me...
D-d-d-ude...
D.B.? It can't...*what happened* to you?
You went missing. Your boat... I thought...
I thought you were *dead.*
Th-thought? Or h-h-hoped? S-sent him...to k-k-kill me... Duuude.
You're *insane.*
B-but now...just the t-two of us...
Come here, dude.
I'll make it *all better.*
click
Dude?

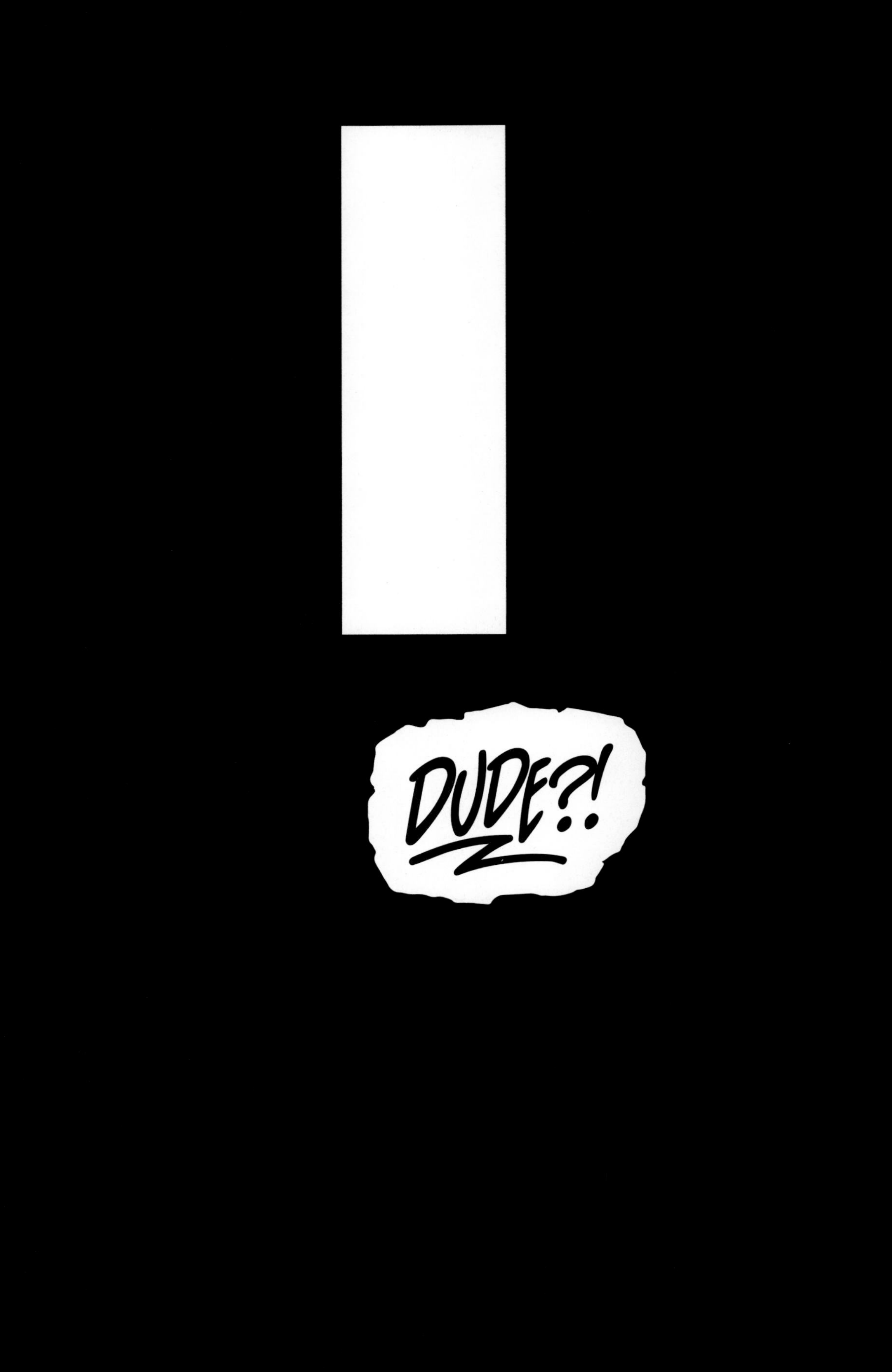
DUDE?!

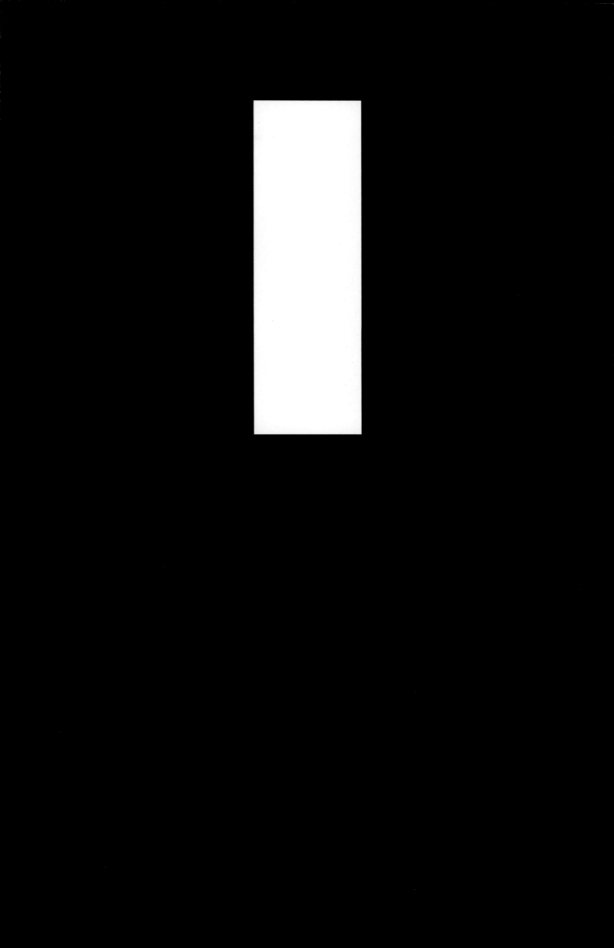

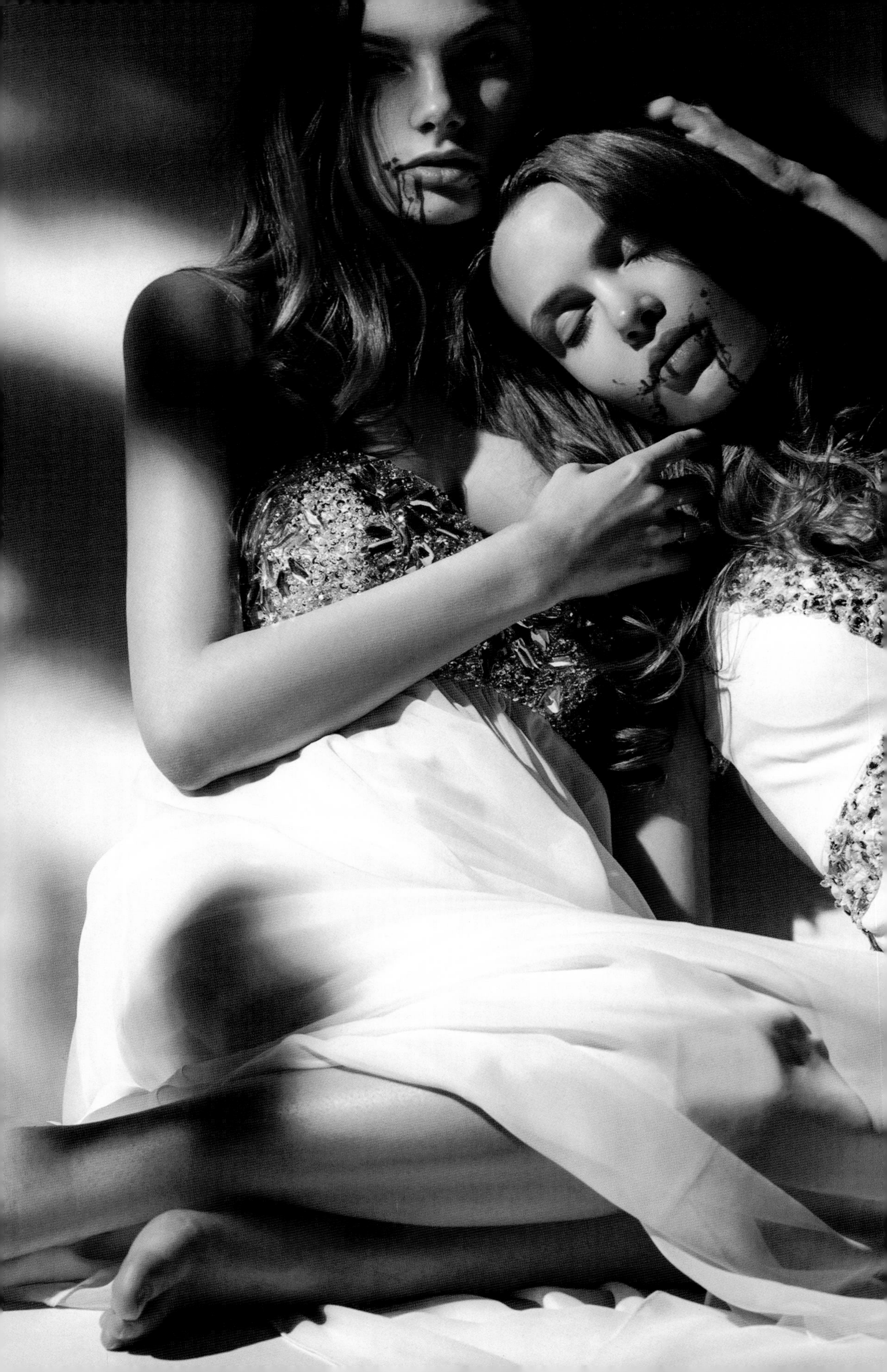

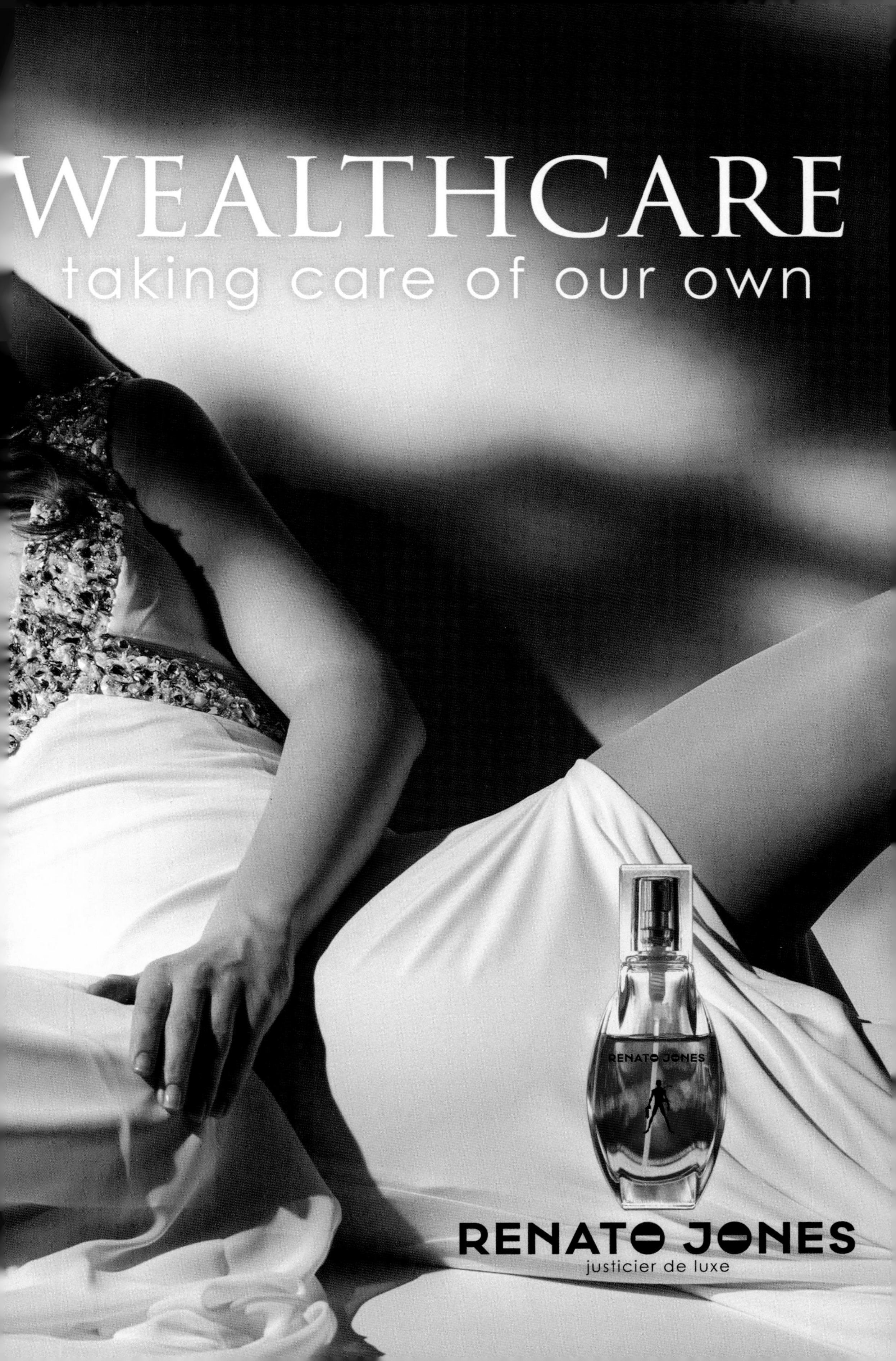
WEALTHCARE
taking care of our own
RENATO JONES
RENATO JONES
justicier de luxe

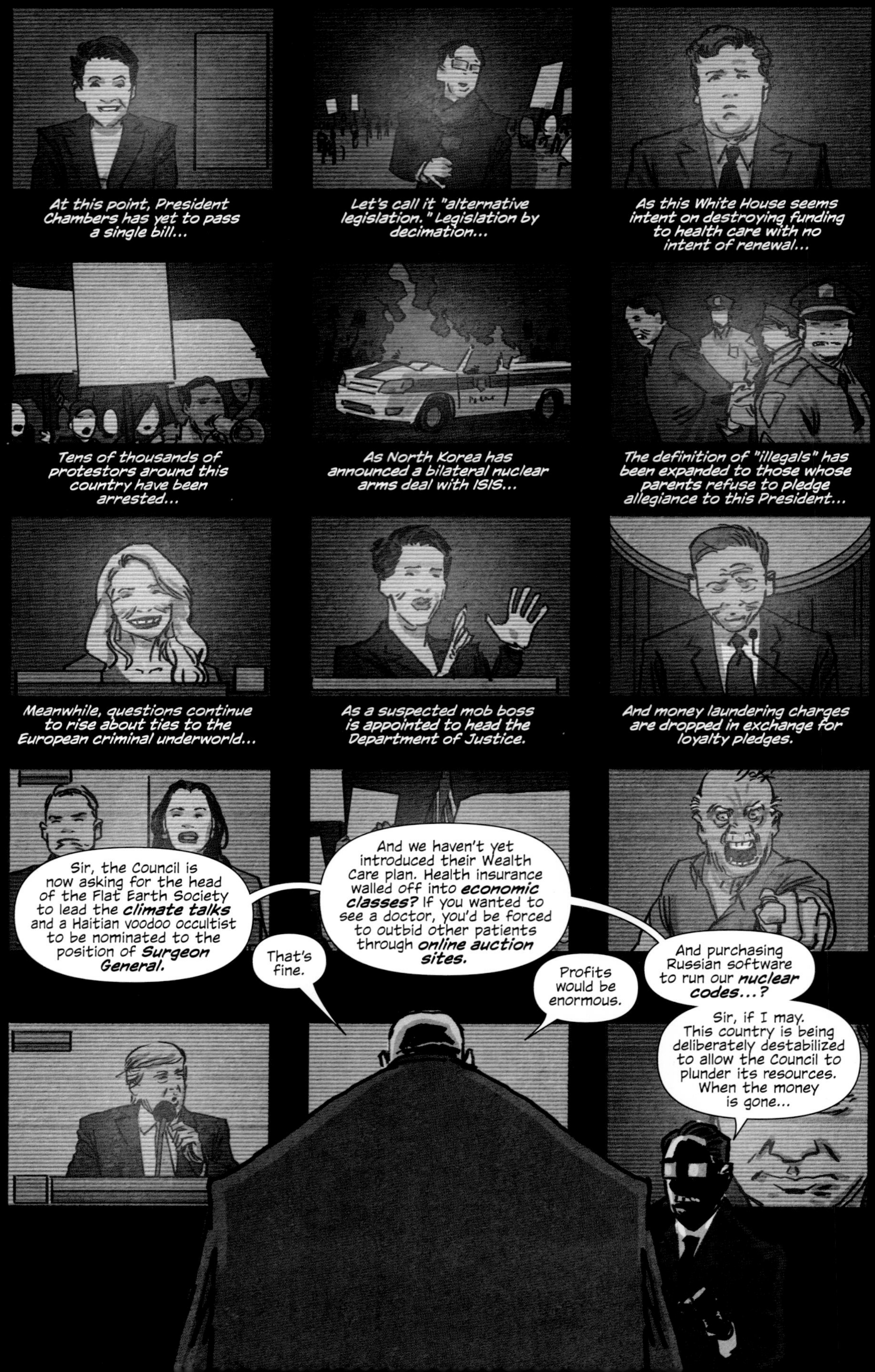

At this point, President Chambers has yet to pass a single bill...
Let's call it "alternative legislation." Legislation by decimation...
As this White House seems intent on destroying funding to health care with no intent of renewal...
Tens of thousands of protestors around this country have been arrested...
As North Korea has announced a bilateral nuclear arms deal with ISIS...
The definition of "illegals" has been expanded to those whose parents refuse to pledge allegiance to this President...
Meanwhile, questions continue to rise about ties to the European criminal underworld...
As a suspected mob boss is appointed to head the Department of Justice.
And money laundering charges are dropped in exchange for loyalty pledges.
Sir, the Council is now asking for the head of the Flat Earth Society to lead the **climate talks** and a Haitian voodoo occultist to be nominated to the position of **Surgeon General.**
That's fine.
And we haven't yet introduced their Wealth Care plan. Health insurance walled off into **economic classes?** If you wanted to see a doctor, you'd be forced to outbid other patients through **online auction sites.**
Profits would be enormous.
And purchasing Russian software to run our **nuclear codes...?**
Sir, if I may. This country is being deliberately destabilized to allow the Council to plunder its resources. When the money is gone...

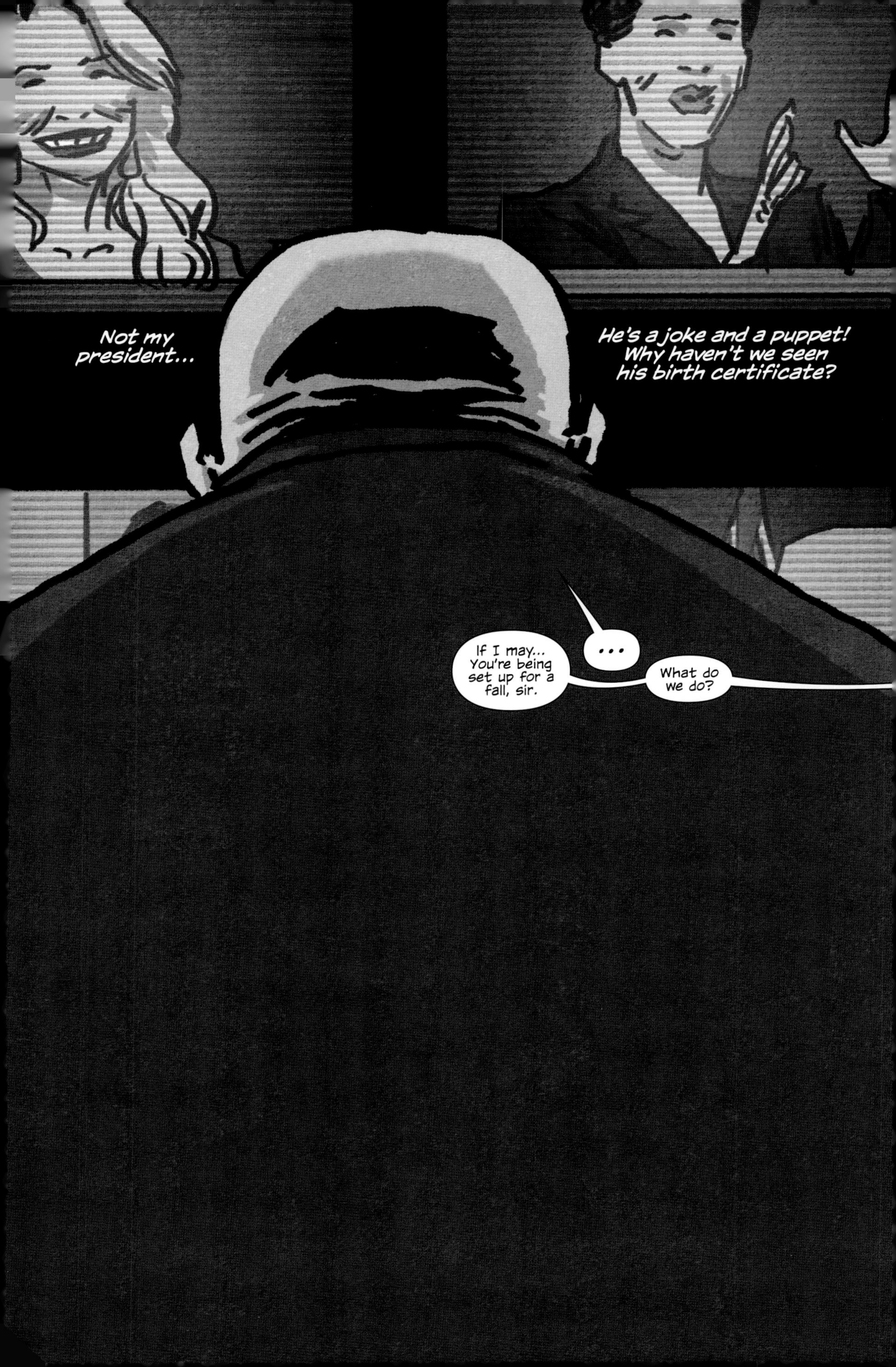
Not my president...
He's a joke and a puppet! Why haven't we seen his birth certificate?
...
If I may... You're being set up for a fall, sir.
What do we do?

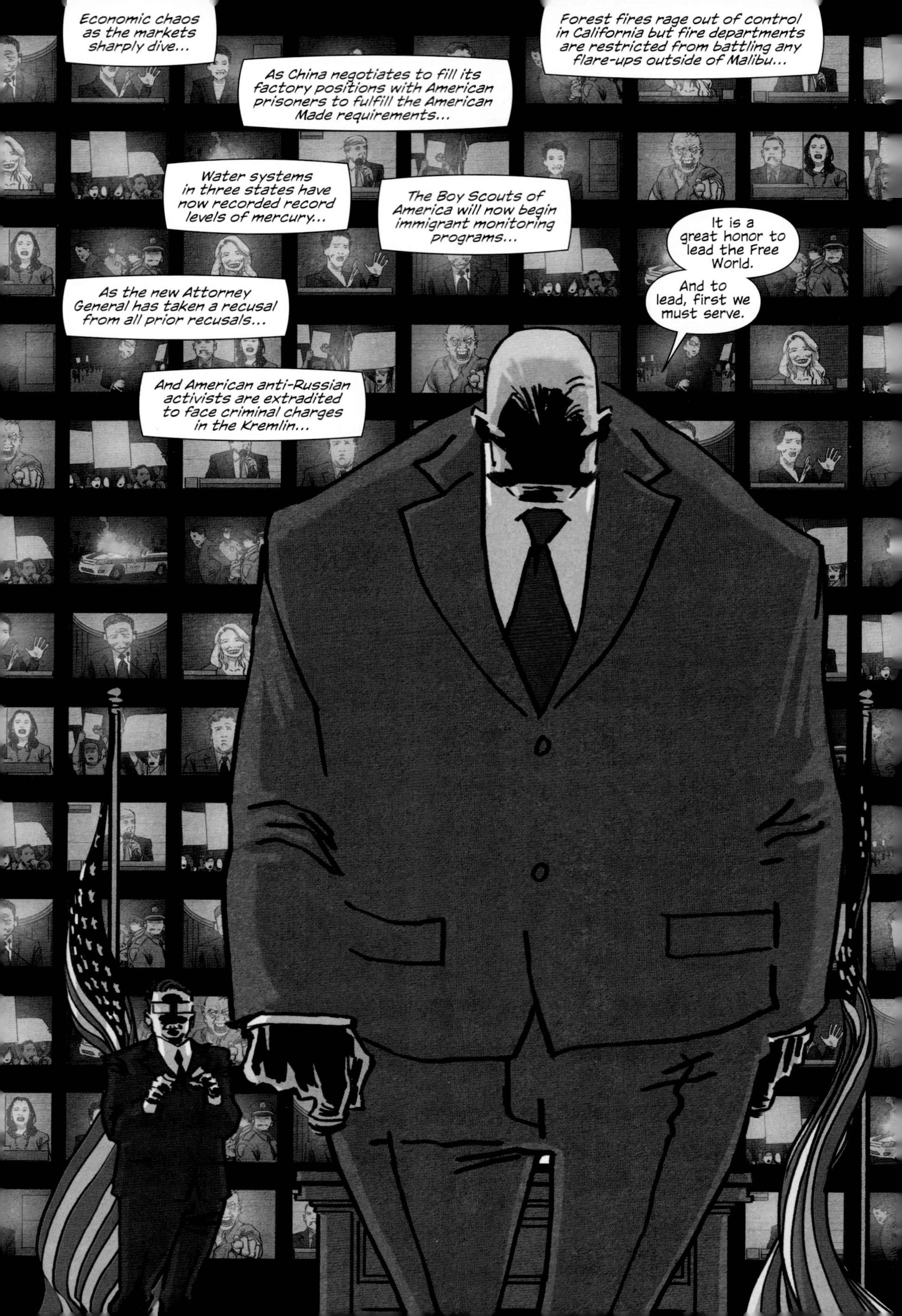
Economic chaos as the markets sharply dive...
As China negotiates to fill its factory positions with American prisoners to fulfill the American Made requirements...
Forest fires rage out of control in California but fire departments are restricted from battling any flare-ups outside of Malibu...
Water systems in three states have now recorded record levels of mercury...
The Boy Scouts of America will now begin immigrant monitoring programs...
As the new Attorney General has taken a recusal from all prior recusals...
And American anti-Russian activists are extradited to face criminal charges in the Kremlin...
It is a great honor to lead the Free World.
And to lead, first we must serve.

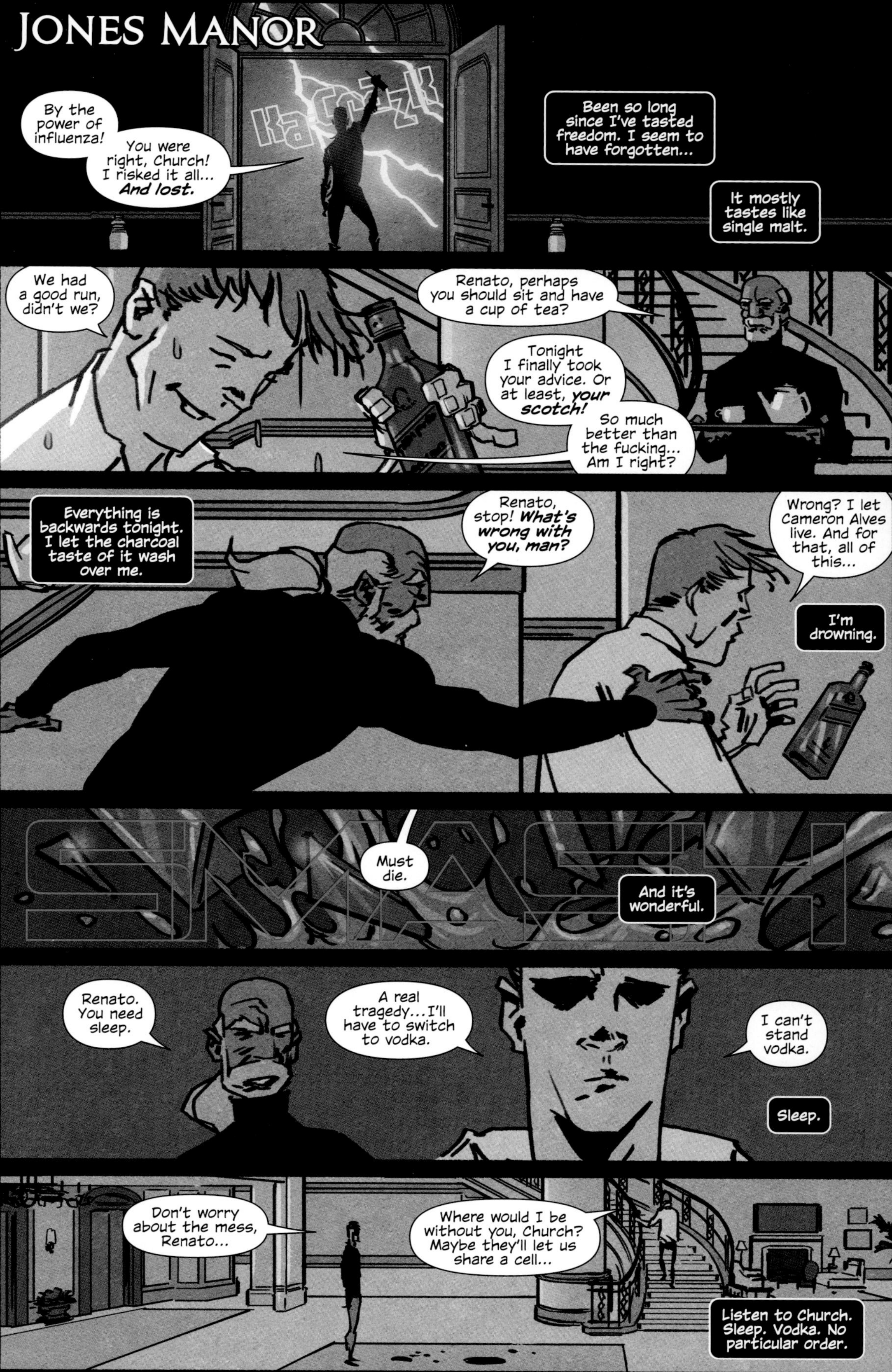
JONES MANOR
By the power of influenza!
You were right, Church! I risked it all... And lost.
Been so long since I've tasted freedom. I seem to have forgotten...
It mostly tastes like single malt.
We had a good run, didn't we?
Renato, perhaps you should sit and have a cup of tea?
Tonight I finally took your advice. Or at least, your scotch!
So much better than the fucking... Am I right?
Everything is backwards tonight. I let the charcoal taste of it wash over me.
Renato, stop! What's wrong with you, man?
Wrong? I let Cameron Alves live. And for that, all of this...
I'm drowning.
SMASH
Must die.
And it's wonderful.
Renato. You need sleep.
A real tragedy... I'll have to switch to vodka.
I can't stand vodka.
Sleep.
Don't worry about the mess, Renato...
Where would I be without you, Church? Maybe they'll let us share a cell...
Listen to Church. Sleep. Vodka. No particular order.

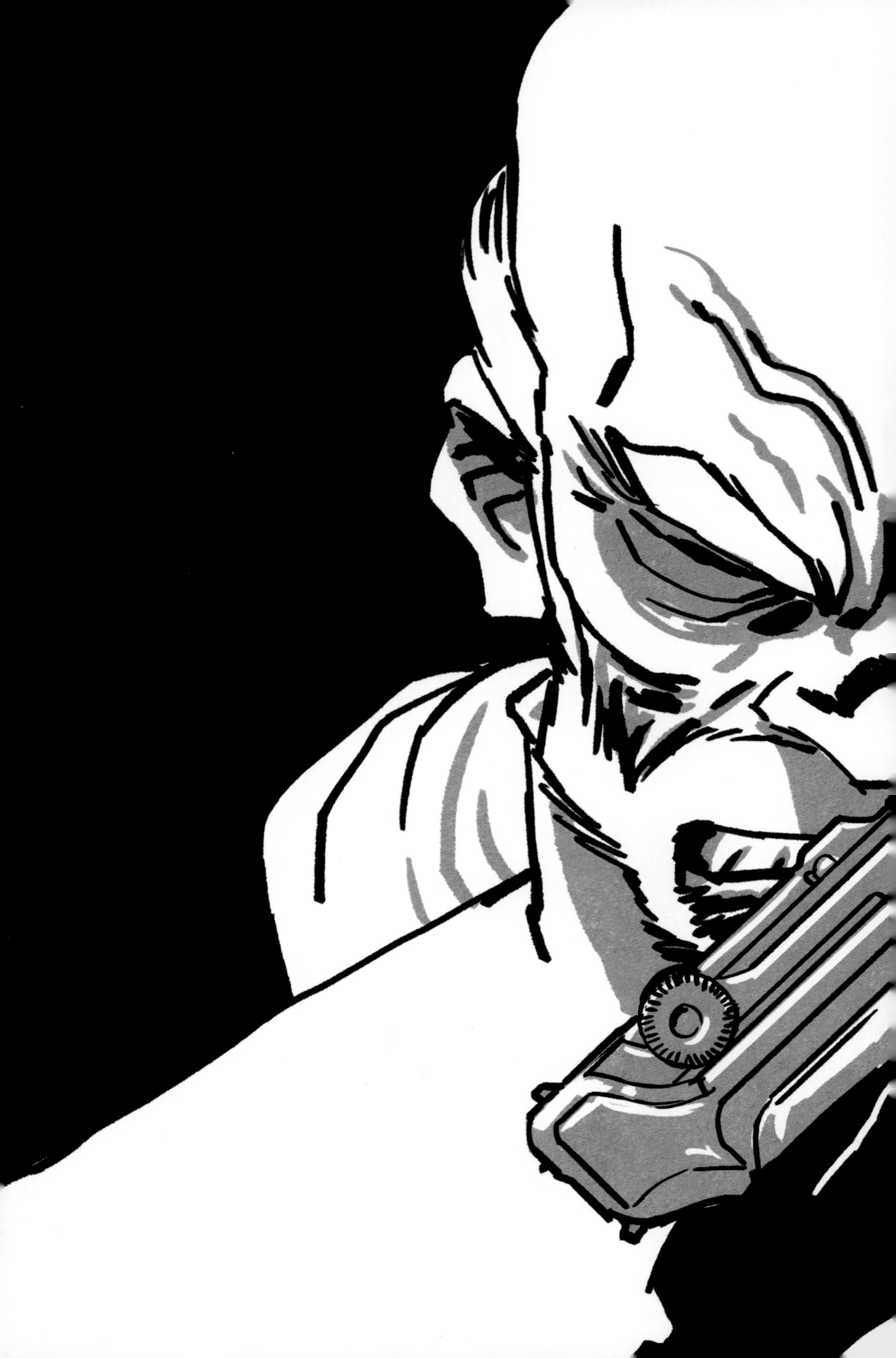

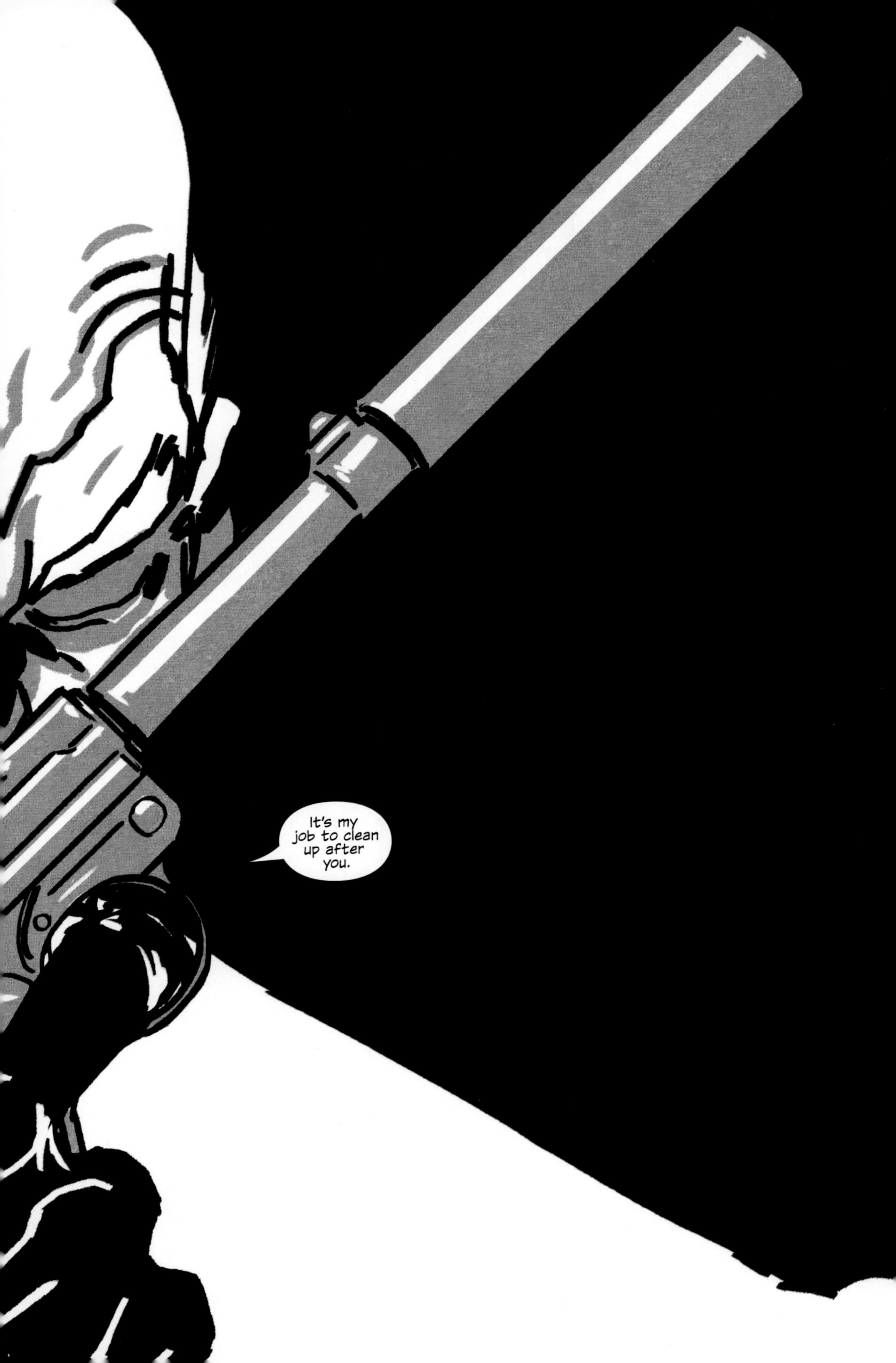
It's my job to clean up after you.

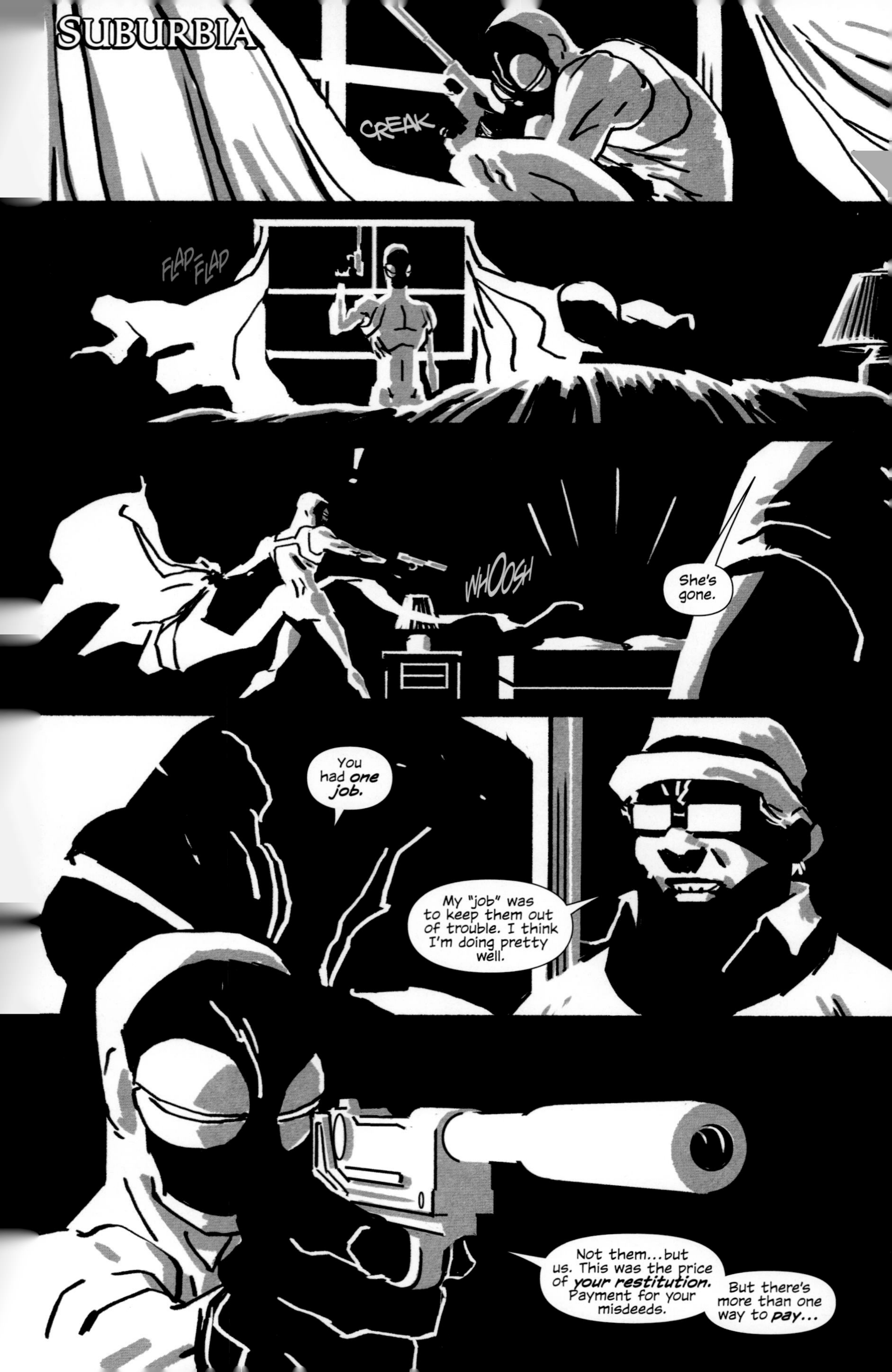
SUBURBIA
CREAK
FLAP-FLAP
!
WHOOSH
She's gone.
You had one job.
My "job" was to keep them out of trouble. I think I'm doing pretty well.
Not them...but us. This was the price of your restitution. Payment for your misdeeds.
But there's more than one way to pay...

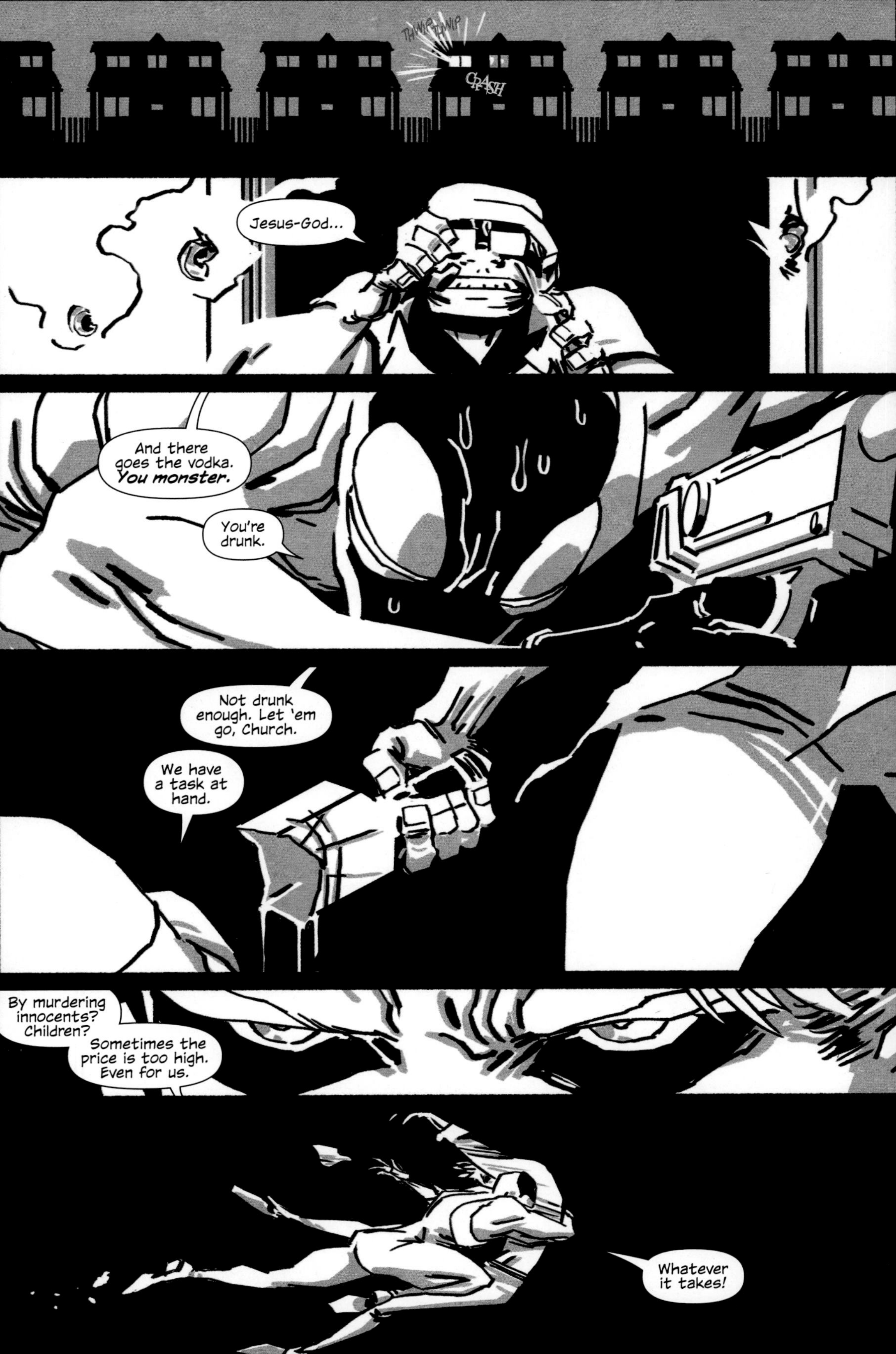
THWIP THWIP
CRASH
Jesus-God...
And there goes the vodka. ***You monster.***
You're drunk.
Not drunk enough. Let 'em go, Church.
We have a task at hand.
By murdering innocents? Children?
Sometimes the price is too high. Even for us.
Whatever it takes!

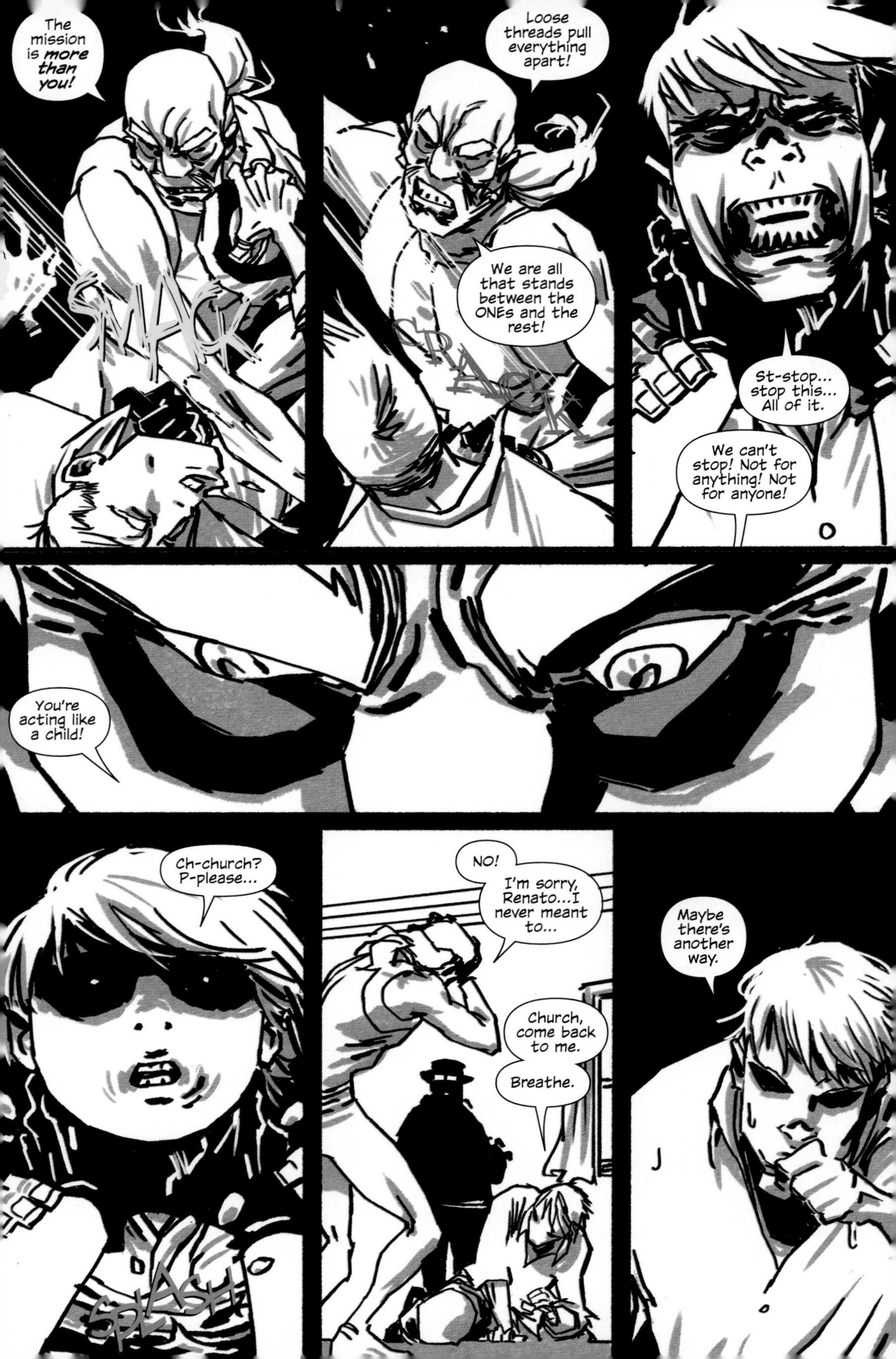
The mission is ***more than you!***
SMACK
Loose threads pull everything apart!
We are all that stands between the ONEs and the rest!
CRACK
St-stop... stop this... All of it.
We can't stop! Not for anything! Not for anyone!
You're acting like a child!
Ch-church? P-please...
SPLASH
NO!
I'm sorry, Renato...I never meant to...
Church, come back to me.
Breathe.
Maybe there's another way.

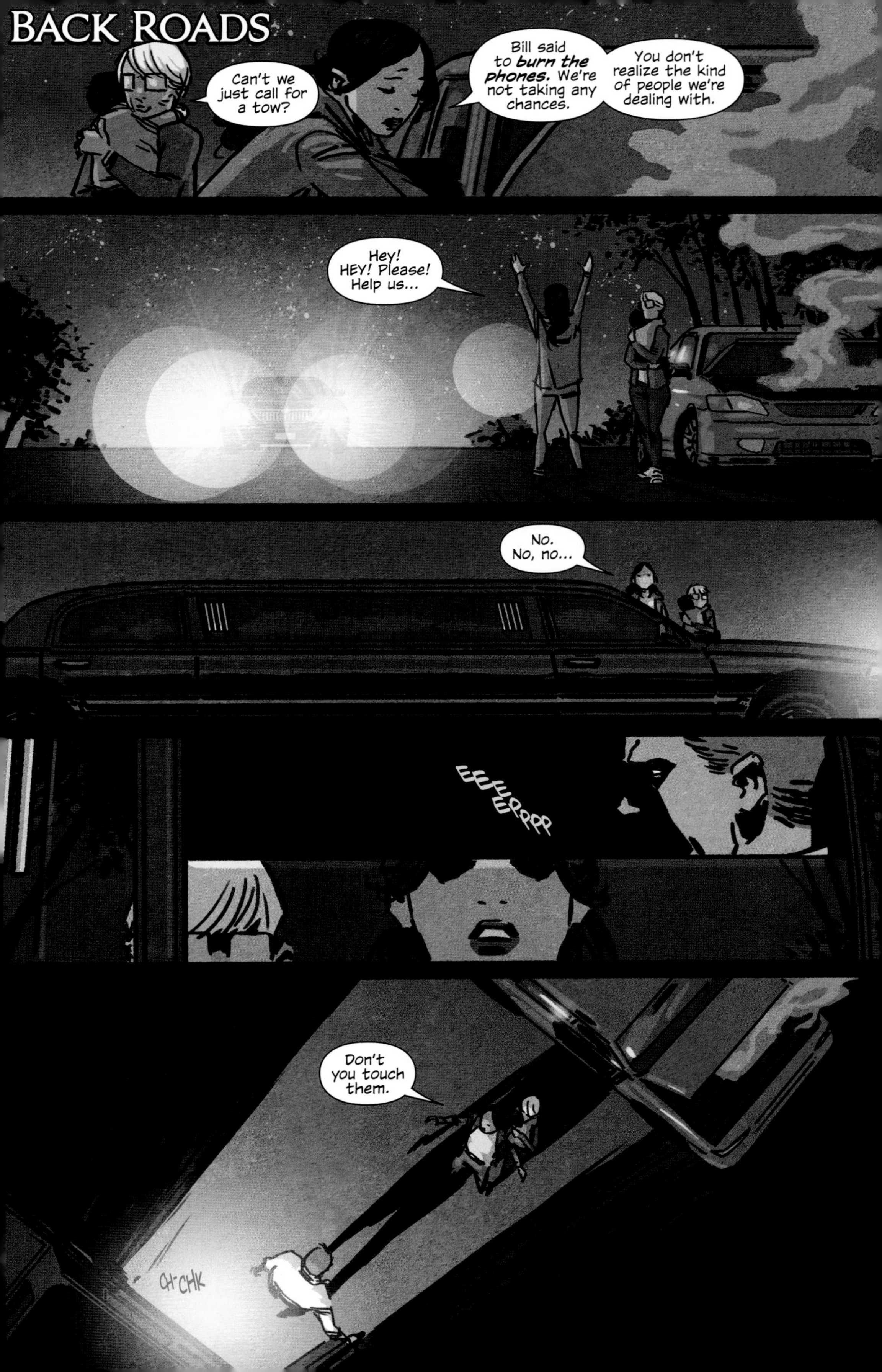
BACK ROADS
Can't we just call for a tow?
Bill said to **burn the phones.** We're not taking any chances.
You don't realize the kind of people we're dealing with.
Hey! HEY! Please! Help us...
No. No, no...
EEEEERPPP
Don't you touch them.
CH-CHK

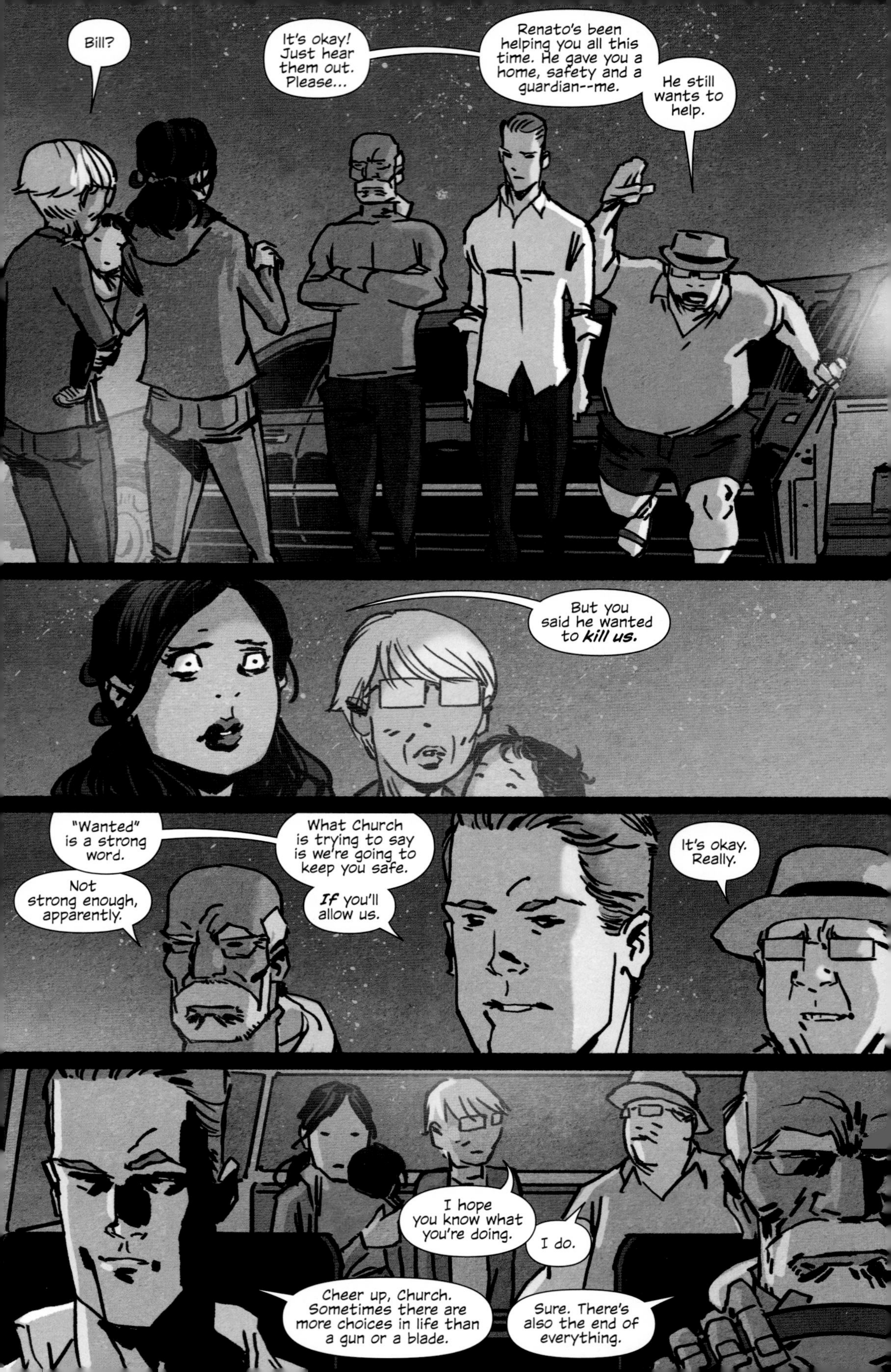
Bill?
It's okay! Just hear them out. Please...
Renato's been helping you all this time. He gave you a home, safety and a guardian--me.
He still wants to help.
But you said he wanted to *kill us.*
"Wanted" is a strong word.
Not strong enough, apparently.
What Church is trying to say is we're going to keep you safe.
If you'll allow us.
It's okay. Really.
I hope you know what you're doing.
I do.
Cheer up, Church. Sometimes there are more choices in life than a gun or a blade.
Sure. There's also the end of everything.

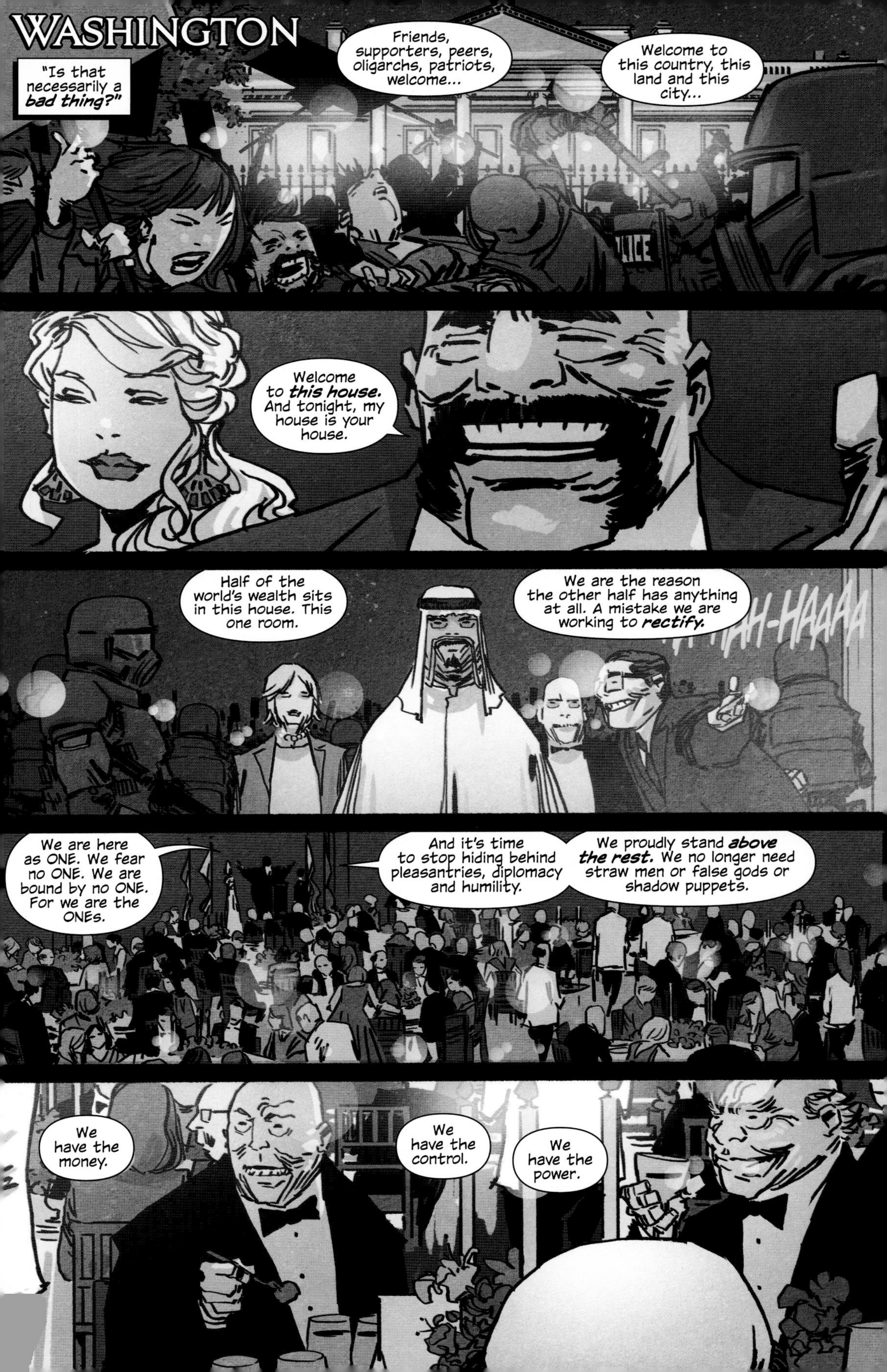
WASHINGTON
"Is that necessarily a *bad thing?*"
Friends, supporters, peers, oligarchs, patriots, welcome...
Welcome to this country, this land and this city...
Welcome to ***this house.*** And tonight, my house is your house.
Half of the world's wealth sits in this house. This one room.
We are the reason the other half has anything at all. A mistake we are working to ***rectify.***
HAH-HAAAA
We are here as ONE. We fear no ONE. We are bound by no ONE. For we are the ONEs.
And it's time to stop hiding behind pleasantries, diplomacy and humility.
We proudly stand ***above the rest.*** We no longer need straw men or false gods or shadow puppets.
We have the money.
We have the control.
We have the power.

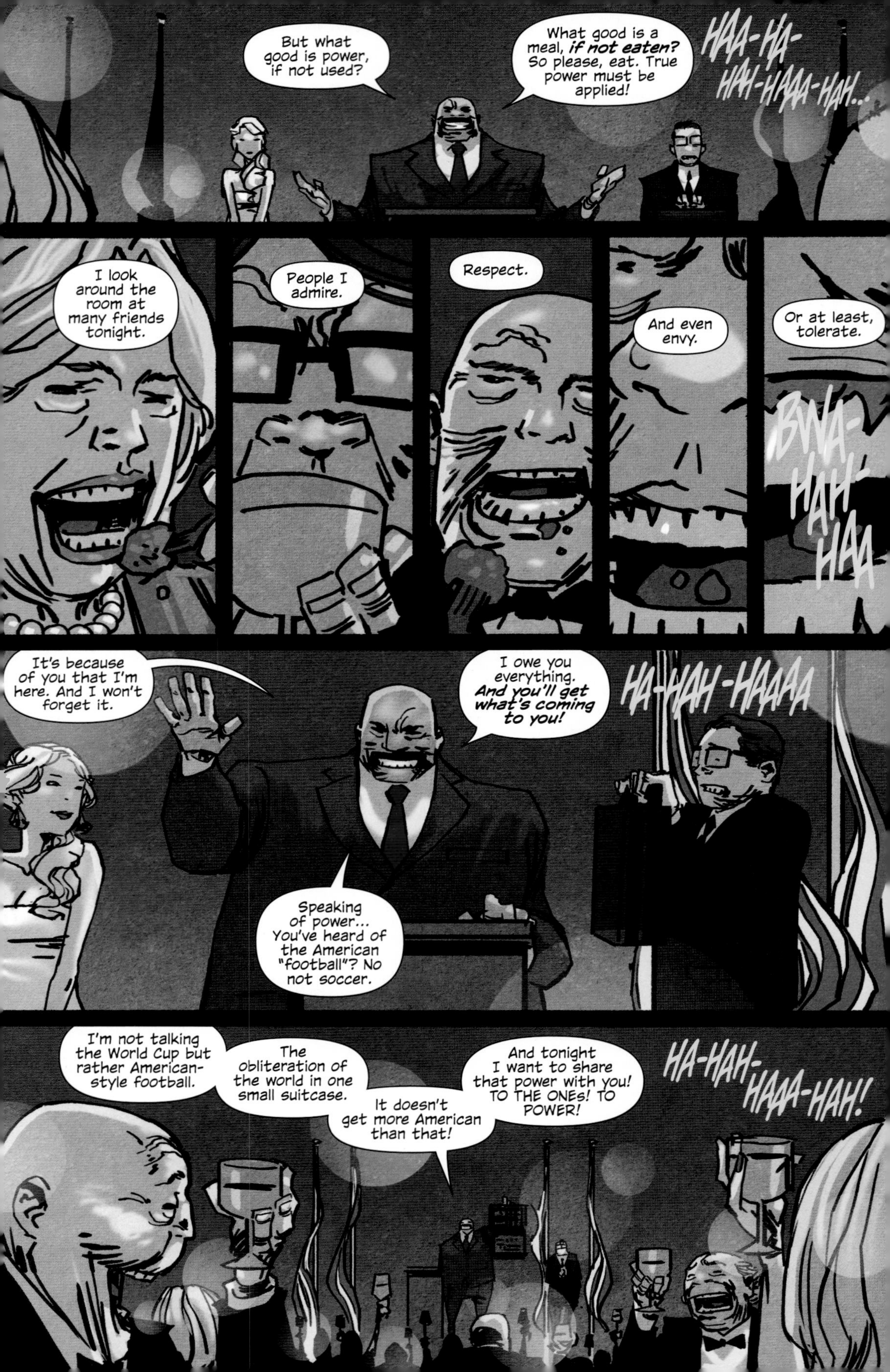

But what good is power, if not used?
What good is a meal, *if not eaten?* So please, eat. True power must be applied!
HAA-HA-HAH-HAAA-HAH...
I look around the room at many friends tonight.
People I admire.
Respect.
And even envy.
Or at least, tolerate.
BWA-HAH-HA-HAA
It's because of you that I'm here. And I won't forget it.
I owe you everything. ***And you'll get what's coming to you!***
HA-HAH-HAAAA
Speaking of power... You've heard of the American "football"? No not soccer.
I'm not talking the World Cup but rather American-style football.
The obliteration of the world in one small suitcase.
It doesn't get more American than that!
And tonight I want to share that power with you! TO THE ONES! TO POWER!
HA-HAH-HAAA-HAH!

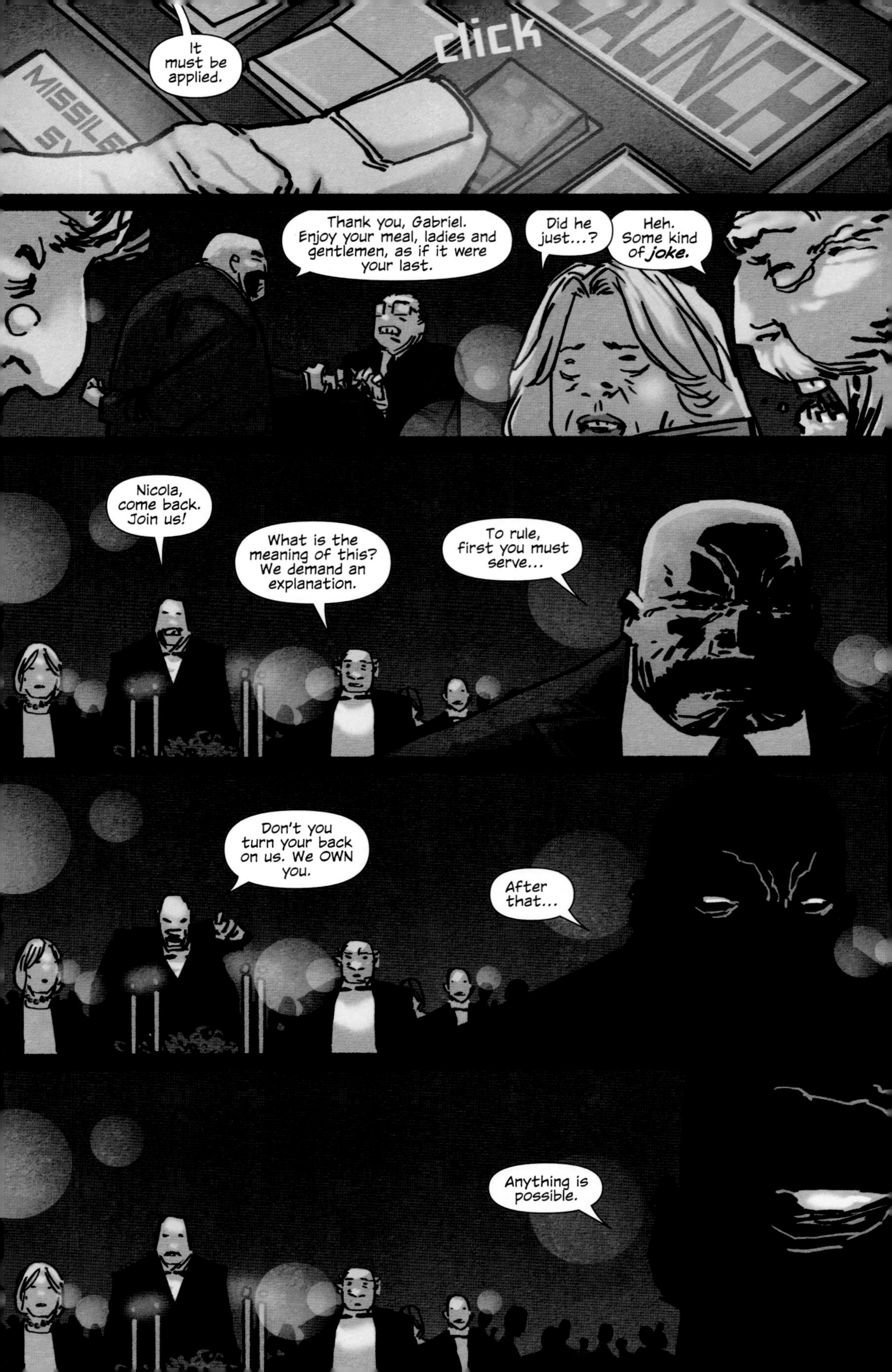
It must be applied.
click
MISSILE SY
LAUNCH
Thank you, Gabriel. Enjoy your meal, ladies and gentlemen, as if it were your last.
Did he just...?
Heh. Some kind of *joke.*
Nicola, come back. Join us!
What is the meaning of this? We demand an explanation.
To rule, first you must serve...
Don't you turn your back on us. We OWN you.
After that...
Anything is possible.

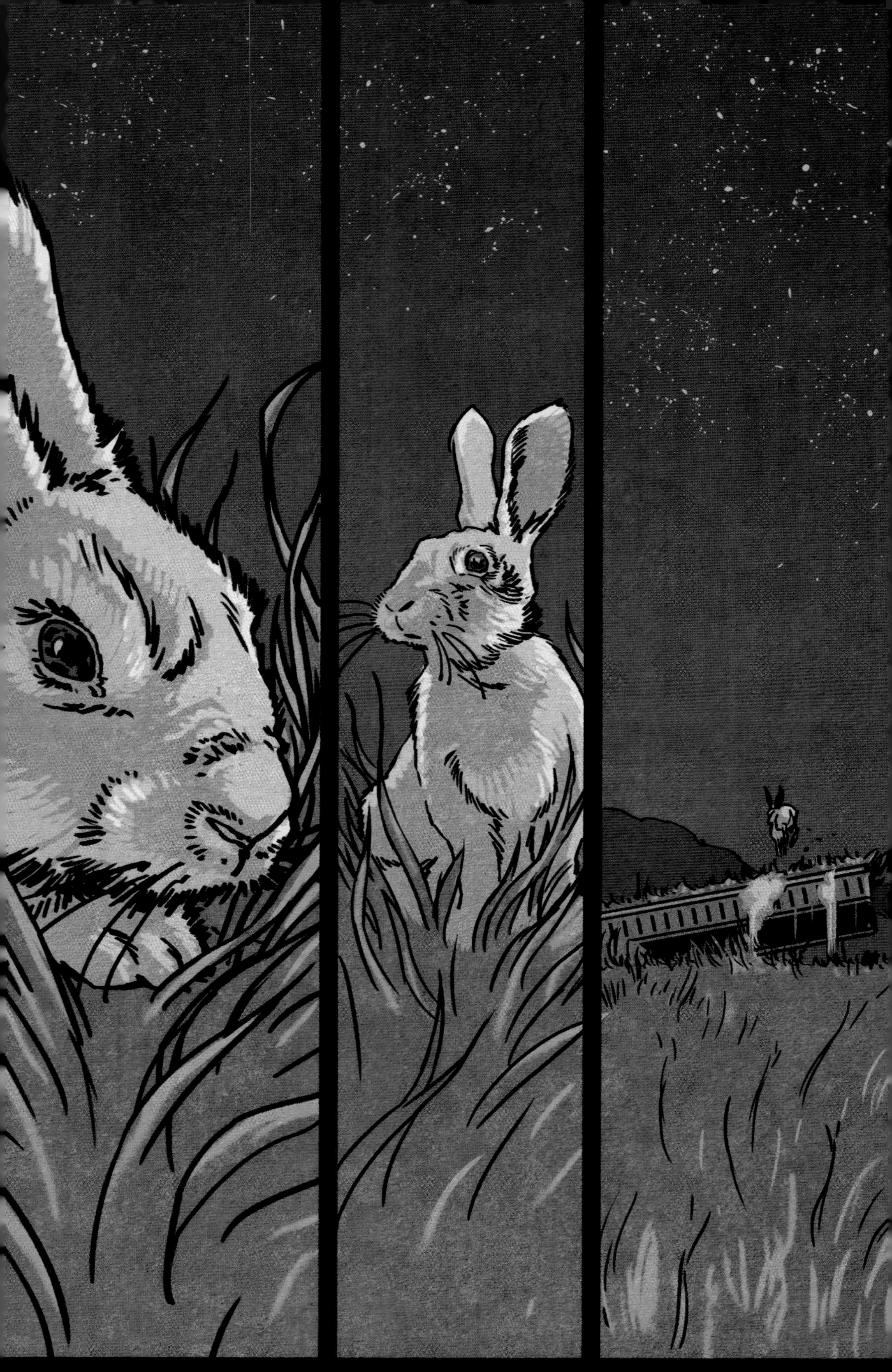

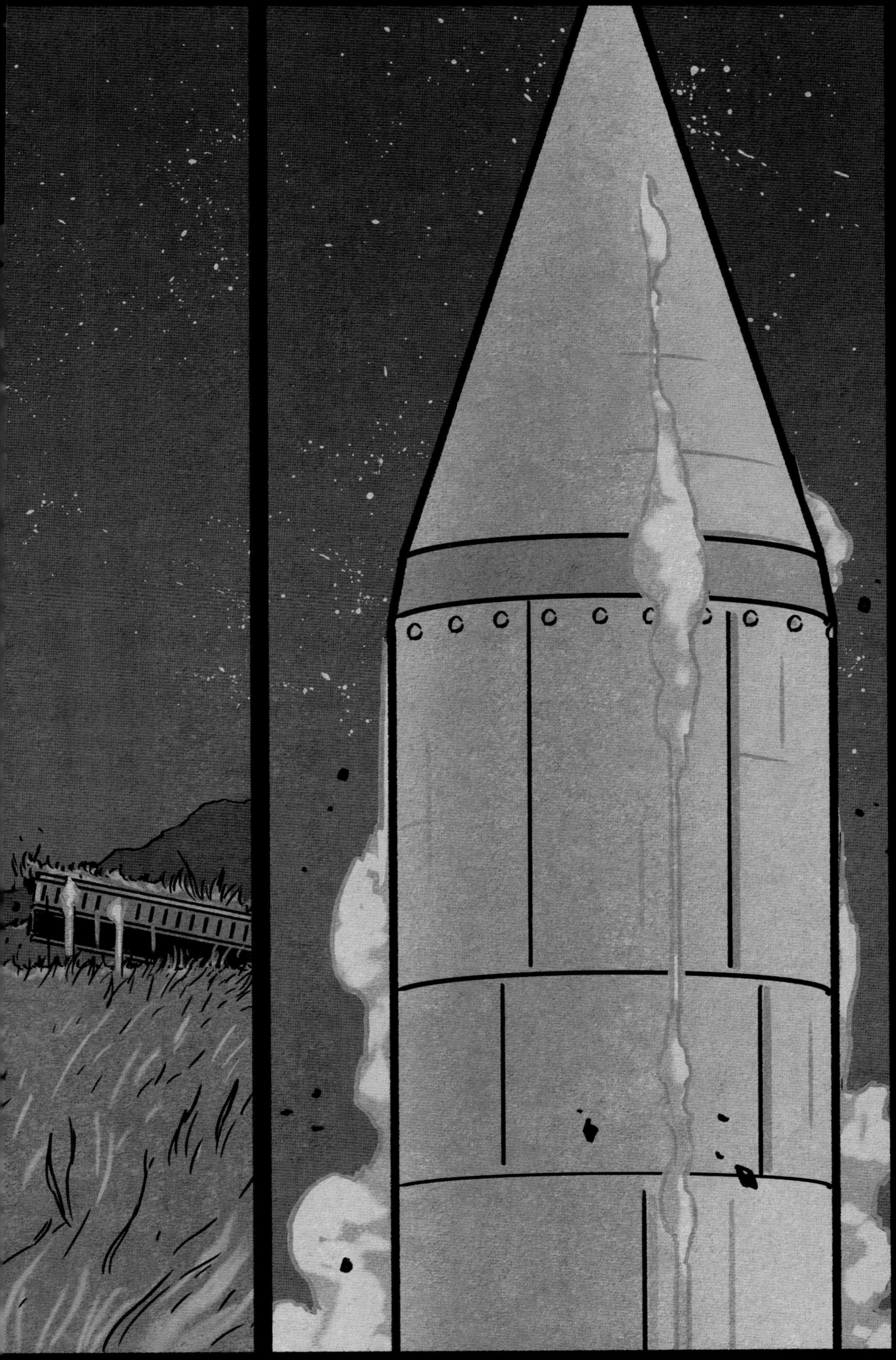

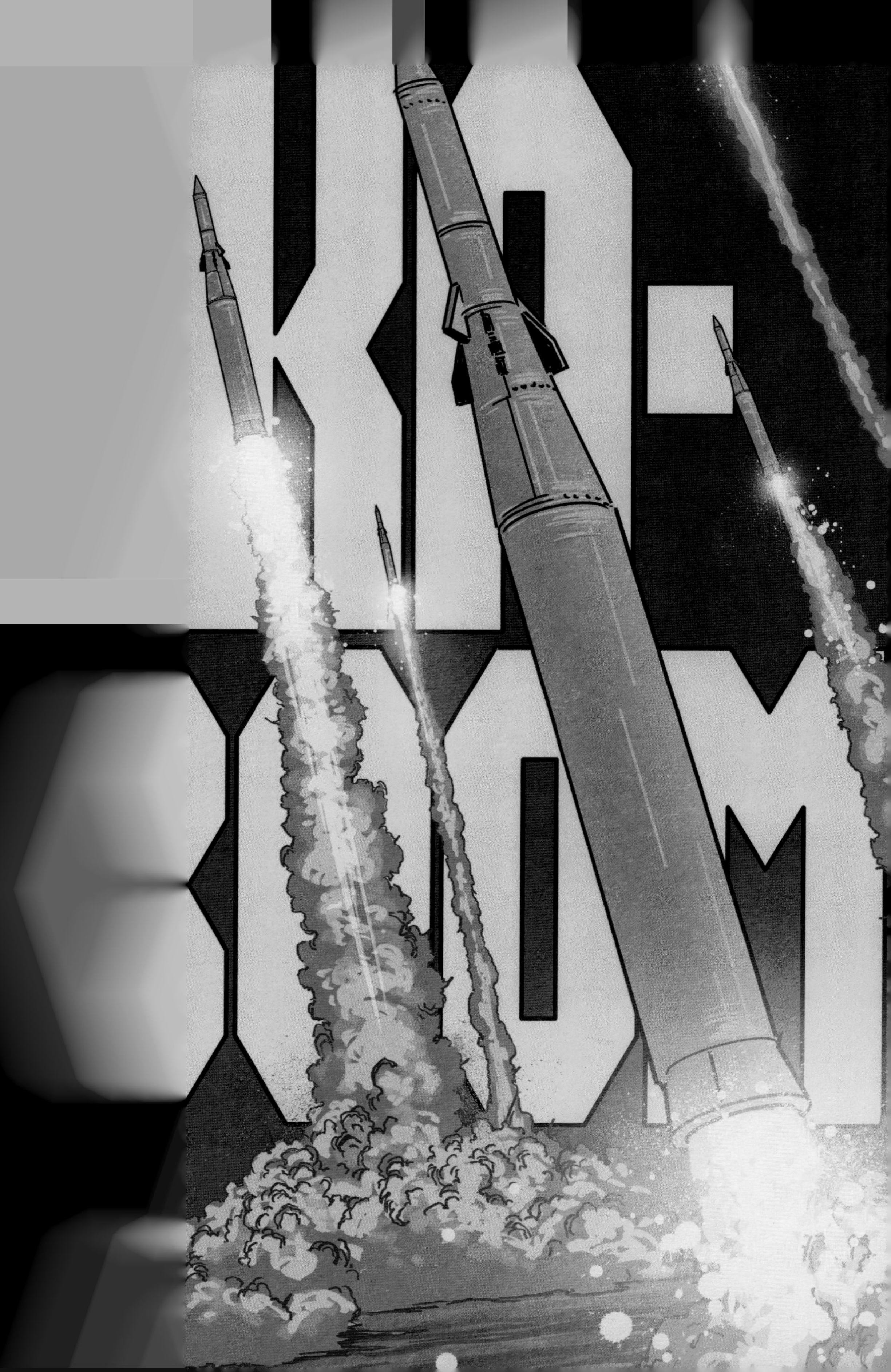

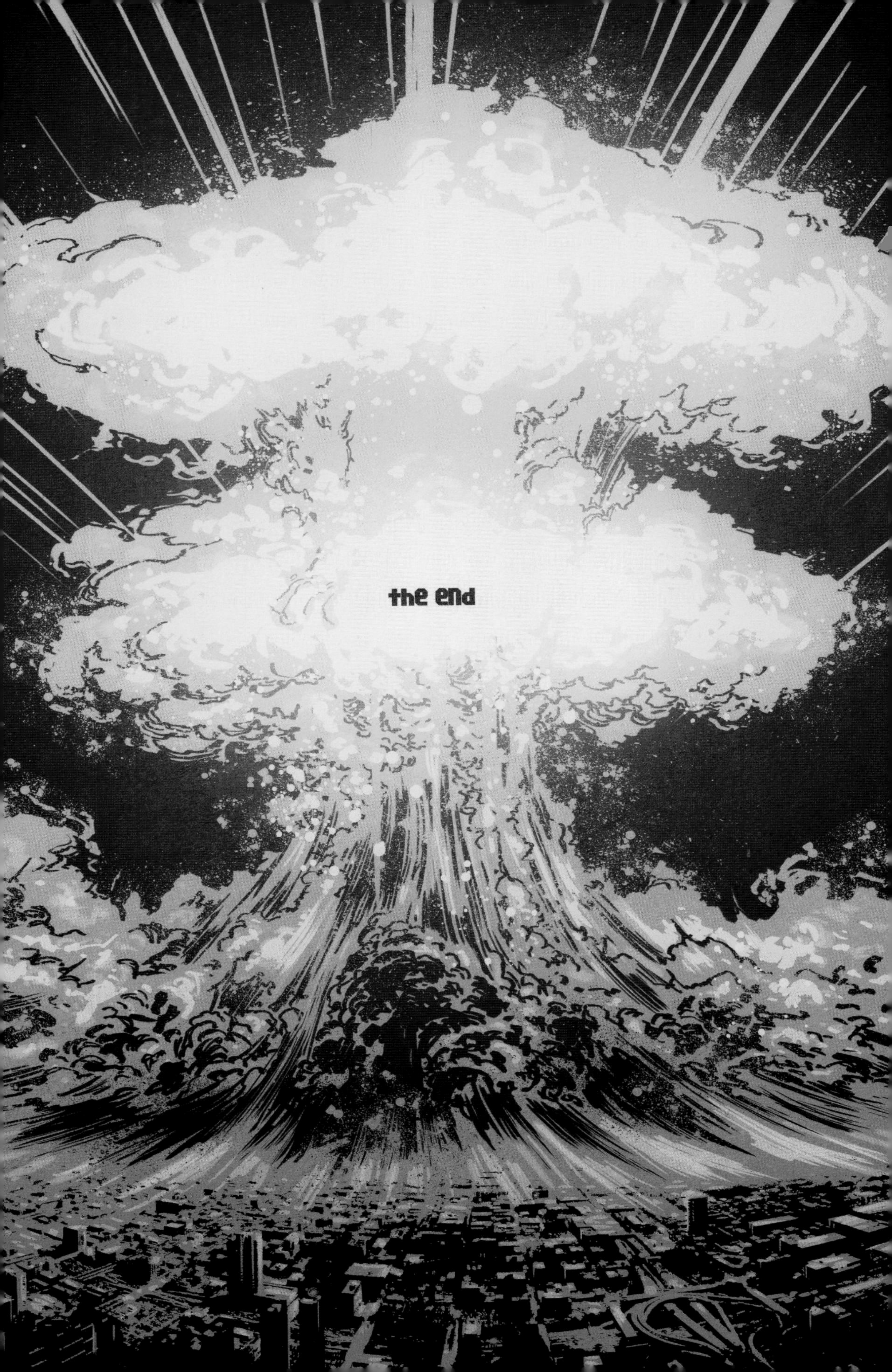
the end

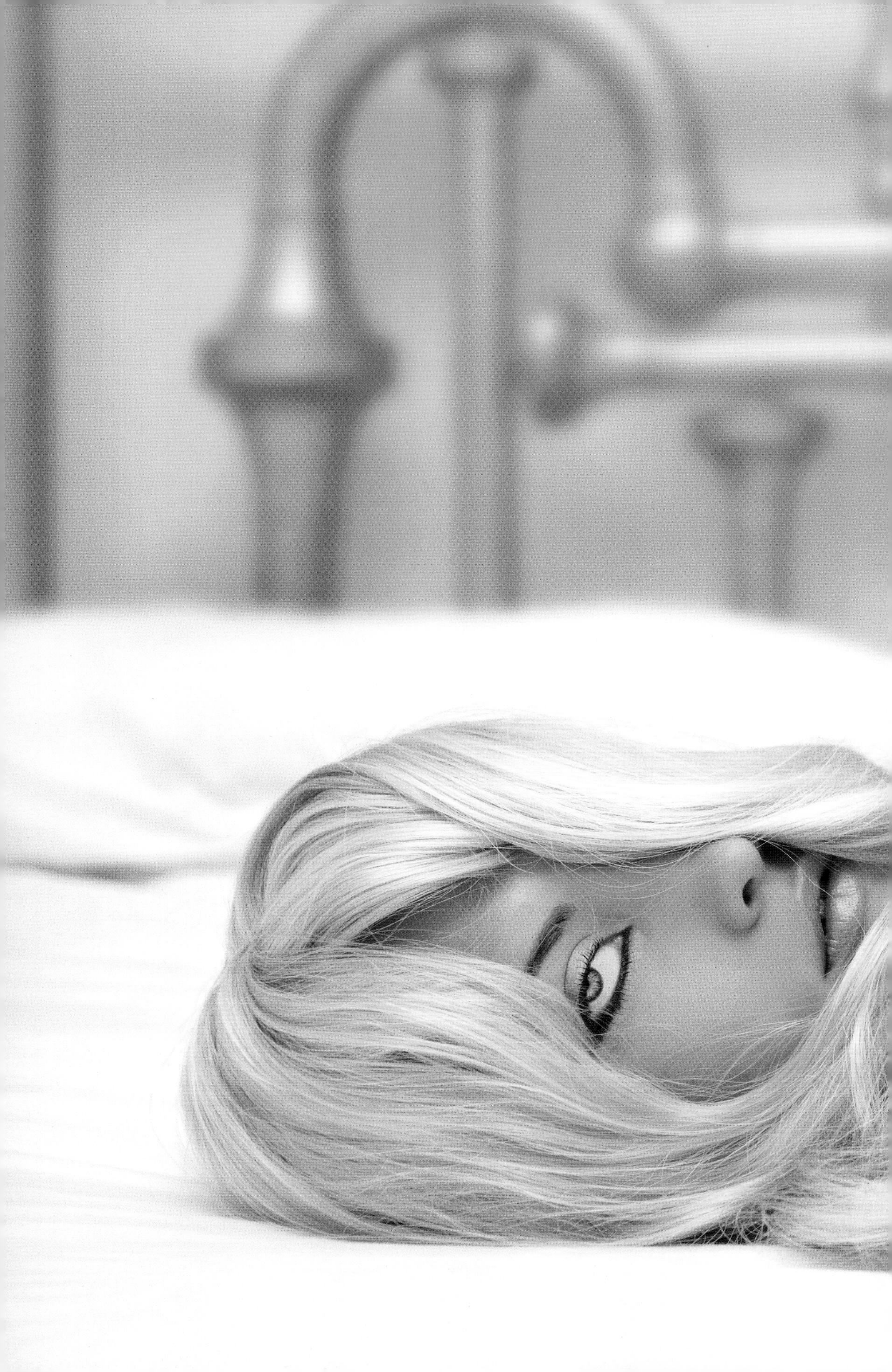

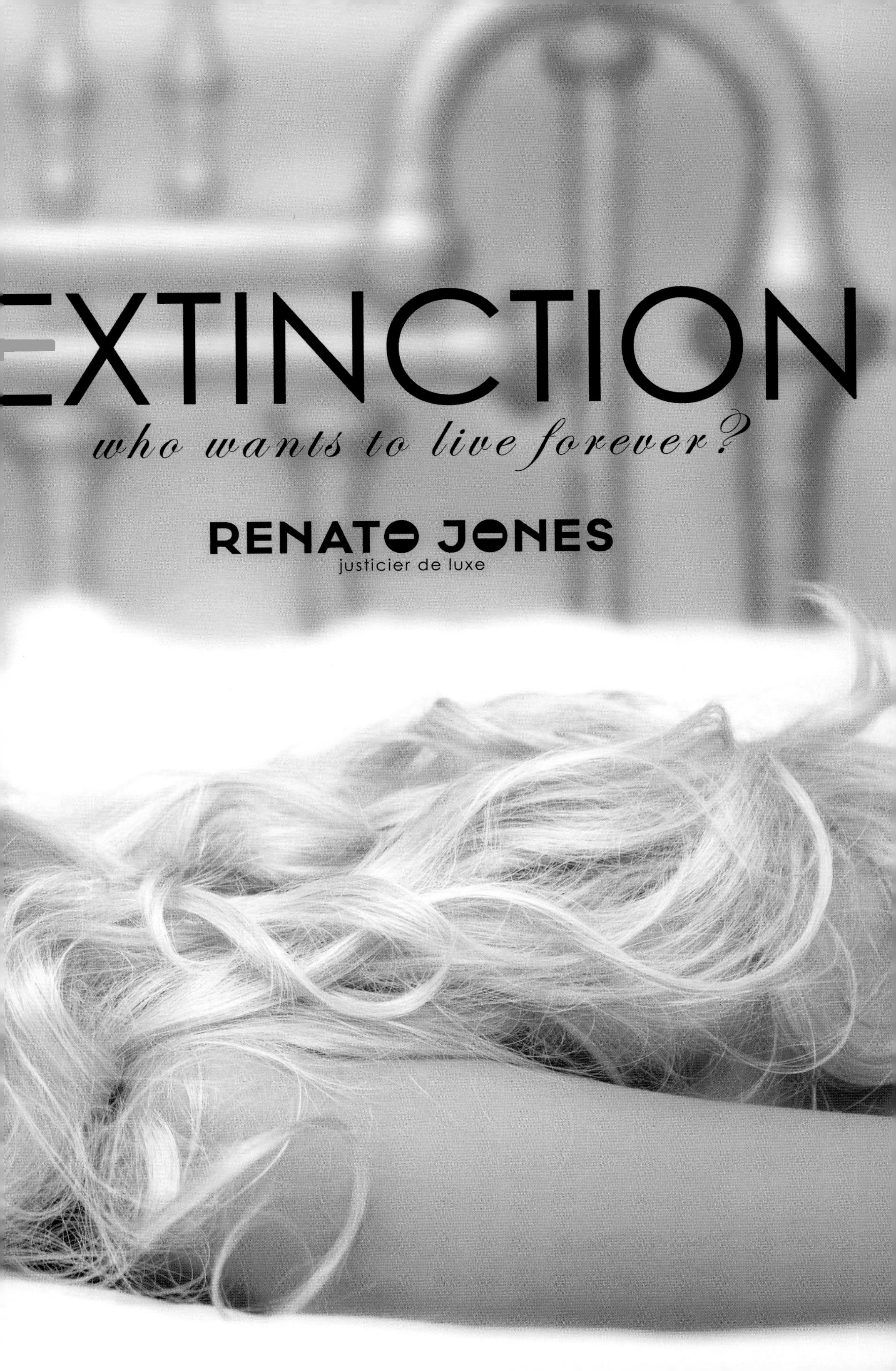
EXTINCTION
who wants to live forever?
RENATO JONES
justicier de luxe

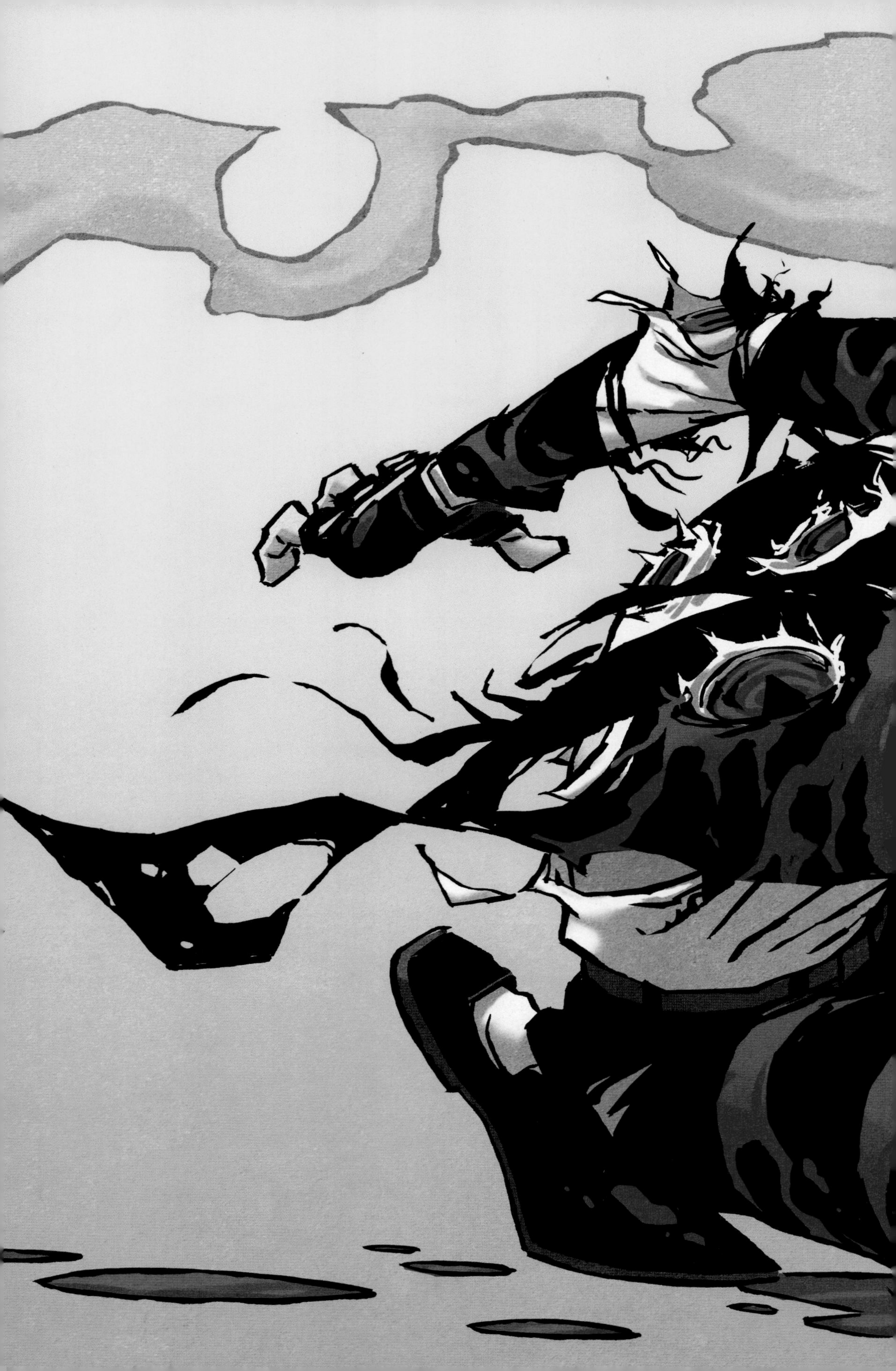

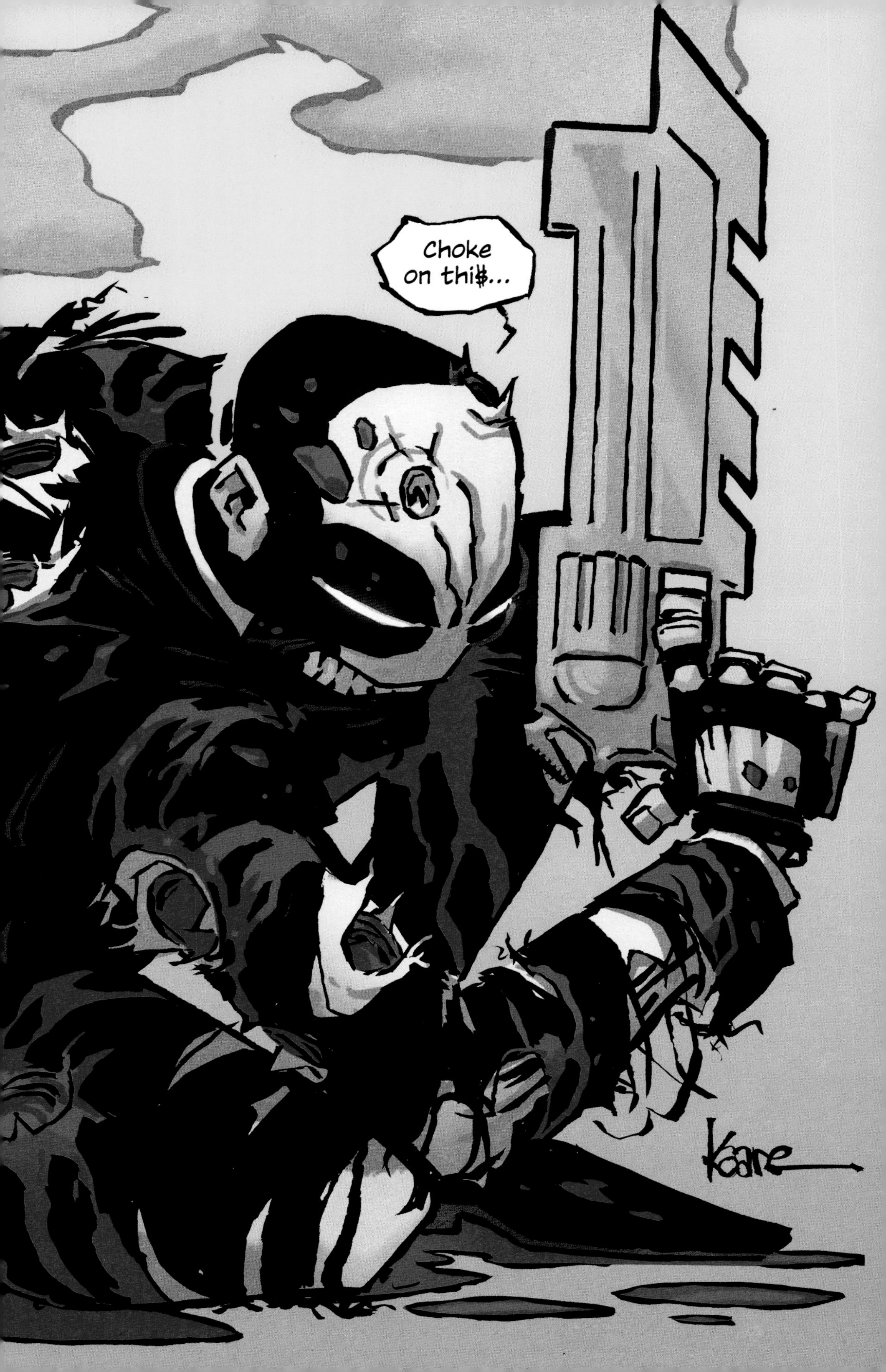
Choke on thi$...
Kaare

4
___

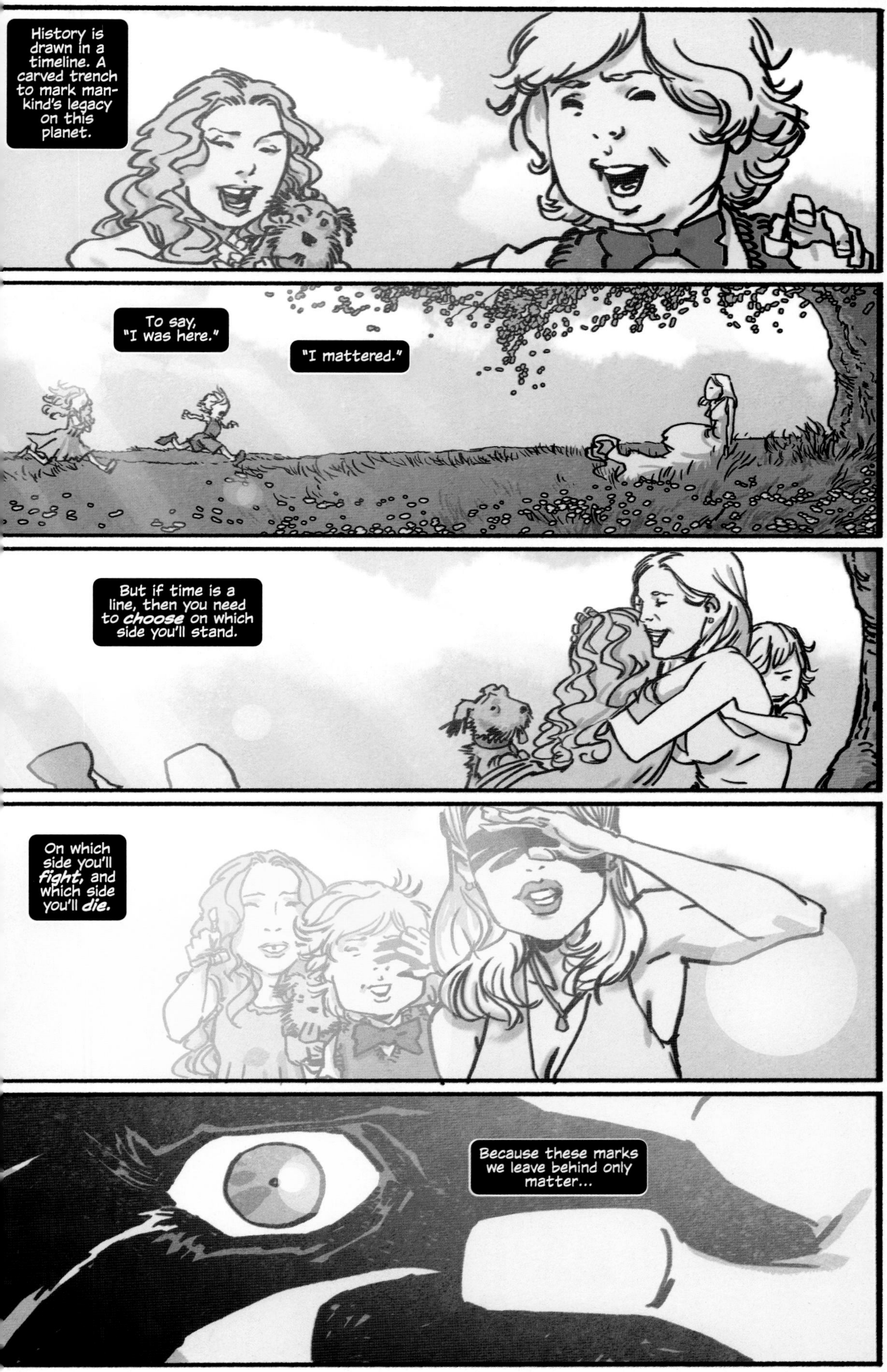
History is drawn in a timeline. A carved trench to mark mankind's legacy on this planet.
To say, "I was here."
"I mattered."
But if time is a line, then you need to *choose* on which side you'll stand.
On which side you'll *fight,* and which side you'll *die.*
Because these marks we leave behind only matter...

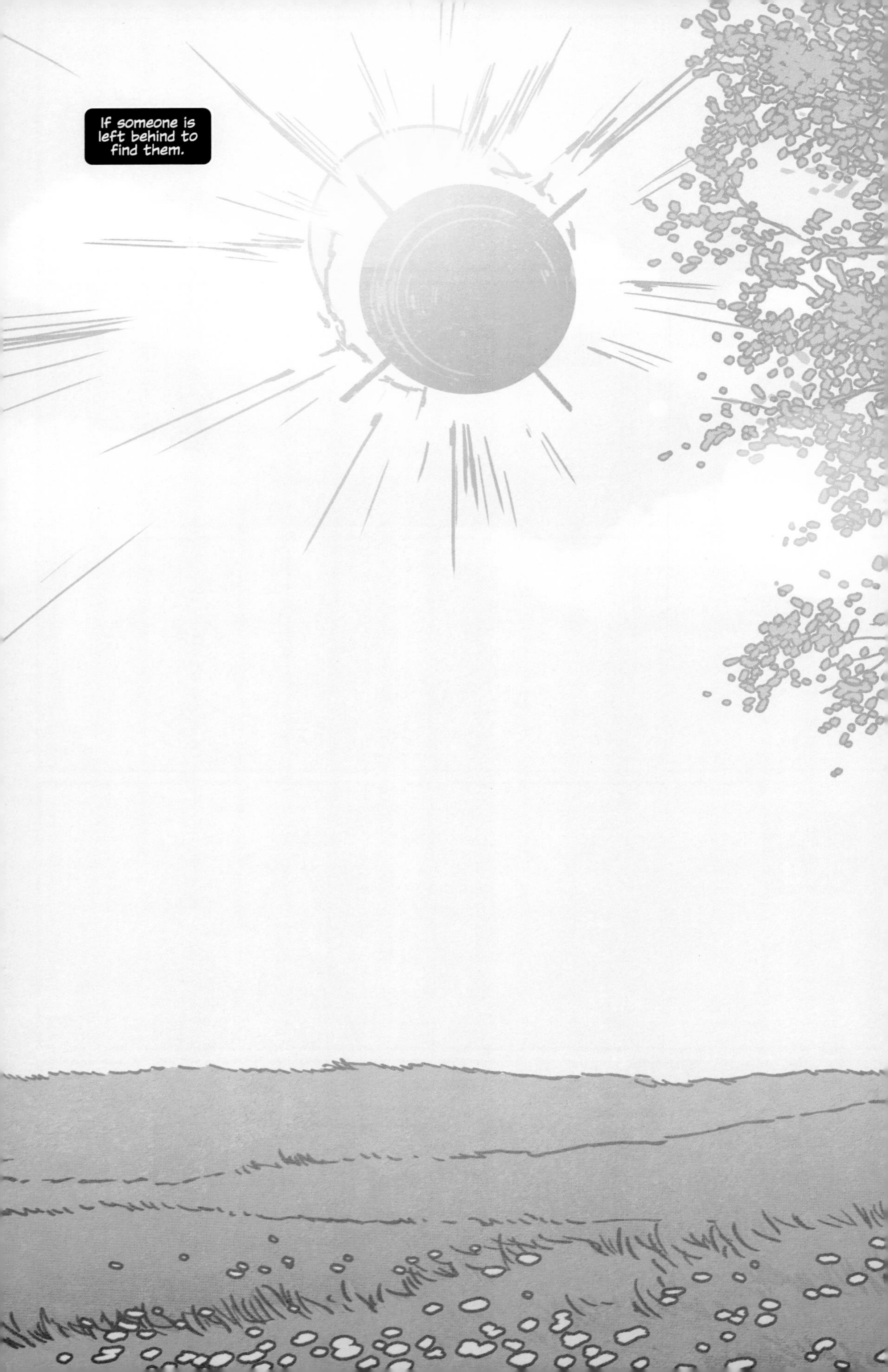
If someone is left behind to find them.

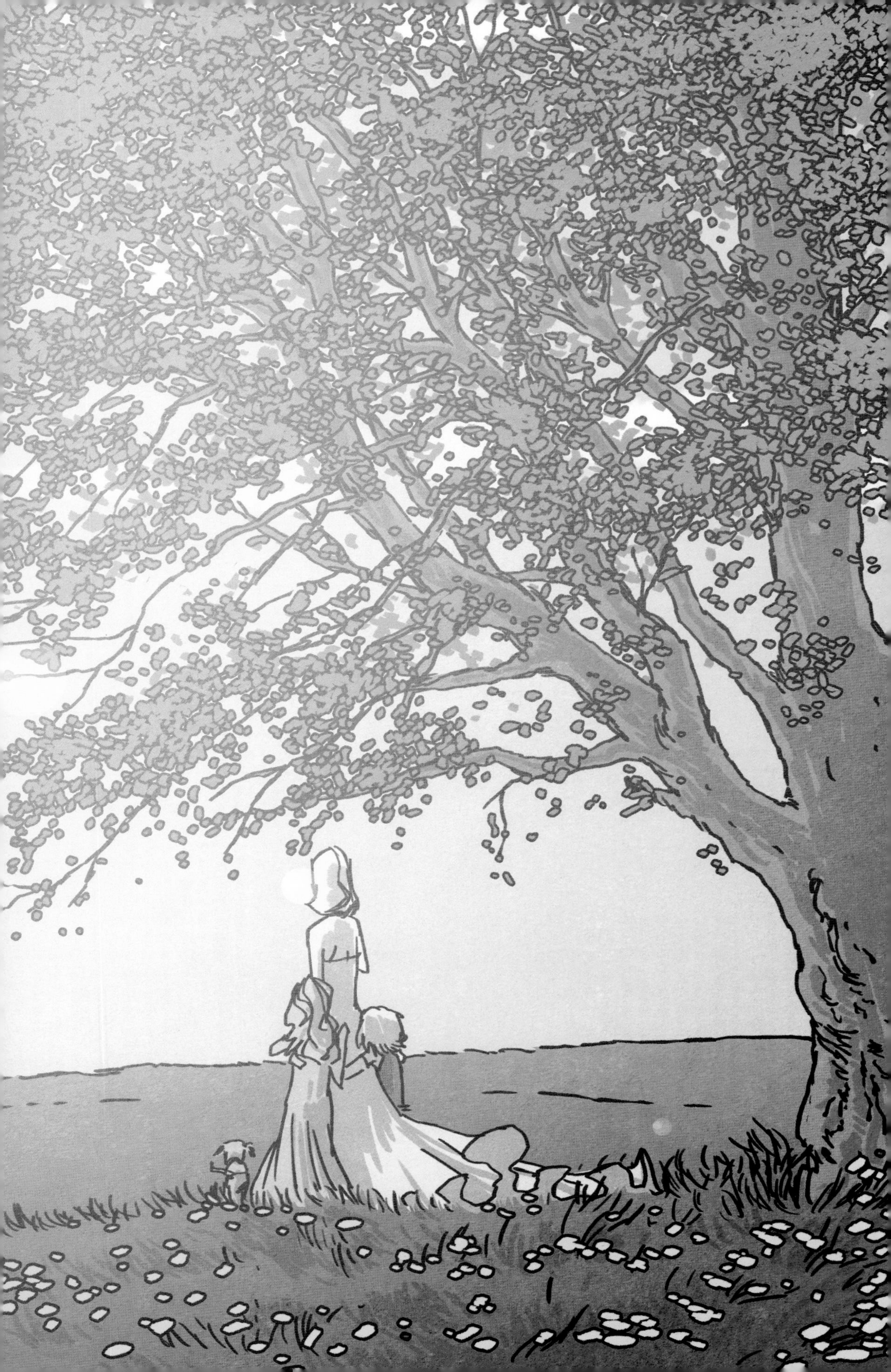

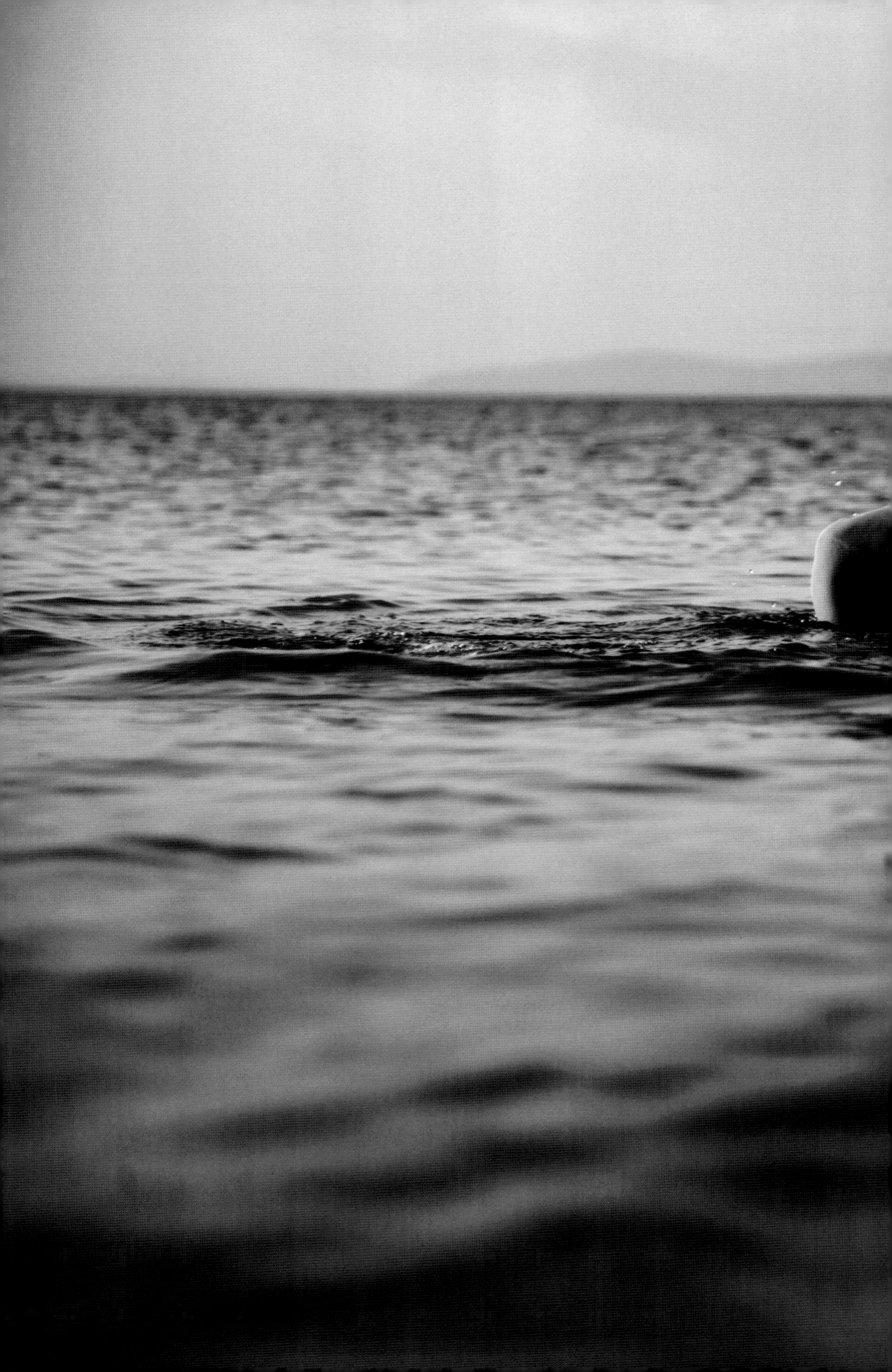

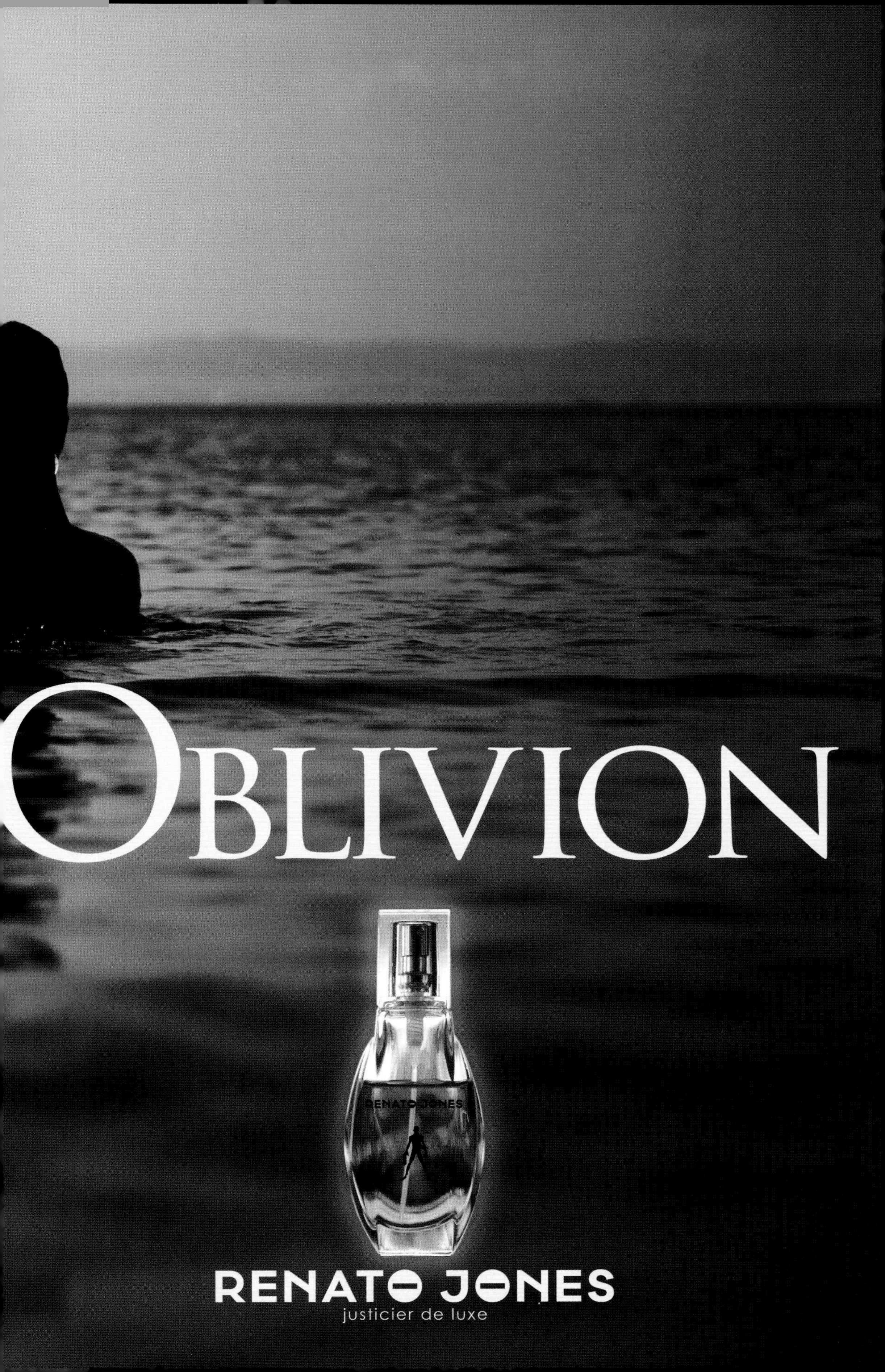
OBLIVION
RENATO JONES
RENATO JONES
justicier de luxe

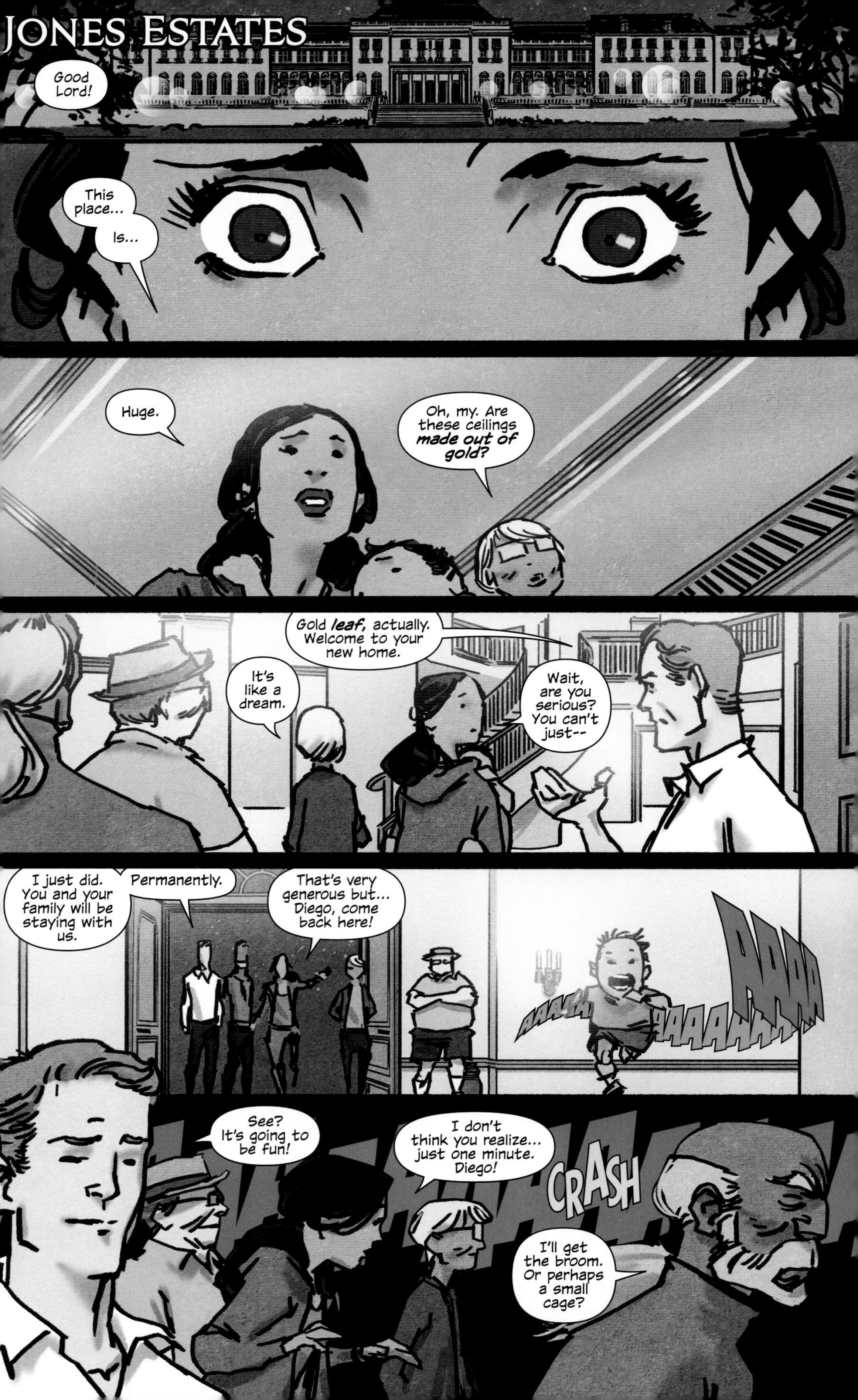
JONES ESTATES
Good Lord!
This place...
Is...
Huge.
Oh, my. Are these ceilings *made out of gold?*
Gold *leaf,* actually. Welcome to your new home.
It's like a dream.
Wait, are you serious? You can't just--
I just did. You and your family will be staying with us.
Permanently.
That's very generous but... Diego, come back here!
AAAAAAAAAA!!
See? It's going to be fun!
I don't think you realize... just one minute. Diego!
CRASH
I'll get the broom. Or perhaps a small cage?

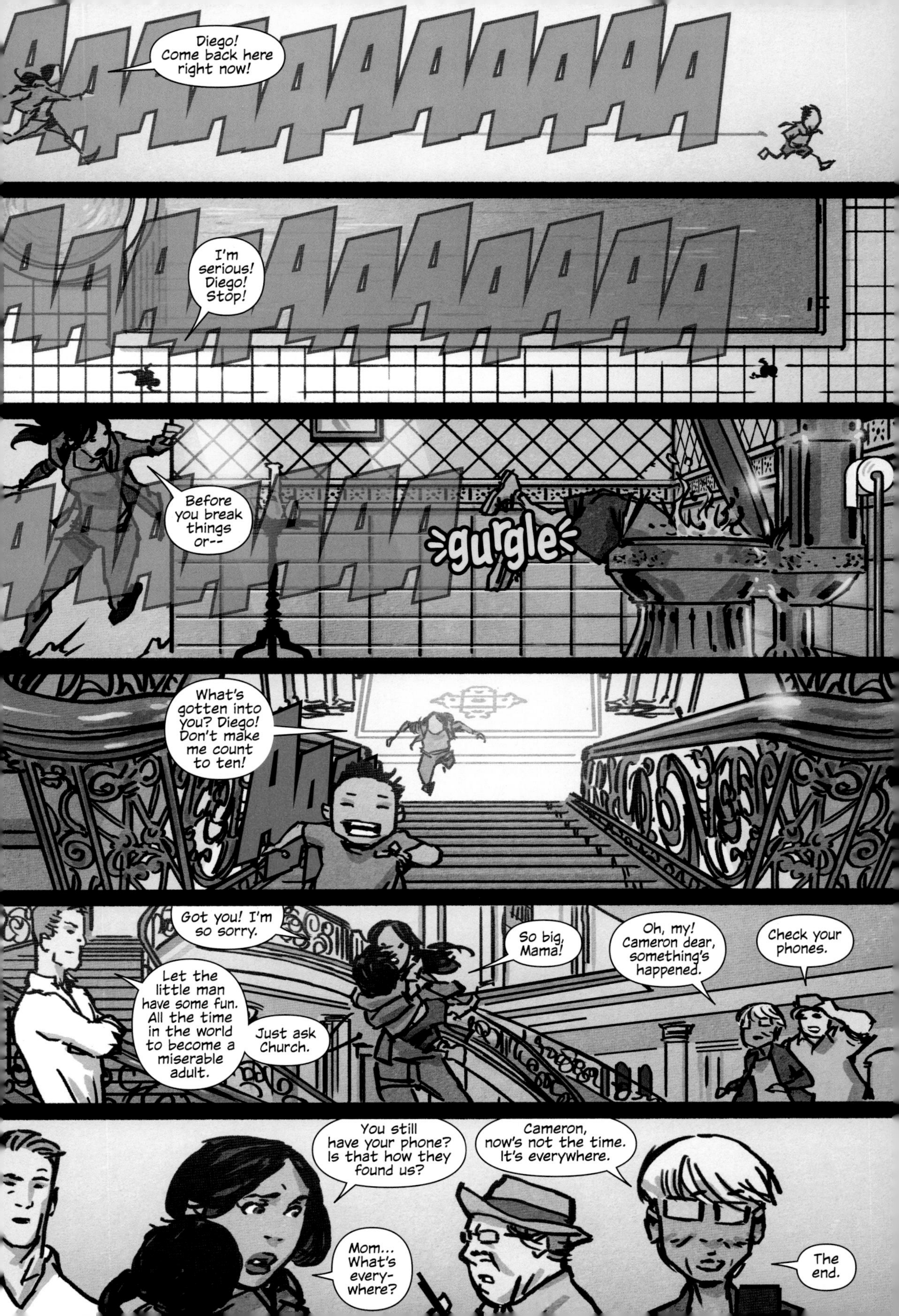
AAAAAAAAAAAA
Diego! Come back here right now!
AAAAAAAAAAAA
I'm serious! Diego! Stop!
Before you break things or--
gurgle
What's gotten into you? Diego! Don't make me count to ten!
Got you! I'm so sorry.
So big, Mama!
Oh, my! Cameron dear, something's happened.
Check your phones.
Let the little man have some fun. All the time in the world to become a miserable adult.
Just ask Church.
You still have your phone? Is that how they found us?
Cameron, now's not the time. It's everywhere.
Mom... What's every-where?
The end.

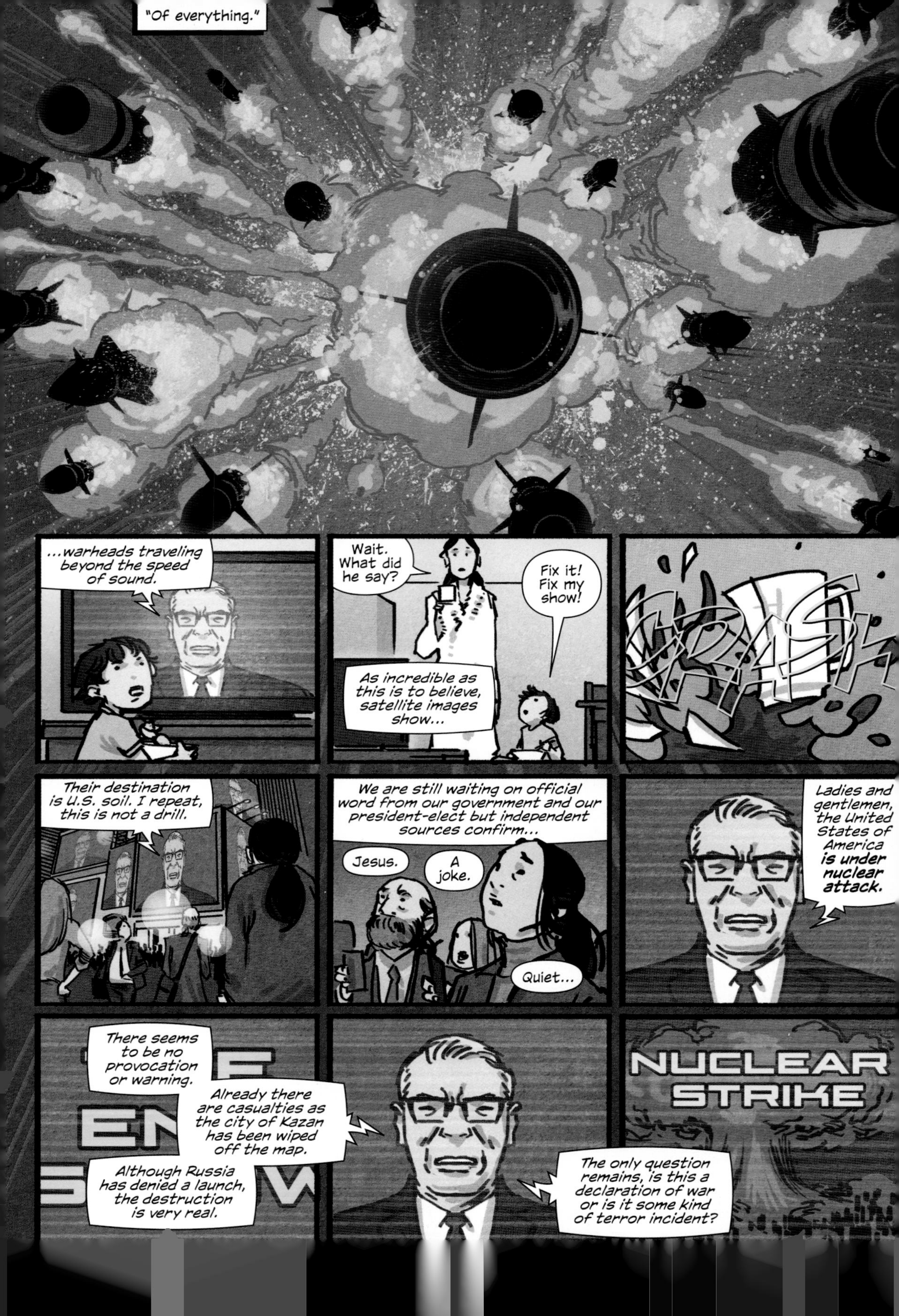
"Of everything."
...warheads traveling beyond the speed of sound.
Wait. What did he say?
Fix it! Fix my show!
As incredible as this is to believe, satellite images show...
CRASH
Their destination is U.S. soil. I repeat, this is not a drill.
We are still waiting on official word from our government and our president-elect but independent sources confirm...
Jesus.
A joke.
Quiet...
Ladies and gentlemen, the United States of America **is under nuclear attack.**
There seems to be no provocation or warning.
Already there are casualties as the city of Kazan has been wiped off the map.
Although Russia has denied a launch, the destruction is very real.
The only question remains, is this a declaration of war or is it some kind of terror incident?
NUCLEAR STRIKE

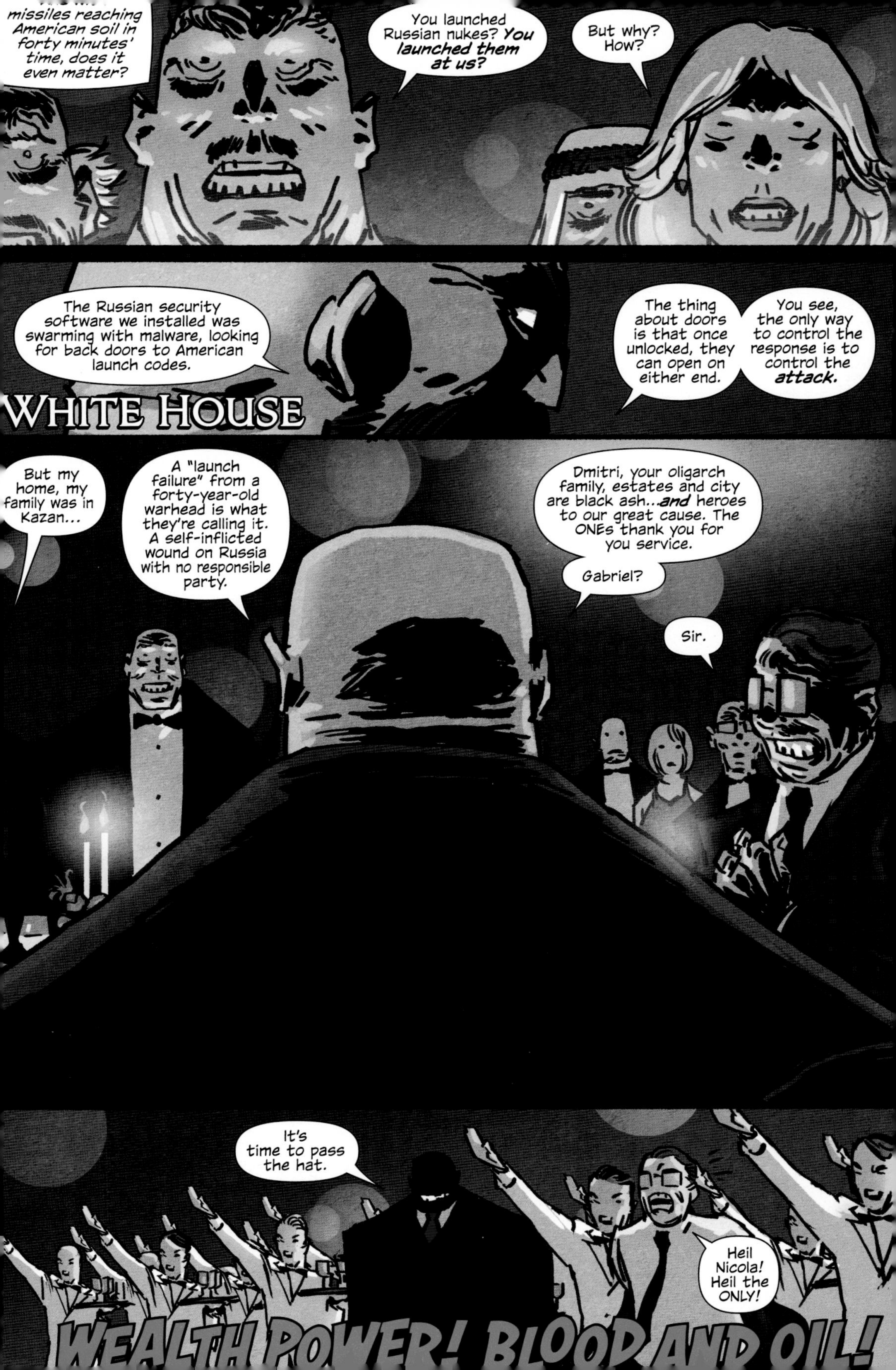

missiles reaching American soil in forty minutes' time, does it even matter?
You launched Russian nukes? *You launched them at us?*
But why? How?
The Russian security software we installed was swarming with malware, looking for back doors to American launch codes.
WHITE HOUSE
The thing about doors is that once unlocked, they can open on either end.
You see, the only way to control the response is to control the *attack.*
But my home, my family was in Kazan...
A "launch failure" from a forty-year-old warhead is what they're calling it. A self-inflicted wound on Russia with no responsible party.
Dmitri, your oligarch family, estates and city are black ash...*and* heroes to our great cause. The ONEs thank you for you service.
Gabriel?
Sir.
It's time to pass the hat.
Heil Nicola! Heil the ONLY!
WEALTH POWER! BLOOD AND OIL!

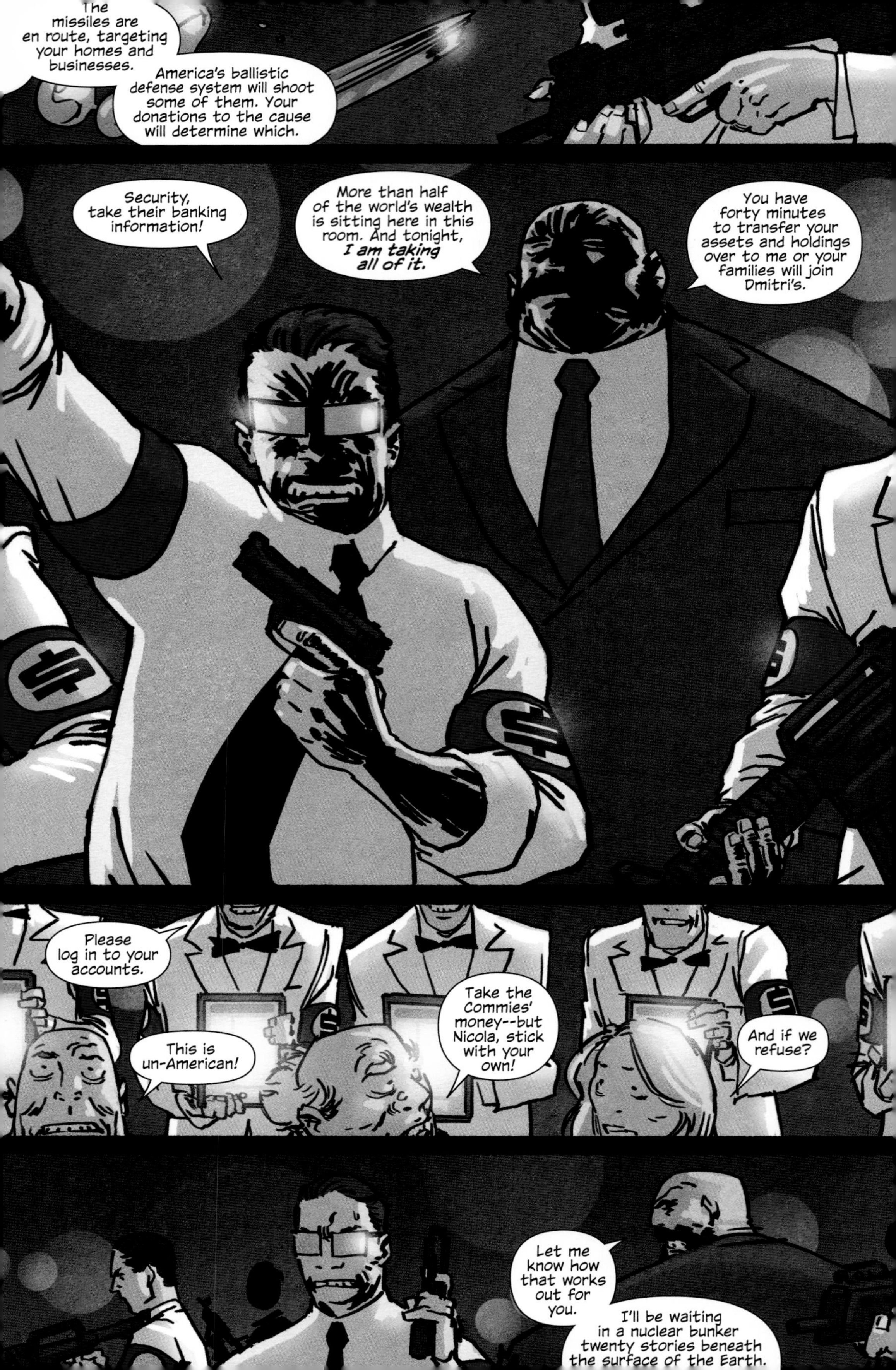
The missiles are en route, targeting your homes and businesses.
America's ballistic defense system will shoot some of them. Your donations to the cause will determine which.
Security, take their banking information!
More than half of the world's wealth is sitting here in this room. And tonight, ***I am taking all of it.***
You have forty minutes to transfer your assets and holdings over to me or your families will join Dmitri's.
Please log in to your accounts.
This is un-American!
Take the Commies' money--but Nicola, stick with your own!
And if we refuse?
Let me know how that works out for you.
I'll be waiting in a nuclear bunker twenty stories beneath the surface of the Earth.

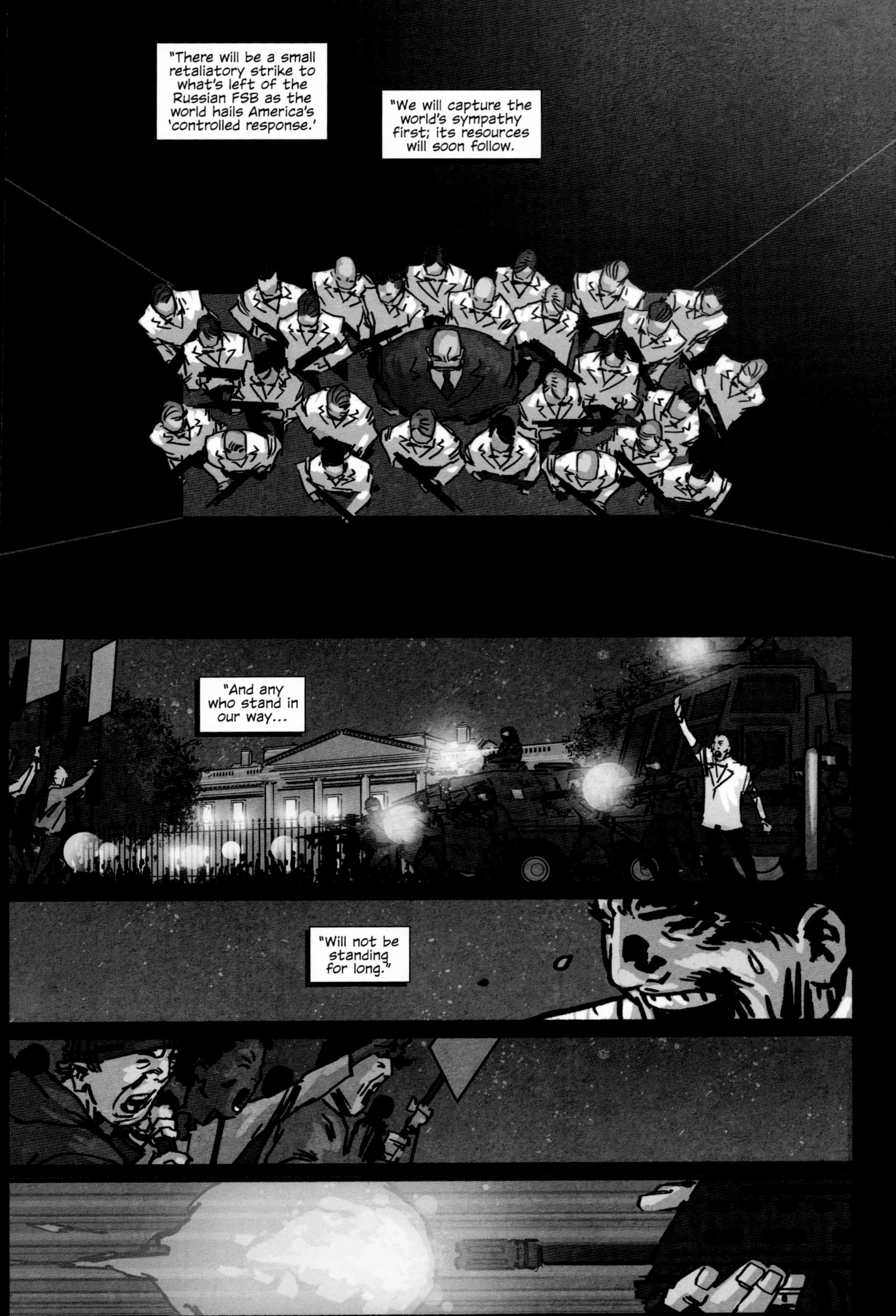
"There will be a small retaliatory strike to what's left of the Russian FSB as the world hails America's 'controlled response.'
"We will capture the world's sympathy first; its resources will soon follow.
"And any who stand in our way...
"Will not be standing for long."

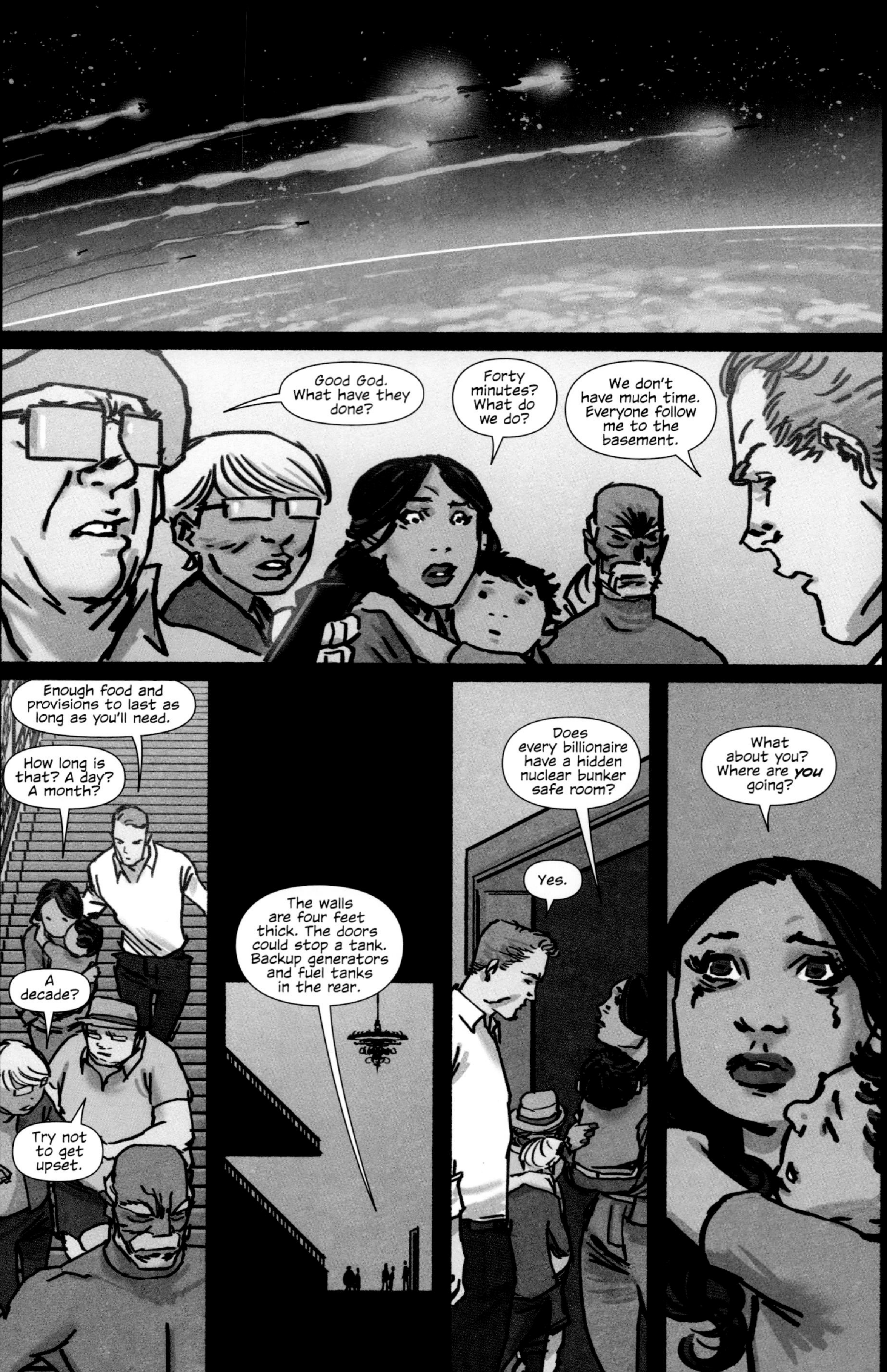

Good God. What have they done?
Forty minutes? What do we do?
We don't have much time. Everyone follow me to the basement.
Enough food and provisions to last as long as you'll need.
How long is that? A day? A month?
A decade?
Try not to get upset.
The walls are four feet thick. The doors could stop a tank. Backup generators and fuel tanks in the rear.
Does every billionaire have a hidden nuclear bunker safe room?
Yes.
What about you? Where are *you* going?

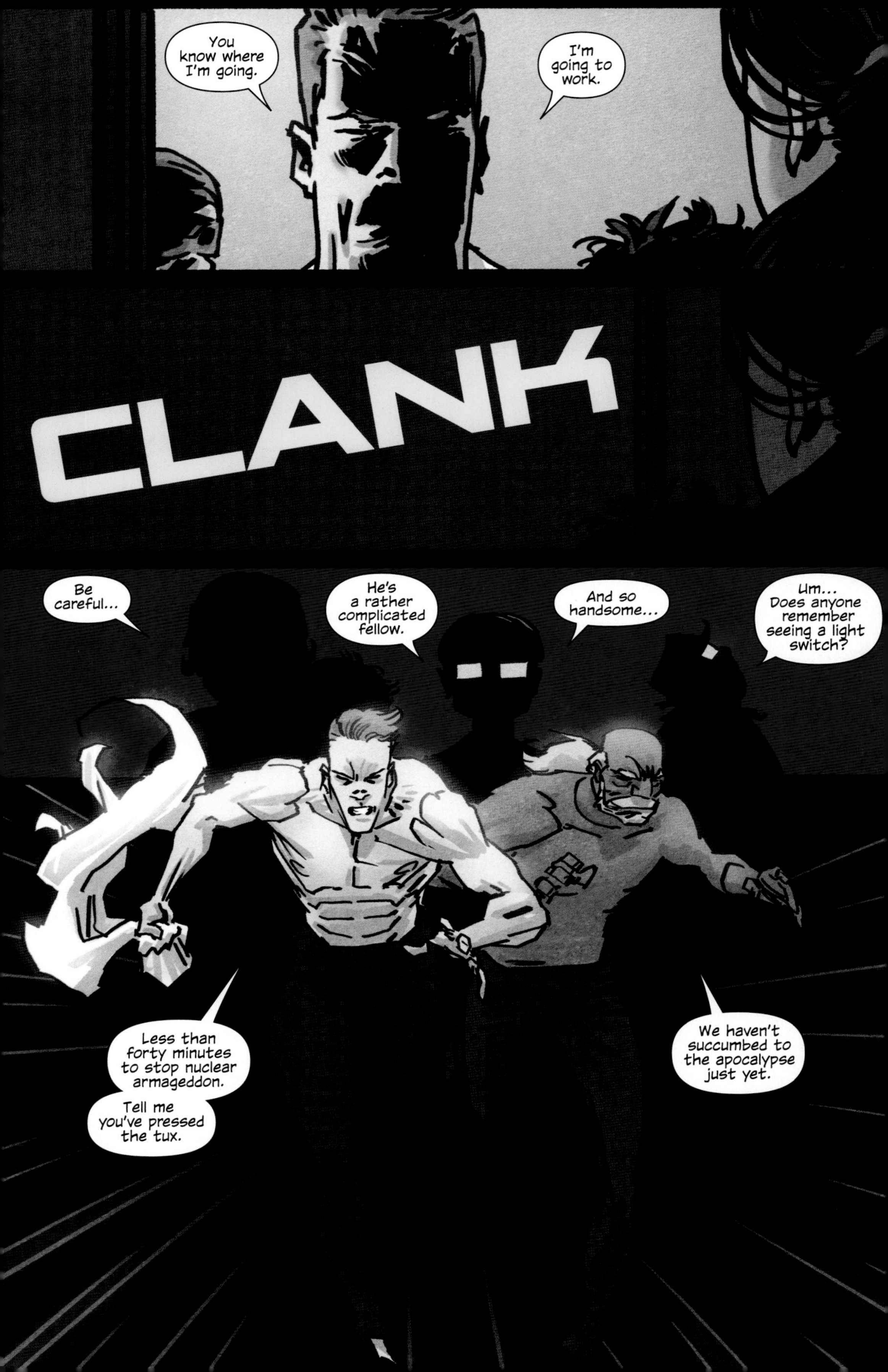
You know where I'm going.
I'm going to work.
CLANK
Be careful...
He's a rather complicated fellow.
And so handsome...
Um... Does anyone remember seeing a light switch?
Less than forty minutes to stop nuclear armageddon.
Tell me you've pressed the tux.
We haven't succumbed to the apocalypse just yet.

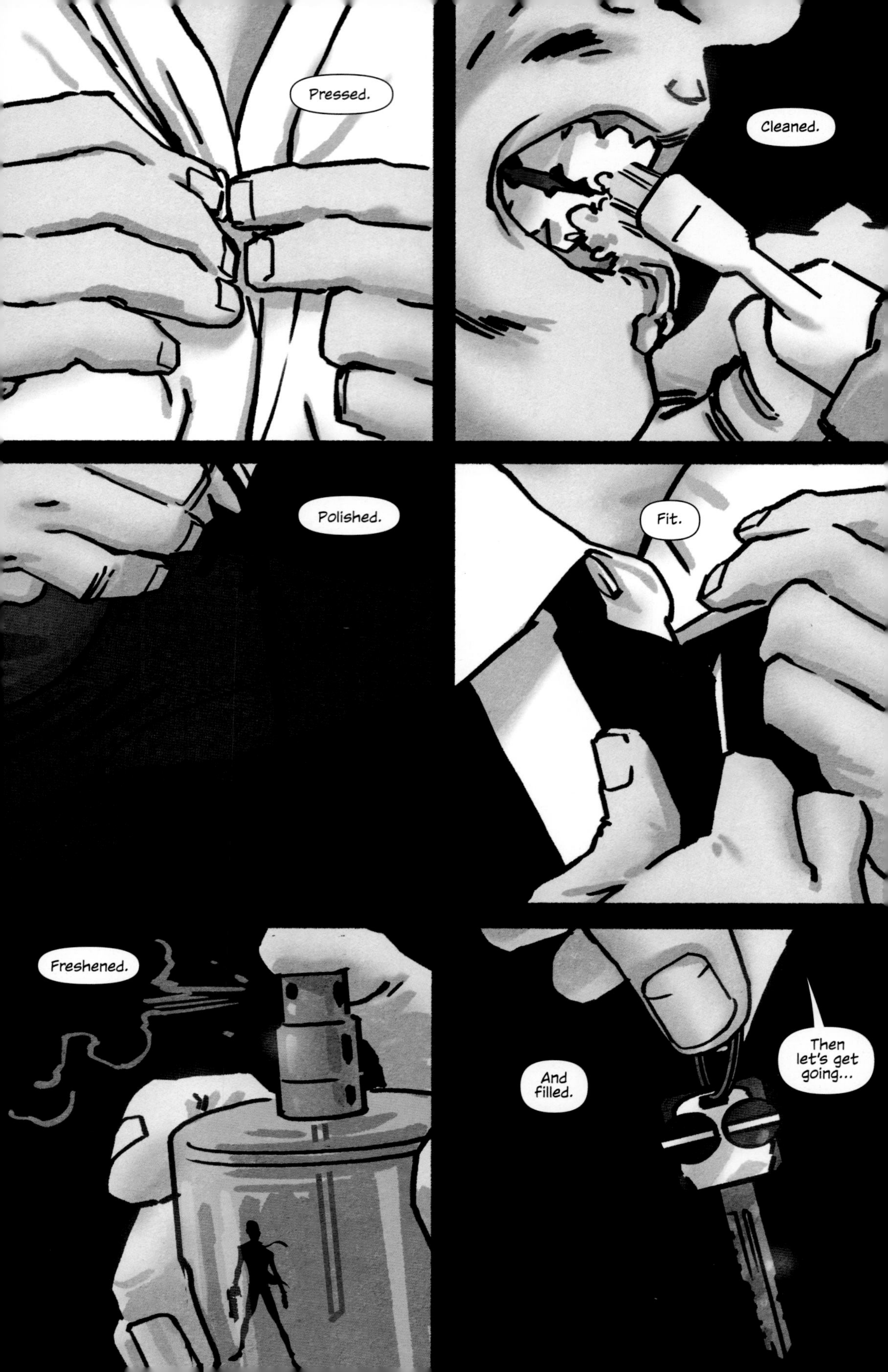
Pressed.
Cleaned.
Polished.
Fit.
Freshened.
And filled.
Then let's get going...

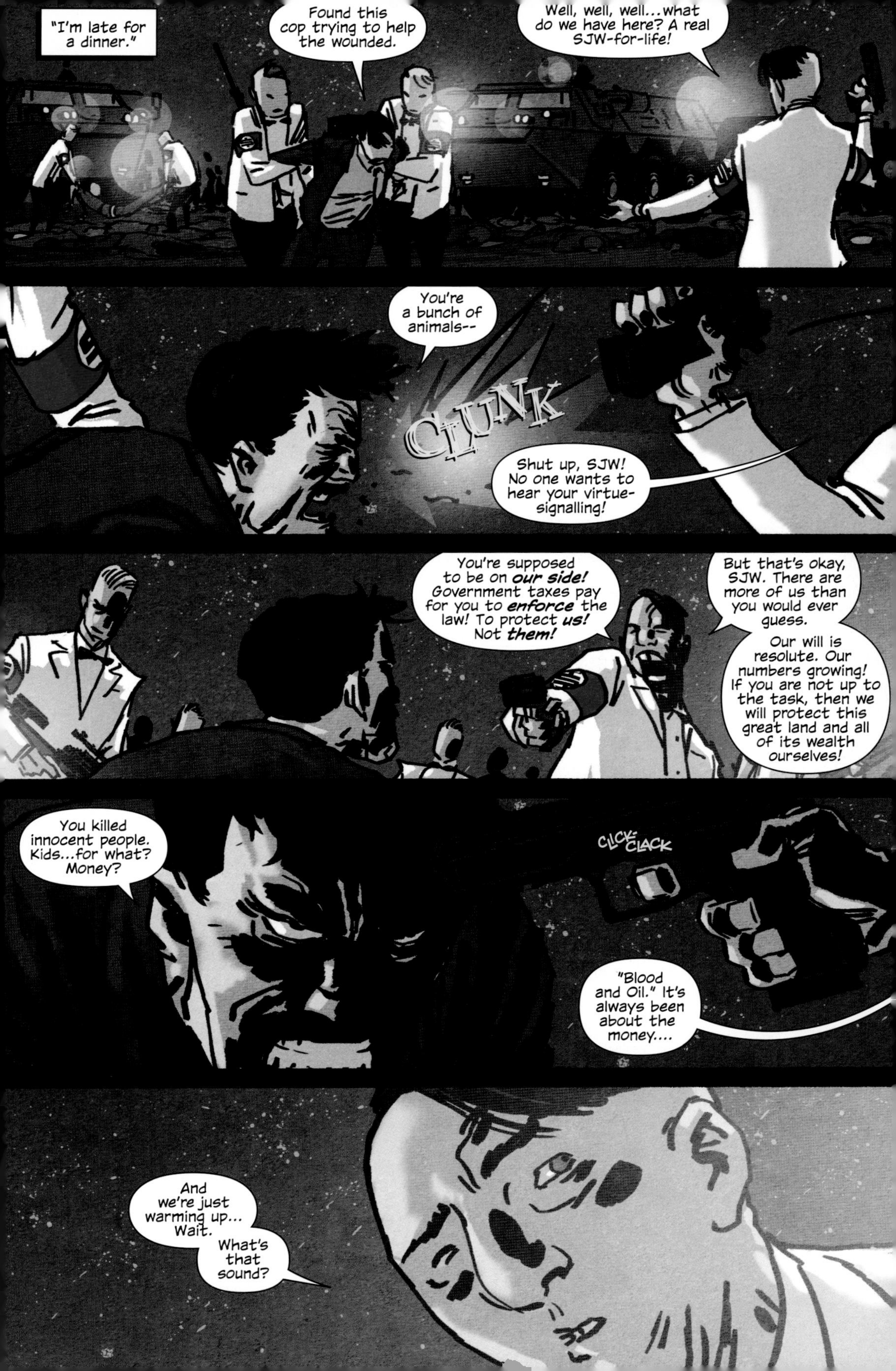
"I'm late for a dinner."
Found this cop trying to help the wounded.
Well, well, well...what do we have here? A real SJW-for-life!
You're a bunch of animals--
CLUNK
Shut up, SJW! No one wants to hear your virtue-signalling!
You're supposed to be on **our side!** Government taxes pay for you to **enforce** the law! To protect **us!** Not **them!**
But that's okay, SJW. There are more of us than you would ever guess.
Our will is resolute. Our numbers growing! If you are not up to the task, then we will protect this great land and all of its wealth ourselves!
You killed innocent people. Kids...for what? Money?
CLICK-CLACK
"Blood and Oil." It's always been about the money....
And we're just warming up... Wait.
What's that sound?

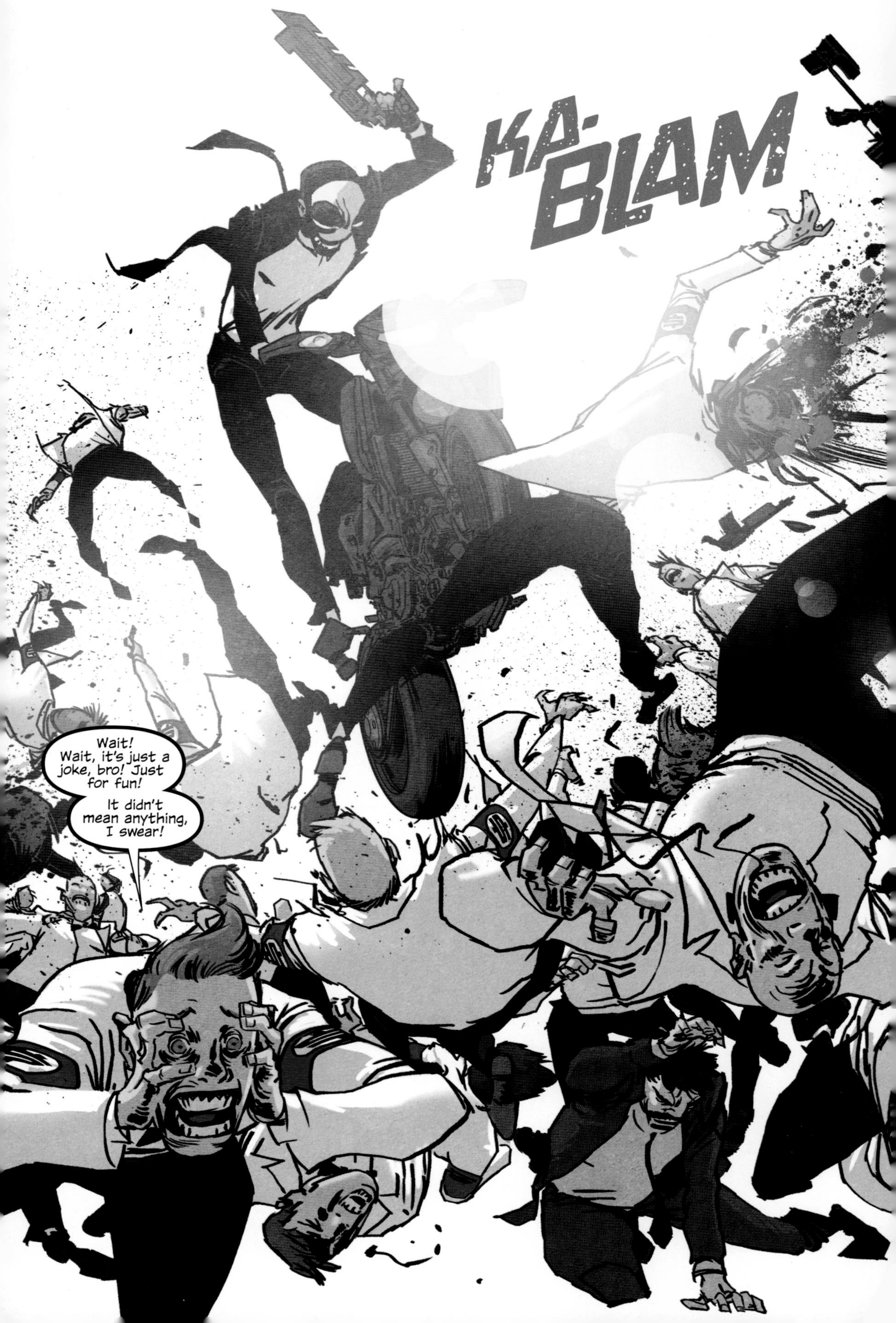
KA-BLAM
Wait! Wait, it's just a joke, bro! Just for fun!
It didn't mean anything, I swear!

CHOKE ON THI$!

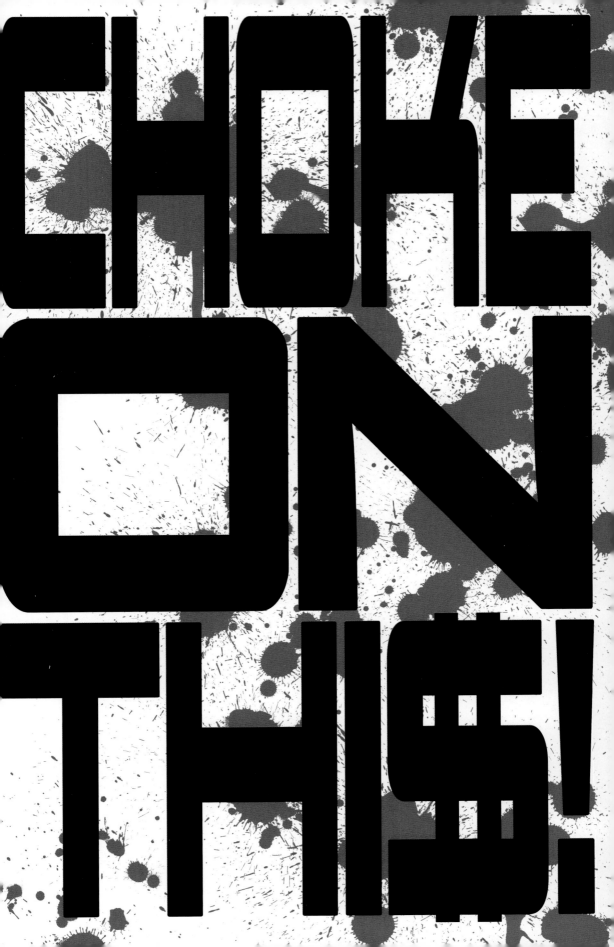

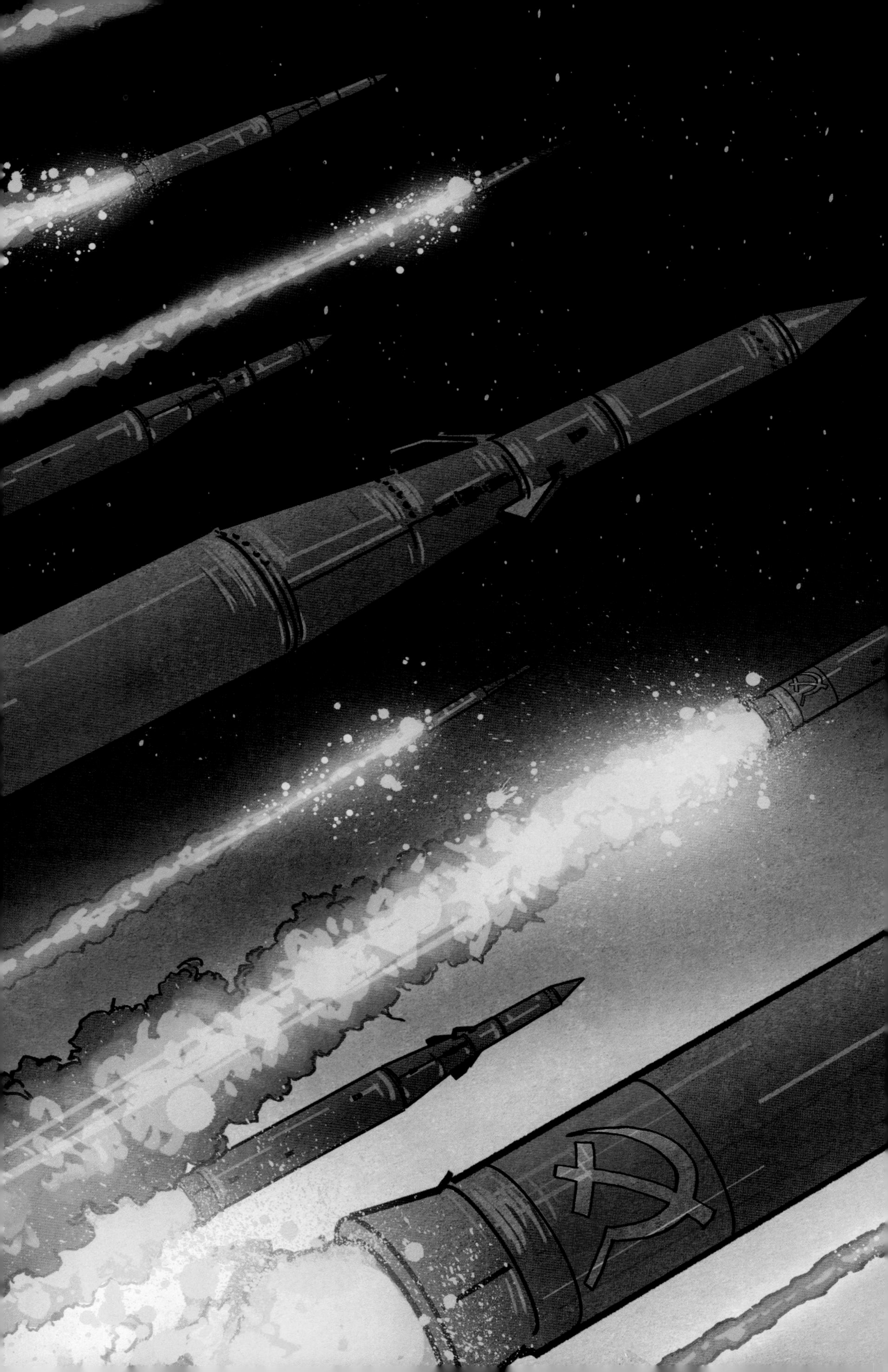

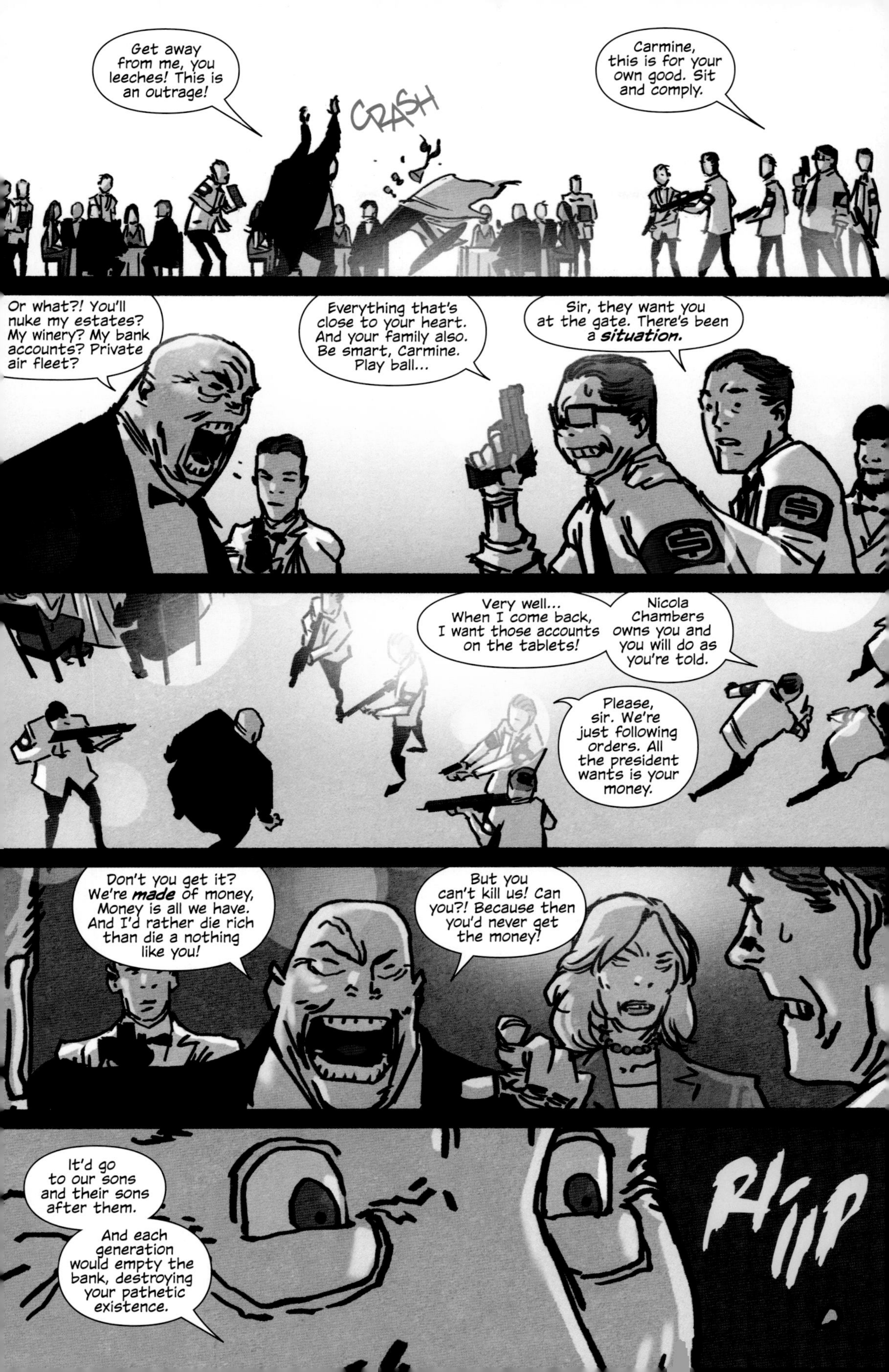
Get away from me, you leeches! This is an outrage!
CRASH
Carmine, this is for your own good. Sit and comply.
Or what?! You'll nuke my estates? My winery? My bank accounts? Private air fleet?
Everything that's close to your heart. And your family also. Be smart, Carmine. Play ball...
Sir, they want you at the gate. There's been a *situation.*
Very well... When I come back, I want those accounts on the tablets!
Nicola Chambers owns you and you will do as you're told.
Please, sir. We're just following orders. All the president wants is your money.
Don't you get it? We're *made* of money, Money is all we have. And I'd rather die rich than die a nothing like you!
But you can't kill us! Can you?! Because then you'd never get the money!
It'd go to our sons and their sons after them.
And each generation would empty the bank, destroying your pathetic existence.
RIIP

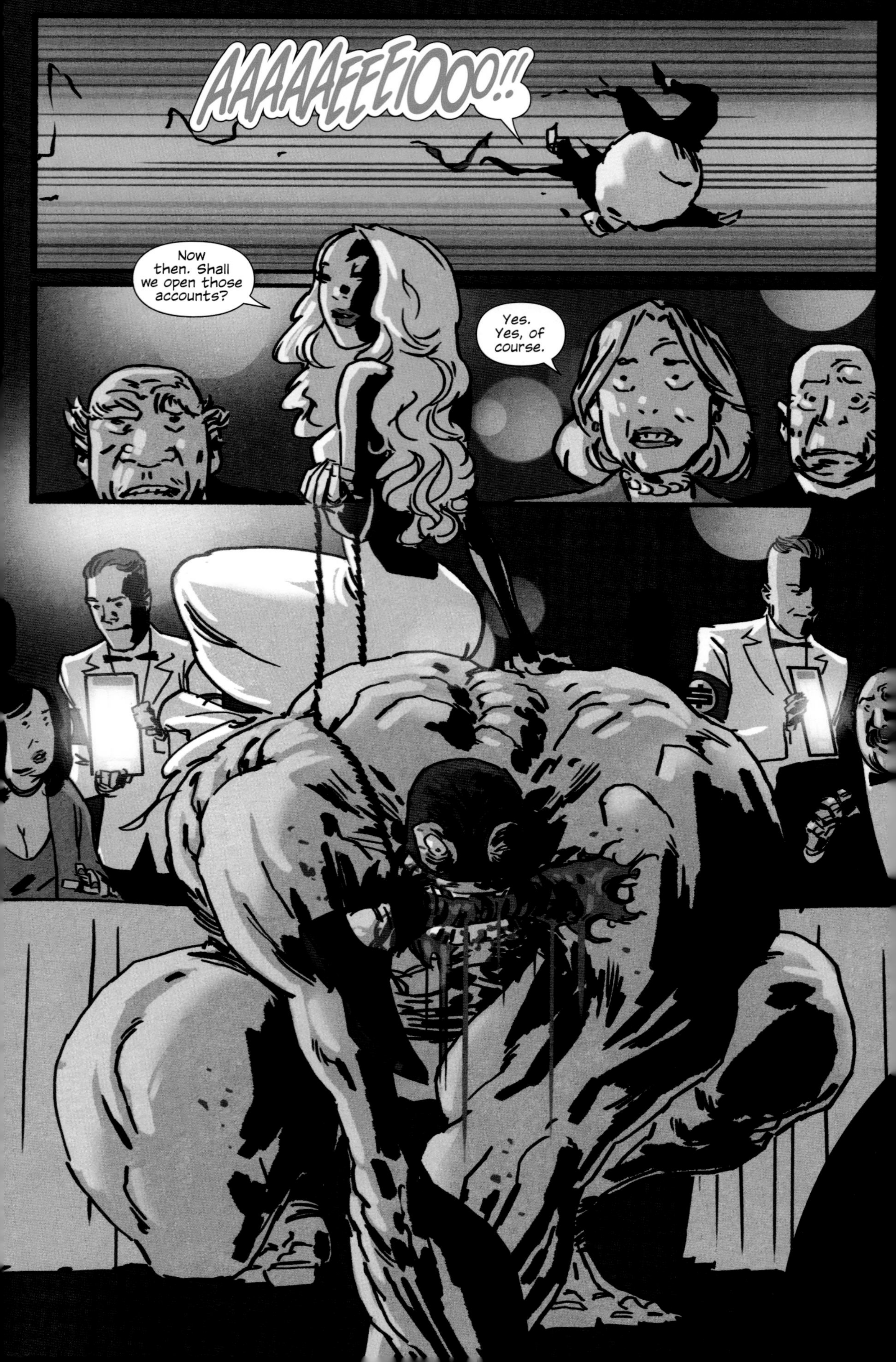

AAAAAEEEIOOOO!!
Now then. Shall we open those accounts?
Yes. Yes, of course.

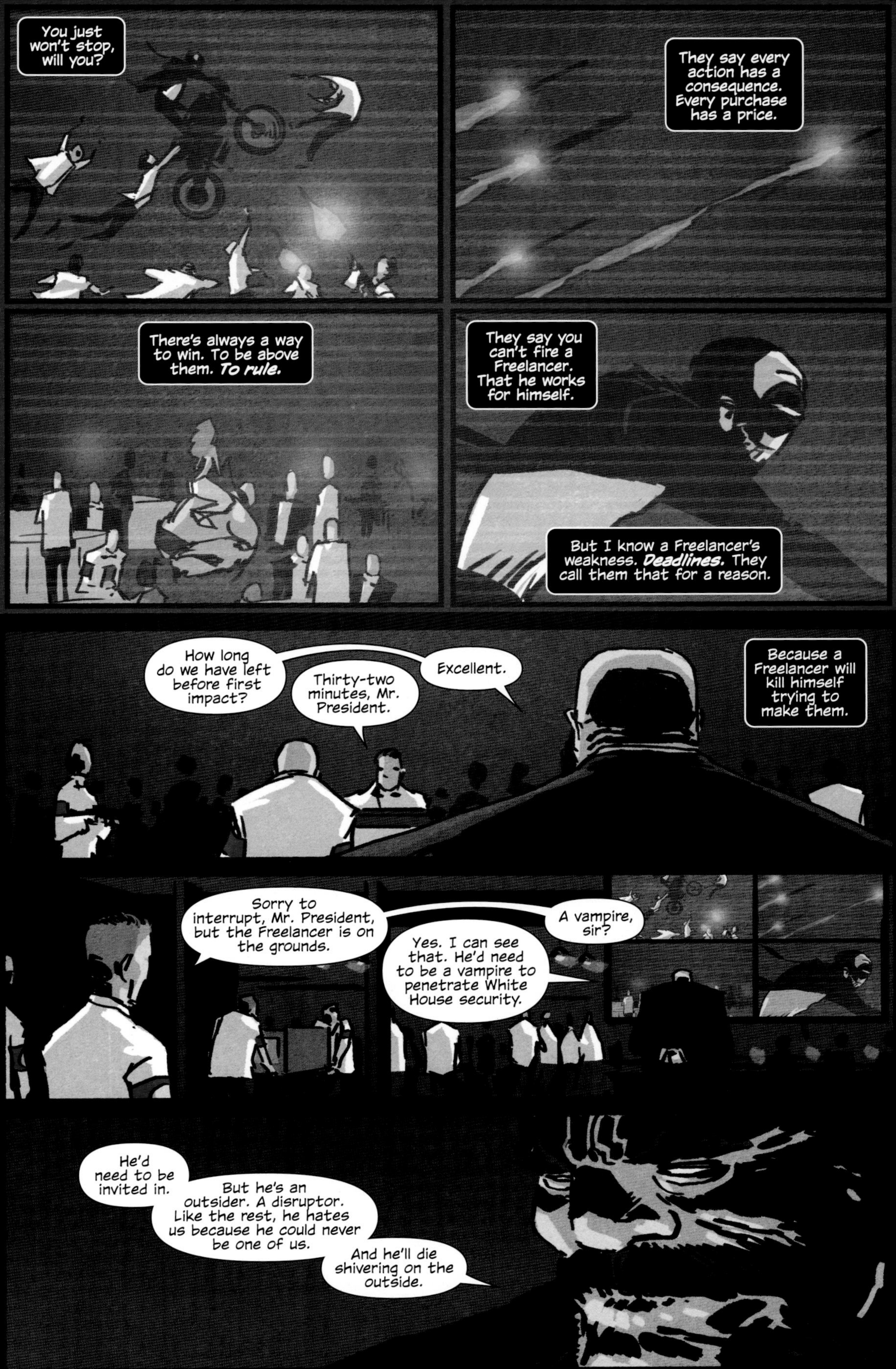
You just won't stop, will you?
They say every action has a consequence. Every purchase has a price.
There's always a way to win. To be above them. *To rule.*
They say you can't fire a Freelancer. That he works for himself.
But I know a Freelancer's weakness. ***Deadlines.*** They call them that for a reason.
How long do we have left before first impact?
Thirty-two minutes, Mr. President.
Excellent.
Because a Freelancer will kill himself trying to make them.
Sorry to interrupt, Mr. President, but the Freelancer is on the grounds.
A vampire, sir?
Yes. I can see that. He'd need to be a vampire to penetrate White House security.
He'd need to be invited in.
But he's an outsider. A disruptor. Like the rest, he hates us because he could never be one of us.
And he'll die shivering on the outside.

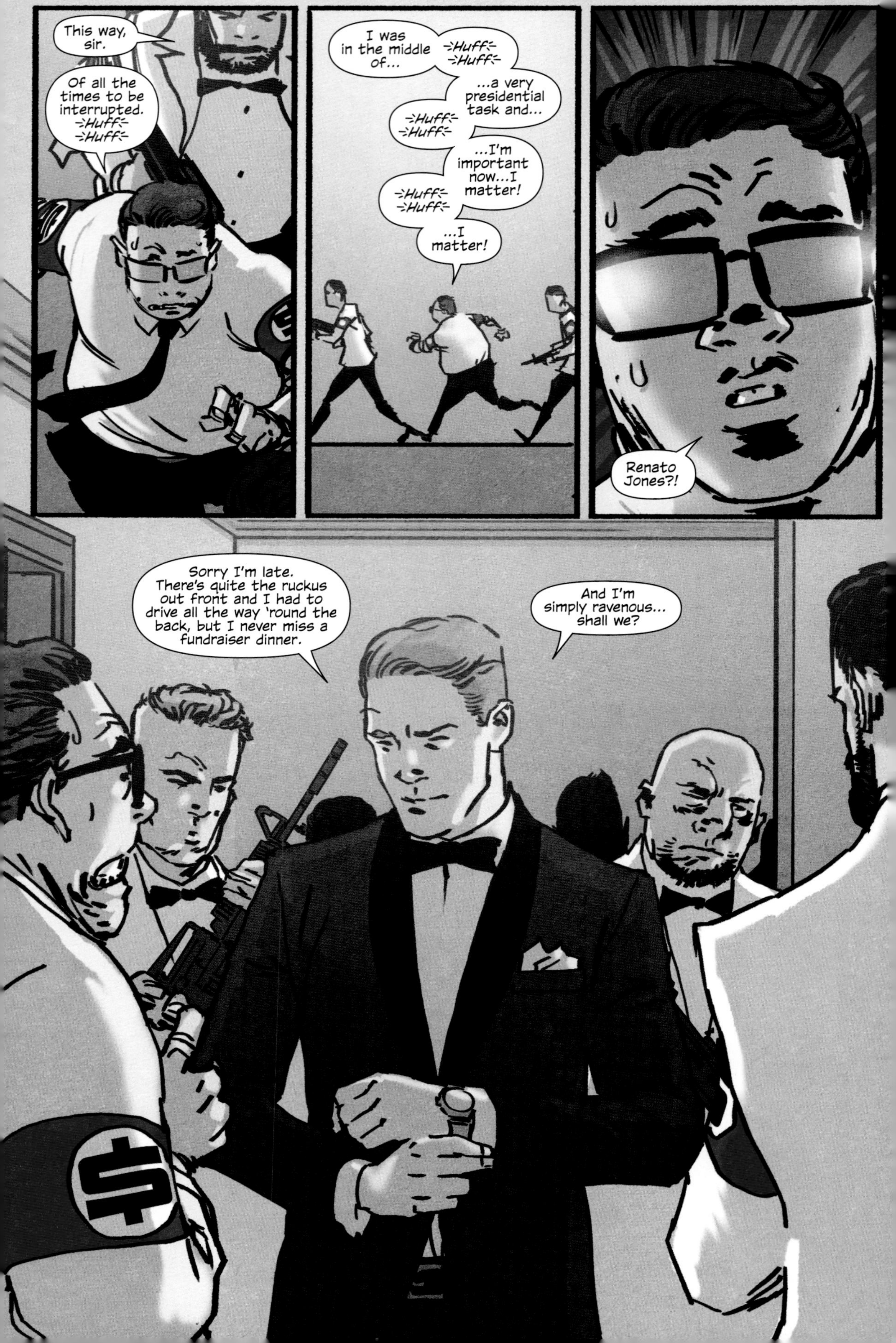

This way, sir.
Of all the times to be interrupted. -Huff- -Huff-
I was in the middle of...
-Huff- -Huff-
...a very presidential task and...
-Huff- -Huff-
...I'm important now...I matter!
-Huff- -Huff-
...I matter!
Renato Jones?!
Sorry I'm late. There's quite the ruckus out front and I had to drive all the way 'round the back, but I never miss a fundraiser dinner.
And I'm simply ravenous... shall we?

"...I know a
Freelancer's
weakness.
Deadlines.
They call them
that for a
reason."

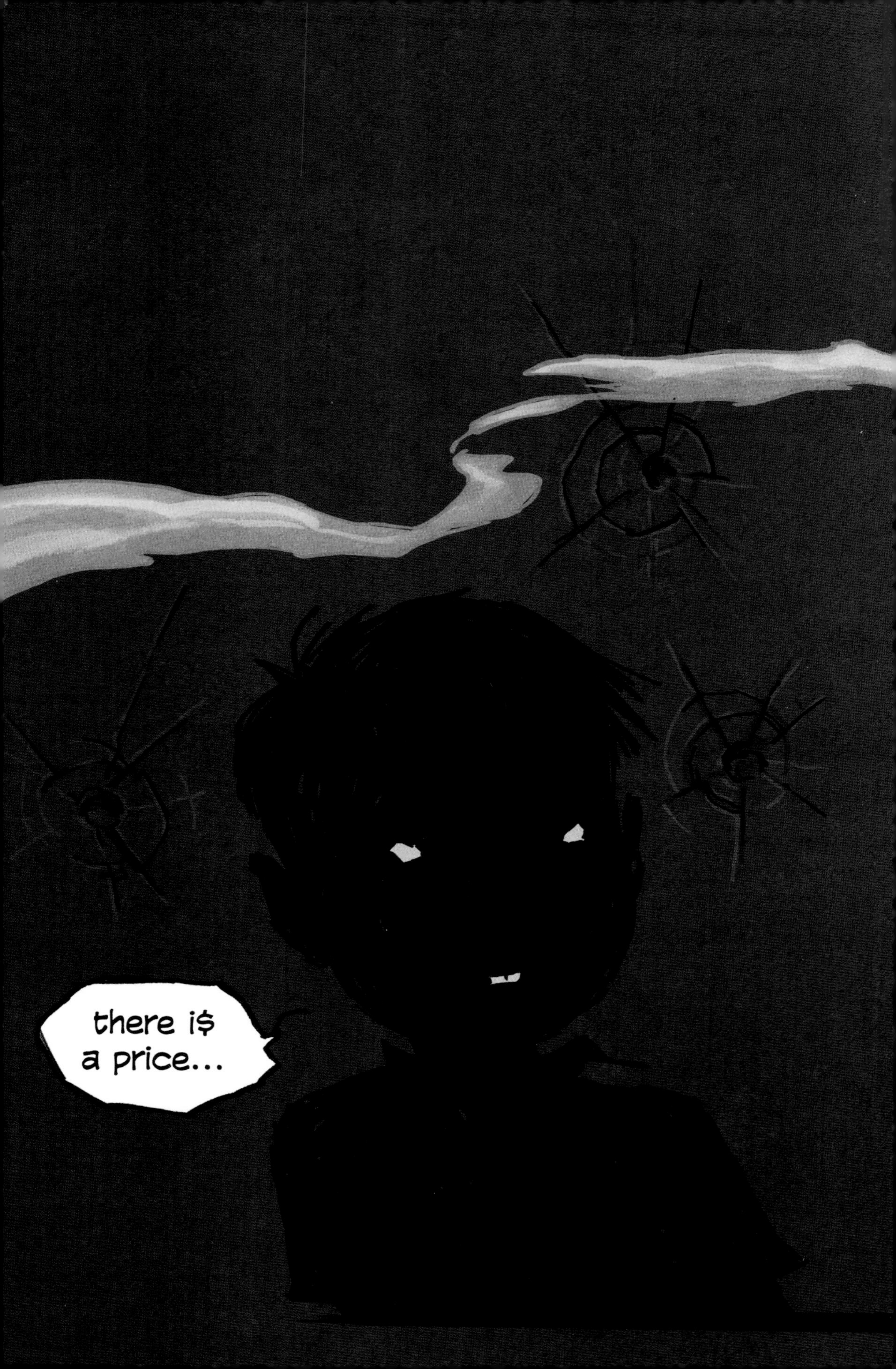
there i$ a price...

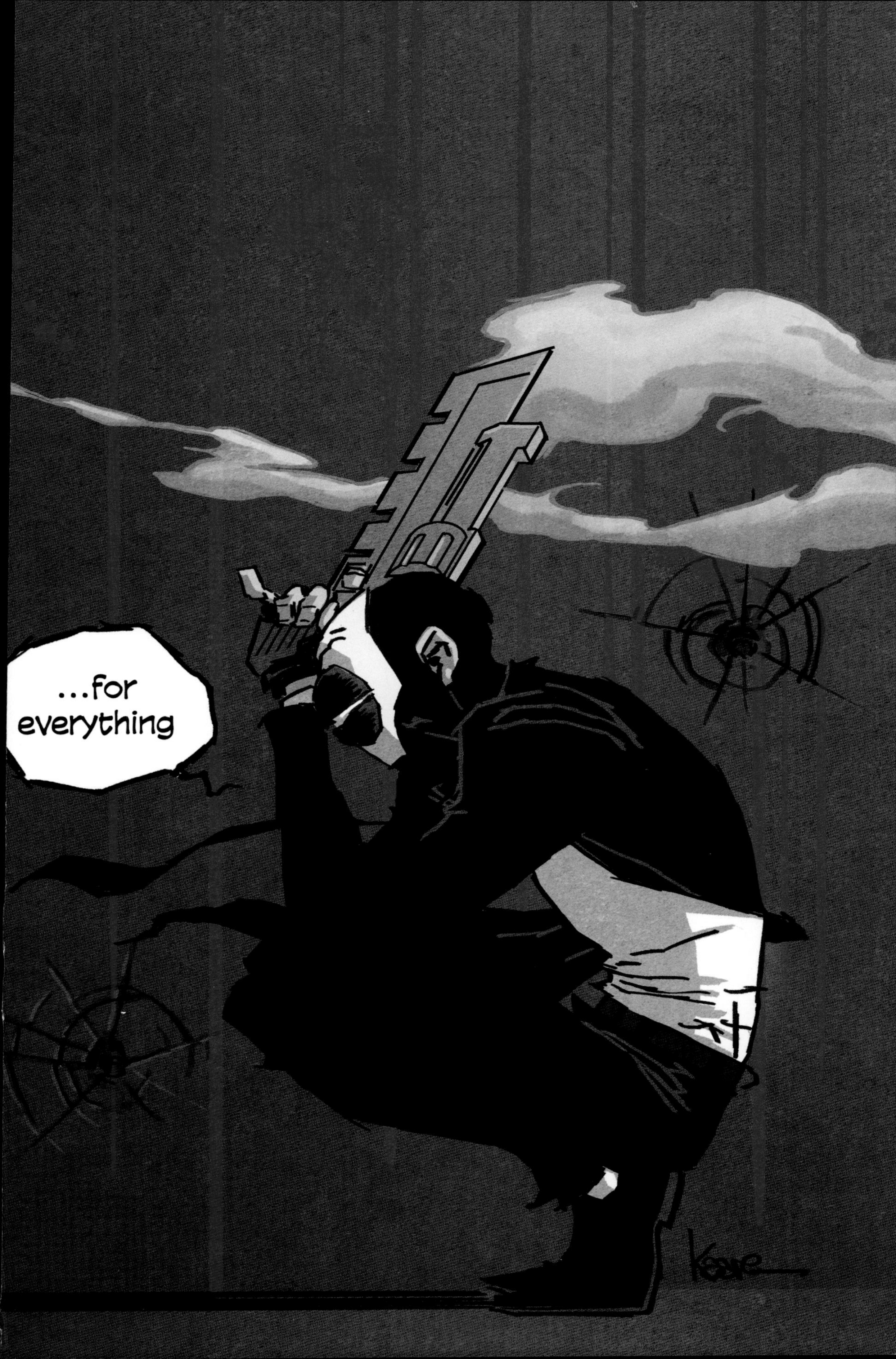
...for everything

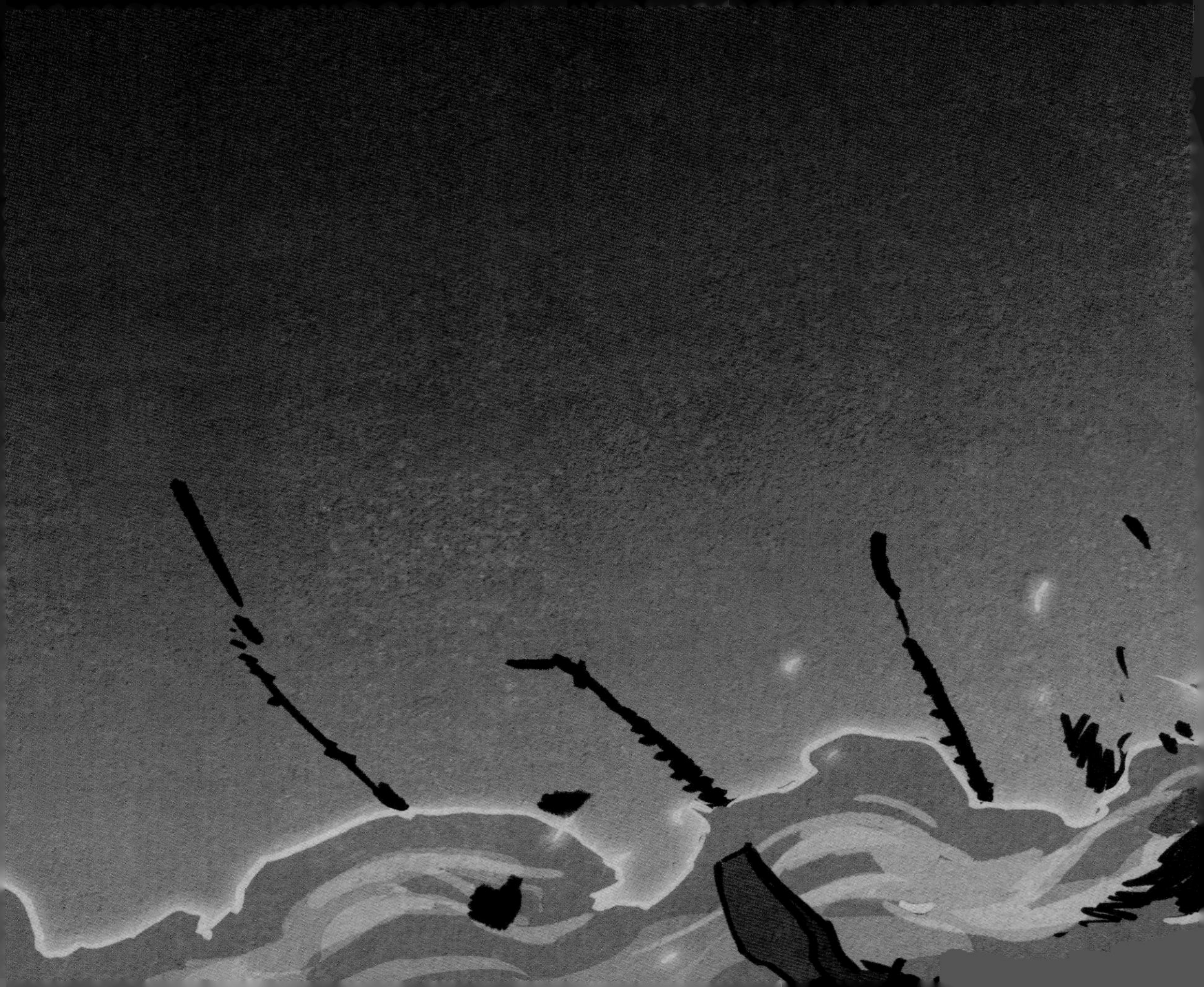

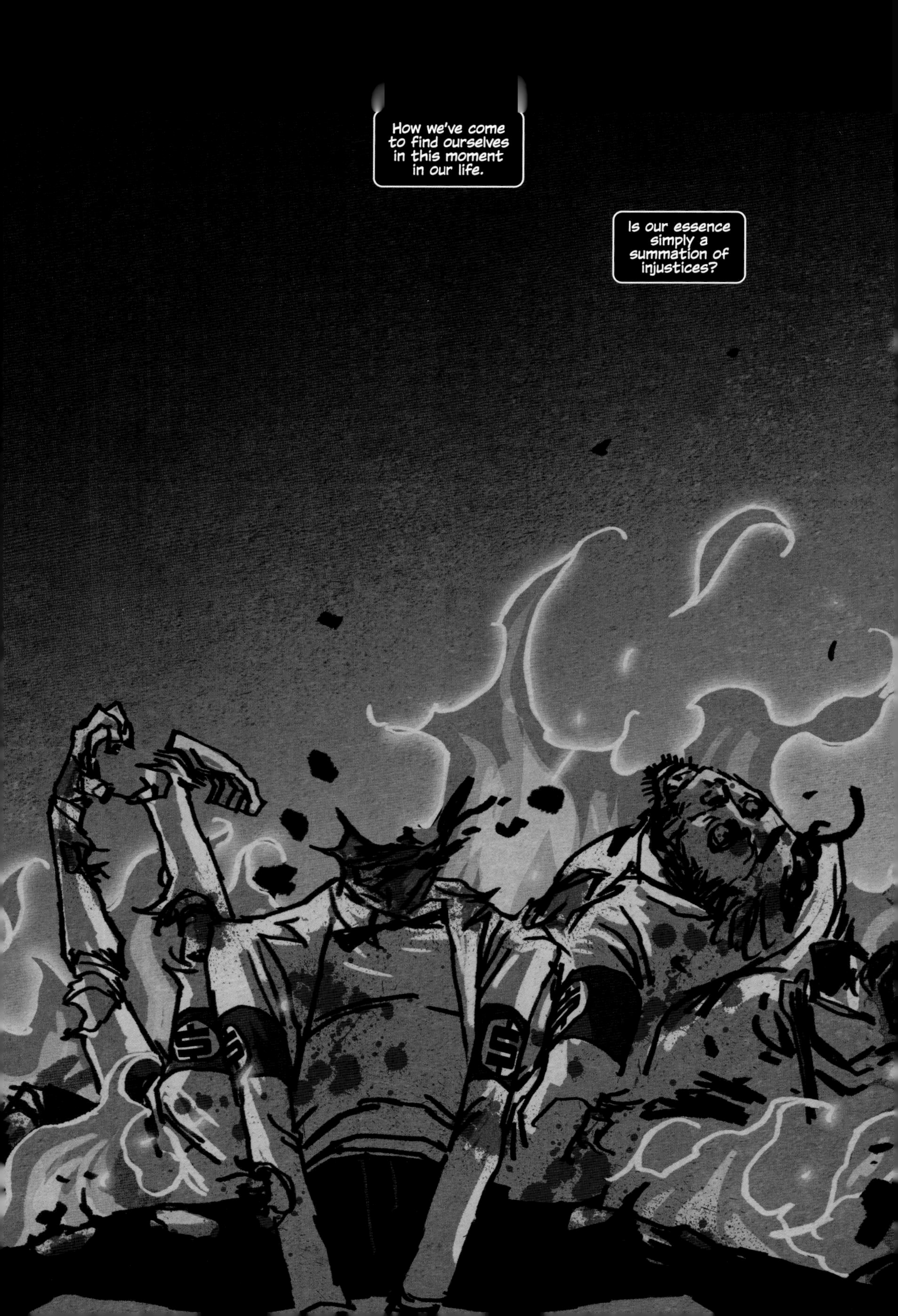
How we've come to find ourselves in this moment in our life.
Is our essence simply a summation of injustices?

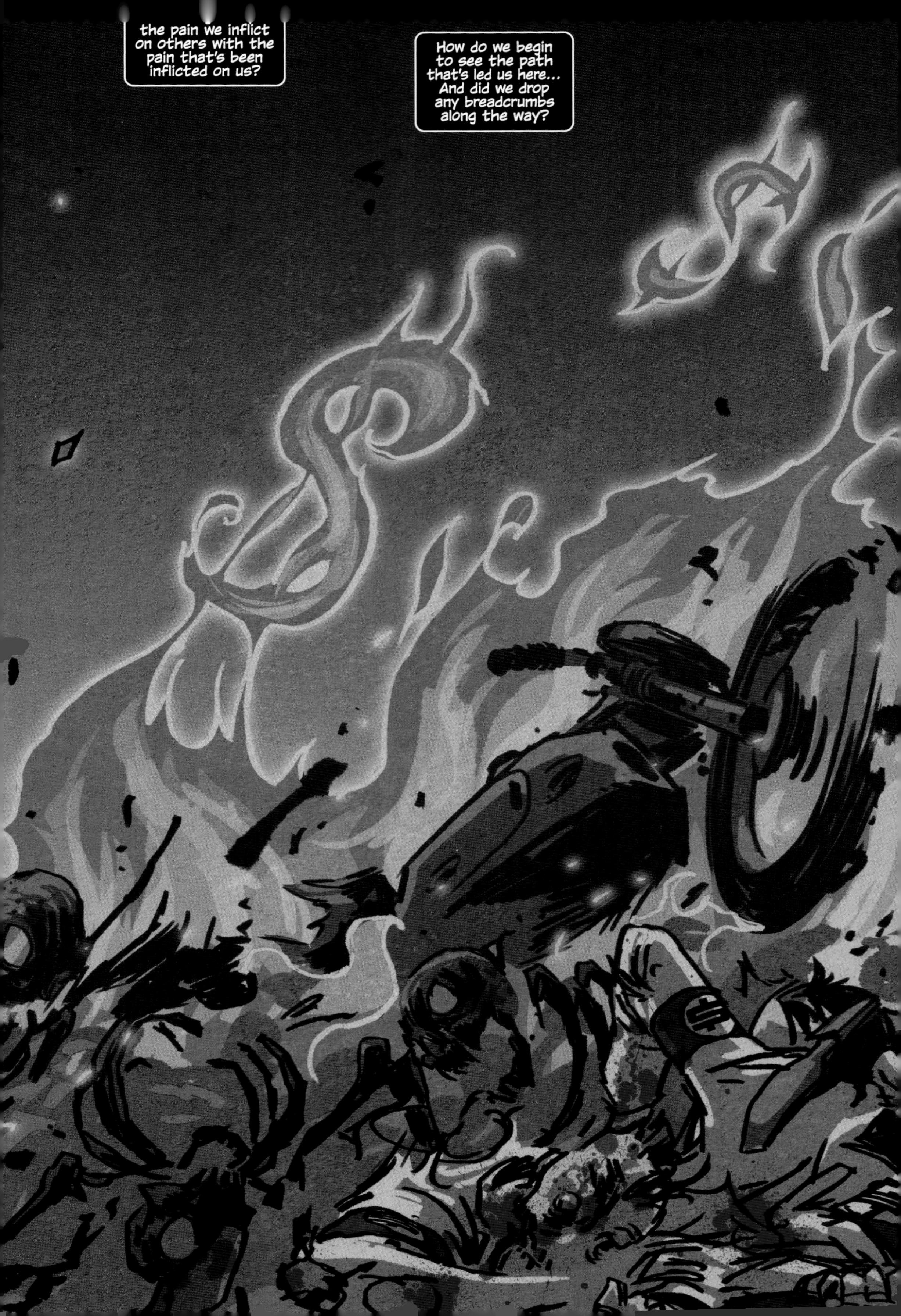
the pain we inflict on others with the pain that's been inflicted on us?
How do we begin to see the path that's led us here... And did we drop any breadcrumbs along the way?

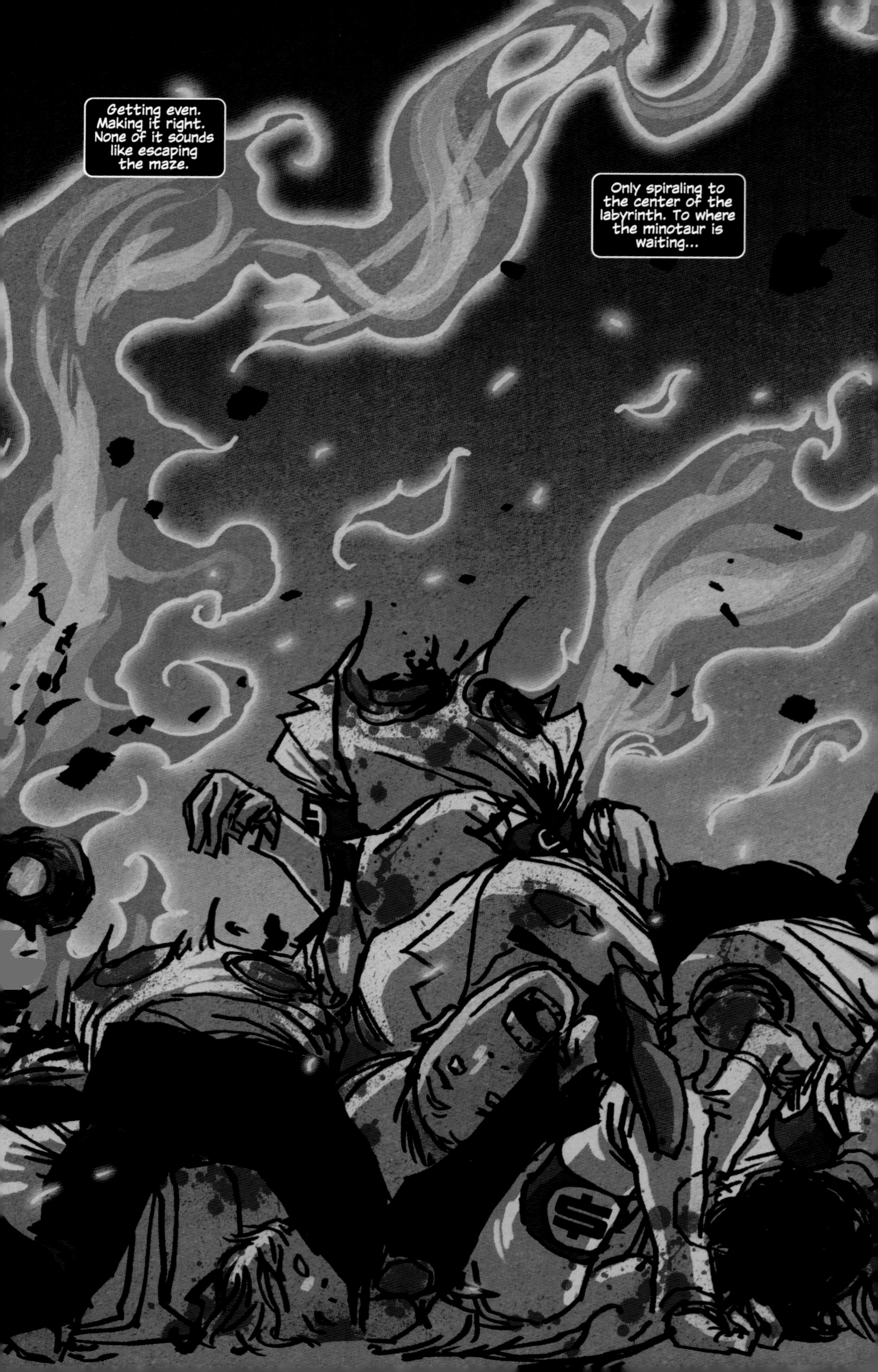
Getting even. Making it right. None of it sounds like escaping the maze.
Only spiraling to the center of the labyrinth. To where the minotaur is waiting...

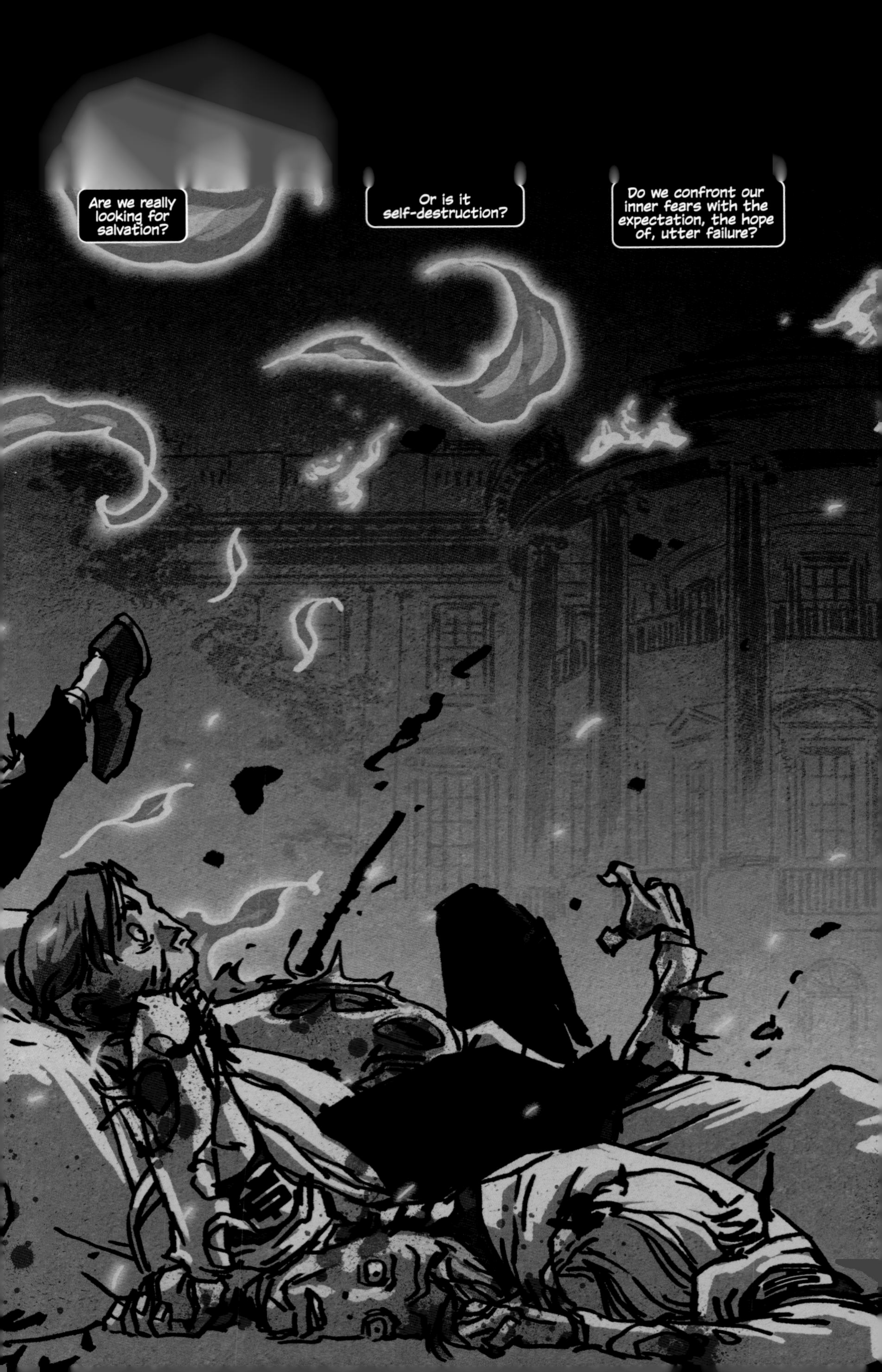
Are we really looking for salvation?
Or is it self-destruction?
Do we confront our inner fears with the expectation, the hope of, utter failure?

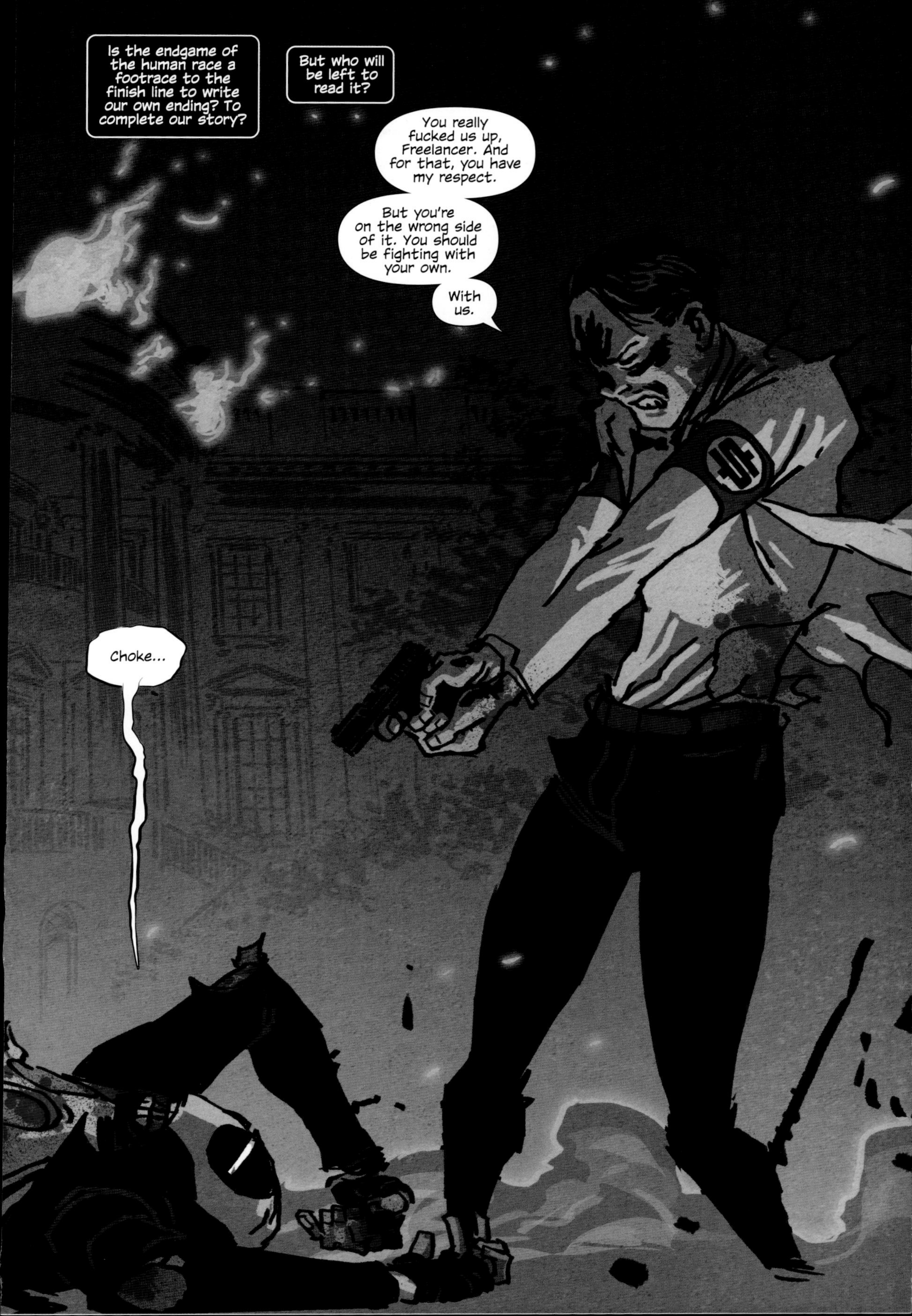
Is the endgame of the human race a footrace to the finish line to write our own ending? To complete our story?
But who will be left to read it?
You really fucked us up, Freelancer. And for that, you have my respect.
But you're on the wrong side of it. You should be fighting with your own.
With us.
Choke...

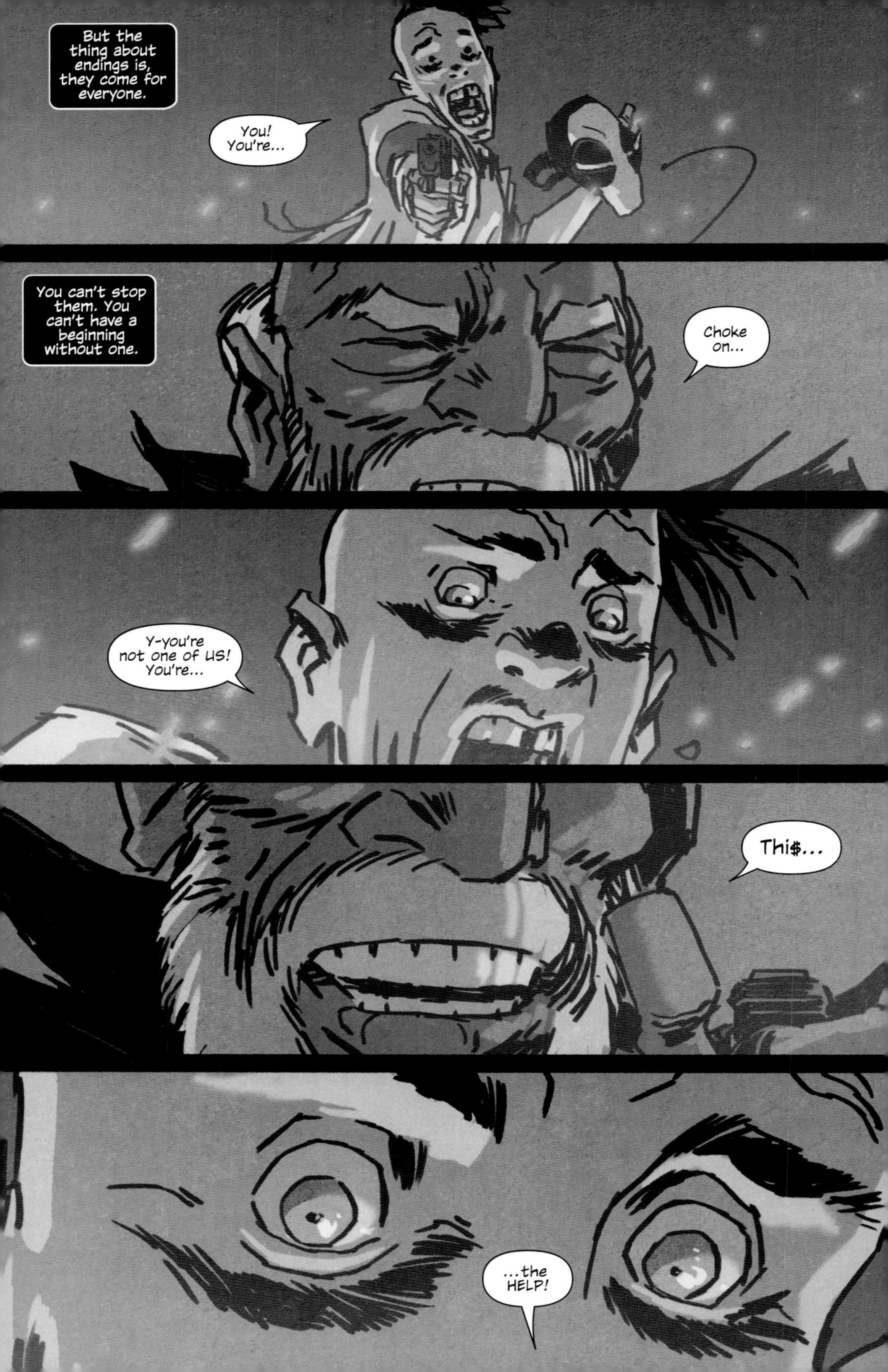

But the thing about endings is, they come for everyone.
You! You're...
You can't stop them. You can't have a beginning without one.
Choke on...
Y-you're not one of US! You're...
Thi$...
...the HELP!

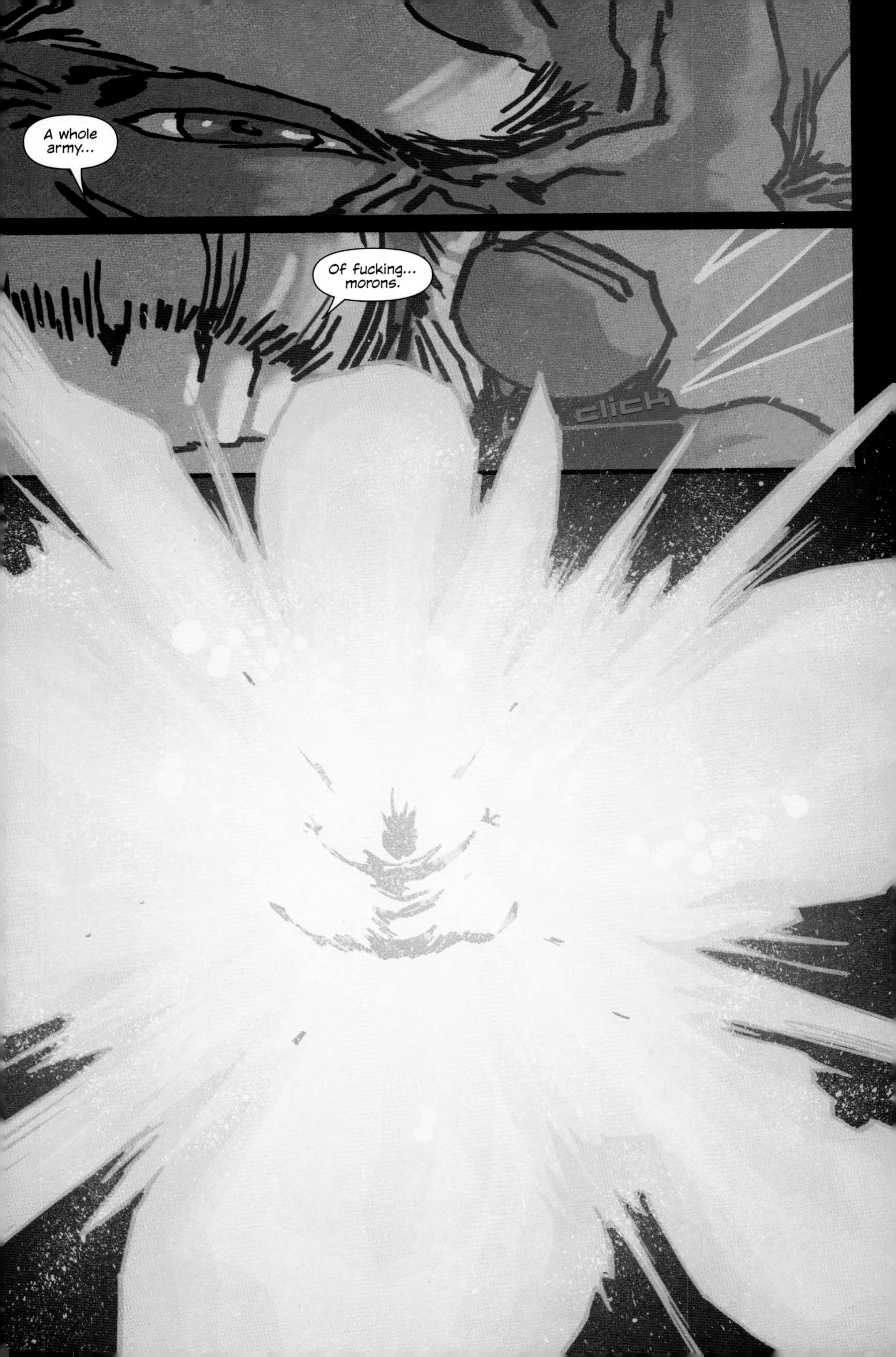
A whole army...
Of fucking... morons.
click

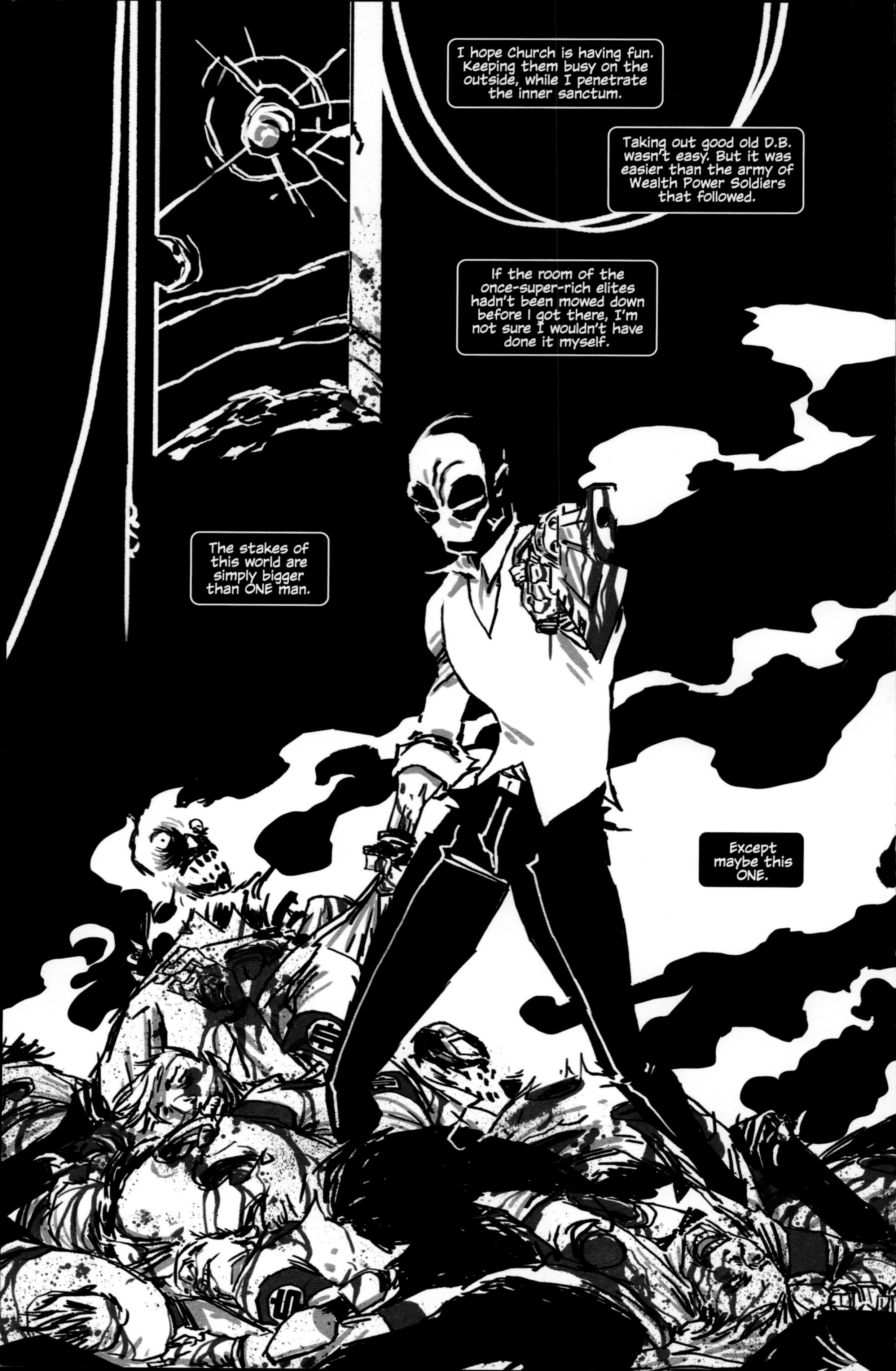
I hope Church is having fun. Keeping them busy on the outside, while I penetrate the inner sanctum.
Taking out good old D.B. wasn't easy. But it was easier than the army of Wealth Power Soldiers that followed.
If the room of the once-super-rich elites hadn't been mowed down before I got there, I'm not sure I wouldn't have done it myself.
The stakes of this world are simply bigger than ONE man.
Except maybe this ONE.

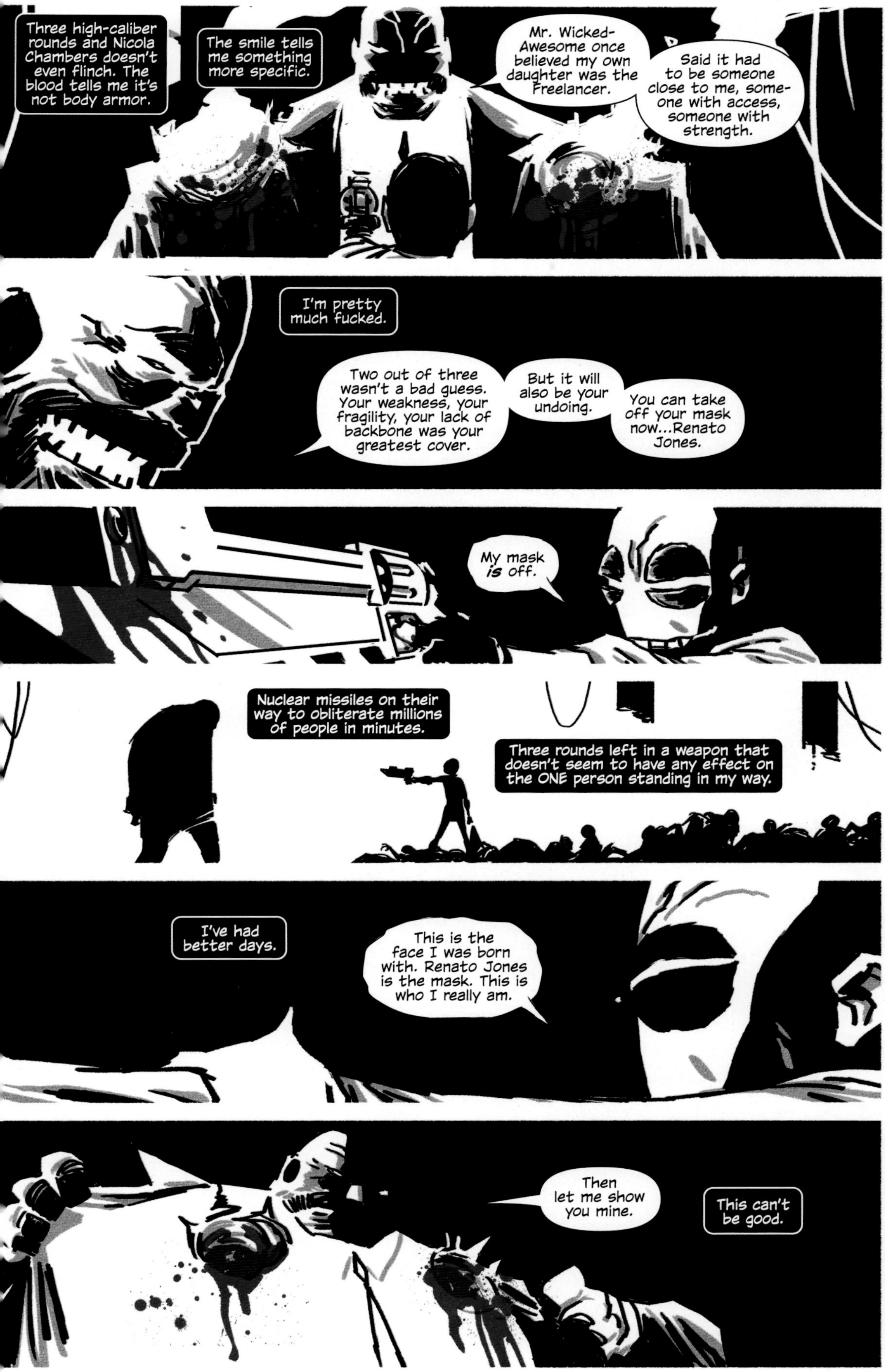
Three high-caliber rounds and Nicola Chambers doesn't even flinch. The blood tells me it's not body armor.
The smile tells me something more specific.
Mr. Wicked-Awesome once believed my own daughter was the Freelancer.
Said it had to be someone close to me, someone with access, someone with strength.
I'm pretty much fucked.
Two out of three wasn't a bad guess. Your weakness, your fragility, your lack of backbone was your greatest cover.
But it will also be your undoing.
You can take off your mask now...Renato Jones.
My mask *is* off.
Nuclear missiles on their way to obliterate millions of people in minutes.
Three rounds left in a weapon that doesn't seem to have any effect on the ONE person standing in my way.
I've had better days.
This is the face I was born with. Renato Jones is the mask. This is who I really am.
Then let me show you mine.
This can't be good.

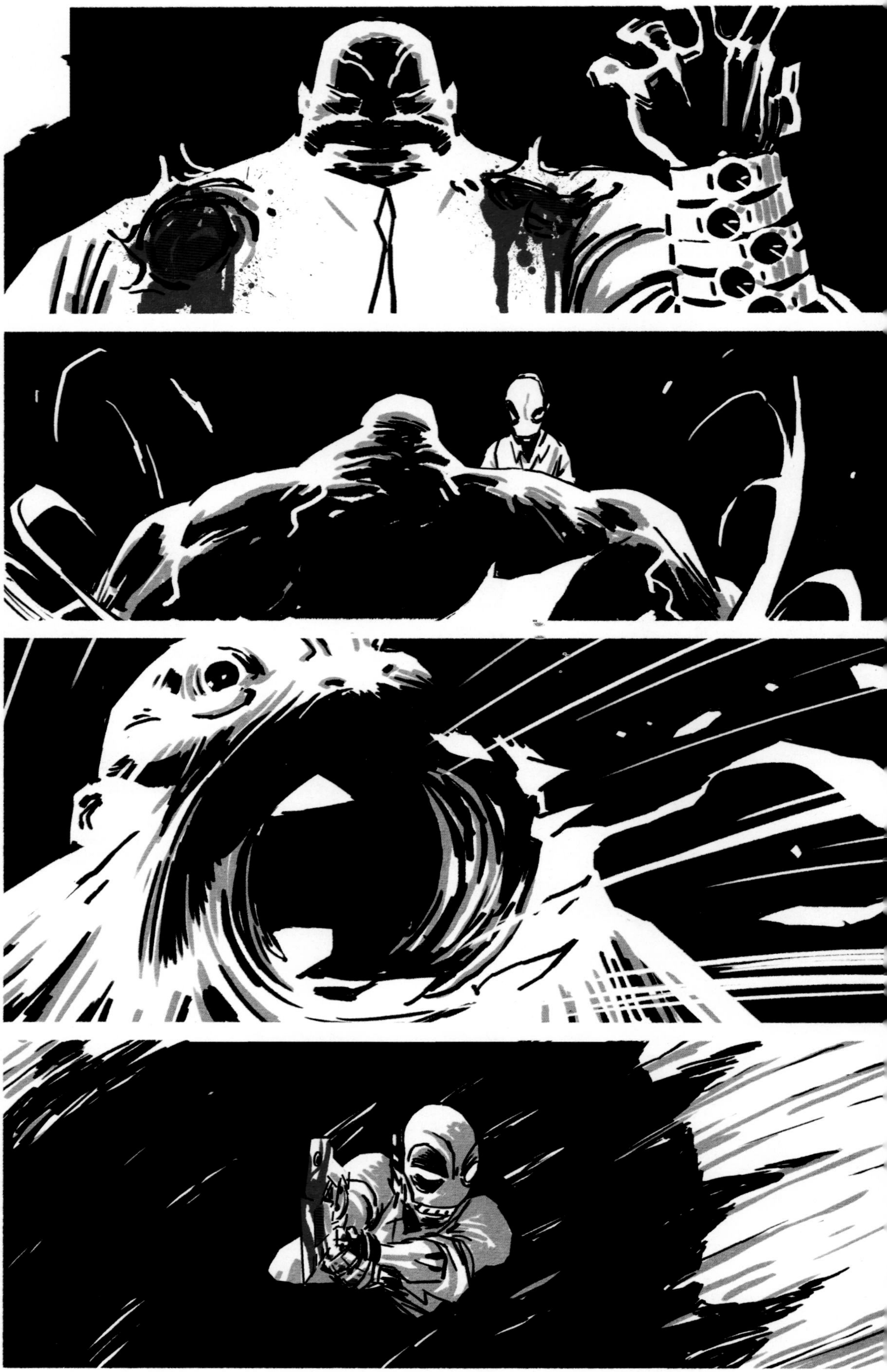

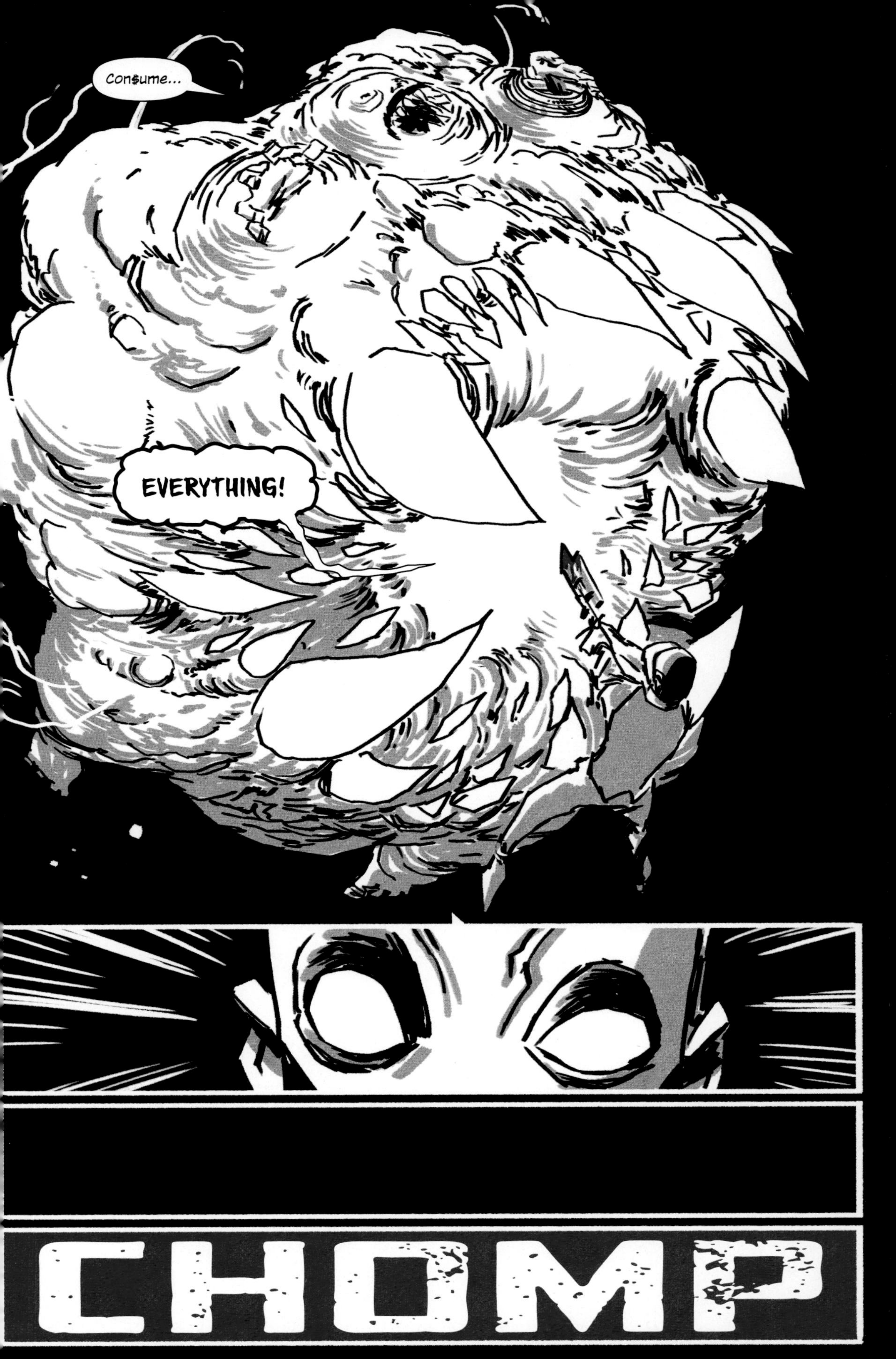

Con$ume...
EVERYTHING!
CHOMP

Death has a certain taste to it. Most wouldn't recognize it, because they'll drink it only once.

But it's familiar to me.

Safe.

In many ways, it's something I look forward to. The ultimate payment for services rendered.

But death not yet ripe is tart. It demands to be aged in the oak barrels of life, fermented, changed and enriched by time.

It has to be earned.

The Taoist proverb goes something like this: "One should look forward to death the way a farmer looks forward to sleep after a good day's work."

But my work isn't done...

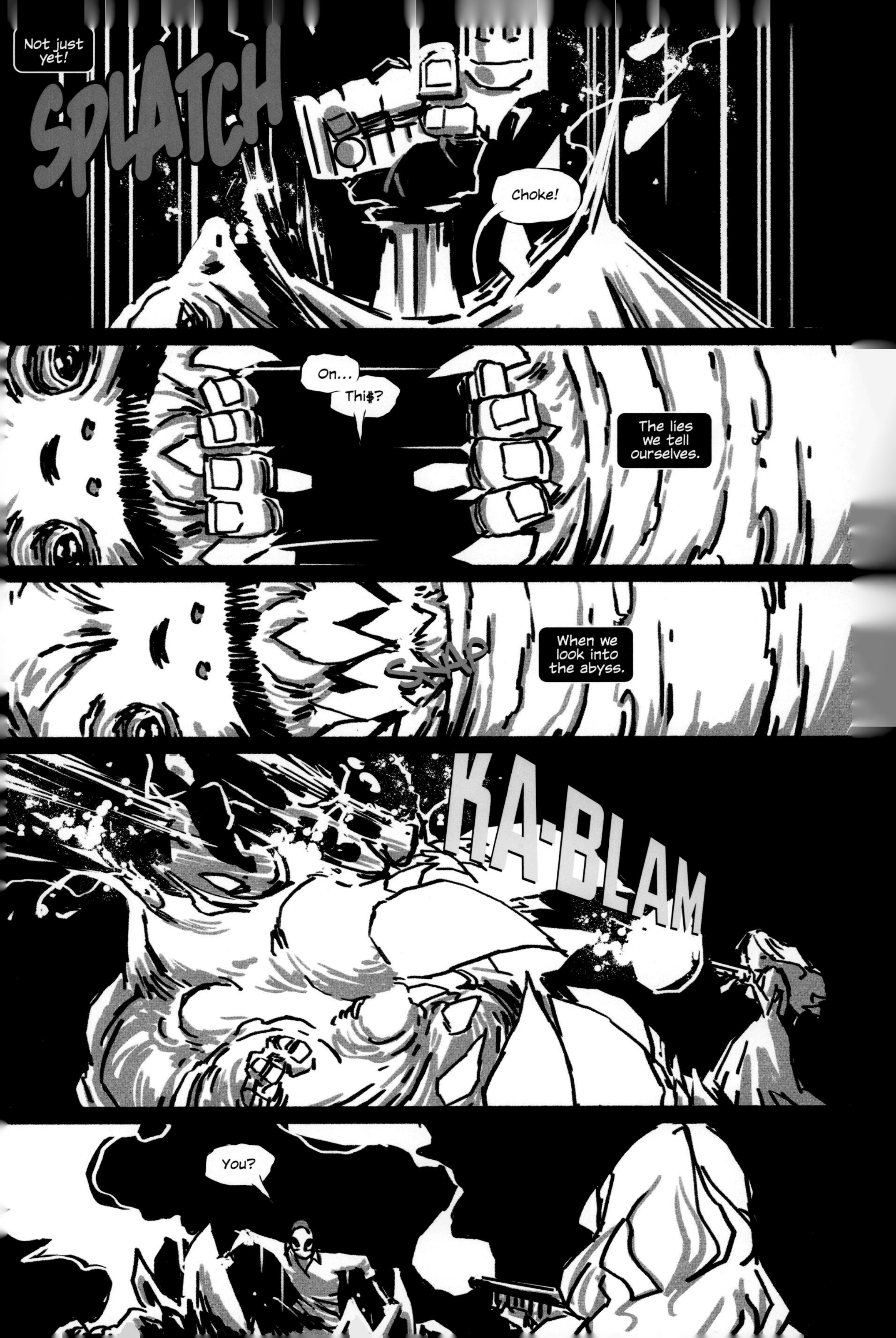
Not just yet!
SPLATCH
Choke!
On...
Thi$?
The lies we tell ourselves.
When we look into the abyss.
KA-BLAM
You?

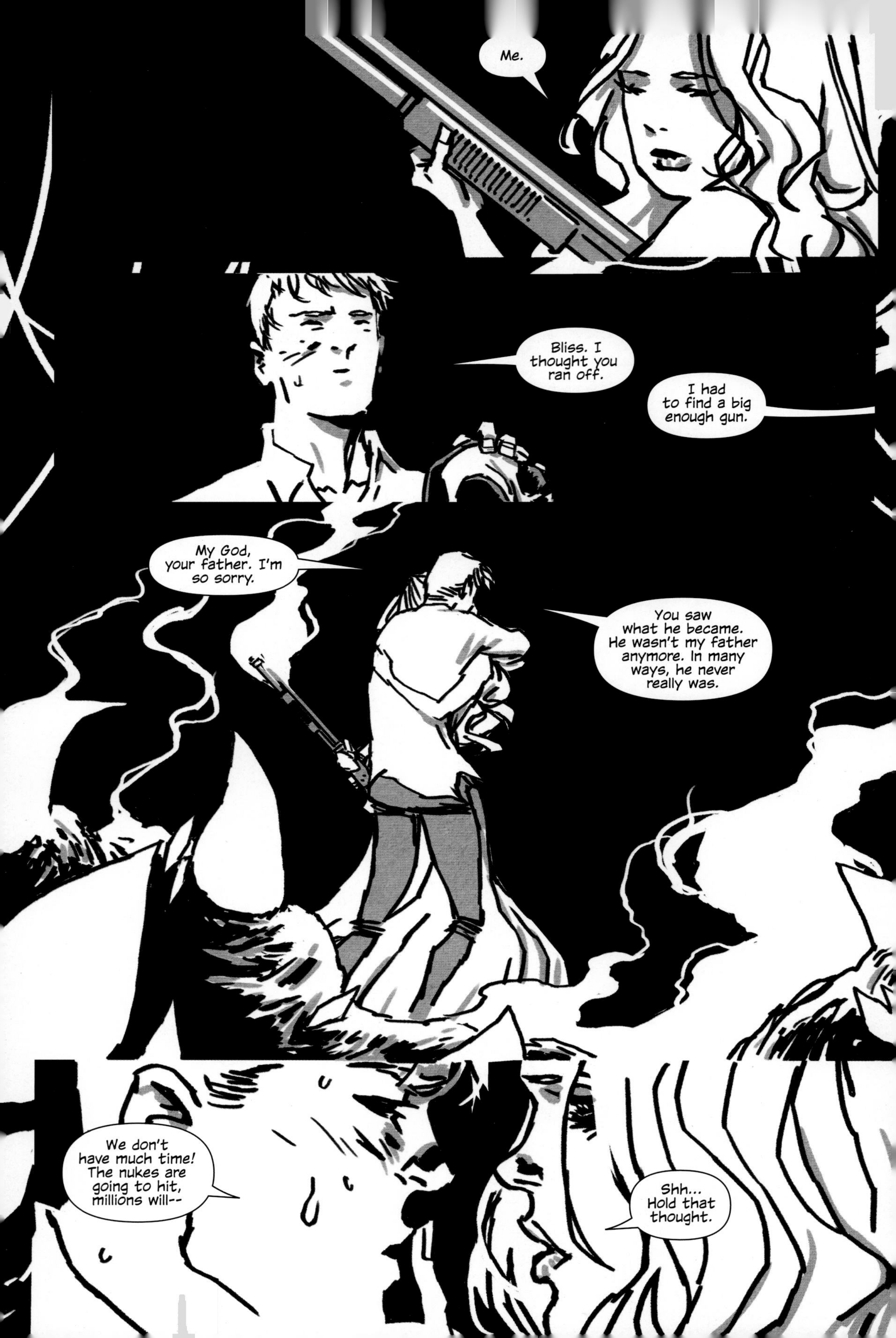
Me.
Bliss. I thought you ran off.
I had to find a big enough gun.
My God, your father. I'm so sorry.
You saw what he became. He wasn't my father anymore. In many ways, he never really was.
We don't have much time! The nukes are going to hit, millions will--
Shh... Hold that thought.

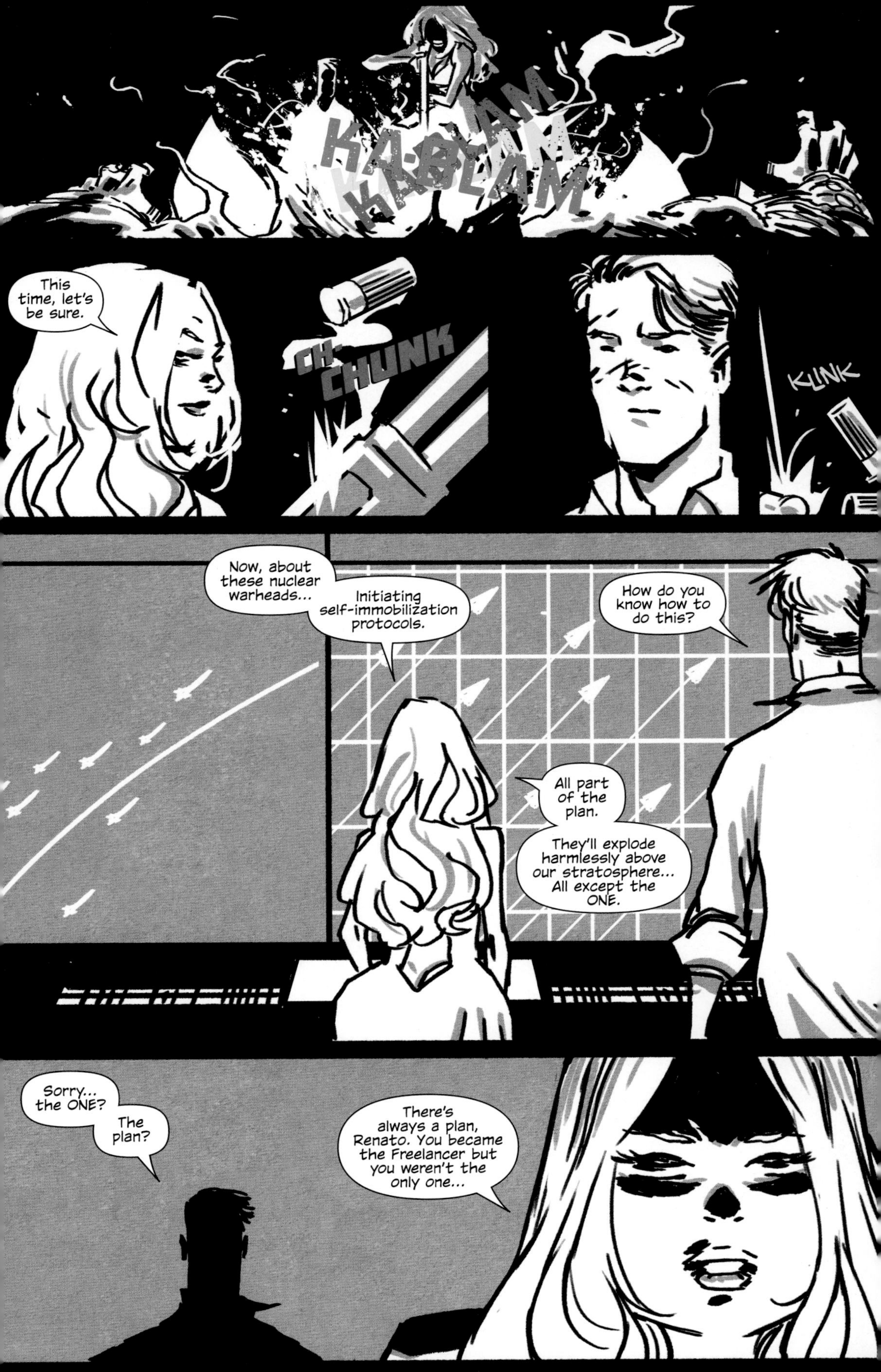
KA-BLAM
KA-BLAM
This time, let's be sure.
CH-CHUNK
KLINK
Now, about these nuclear warheads...
Initiating self-immobilization protocols.
How do you know how to do this?
All part of the plan.
They'll explode harmlessly above our stratosphere... All except the ONE.
Sorry... the ONE?
The plan?
There's always a plan, Renato. You became the Freelancer but you weren't the only one...

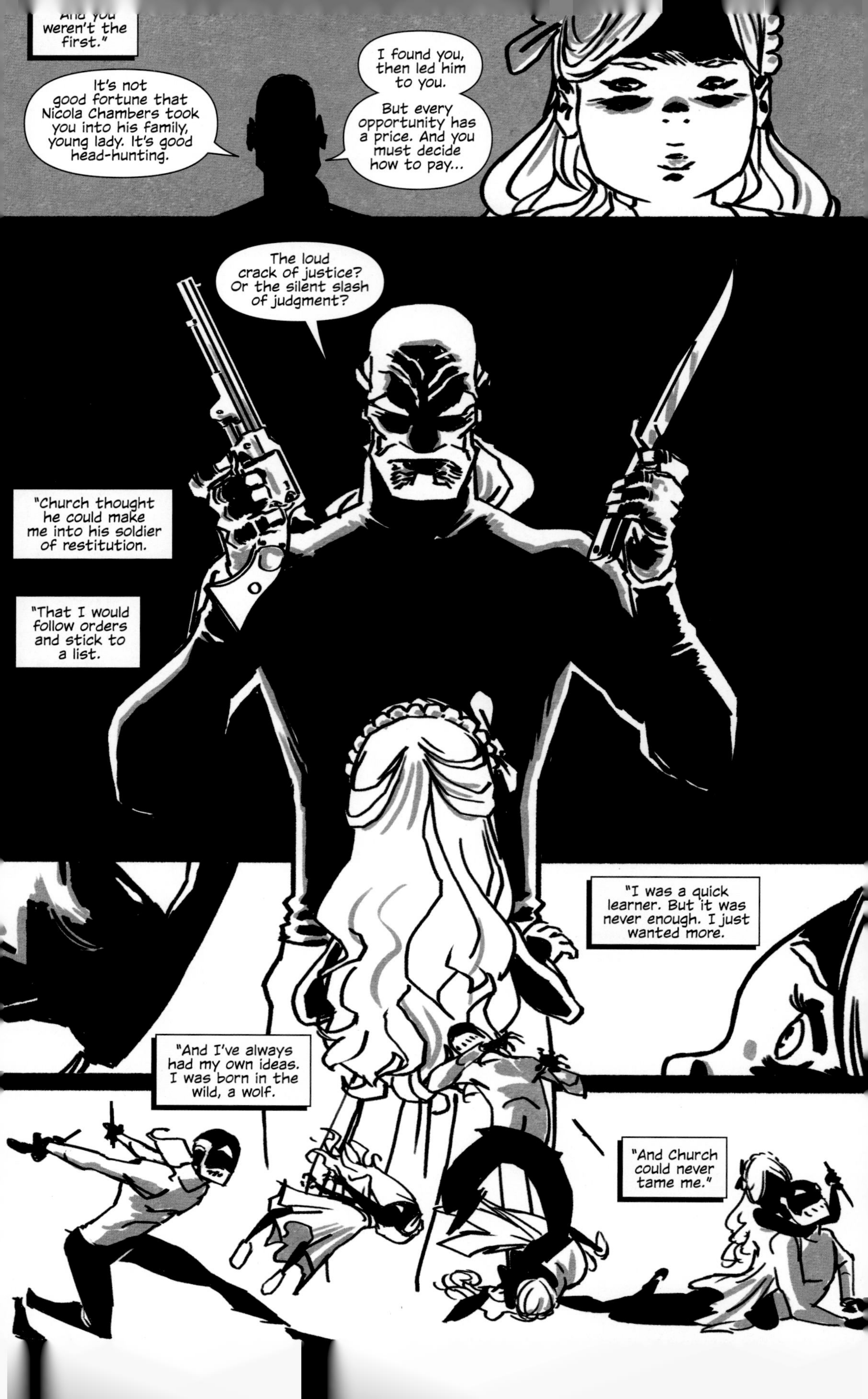

"And you weren't the first."
It's not good fortune that Nicola Chambers took you into his family, young lady. It's good head-hunting.
I found you, then led him to you.
But every opportunity has a price. And you must decide how to pay...
The loud crack of justice? Or the silent slash of judgment?
"Church thought he could make me into his soldier of restitution.
"That I would follow orders and stick to a list.
"I was a quick learner. But it was never enough. I just wanted more.
"And I've always had my own ideas. I was born in the wild, a wolf.
"And Church could never tame me."

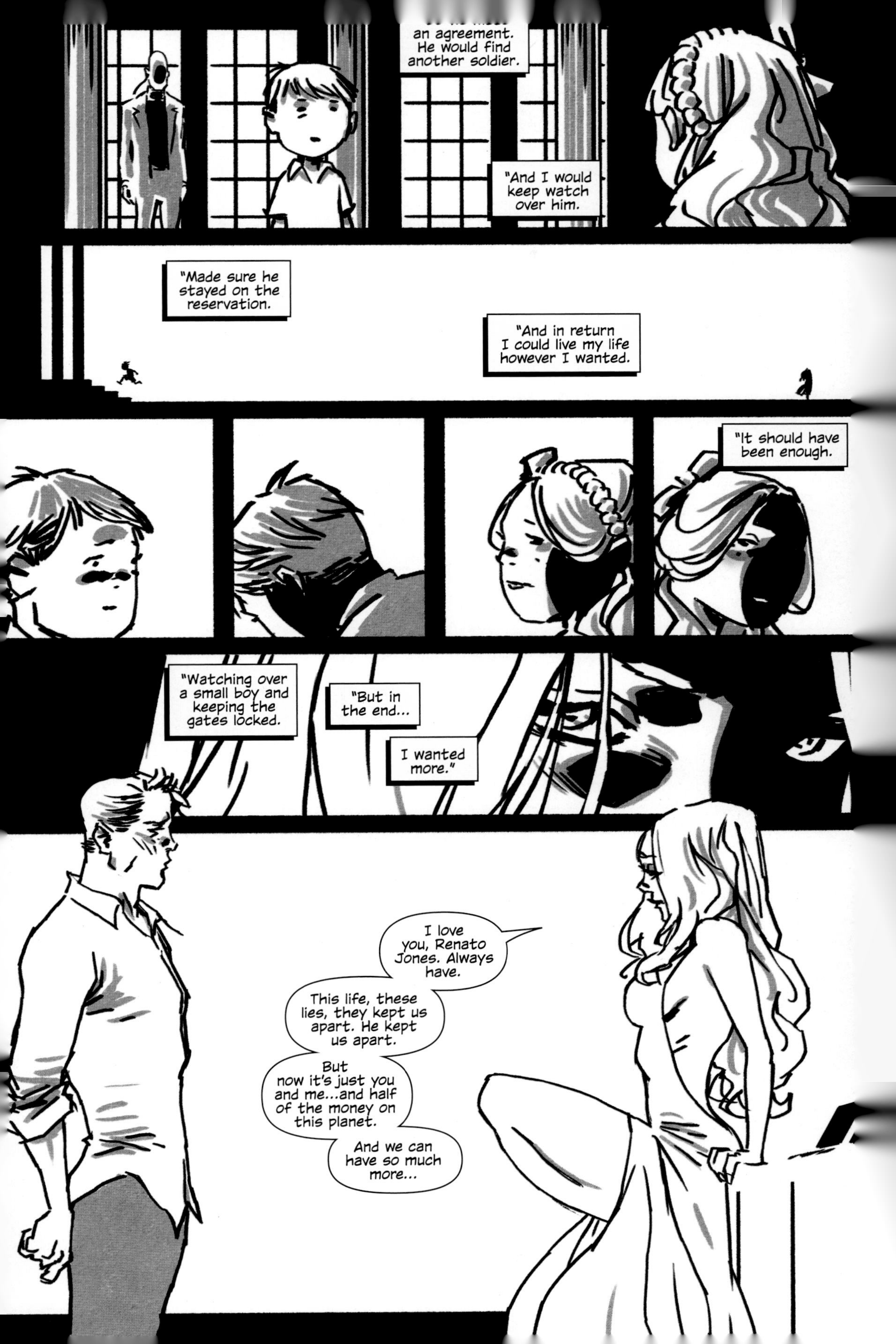
an agreement. He would find another soldier.
"And I would keep watch over him.
"Made sure he stayed on the reservation.
"And in return I could live my life however I wanted.
"It should have been enough.
"Watching over a small boy and keeping the gates locked.
"But in the end...
I wanted more."
I love you, Renato Jones. Always have.
This life, these lies, they kept us apart. He kept us apart.
But now it's just you and me...and half of the money on this planet.
And we can have so much more...

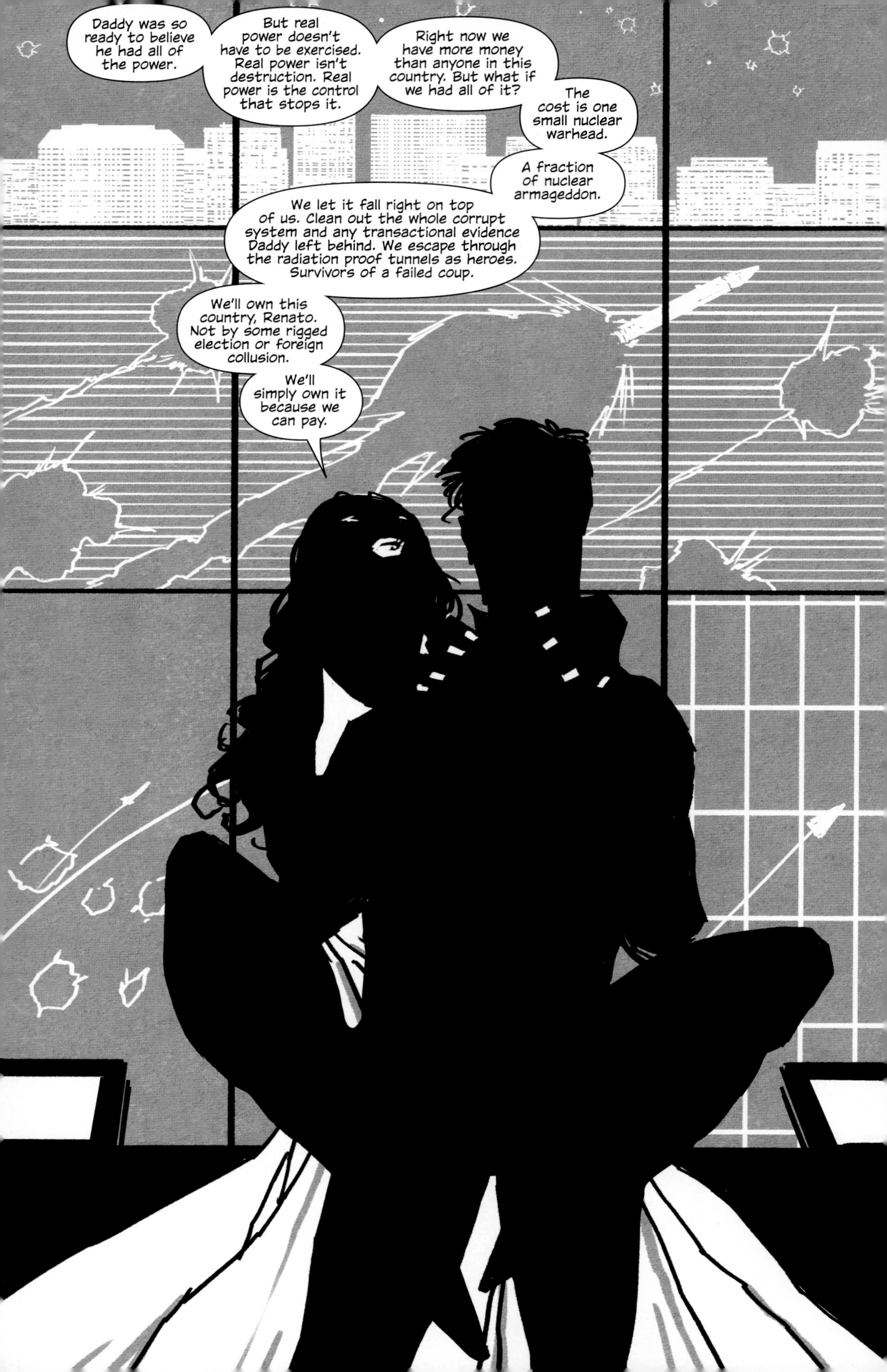
Daddy was so ready to believe he had all of the power.
But real power doesn't have to be exercised. Real power isn't destruction. Real power is the control that stops it.
Right now we have more money than anyone in this country. But what if we had all of it?
The cost is one small nuclear warhead.
A fraction of nuclear armageddon.
We let it fall right on top of us. Clean out the whole corrupt system and any transactional evidence Daddy left behind. We escape through the radiation proof tunnels as heroes. Survivors of a failed coup.
We'll own this country, Renato. Not by some rigged election or foreign collusion.
We'll simply own it because we can pay.

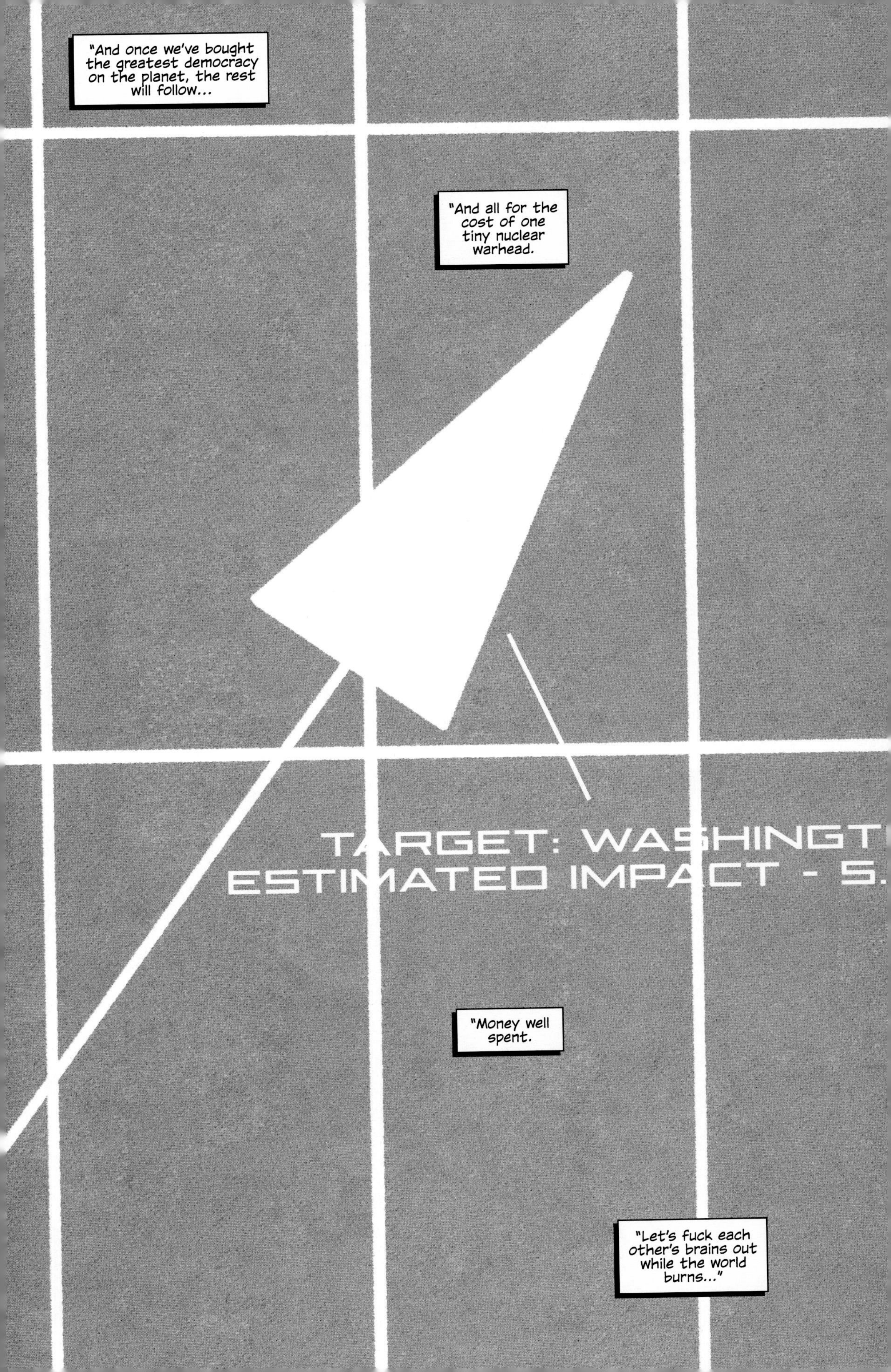
"And once we've bought the greatest democracy on the planet, the rest will follow...
"And all for the cost of one tiny nuclear warhead.
TARGET: WASHINGT
ESTIMATED IMPACT - 5.
"Money well spent.
"Let's fuck each other's brains out while the world burns..."

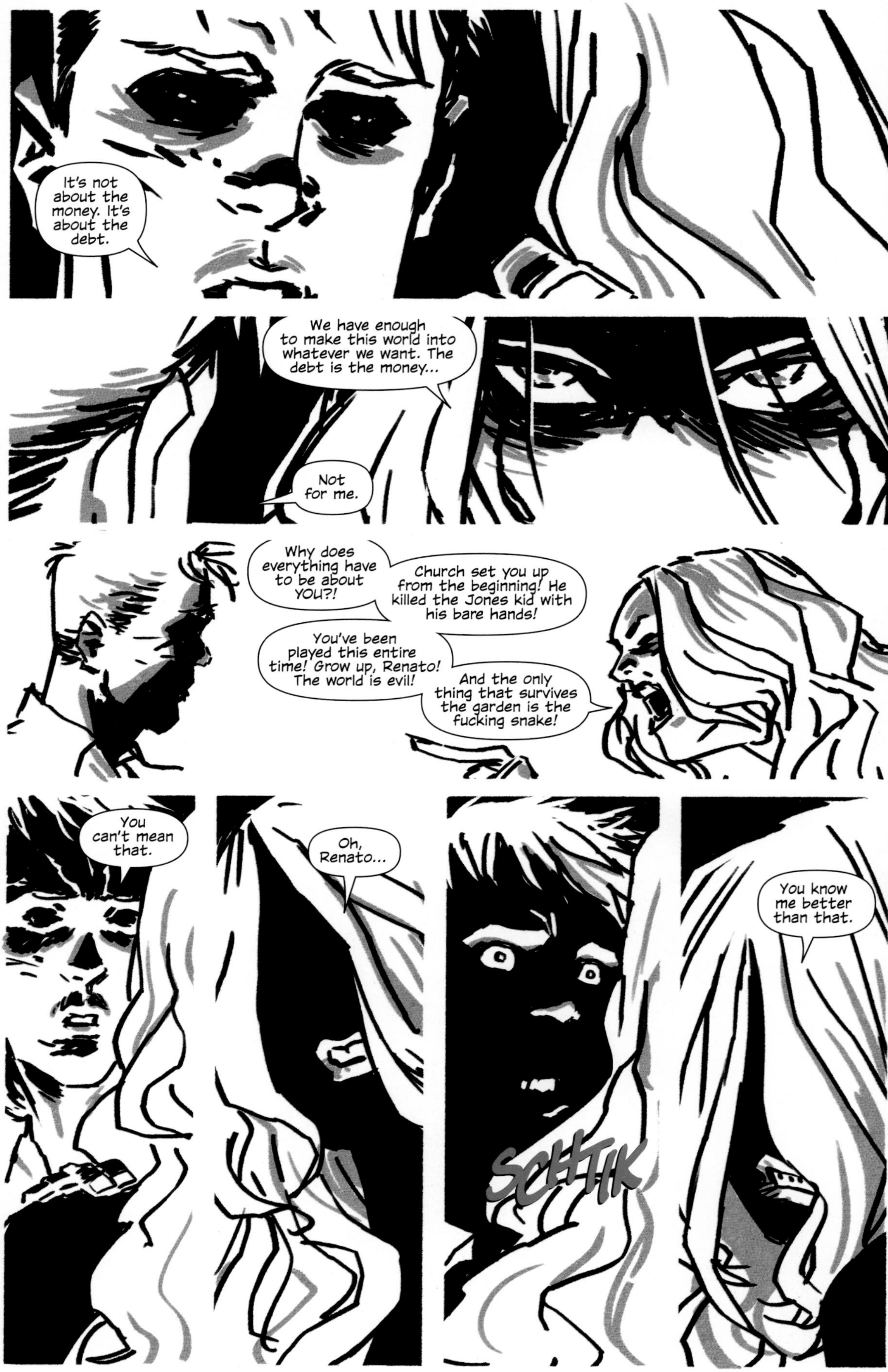
It's not about the money. It's about the debt.
We have enough to make this world into whatever we want. The debt is the money...
Not for me.
Why does everything have to be about YOU?!
Church set you up from the beginning! He killed the Jones kid with his bare hands!
You've been played this entire time! Grow up, Renato! The world is evil!
And the only thing that survives the garden is the fucking snake!
You can't mean that.
Oh, Renato...
SCHTIK
You know me better than that.

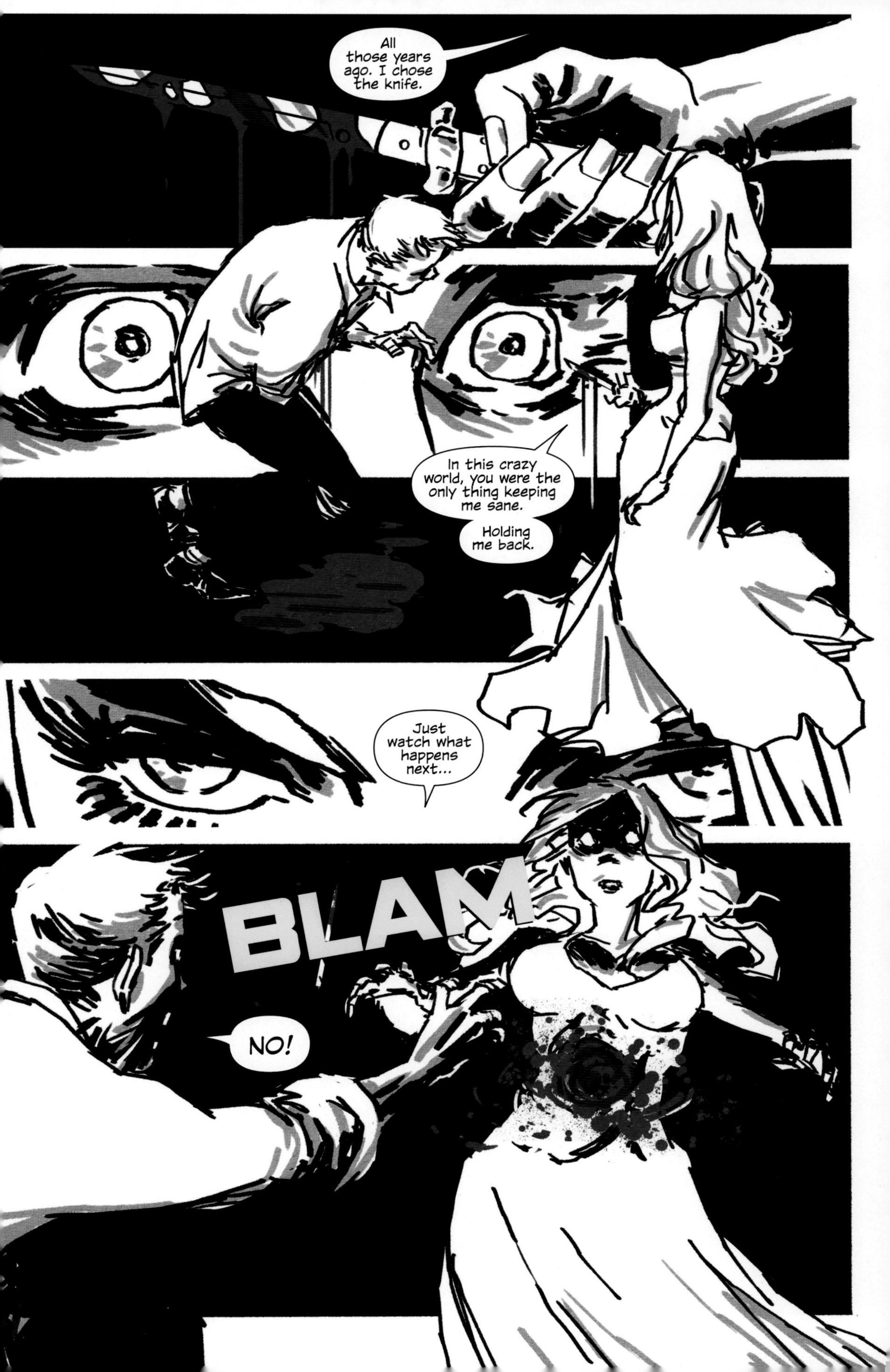
All those years ago. I chose the knife.
In this crazy world, you were the only thing keeping me sane.
Holding me back.
Just watch what happens next...
BLAM
NO!

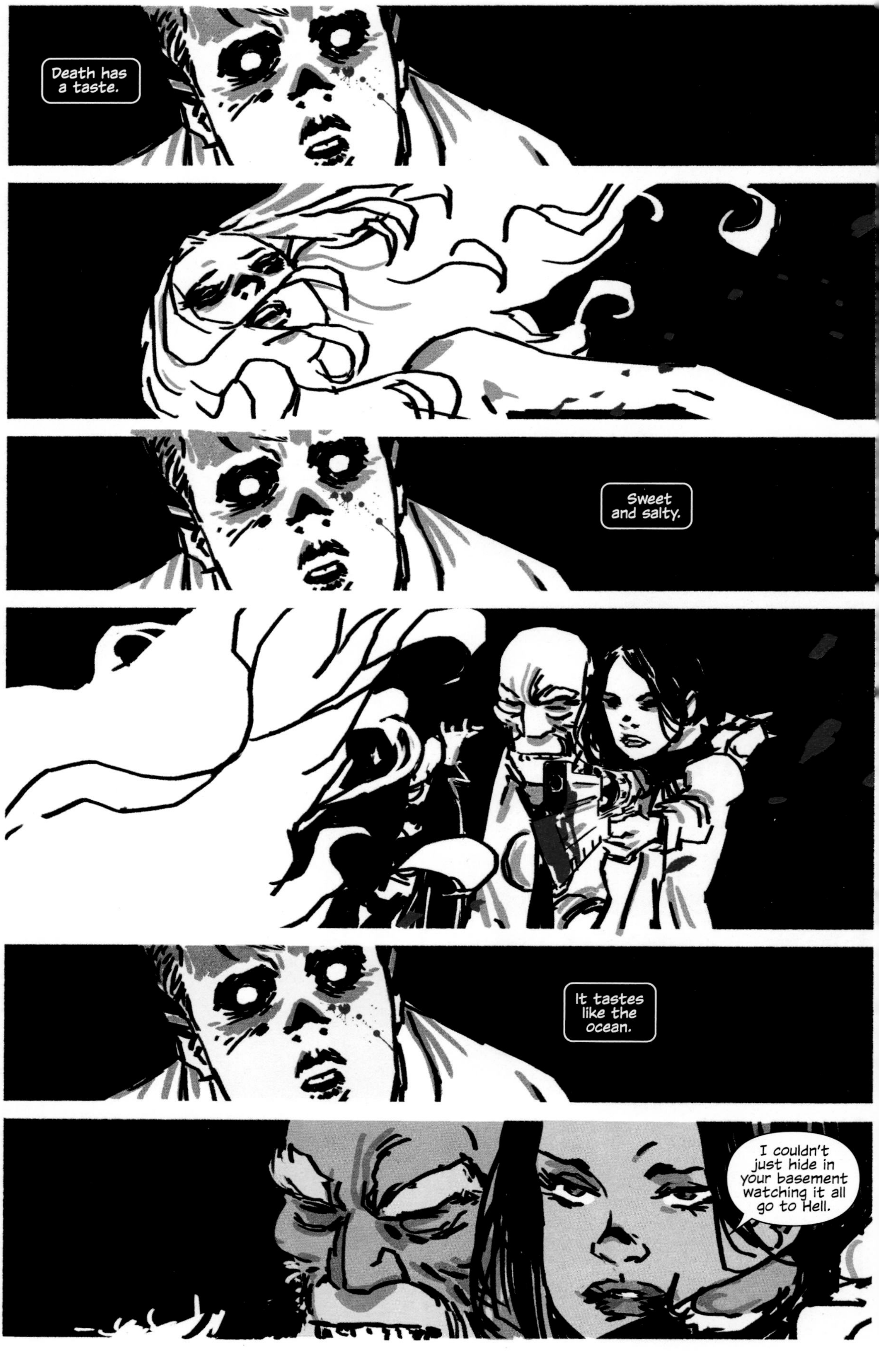
Death has a taste.
Sweet and salty.
It tastes like the ocean.
I couldn't just hide in your basement watching it all go to Hell.

And it's all around me.

And the new election cycle is underway with both candidates vowing to uncover...

World banks have now been subpoenaed to testify in court...

As Russia rebuilds, after the devastation of their own nuclear warhead exploded last fall...

Cyber security now seen as the next battleground of warfare, paid for in secret by cryptocurrencies...

And so-called Wealth Power groups are charged with treason...

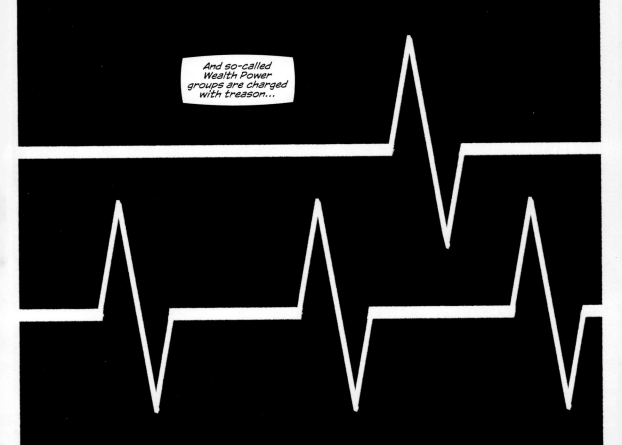

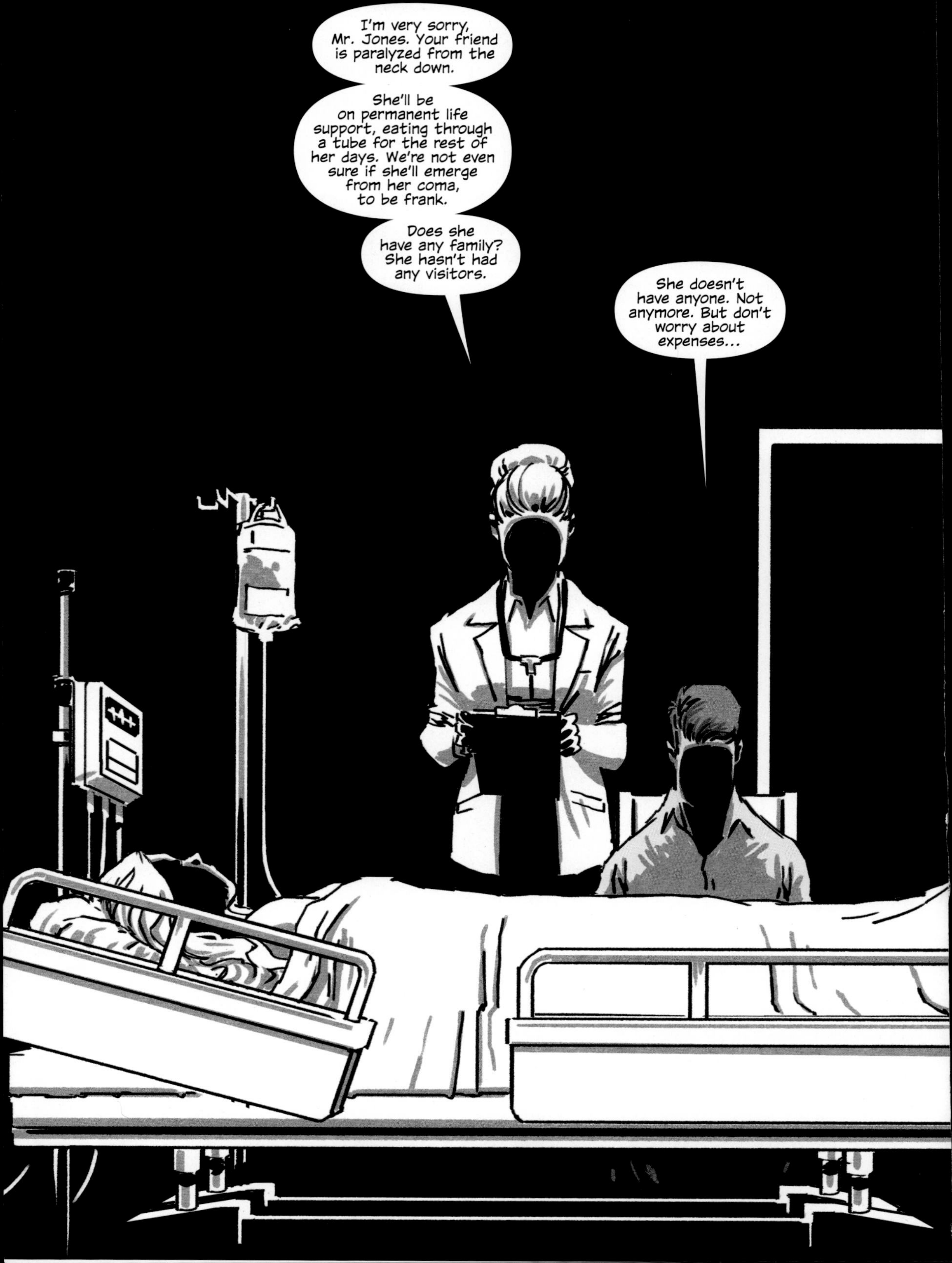
I'm very sorry, Mr. Jones. Your friend is paralyzed from the neck down.
She'll be on permanent life support, eating through a tube for the rest of her days. We're not even sure if she'll emerge from her coma, to be frank.
Does she have any family? She hasn't had any visitors.
She doesn't have anyone. Not anymore. But don't worry about expenses...

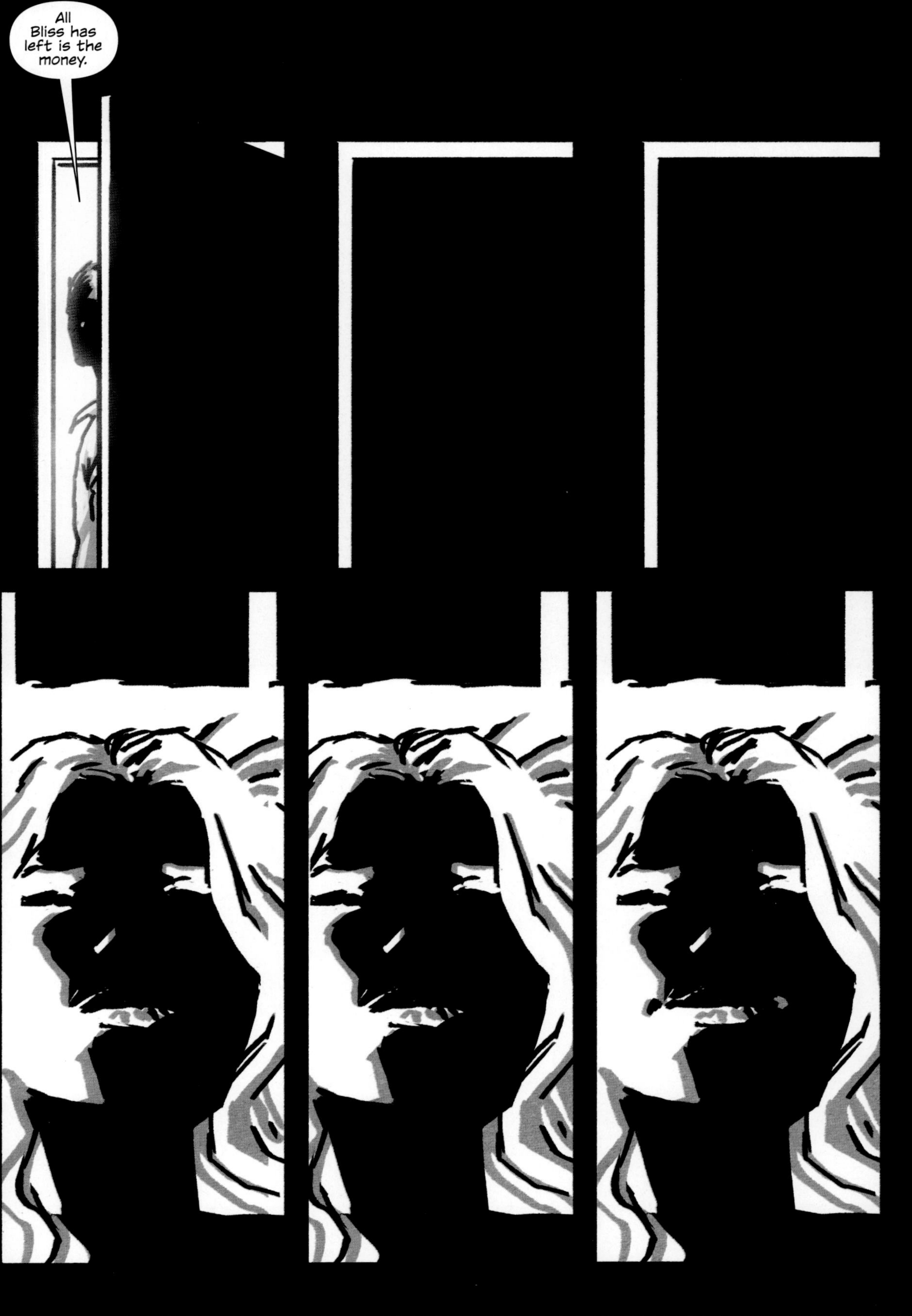
All Bliss has left is the money.

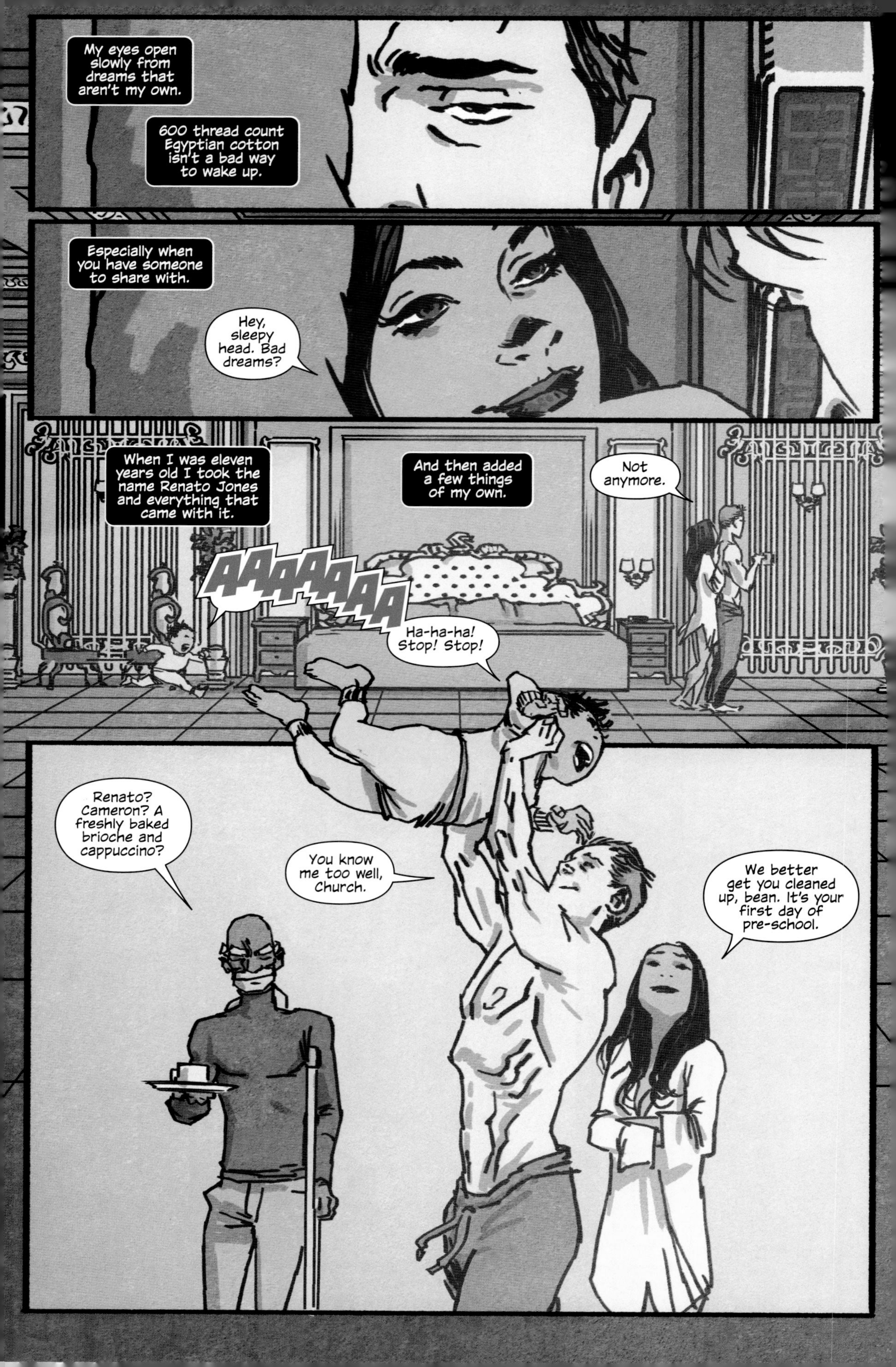

My eyes open slowly from dreams that aren't my own.
600 thread count Egyptian cotton isn't a bad way to wake up.
Especially when you have someone to share with.
Hey, sleepy head. Bad dreams?
When I was eleven years old I took the name Renato Jones and everything that came with it.
And then added a few things of my own.
Not anymore.
AAAAAAAA
Ha-ha-ha! Stop! Stop!
Renato? Cameron? A freshly baked brioche and cappuccino?
You know me too well, Church.
We better get you cleaned up, bean. It's your first day of pre-school.

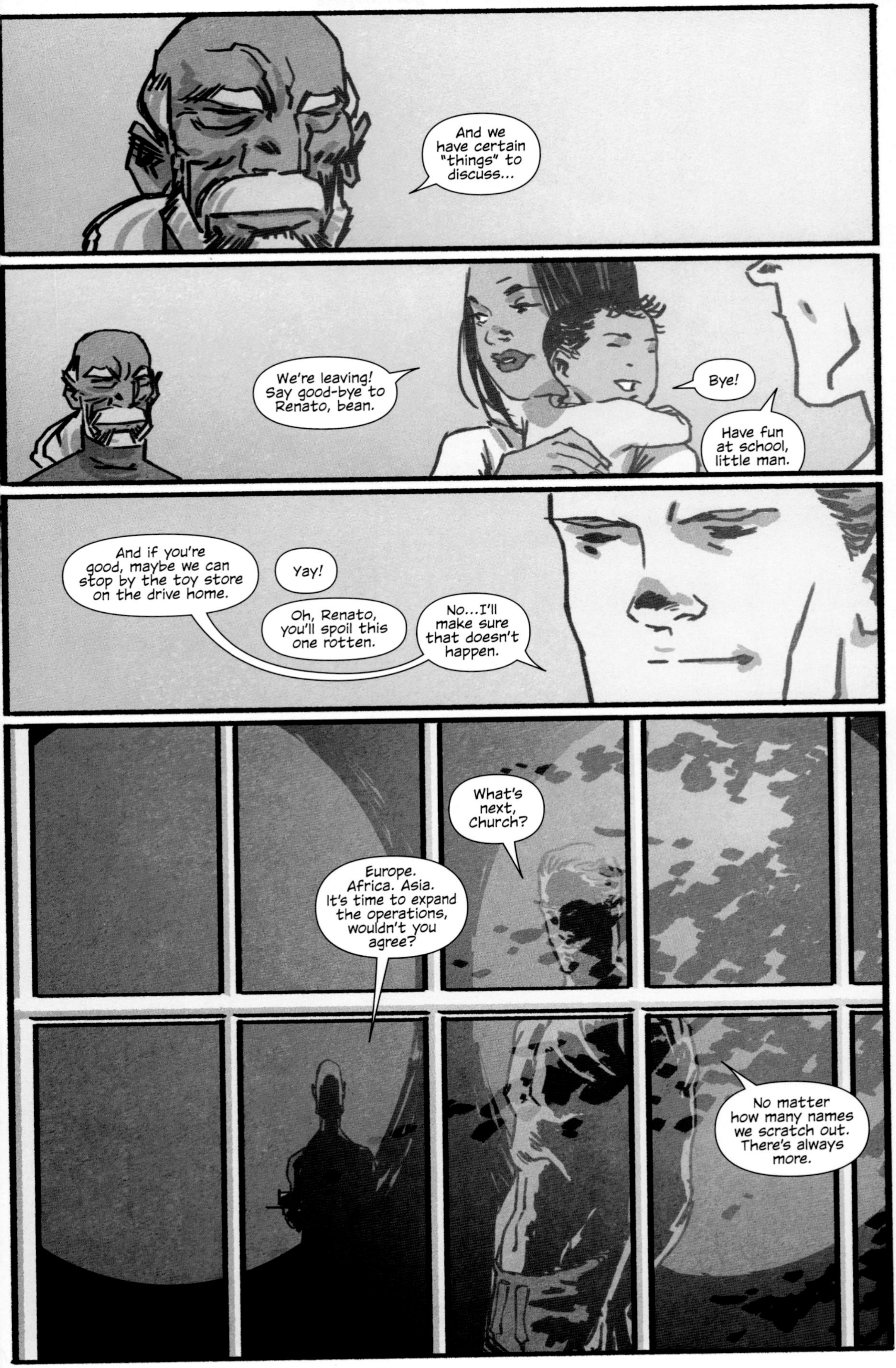
And we have certain "things" to discuss...
We're leaving! Say good-bye to Renato, bean.
Bye!
Have fun at school, little man.
And if you're good, maybe we can stop by the toy store on the drive home.
Yay!
Oh, Renato, you'll spoil this one rotten.
No...I'll make sure that doesn't happen.
What's next, Church?
Europe. Africa. Asia. It's time to expand the operations, wouldn't you agree?
No matter how many names we scratch out. There's always more.

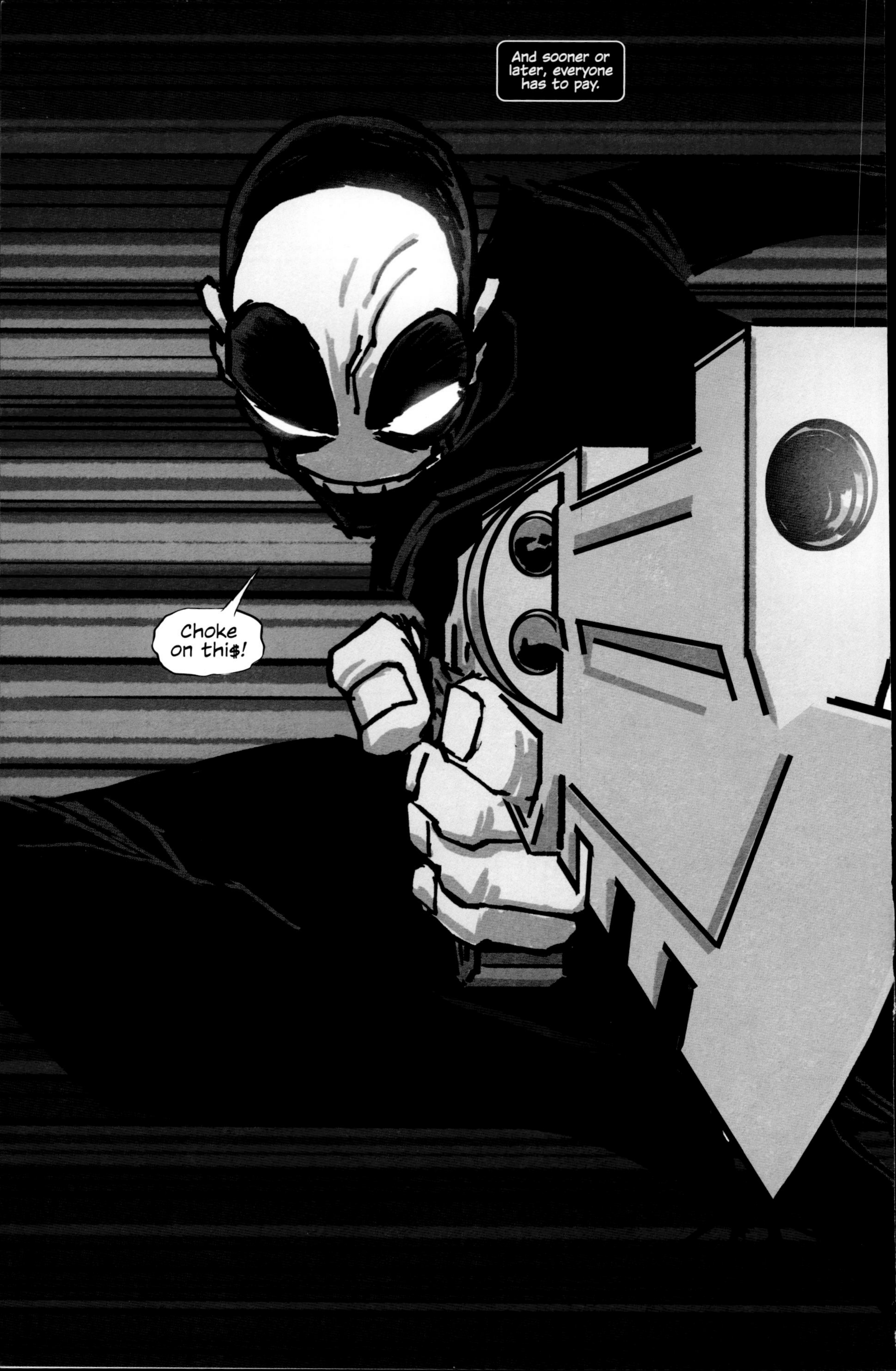

And sooner or later, everyone has to pay.
Choke on thi$!

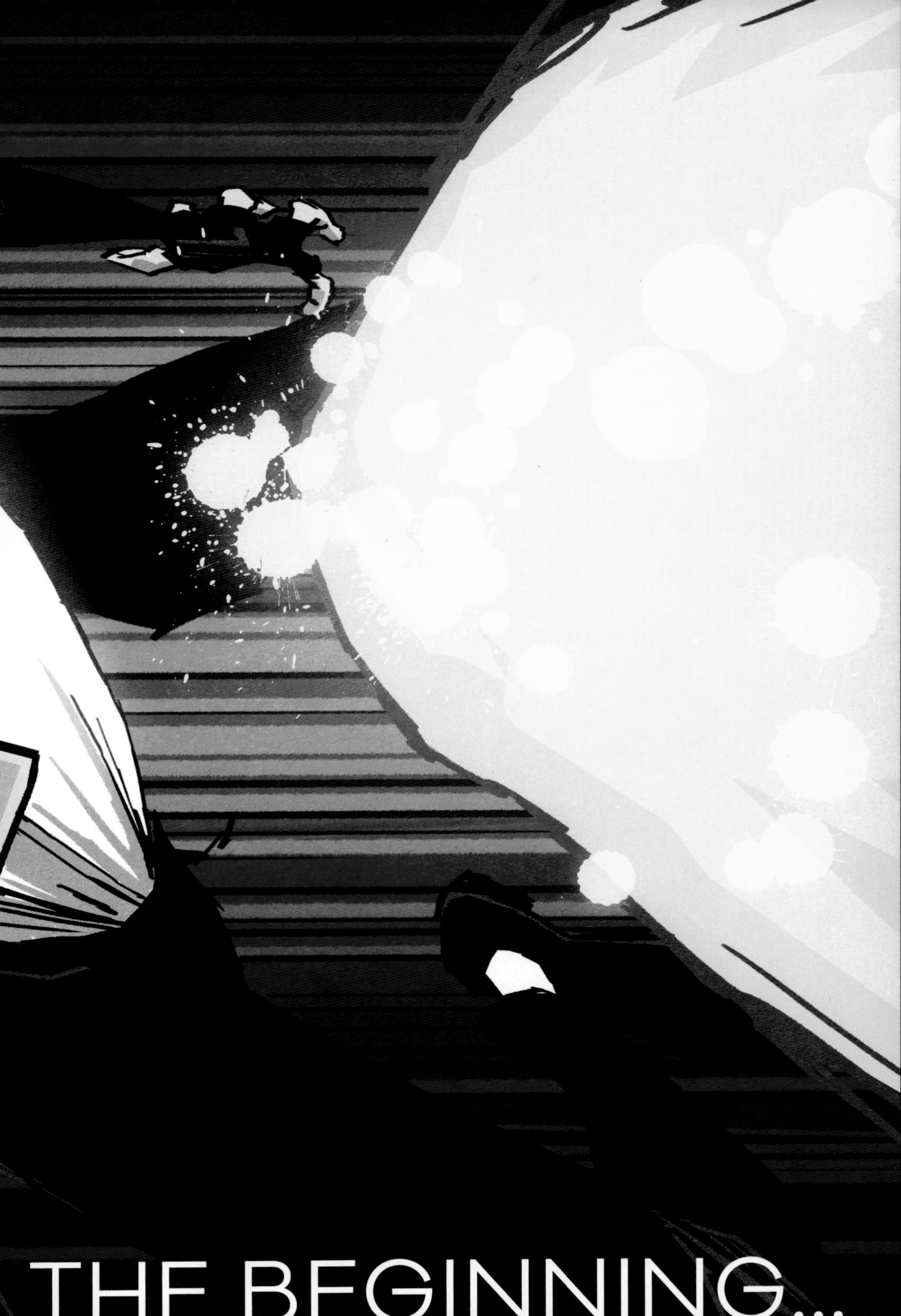
THE BEGINNING...

The World is on Fire

Renato Jones was always a character created by the times we live in, a reaction to the increasingly disparate wealth gap of our world. But back then we were ready to welcome the first female President of the United States of America. A time of progressive change, where it might be just good old fun to "go after" the kind of evil that hides behind money.

And then somewhere along the way, everything started turning upside down.

Disparate become desperate. The gap became a chasm. The outrage become outrageous. We began to tear each other apart faster than we could hold each other together. And my wealth-fueled action-adventure comicbook became something else.

You see, Renato Jones was written to be a satire. A dark humor reaction to the "what might"… before it became the "what happened." And after it happened, the only way to keep Renato Jones a satire was to try to out-do, to out-race the current events. Russia, North Korea, nuclear Armageddon, and the loss of all reason and debate. Truth fell out of favor, in place of whoever could yell the loudest. Corruption, anger, moral decay and the backlash to all of it became an ocean of madness. Swirling. Drowning. Madness. And Renato Jones turned into a way for me to survive it.

This book has now ended, but I still believe in people. I believe in goodness. And in change. You see, while fire consumes tinder it also tempers steel.

It's moments like these where you ask yourself, what are you made of?

I believe that one day we'll look back at everything that's happened as one more crazy time when the world had to figure out what it needed to be. Because everything I've learned in life has taught me that we get through the tough times. That despite the efforts of those to divide us, we stick together.

And no matter how loud any one person is screaming…

Truth still matters.

We still matter.

You matter.

Thanks for sticking with me on this crazy adventure, and I'll see you on the next one.

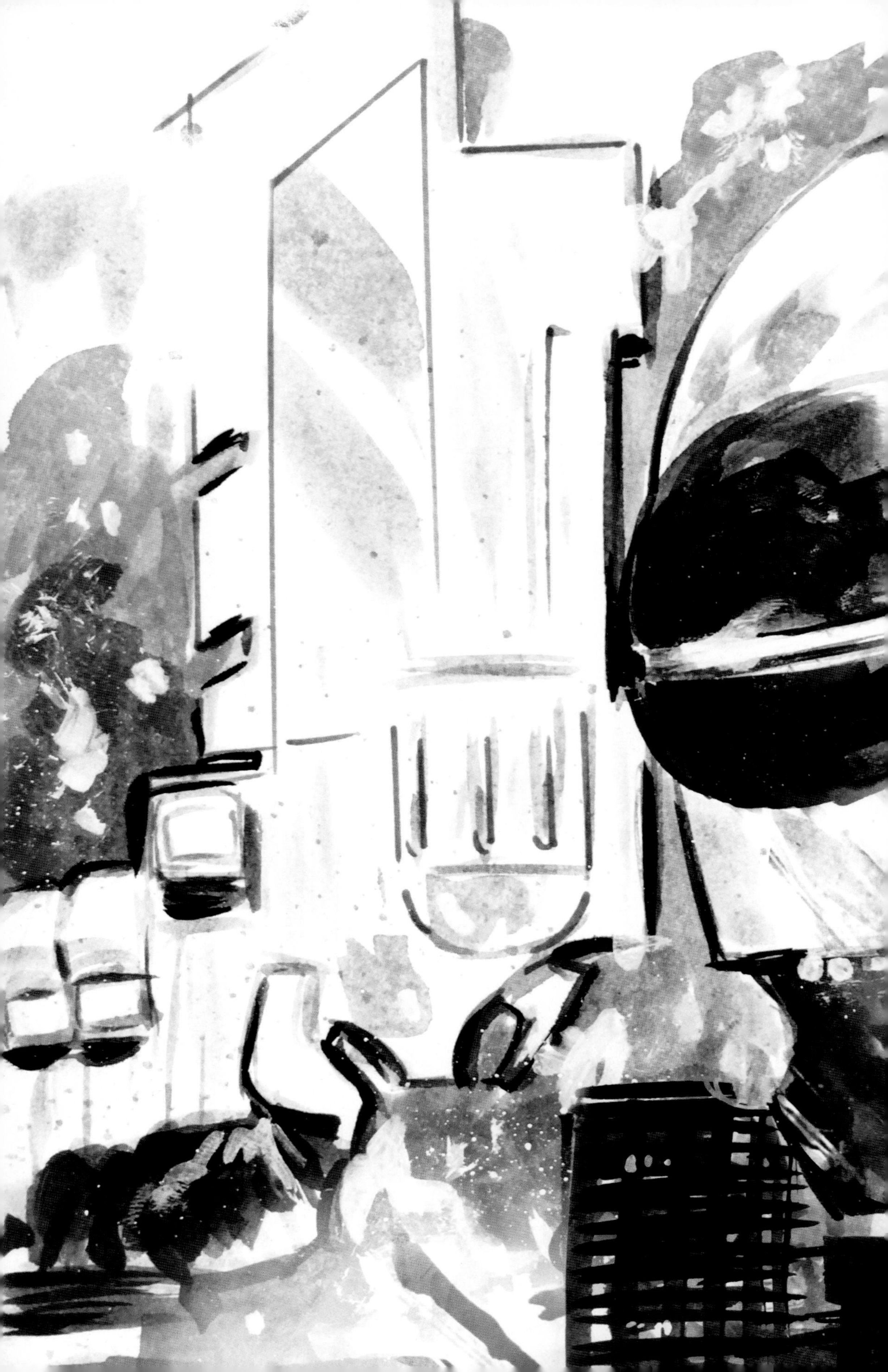

SKETCHBOOK

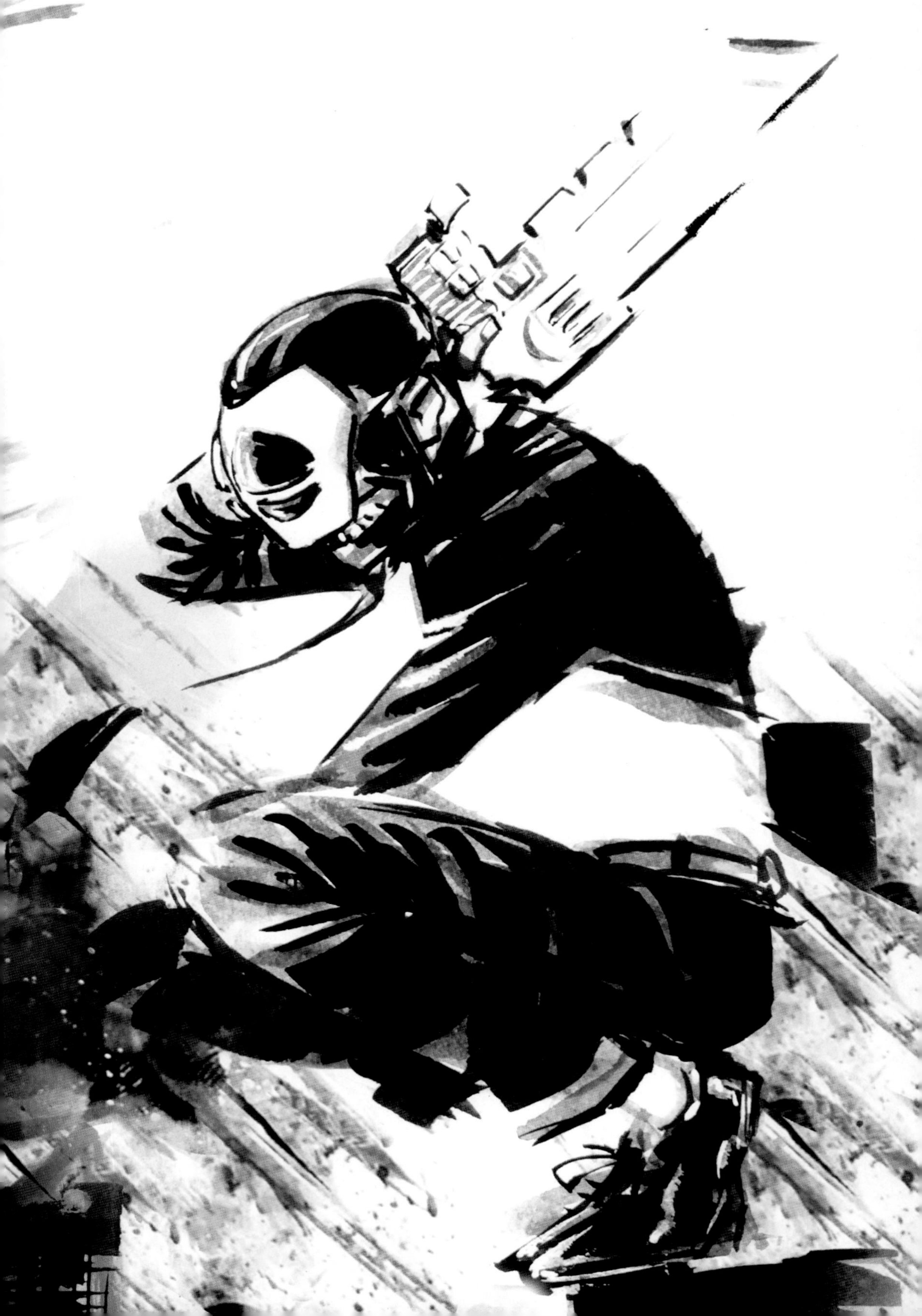

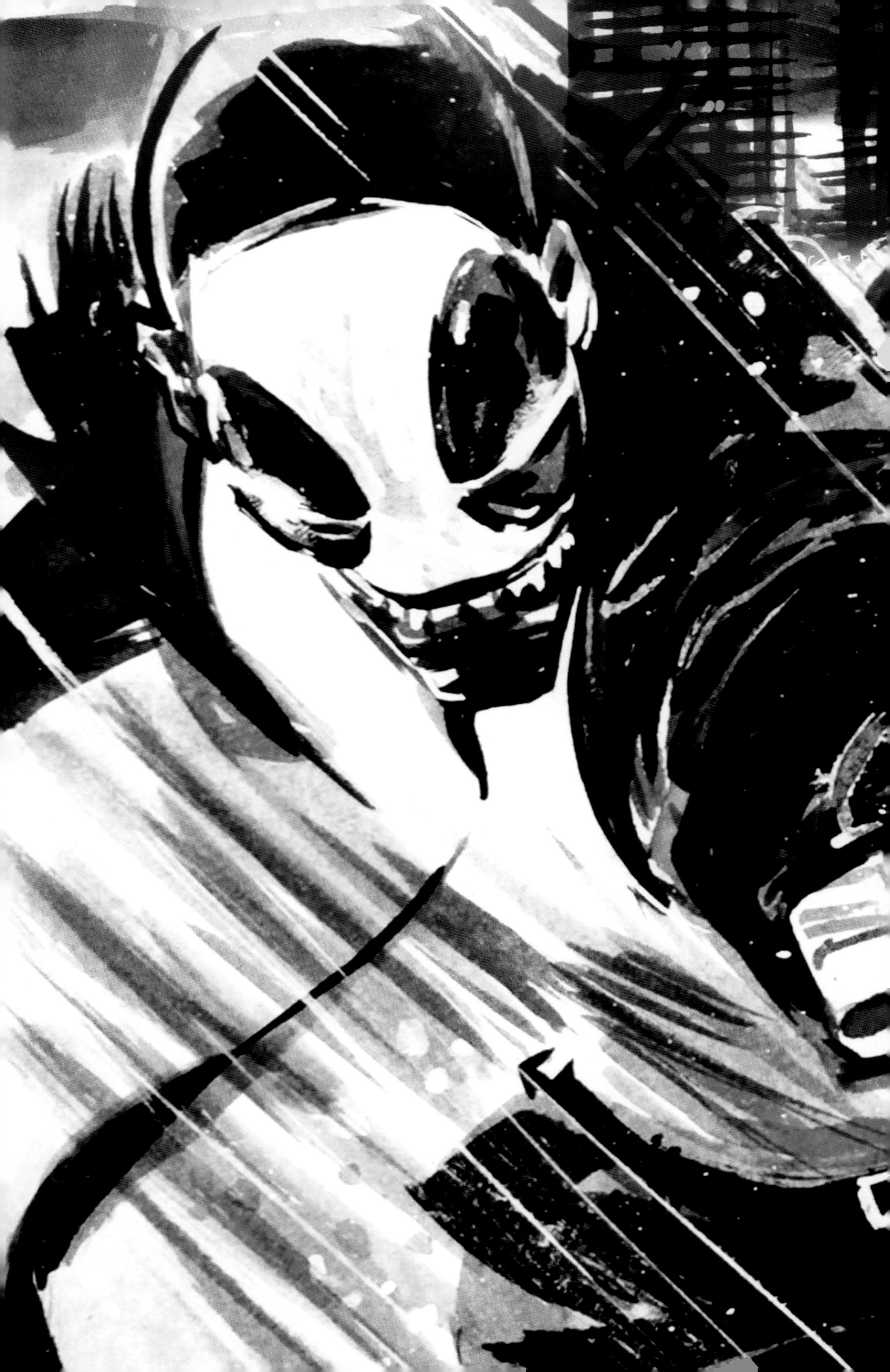

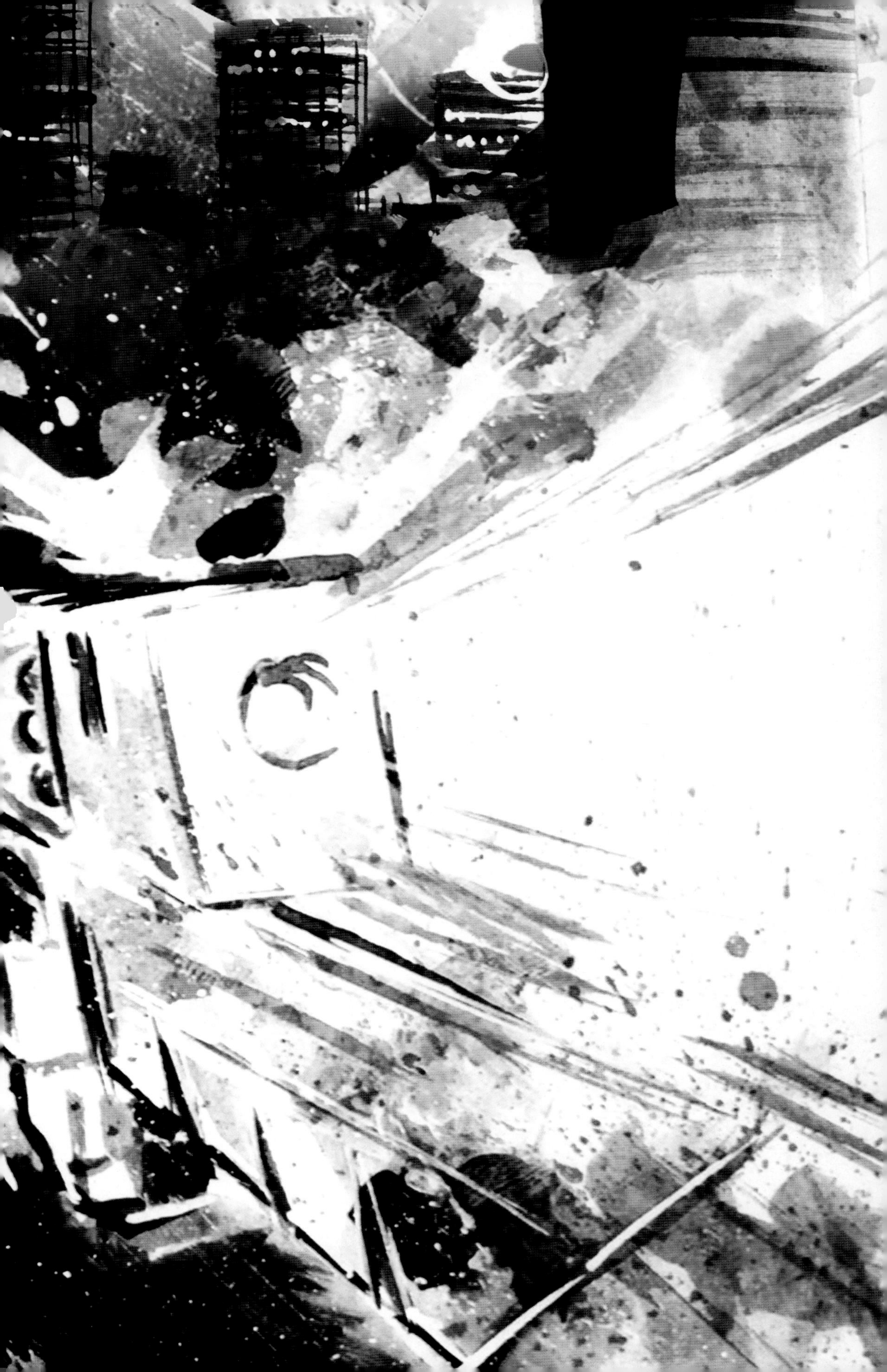

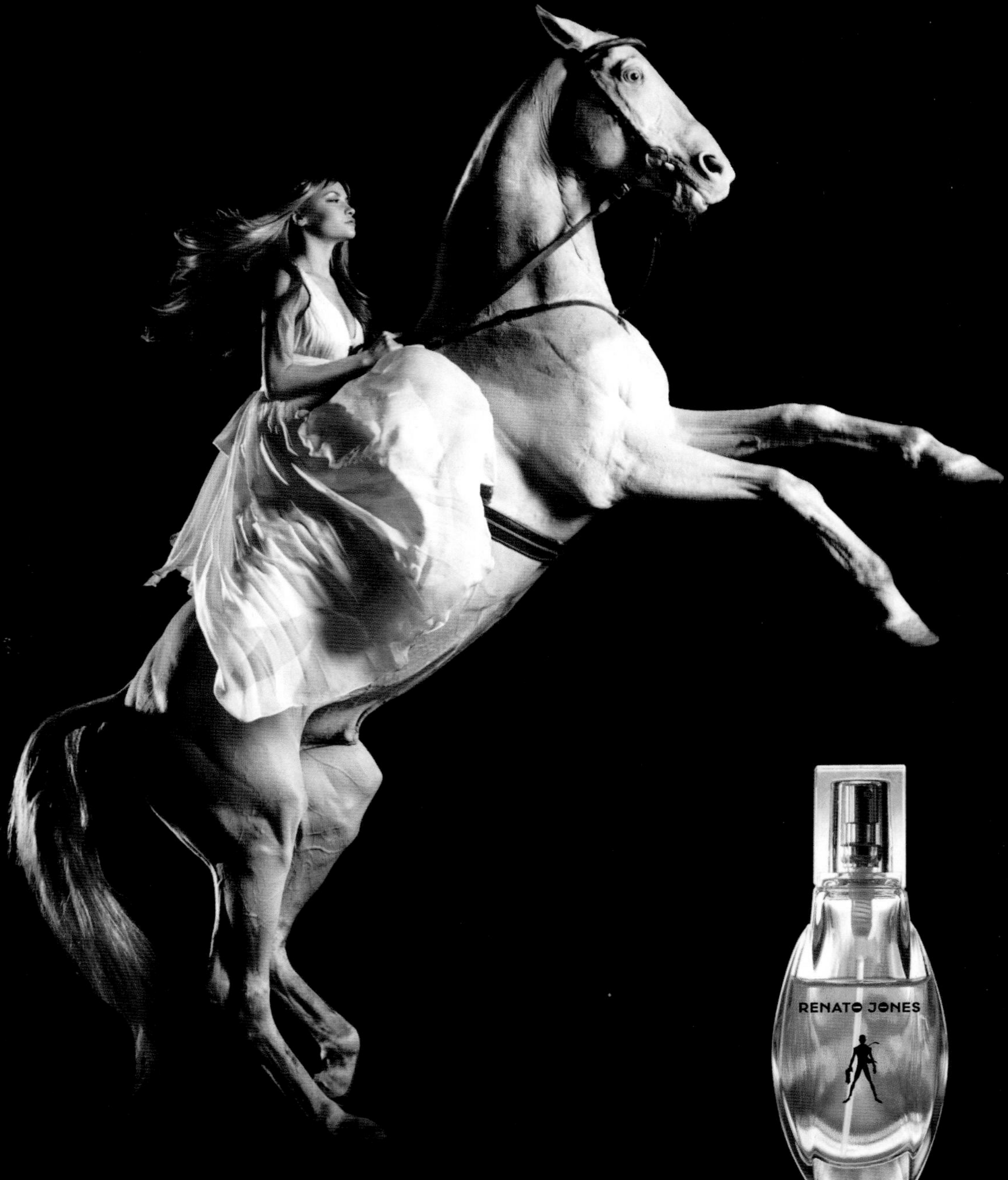
RENATO JONES

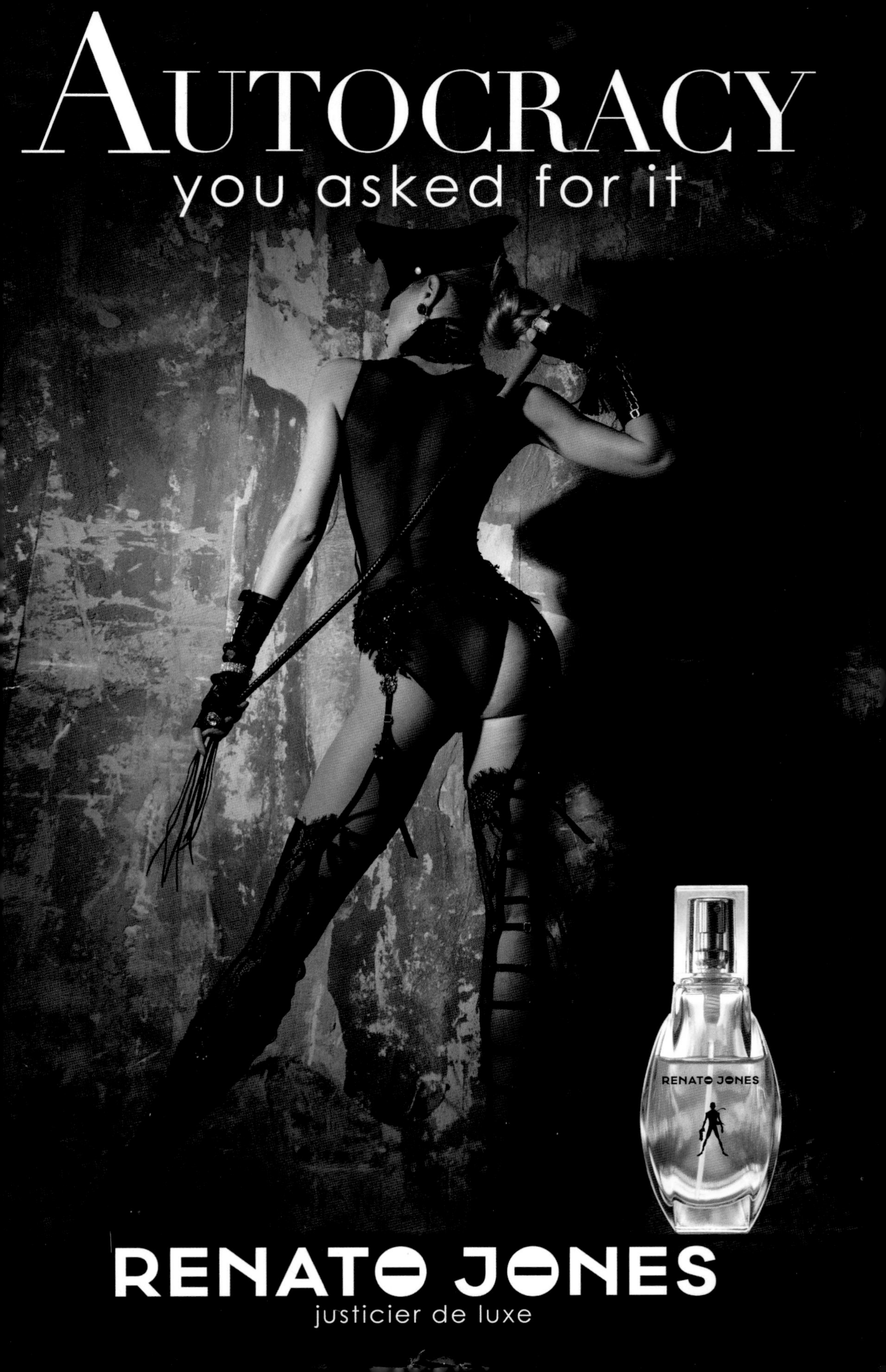
AUTOCRACY
you asked for it
RENATO JONES
RENATO JONES
justicier de luxe

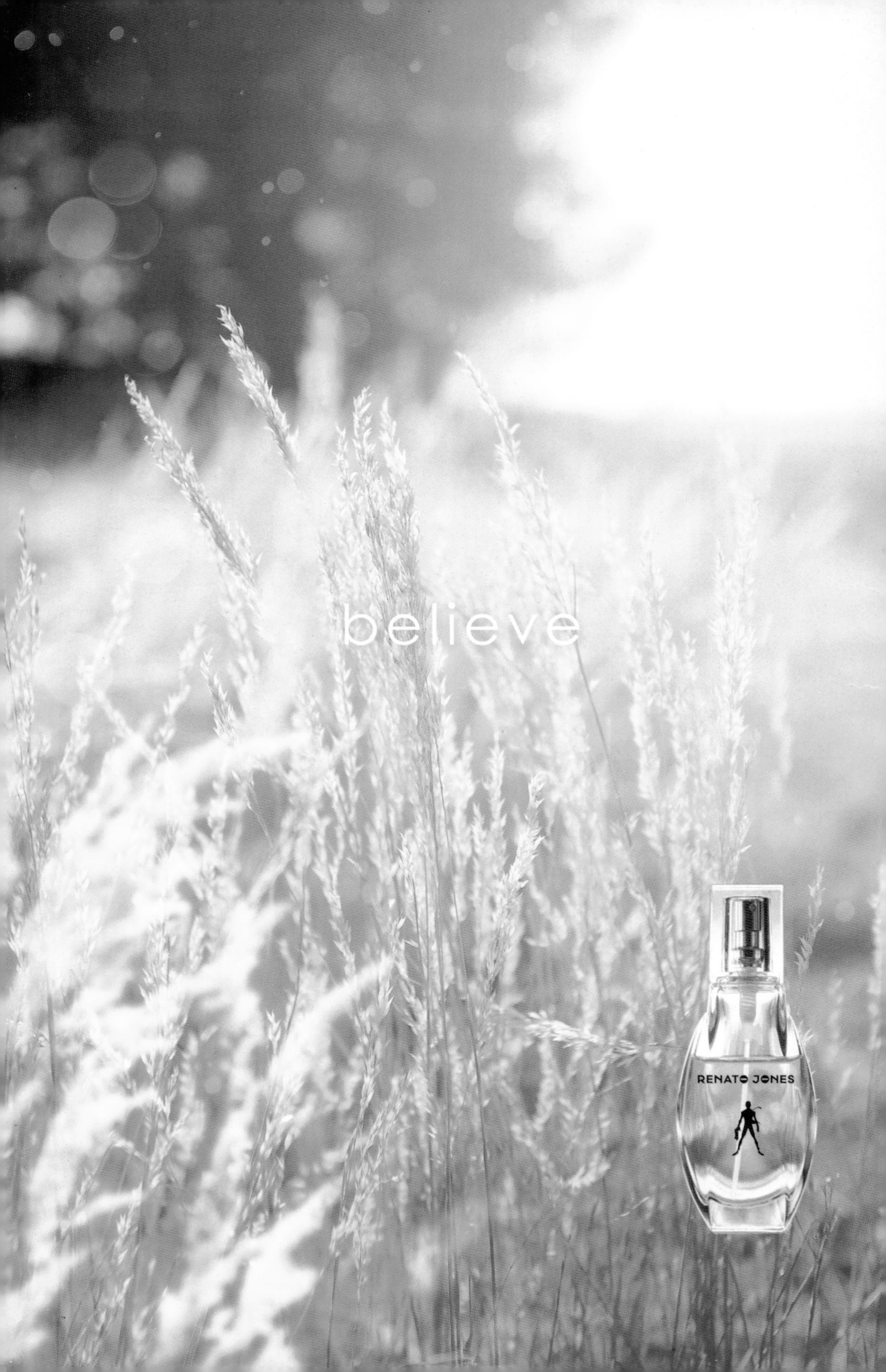
believe
RENATO JONES